THE NEW WORLD
BENEATH THE SEA . . .

Plunge toward a land many miles below the surface of the ocean as one of Earth's greatest adventures begins . . .

Down . . . down . . . to where the sea has no bottom . . . and science has no answers to the secrets of the deep . . .

Where awesome currents, monstrous creatures and crushing pressure create impossible barriers to human exploration . . .

Where incredibly brave men and women risk the enormous perils of a great new world . . .

AQUARIUS MISSION
The electrifying new superthriller by
MARTIN CAIDIN

Bantam Books by Martin Caidin
Ask your bookseller for the books you have missed

AQUARIUS MISSION
WHIP

Aquarius Mission

~~~~~~~~~~~~~~~~~~~~~~~~~~~~~~~~~~~~

A Novel by
Martin Caidin

~~~~~~~~~~~~~~~~~~~~~~~~~~~~~~~~~~~~

BANTAM BOOKS
TORONTO · NEW YORK · LONDON

He dreamed it.
We did it.

This book is for
Howard Minsky

AQUARIUS MISSION
A Bantam Book | April 1978

ISBN 0–553–11267–8

Published simultaneously in the United States and Canada

Bantam Books are published by Bantam Books, Inc. Its trademark, consisting of the words "Bantam Books" and the portrayal of a bantam, is registered in the United States Patent Office and in other countries. Marca Registrada. Bantam Books, Inc., 666 Fifth Avenue, New York, New York 10019.

PRINTED IN THE UNITED STATES OF AMERICA

BOOK
I

1

The horizon curved in a blanket of burgundy. The bend and hue tugged vision to the edge of vertigo. Then, other colors glowed softly, averting eye-twisting unbalance. Pale yellow, green, amber, blue white; bars and circles and squares and quivering needles and triangles and target rings; digital numbers and letters ghosting in a disciplined spray of light and color. Very gently, the new illumination gave the reddish horizon familiarity. Dr. Matthew Chadwick of the Scripps Oceanography Institute rested comfortably in a padded contour seat facing the subdued artificial coruscation of the tiny submarine world. Padded straps and belts held him easily, secure but not tightly bound, although any severe motion would immediately clutch him in a protective web.

Chadwick clenched an old briar pipe between his teeth with easy pressure. The pipe was not for smoking in this atmosphere of controlled pressure, but the memory of the sweet flavor provided a measure of comfort. There could be little relaxation of discipline within this sharply confined world —no more than a bubble of steel, glassite, and alloyed armor—yet Matthew Chadwick wore his discipline like a comfortable robe and slippers. Bare inches from his body, water was grinding with crushing pressure against the glassite hull of his small research submarine. He did not begrudge the unlit pipe, or anything else for that matter, for it was a small price to pay for a man who had an "Earth II" planet to explore.

The abyssal deeps had long beckoned to Matthew Chadwick, who had spent most of his life on and within the sea. Despite his reputation as one of the planet's leading oceanographic scientists, Chadwick knew that he understood only the barest fraction of the secrets the deep sea had kept from man. Unimpressed by the pompousness of the academic world, he was far more at home at this moment, gliding effortlessly downward, three thousand feet beneath the choppy and frigid waters that flowed along the forbidding mountain chain known as the Aleutian Islands.

The muted lights in the submarine cabin softened the weathering wrought by salt, wind, and sun on the fifty-six-year-old face of this man who had joined his soul deeply with the dark brine. Crow's-feet pressed along the corners of Chadwick's eyes, and unruly brows and wisps of hair fallen from his forehead covered scars and wrinkles.

The two-man submarine, *Sea Search*, eased down through the level of five hundred fathoms. Strapped in the right seat was Larry Templeton, twenty-six years old, a willing, enthusiastic, and almost worshipful disciple of Dr. Chadwick. Templeton's awareness of events about them quivered at its highest possible peak. Templeton—intense, almost brooding—would have been surprised, if not mildly shocked, to have known Chadwick's high opinion of his younger assistant.

Prior to the short-lived but furious nuclear war —that started with fireball-shattering terror in late 1994 and ended with a whimper a scant four months later—the technological push had produced a generation of scientists who wore blinders. In their individual pursuits, they had suffered tunnel vision that was valuable under the most exacting circumstances, but let there come a situation when their own specific skill was thrown into uncertainty or blacked out because of equipment failure, and they became sightless maggots with no purpose other than that of technological janitors or errand boys.

Not so the breed represented by Larry Templeton. The savage "little" nuclear war was five years behind him; it remained, in the form of shattered cities and devastating radioactive debris spread willy-nilly by capricious winds, but the lessons had been learned, and, in the compression of training and education needed to make up for all the brilliant young minds sacrificed to the nuclear gods in those four months of madness, diversity was a keynote never again forgotten. Aided by computer facilities, by drugs to stimulate the memory receptors of the brain, by a long overdue dose of hard common sense in educational practices, the young people burgeoning their way into the postwar world heralded an era where multifaceted skills were developed as fully as possible.

Thus, Larry Templeton was a hydrographic authority as well as a man who followed a natural bent and could speak, read, and write eight separate languages. His leaning for biology was nurtured in the cross-referencing of scientific knowledge in related subjects. This kind of education resulted in individuals who were highly skilled in their own field or fields but also well grounded in other subjects, thereby preventing their isolation from the "whole" of a world that relied ever more heavily on science and technology to survive its near-Götterdämmerung.

A billion dead; twice that many suffering from radioactive poisoning and abortive germ warfare; and the remainder struggling with shattered agricultural systems, diseased flora, devastated animal stocks. It was a world that sorely needed attention.

Food, of course, headed the list of priorities for survival. Food, and new sources of petroleum to ensure the functioning of the technological systems so desperately needed to hold together the framework of industry that had to mend, rebuild, and expand in an atmosphere of bitterness and cynicism. The aftermath of any war in which there is no clearly defined victor, as was the case now, produces no era of largesse or increased personal freedom, but precisely the opposite. Out of that brief insanity had emerged a new China, strong not so much in nuclear weaponry (for her nuclear missiles and aircraft were worth less than the remaining arms of the United States and the Soviet Union) but in nonnuclear arms, and still the world's greatest reservoir of manpower.

Reality stared at the planet with increasing bleakness each day. The problems involving food, petroleum, and the distribution of same, needed immediate solution, or the international community must sink again into savage conflict for the few remaining bones of sustenance. It was a strange dichotomy: The gap between the heavily technologized nations and the have-nots had become ever greater; and men who have nothing to lose are quite willing to throw away their lives in a final spasm of self-respect.

Yet hope remained. Not some distant tendril drifting beyond reasonable grasp, not some dreamed-of charitable windfall, but a new science that could plumb the depths of Earth's neighboring planet for the food to feed billions and the lubricants so critical to industrial and engineering systems.

The planet was sometimes referred to as Hydroworld: the ocean depths of our own globe. Between the dark brine and the sun-splashed upper layers of the sea were the riches men sought to suspend further deterioration of their planet. The solution for daily life, especially in the coming future, was simple: Either find, claw free, and distribute what the world needed, or accept the fact that those who remained would have to savage one another in order to survive on what was left.

Thus, Dr. Matthew Chadwick and Larry Templeton were sliding down a gentle gravity chute into the ocean deeps off the Aleutians, easing through a level of 3,000 feet, with more than 23,000 feet lying beneath them, as they guided their teardrop submersible toward the Aleutian Trench, a sheer-walled fissure in the ocean bottom that promised thick and syrupy riches of raw petroleum.

The gravitational anomalies from orbiting satellites had titillated geologists, had hinted of subtle shifts in the makeup of the crustal floor of the ocean, but even in this day and age there was no easy voyage to the bottom of a sea five miles straight down. Old-fashioned bathyscaphes and other pioneering diving systems might plumb those depths, but their voyages were little more than games of blindman's bluff, groping through stygian darkness pierced by short-ranged lights, too often at the mercy of unknown currents, upflows, avalanches, and sea terrain pitifully charted.

The two-man sub, *Sea Search,* was one of the newer vessels—not that distant from the experimental category. Its composition of glassite and alloyed armor gave it a strength of more than 70,-000 pounds to the square inch, far beyond any pressure that would be encountered in the deeps. It was also a triumphant departure from the positive buoyancy "gasbags" that characterized all submersibles of earlier years. Negative buoyancy was the name of the new game in probing the ocean depths. It gave high speeds, unprecedented maneuverability, and a freedom the old submariners could find only in dreams or cherished hopes for the future. It carried with it the same penalty of any machine that moved through the fluid medium we call the atmosphere. When your power quit, you were on your way down. Period.

The tiny *Sea Search* that carried Chadwick and Templeton was too diminutive to impress anyone save those familiar with such undersea vehicles. Two men and no more could fit in its cramped cabin, but those two men operated their submarine like a small observation aircraft; they were able to dive, ascend, turn, or hover as they so desired. Most of the equipment, beyond propulsion and fuel, consisted of instruments and probes that would enable Chadwick and Templeton to test the nature of what men everywhere sought so desperately—a single find of petroleum that could change international politics.

As the two men slid away from the place where ocean and atmosphere meet, they were surrounded by a world of sound that most men are never exposed to—a cacophonous array of screeching, groaning, chittering, clicking, rolls and reports, booming thunder, and grating—the medley of life in the sea, all the louder because of the medium through which it moves. Sound within the oceans is stronger and carries much farther than comparable concussion waves in the atmosphere. Below three thousand feet, beyond that level where even the tiniest ghost of sunlight can penetrate, life swelled and roared and whispered about them. The sounds penetrated the hull of the submarine, but the two men, enjoying the orchestration, listened more clearly because of the hydrophones on the exterior hull that carried the sounds in through cabin speakers.

Chadwick and Templeton descended through a night that was always present. No last wisp of sunlight could reach them here, but they were expert in the art of groping with optical myopia in this world of eternal darkness. If the two men wished to make visual observations, they needed to switch on brilliant searchlights, for all their power like flashlights in a dense fog, where much of the light gets lost through scattering and reflection. The men could also extend their visual reach by sending out small projectiles carrying either searchlights or powerful flare bombs. The flare bombs hissed wildly in the thick pressures of the deeps, sputtering and growling as their chemicals combined furiously to emit a great bowl of light that was as limited as it was intense.

Yet there could be natural light in these dark waters, created through the act of bioluminescence. The deeps at times exploded in silent isolated glory as all manner of creatures pulsed and flickered or shone with dazzling colors and varieties of patterns. Best of all, one could never anticipate what would be encountered, no more than one might predict the pattern of the next snowflake to alight on a fingertip.

Templeton shifted his gaze from the viewport directly before him to the curving bank of instruments and controls. His eye moved expertly across the shaped plastic colors to SONAR SCAN, which at the moment was absent of activity on the viewscope. He continued his scan, much as would a pilot flying blind on instruments, to cover DEPTH, DESCENT RATE, SALINITY, TEMPERATURE, RANGE, and other information readouts. The digital numbers and letters shone or flickered or changed, obedient to the information coming in from instruments and sensors, and in his quick scans Templeton would be alert to any minor changes. Were there a sudden change that might require him or Chadwick to apply full attention, a warning chime would sound, and the light intensity of the readout would flare at once to the eye-commanding level.

It happened at that moment. A sonar contact was

made. The modulated sound waves pulsing from the submarine had "found" an object, bounced back the information, and the digital RANGE blossomed into light as the chime sounded. Both men studied the instrument panel calmly.

"Whatever it is," Chadwick said through the pipe-stem in his teeth, "there's a lot of it. Interesting."

Templeton leaned forward to adjust the panel controls. For several moments he kept silent, concentrating. "There," he said finally, "we're locked on. I'll try to narrow the range."

Chadwick gestured easily. "Don't be too concerned with it, Larry. We've got some temperature inversions around us."

"Well, I think, if I can—" He straightened up, showing surprise. "Dead on, Matt. No more than two hundred yards out."

Chadwick's hands stirred to his controls. "Very good. Stand by for floodlights. I don't think we'll need any flares."

"Yes, sir."

"Oh, yes," the older man continued, "we'll want autocamera also. This could prove interesting."

Templeton glanced quickly at him. "You know what's out there?"

A smile teased at Chadwick's lips. "I believe I do," he said slowly. He studied the gauges and the scope, relaxed, patient, almost certain he would be seeing "old friends."

"All set," Templeton reported. "We've got a bearing of, ah, zero three zero, closing steadily. You want the lights now?"

Chadwick shook his head. One finger tapped the sonarscope. "Not yet. But activate the cameras. I think our friends out there are about to start talking to one another."

Templeton's blank stare was more eloquent than any question he could have asked.

Chadwick smiled. "Watch carefully, now—"

They were acutely aware of the sound of water moving heavily past the hull, the continuing sound of ocean life, the hum of power within the submarine. On an impulse, just as Chadwick brought up the floodlights, Templeton switched off the cabin speakers.

The motions were almost simultaneous. The brilliant lights splashed through black water, the cabin went quiet, and, just as quickly, Chadwick turned off the lights so that they were looking into darkness. But only for an instant.

In utter silence they watched a series of multicolored explosions in the near distance. Templeton sucked in his breath, started to speak, changed his mind, and surrendered himself to the moment, for he saw a beauty encountered by very few men: the silent exchange of messages between creatures in permanent natural darkness who produced light in a scarcely credible range, in brilliant flashes and subtle hues.

Templeton stared at great octopuses clamoring silently, calling one another, sending their signals by way of body luminescence. Light rippled from the central bodies out along the tentacles in definite patterns, intelligent rhythms. The creatures glowed eerily. Most of the animals slipped behind and above the small submarine as it continued its descent, but several moved suddenly, leaving behind them trails of sparkling mites, a mixture of their own fluids swirling through the phosphorescent particles of the deep sea.

As he turned to the older man beside him, Templeton's face reflected a sense of wonder. "I had no idea. I know about the octopuses, of course, and that they—it still overwhelms me. They were communicating. There was a pattern, signals sent between them, and—"

"They were talking about us, Larry." Chadwick removed the pipe from between his teeth, smiled at his assistant. "You saw how most of them simply ignored us after a few moments. Only a few went with us, followed our descent."

He smiled as Templeton returned his gaze to the viewport. "You won't see them anymore," Chadwick went on. "They've determined we're no danger to them, so they've gone about their affairs."

"You've seen this before."

Chadwick nodded. "Many times. I wish I could have the opportunity to research their light patterns, establish the intelligence factor. It's high. They're some of the smartest creatures in the sea."

Templeton chewed his lower lip. "Have we ever tried to communicate with them?" he asked. "I mean, like we have with the whales?"

Chadwick shook his head slowly. "We've never had the chance. We have submarines like ours," he gestured, "but we don't have the time to spend chasing deep ocean rainbows. One thing appears certain, though. These creatures have been communicating in this fashion for perhaps millions of years. Certainly long before the human race got off its foreknuckles and walked on two legs."

Templeton glanced through his viewport, spoke without turning. "They're still with us," he said.

Chadwick's attention was immediate. "That's odd. Quickly, Larry. Let's get them on film. Hit the lights and the cameras for—"

No need to finish. Templeton's hands worked the controls and, in an instant, dazzling lights flooded the ocean and cameras whirred into action. In the shocking white beams the bright octopus colors faded, and then the animals became dimly visible. The two men had a brief glimpse of whitish bodies and swirling tentacles, and then everything vanished behind clouds of inky liquid as the octopuses fled.

"Shut down the systems," Chadwick said.

The floodlights glowed away, and once again their world consisted of the burgundy light of the cabin and the spattering glows of color from the instruments and consoles.

"Six hundred fathoms," Chadwick noted. He leaned back in his seat, adjusted his body for comfort, reached out for a microphone, and pressed a switch marked ANTENNA RELEASE. "We'll never find any petroleum way up here, Larry. Increase our rate of descent."

He paused as Templeton adjusted the power. The small submarine trembled as the hydrojets increased their speed.

"We're through 600 fathoms, our descent coming up to 130 fathoms a minute," Templeton recited.

"Very good. Stay with it. I'll talk to the people upstairs."

He waited for the antenna release indicator to show a green light, then he spoke quietly into the microphone.

Nearly a mile above them, his voice drifted as a radio wave through the air.

2

~~~~~~~~~~

The sun sprayed burnished copper across a sea unusually quiet for the northern waters off the Aleutians. This was a rare moment, especially appreciated for its quiescence and splendor by the crewmen of the great triple-hulled S.S. *Windward*; they had endured more than their fill of explosive winds and roiling seas. Just now, however, the *Windward* idled through gentle swells and dappled reflections, its crew waiting while the captain of the deep-ocean research vessel listened to a voice far beneath the very waters he cruised.

Captain Lars Svenson, like his crew, wore a synthetic garment that was something of a cross between a diver's wet suit and a pilot's jump suit—gear for all seasons, with temperature-sensitive plastic beads inside of lining that adjusted to ambient temperature as though the wearer had thermostat control available for his comfort. The only insignia of Svensen's rank was a double orange stripe running down one side of the dark blue jump suit. The *Windward* was a vessel in which close and willing coordination displaced familiar chain-of-command authority. Svensen leaned easily on a bridge railing, his eyes drifting vacantly, yet he was busy, communicating through a tiny lip microphone at the side of his mouth and listening through a speaker embedded in the bone behind his ear. For someone who spent years handling communications, the quick and easy operation was tremendously efficient.

Lars Svensen enjoyed a sense of detachment, feeling the wind through the open sliding glassway of the bridge, absorbing the rare quiet of the Aleutian waters, conscious of the sun's warmth, and he pictured the tiny submarine slipping downward. He had launched that same vessel from his ship; *Windward* was its mother ship and custodian and command post, and it was to a later rendezvous with Svensen that Chadwick would return. Chadwick's voice ghosted now into his ear—a voice that began at a microphone thousands of feet below the surface, raced upward along the thin wire trailed by the *Sea Search,* and converted to radio signals at the surface before it reached the homing antenna of *Windward* and found its way with a vibrating pulse to Svensen's own ear. A small enough miracle at the brink of the twenty-first century, but one still not lost to the consciousness of Lars Svensen.

"You're coming in very clear, Matt," he said in response to the trickle within his ear. "How's the ride down there?"

"Very good. Quite smooth so far, in fact. We've had some company with us for a while."

Svensen nodded to himself. "We know. But sonar couldn't make out what it was. Our guess was squid."

"Close enough," his ear said to him with Chadwick's voice. "Octopus. Almost an entire tribe. We may have gotten some nice film."

"Matt, give me a depth check, will you, please?" Svensen glanced at the instrument readout panel reporting on the progress of the submarine.

"We're exactly at six hundred fathoms, Lars."

Svensen studied the depth readout—3,600 feet on the nose. The ship's instruments were tagging accurately after the sub.

"Very good," Svensen said after scanning the bridge gauges. "You're right on track. How's Templeton enjoying the ride?"

"Fine, fine. Lars, we've started to get some indication of inversion layers beneath us. The sonar echo seems to be distorted, that sort of thing. Do you have anything up there?"

Svensen nodded. They had anticipated just what *Sea Search* was encountering when they'd sent a small high-speed probe down to report different conditions at the changing depths. Few people realize that the vast multidimensional mass of the oceans—which must be considered in its true form of *cubic* space—is anything but quiescent. "The deep," the ocean far beneath the surface, seems to connote a deadening of physical forces. The truth is almost precisely the opposite, for the upper layers of the ocean conceal energy that is eternally surging, marching, tumbling, carrying waves and fronts and currents involving tremendous forces. Far below the area where man's naked vision becomes useless, currents flow with the grinding impact of a thousand rivers. Deep tributaries snake unpredictable tendrils in every direction. It is a common enough occurrence to find a river miles in width coursing powerfully from north to south—and to discover another heavy flow, only scant feet beneath the first enormous stream, moving in precisely the opposite direction. The levels of the hydroworld are much like the jet streams and other air currents of the atmospheric ocean, sometimes mild and variable and other times fierce and irresistible. The nature of the ocean deeps permits huge rivers to move almost side by side but in a constantly changing panorama, and it is impossible to predict just what will happen, or where, or when.

Thus any deep-ocean penetration must be made with caution, with enormous strength and power contained in whatever vehicle is used, and with every scrap and ounce of knowledge about the hydroworld. Even then there is no avoiding the risks in broaching ocean rivers that move billions of tons of seawater every minute of the day, endlessly, year after year. The deeps through which Chadwick and Templeton even now moved were alive with eddies and streams, great mountain ranges of water rising vertically and sliding down with ponderous force. Closer to shorelines there were fast-moving cataracts tumbling and roiling down escarpments, plunging away from submerged cliff walls miles in height with so mighty a push that house-sized boulders were tossed about as if they were mere pebbles.

These were facts Chadwick knew as much by the instinct of long experience as by study. To his young assistant, the depths were still a comparatively new challenge, as fascinating as they might be dangerous.

Men who had ventured into space had to train themselves to think of a vacuum not as an absence of something, but as a force that would kill them instantly upon exposure. Far down in the dark-frozen waters, much the same rule must be applied. The awareness might have been more subconscious than in the forefront of his brain, but it was never ignored by Chadwick.

There was yet another cruel demand—cruel because a lapse of attention could easily prove fatal. It is easy to think of air as air and water as water, and the generalization is usually odious in what it ignores. The density of the hydroworld is scarcely comprehended by those of us who live under the naked thinness even of an atmosphere a hundred miles high. Water in the hydroworld is not something cool and refreshing as it springs from a fountain, nor is it a gently heaving surface to entertain dappled sun reflections; it is neither the liquid the baby splashes happily, nor the stuff we use for cooking, nor the thousand and one other things we use it for every day of our existence. In the deeper oceans, water is as hard and tough as steel, and it punishes any failure in structure with an implosion that has all the force of an atomic fireball. It is literally the substance of some alien world, and it must always be held in regal respect.

Water has a density *eight hundred times greater* than that of the thickest air we breathe on the surface of this planet. It has a viscosity that is fifty times greater than air. If the numbers beggar comprehension, as truly they must, then picture a man trying to swim or run through thick, gooey, mucky, leg-grabbing oil. In the ocean depths the thickest oil —sludge with perhaps the texture of rumbling magma—is wispy and gossamer in comparison with the savage, crushing pressures prevailing everywhere.

When men accelerate their magnificent vessels through this bizarre fluid they must never forget the nature of their adversary—monster pincers ready to crash with the impact of mile-long battering rams.

Matthew Chadwick and Larry Templeton accepted these concepts with the same calm and serenity as a sky diver who experiences the stunningly swift yielding of thin air before his plummeting body.

Every attempt had been made to assure their safe passage through the tremulous and potentially dangerous waters. Lars Svensen in the *Windward*—high above them in what was by comparison an atmospheric vacuum—used the services of an elaborate computer into whose memory box had been crammed every available scrap of data on undersea activity. Yet all the wiles of the gods of science could instantly lead to acute myopia, for thousands of feet beneath the ocean surface there are waves hundreds of feet high, enormous hills of that cruelly dense water inexorably thundering along, rising and falling like some Appalachian Mountains suddenly gone fluid as they marched across the land, capable of buffeting and tossing about a submarine as easily as a great thunderstorm can make a broken child's toy out of an airplane.

But at this moment, the sea presented an almost indifferent acceptance of this tiny artificial sliver that probed its depths, and whatever fluid motions were encountered passed without tremor along the *Sea Search*'s smooth flanks.

Lars Svensen wanted another final few words during this contact. He glanced at the gauges that presented a real-time readout of what was happening to the submarine descending beneath his own hulls.

"We'll probably get some distortion soon, Matt. I just wanted to remind you to bring in a gusher. The crew says they could use the bonus, and we all know there's oil somewhere down there."

A chuckle drifted along wire, through air into waiting electronics, and it tickled the bone behind Svensen's ear. "If it's there, we'll find it, old man," Chadwick replied cheerily. "And if it's anywhere, it's in that trench right below us. I—"

Silence. Svensen stiffened with the sudden break in words.

"Matt," he said. He kept his voice calm. Anything to break communications could spell trouble. But it could also be a glitch, a momentary interruption. "Matt, you were cut off. Do you read me?"

Chadwick heard Svensen; the link was still open. But at this moment he was engrossed in his sonarscope and other instrument readings. Chadwick spoke, not to Svensen, but to Templeton at his side. Fortunately, the communications lines were still open to transmit, and Svensen on the surface could listen to the exchange between the two men.

Chadwick tapped the Plexiglas sonar screen. The liquid crystal material had brightened in different areas, in a pattern they found wholly unexpected. "Look at this, Larry. Do you get anything familiar? Especially at this depth?"

Templeton shook his head slowly. He felt he recognized the scope pattern, but Chadwick's last question threw him. "Not down here," he replied carefully. "It simply doesn't fit."

The crystal indexes brightened. Chadwick motioned with his pipestem. "It's big," he said quietly. "It's just too damned big," he added with sudden emphasis. He made a decision. "Set up lights and cameras to kick in with a single command. Then go to transparency for the bow."

Templeton's fingers moved the appropriate controls. Now, with a single switch, they would get flare bombs, floodlights, and camera operation all at the same moment. The bow was something else. The entire foresection of the small submarine was of glassite, stronger than Carboloy steel yet transparent when a very low electrical charge was transmitted to the rounded bow. Sandwiched between thick layers of glassite was a liquid crystal that remained opaque until that moment when the current, of specific voltage and the barest amps, neutralized the light-absorbing qualities of the crystal and rendered it fully transparent. By doing no more than switching the system to CURRENT ON, the entire bow became a window to the ocean. At this moment, the octopuses gone, when the bow went transparent they saw only darkness—and dim distorted reflections of themselves curving back at them. But any light that appeared outside in that utter darkness would also become visible to them, and they had a sweeping "eye bubble" view of whatever might happen.

By now Chadwick could hardly ignore Svensen's repeated calls, and he shook himself free of his preoccupation with events at hand. "Lars, sorry about the delay. We're getting some rather large targets on sonar. They seem much too big for anything we might expect at this depth. What do your instruments show from up there?"

Svensen sighed with sudden relief; he'd wondered when Chadwick was going to speak to him. "Matt, we can't help you. You're beneath some sort of scattering layer. Temperature inversion, maybe. I don't know. We show targets also, but nothing with any clarity. From the size of them they look like whales. Big ones, too, but we both know that's impossible at that—"

"Damn!"

Chadwick's exclamation almost rattled Svensen's skull bones. Far beneath the ocean surface, Chadwick and Templeton had encountered a new element. The "vision of the deeps": sound. The echo-ranging biological sonar of the deep-sea creatures.

"Matt, what is it?"

"Lars, they not only look like whales on the scope, but—"

Svensen couldn't miss the excitement in Chadwick's voice, and that alone told him more than any words. That old sea dog showed excitement on very rare occasion.

"By God," Chadwick's voice came in, "they *are* whales!"

Svensen listened; Chadwick and Templeton were involved in a rapid-fire exchange.

"But that's impossible," Templeton complained. "Look here. Look at the depthometer. Matt, we're down to almost six thousand feet! You don't get whales down here, and—look at the scope. That's a formation of some kind out there."

"I know, I know," came Chadwick's voice, and Svensen detected the chuckle in his response. Faced with the unknown, or even mortal danger,

Chadwick was wont to respond with whatever humor he might find in the situation. It was a trademark of the tall and seemingly frail scientist, and he'd lost none of his past characteristics. He seemed able to disassociate himself physically, even from the imminence of his own destruction, just so that he might study whatever was happening. He tapped Larry Templeton on the arm, and the young man showed surprise at the bemused expression on Chadwick's face.

"Never mind what's impossible, Larry," Chadwick said in mild rebuke. "Focus on what's here, now. Study the scope and relate to that only. My guess is that they're either great blues or sperm whales." Something on the scope struck a chord in him. He made a sucking sound on the cold pipestem. "My bet is on the sperms."

The sea cooperated with his conjecture; almost as quickly as he spoke the cabin speakers came alive with the calling medley of great whales, a running tumble of rapid high-pitched clicks, deep groaning cries, sounds in between.

"There! Hear them? *Sperms*, by God! That's their battle cry! I've heard it for years. I'd know that sound anywhere. I—"

But Templeton had pushed aside the savory cries of proof from Chadwick. He had sent out a flare bomb without commenting to his companion, and in the sputtering glare he had a glimpse of enormous shapes moving inexorably toward them. There was still little to see with any clear definition, but Templeton didn't need much beyond what had struck instant alarm in his bloodstream. His hand slammed full forward on the power lever, and a deep thrumming sound groaned through the sub as the hydrojets spun to full speed. The small sub accelerated with a rush great enough to press them against the backs of their seats. In the same expert motion, Templeton was pushing forward on the control stick to increase the angle of their dive. He slammed the stick to the left as well, maneuvering the sub down and away.

High above them, the application of full power and the emergency maneuvers were registering on the instrument console in front of Svensen. His own reaction was immediate; his hand slammed onto a red button, and the emergency alarm clamored through the *Windward*. Men ran to their stations and Svensen turned to a bridge officer.

"I don't know what the hell's going on down there—whales or what—but it's trouble," he snapped. "Get me a lock on their position. Fire a comm torp to pass close by with the emergency ascent signal. Move it, man!"

They worked as what they were—a precision team. The engineer to Svensen's right motioned to him. Svensen went to his side, sharing his view of an electronic display chart of the area. Contour lines and depth soundings showed clearly, as did glowing threads that marked latitude and longitude. A small yellow light blinked steadily; that would be the sonar position of the *Sea Search*. The yellow light began to trace a curving pattern.

The engineer looked up. "They're diving, turning to the left. Maximum power, full acceleration."

"Goddamn it, something's after them." Svensen spun around, back to his own panel, his voice harsh as he spoke into the tiny lip mike. "Chadwick, come in! Answer me, damn it!"

His voice went unheeded in the sub. Chadwick and Templeton stared in mixed awe and growing fear at the great shadowy things rushing toward them. Templeton hit the floodlights, and the darkness yielded grudgingly.

They could hear what they perceived so poorly with their eyes: a heavy drumming thunder, the powerful thrashing of enormous flukes.

"My God! There must be a dozen of them!" Templeton's cry needed no response. There were a dozen in sight from only one direction. The pinging sounds of the great creatures might have come from a hundred such animals.

And then one of them was close enough for the powerful lights to reveal in heart-freezing detail. An eye from one side staring into the floodlights, the mouth slightly open, the enormous row of teeth showing beneath the blunt head. The creature hurtling at them seemed to fill the ocean. Templeton had time enough to slam his hand to the switch marked COMPUTER EMERGENCY ASCENT, in that instant taking control away from his own body and mind and handing it over to the electronic system of the sub.

He had only that one instant. The shock of the great sperm whale smashing into the sub hurled both men unconscious.

3

<hr>

Captain Arnold Switek, USN, stood patiently before the sprawling communications computer that filled one wall of the large office. Glowing lights rippled in a pattern whose meaning was known only to the computer; the man ignored them, interested only in the readout card even then being processed in the bowels of the system. Fluted sounds, the strange melodious chirpings of electronic touchings around the planet, played gently against his ears. He glanced into a sheet of polished metal, and in its reflection he saw the office windows and beyond them the expanse of Pearl Harbor: buildings, cranes, ships at dockside, areas of greenery and trees, and the inevitable dragonfly shapes of hustling helicopters against white clouds. The computer blinked, adjusted its fluting tone, and ejected a printed card. Switek scanned the message, turned, and walked across the long office to a desk that held a model of a three-masted schooner and other memorabilia of decades past. From behind the desk, Vice Admiral Timothy S. Haig, USN, stared at Switek with unblinking eyes.

Tim Haig deigned to squint, and the facial movement accented the leathery wrinkles in the skin that had been scoured by wind and sun, and oil and smoke and steam and God knew what else in a naval lifetime. Haig sat in a semisprawl like an old cougar, chewing an unlit cigar, the eyes behind the cold tobacco locked onto his aide. Switek held forth the message card.

Haig didn't move. "Read it," he said tersely.

"I have, sir."

"And?"

"It's hard to believe."

"The same as before?"

"Yes, sir."

Haig snorted, disdain and disbelief mixed equally in his wordless exclamation. He shifted in his seat and his voice growled at Switek. "Well, *I* don't believe it. I've been in subs and at sea for more than thirty years, and," he gestured suddenly, "there isn't a damned thing in that report that any sane man would believe."

He stood, his chair still turning from his sudden burst of energy, and walked angrily to a far window, hands clasped behind him, staring across the naval bastion. He didn't turn when he spoke again.

"Do you believe it, Arnie?"

"I don't know, admiral. It sounds crazy."

Haig spun about. "It *is* crazy." He pointed to the computer. "Use the satellite links. Get me Chadwick on the *Windward*."

Switek addressed the computer, punched in the appropriate controls. Haig watched from across the room. Arnie could play that thing like an expert typist or an accountant whose fingers flew over keyed numbers. While his aide set up the call through communications satellite relay to the trimaran in the Aleutians, the admiral reread the report, his cheek muscles working. He went back to his desk as Switek gestured to the blinking light on Haig's phone.

"It's no go, sir," Switek told him. "Dr. Chadwick is still under sedation. No broken bones, but severe bruises and shock. It'll be at least six hours before he can—"

"The muddling old fool! His entire report is preposterous! Who the hell ever heard of sperm whales at a thousand fathoms? And if that isn't enough—" Haig cut himself short, preferring silence to his own frustration. He tore the computer card to shreds, took a deep breath. "His report, or at least what we received here, said something about the whales working in concert, in some sort of formation. I could believe almost anything else, but that one tears it."

Switek glanced across the room, then he returned his gaze to his superior. "Sir, if I may?"

"Stop being so goddamned military, Arnie."

"What you just described came as a statement from Svensen on the *Windward*, admiral. He was putting together what information he could gather from Chadwick when the *Sea Search* was still underwater. Sonar indicated a grouping of the whales, but the word *formation* might not be what they intended, and—"

"How do you explain the thousand fathoms? That wasn't garbled."

"Sir, you know Chadwick isn't anyone's fool. He's got as much salt water in his veins as you do. He's been top dog at Scripps Oceanography for a long time, and he's the best scientist in the deepwater business."

Haig gestured for silence; Switek waited. The sigh he expected from the admiral finally came. "I know, I know," Haig said quietly. "I've served with the man, Arnie. I know he's the best. But this is all so damned important I can't afford even the slightest misinformation. I—"

He interrupted himself, and in a rare gesture struck a match to his cigar, sending out a cloud of thick smoke. It was a ritual Switek well recognized. Decision time.

"All right, Arnie," Haig went on. "Let's assume the reports we have from Svensen are true. According to what he said, the minisub was banged up pretty badly. Internal and external damage. That tells its own story in a boat designed to withstand pressure in more than forty thousand feet of water. Yet it's not as important as what the report on the big animals could mean. If—and it's a very big and fat *if*—Svensen passed on information that's accurate, we're now faced with the problem of sperm whales diving three thousand feet deeper than we ever believed, and doing so in a group, and—"

"Excuse me, sir. We can't overlook another part of that report. Svensen also said that their pickup of echo ranging from the whales indicated intelligent calls between them—"

"We know they're intelligent," Haig said with unintended sarcasm. "We've communicated with them ourselves."

"That's not what I meant, admiral. Svensen seemed explicit that the sonar signals were clearly aggressive." Switek paused, as if he were chewing the end of a distasteful thought. "It would also seem," he said, adding caution to his tone, "as if the sperms were actually coordinating their attack on the sub."

To Switek's surprise—although the admiral often surprised him when he least expected it—Haig failed to evince the angry rejection Switek believed his words would bring.

"That," said the admiral, "is the wildest part of all. It reeks, it stinks to high heaven of the impossible, and yet I can't reject the consistency that runs through these reports. At the same time," he added with a frown, "I also cannot accept at face value information that runs wildly counter to everything we know about these animals."

Switek nodded, eager to continue the line of conjecture. "I wish I could find something from Chadwick or Svensen to argue with, sir, but I can't. I did some additional checking on my own."

"Never mind the dramatic pauses." Haig glared at him.

"Admiral, I didn't mean—"

"Go on, go on, man."

"Yes, sir. Everything else checked out. The *Windward* departed Constantine Harbor in Amchitka Island right on schedule. Svensen maintained his program down to the last degree. As you know, his crew is pretty evenly split between the people from Scripps and from our own deep-sea program. So we've had monitoring from both groups, and they both reported their dive position at precisely 253 miles west of Amchitka—confirmed with satellite tracking—where they released the *Sea Search* minisub."

Tim Haig felt an angry rumble beginning deep in his chest, pushed it down, and spoke quietly. "Why are you spelling it out like that, Arnie?"

"I don't want you to have any questions unanswered, admiral. Everything seemed right up to snuff, and—"

He watched the other man lean forward, resting his weight on his elbows. One eyebrow came up slowly in a gesture well known to Switek, and when Haig spoke it was with a candor that had been missing from their exchange so far. Not that the admiral had been playing word games; it was simply the old tried and true military system of not passing on information without a clear "need to know." Now, Haig had apparently decided that it was time to clue in his aide.

"Everything was *not* up to snuff, captain." Haig hesitated, and his brow went up another notch. "Do you know why Chadwick was going down more than five miles into the Aleutian Trench?"

"Well yes sir. There's a good chance we can make a major petroleum find there and—"

"Chance, hell, Arnie. We've *got* to find that oil. We're not even competing anymore with the Russians. No matter what," he added with a touch of scorn for what was fed to the public, "anyone in this country or theirs might think."

Switek's brow furrowed in open question. "I don't understand, sir."

"We can't afford to fight one another about oil reserves. We both need petroleum too badly to get into a snit about who owns what or where. Look, Arnie, it's been five years since we had that atomic bash. A war that for all intents and purposes lasted about a week. The real punch, anyway. And what happened that week? We were afraid the Russians would get the Arab oil fields, and they felt the same way about us, so we slammed into those fields with earthquake bombs."

Switek nodded, his face grim. "Yes, sir, and they did the same thing."

"That's right, and we ended up with the biggest radioactive desert in the world, a couple of million Arabs dead, more millions hurt, and a fire that burned for nearly two years because no one could get near the area. It was radioactive hell for our side *and* their side. Sure, sure, the war went on for a couple more months, but it was all jockeying for position, and we all knew it was quits months before we signed our treaties."

Haig rose from his desk, trailing cigar smoke, stopping before a wall switch across the room. He depressed the switch and the room darkened. A glowing three-dimensional globe sprang into view, the Pacific Ocean side of the planet gleaming at them. Haig gestured to dots and markers of varying colors.

"There's our problem, Arnie. Chinese subs. Chinese warships. Chinese all over and under the damned ocean. We and the Russians were so busy tearing each other apart that we never realized the

Chinese were laying low. They blew the hell out of Taiwan—nobody on either side really cared because we thought the Red Chinese were so busy. But they were laying their groundwork, and *now* they're making their moves. They're going after oil anywhere they can find it, and they won't stop at anything to get the upper hand."

They looked long at one another, two men intimate with shared silent thoughts, until Switek spoke. "Admiral, do you believe the Chinese are involved in this affair with Chadwick?" His expression clearly carried his own disbelief at the suggestion.

"You mean the whales?"

"Yes, sir. We've controlled porpoises and especially the killer whales for years. So have they. I'm wondering if they've managed to get intelligent control of the big whales. The sperms."

"Anything is possible, Arnie. There's a problem with the sperms, though. They're aggressive as hell, they're fighters, but they don't have the instinctive intelligence of the humpbacks or the blues or even the gray whales. And they're very independent; so there's another possibility to consider. Can you figure it?"

"In all honesty, no, sir."

"Think on it then, captain. Think about a situation where Chadwick's boat may not have been attacked by whales at all."

"I—I don't understand, admiral."

"Arnie, it could have been a sub configured to whale size and shape. Bionics systems, articulated frame, powered flukes, plastiskin covering, but all of it just as artificial as any boat that ever went into the sea. Anyone can transmit recordings of whale echo ranging so that even Chadwick, and Svensen on the surface, would *have* to believe they were picking up whale signals." His teeth clamped tighter on the cigar. "But there's no way to tell while we're sitting here like wax dummies." Haig spun about abruptly and stabbed a finger in the direction of his aide.

"It's decision time, captain. Here's what we do. Get our people to load a *Swimmer* boat aboard a C-14 and fly the damn thing directly to Amchitka. Give it red priority all the way. Get Ritter. Let him pick his own crew. Give him anything he wants, but I want that boat in the air *today*."

Switek held his breath, let it out slowly. "Yes, sir."

"Tomorrow morning I want an armed catamaran moving out from Amchitka. They're to repeat—step by step—everything Chadwick did in his own boat. Punch it all into the computer. They follow the same road map to the last foot. And they're to feed back to us everything that happens *as* it happens. I want real-time transmission right into this office. I want to know everything that goes on down there."

Haig turned away again, slipping into a reflective mood, pausing only long enough for one final command.

"Get with it, captain. *Now*."

4

~~~~~~~~~~~

The pilot kept his toes on the brakes, a ridiculously puny action in comparison with the effect his gentle toe pressure had on the shaped metal pads. Just that slight nudge, boosted by electrical and hydraulic systems, was enough to keep the C-14 cargo transport locked solidly to concrete as the copilot spooled up the great engines. Seven hundred tons of airplane vibrated and trembled, the enormous swept wings flexing as power strained to break free. Behind the two men in the cockpit high above the ground, the flight engineer satisfied himself with the readings of multiple rows of gauges. He nodded and spoke into his lip mike.

"It's time to fly, boss. She's all in the green."

The pilot's nod was barely perceptible, but he rotated his feet to remove the pressure against the brake pedals, dropping his heels to the metal floorboard. With the groan of an imprisoned dinosaur shaking free from confinement, the huge machine accelerated. It seemed too big to move fast enough to fly, but the engines hurled back screaming air and sped the giant faster and faster down the long runway. The flight crew worked quietly, expertly, gnats riding in the brain cavity of a winged mammoth. The copilot called out the critical numbers:

the point beyond which they could no longer stop on the runway remaining; the next point at which they reached safe speed should an engine fail; and the final quiet word, as much a command as if someone had screamed *Fire!*

"Rotate," the copilot said calmly, and the yoke in the pilot's hand came back steadily until the nose of the giant was lifted precisely seven degrees above the horizon. For suspended seconds the great airplane continued, riding its main gear only, the changed angle of the wings modifying the flow over the upper surfaces until the lift generated by the airfoil exceeded the weight of the aircraft. Tugged by forces invisible to the eye yet unchanged from the moment when the Wright brothers lurched into the air ninety-six years before, the great birdlike monster lifted magically away from the hard concrete. With every passing instant, lift increased and thrust increased, and what had been a shaped mountain of inert metal only moments before was now a winged wonder slicing upward into the lower stratosphere.

The miracle of what took place was an everyday occurrence to these men, and the flight crew went through the motions of hands and eyes and ears and minds with practiced skill, with as much reflexive action as conscious attention. As the C-14 thundered into thinner and less resistant air, Lieutenant Colonel John Hughes in the pilot's seat studied the computer autopilot system, tapped in numbers that had been determined well before he left the flight operations office, and turned control of the plane over to the black boxes that were buried in the machine's nose section. The computer, working with accelerometers and other gyroscopic and inertial systems, would now fly the aircraft with robotic precision; the crew was content to sit back and drink coffee in their pressurized windowed world, keeping alert for any malfunctions that might arise. The robots that guided them, although aspiring to great electronic heights, were still subject to glitches that tweaked the aircraft's movement. At subsonic speeds, even a small tweak can produce an instant and gut-clenching pucker factor, but, at the moment, tranquillity and performance matched, so the crew could relax.

However, their cargo made them uncomfortable, caused some physical squirming and also some mental gymnastics. Hughes sipped his coffee and glanced at his copilot. Major William Bagwell nodded. The question had been with both of them from the very moment they entered their airplane and saw their Q-Secret cargo.

"I've heard of them all, but this one is a record."

Hughes held his cup gingerly for a moment during a gentle roll through mild turbulence. "Well— there's a first time for everything."

Their flight engineer leaned forward. "Sure, sure, but who'd believe a submarine in this thing at fifty thousand feet?"

Hughes turned in his seat, looked back through the open hatchway into the cavernous hold. "To hell with the tin can—you people get a close look at the bunch *with* that underwater lizzie?"

Bagwell shuddered. He was a wiry, intense man who'd been in the thick of nuclear hell only five years before. "Jesus, yes," he said after a long pause, "they're killers. Every one of them."

He was right. They were killers, and they looked up, a hundred feet distant, and stared unblinking at the flight crew studying them through the small hatchway. They sat or stood around the long slim submarine that was chained and cabled securely to the cargo deck of the C-14. Twelve men. Four of them crew of that sinister *Swimmer IV* killer sub, and eight security guards, every one of them holding rapid-fire submachine guns. Which the pilots of the C-14 knew, because they had been told, were loaded and ready to fire.

Their orders had been blunt. Take your cargo to your appointed airport. Don't try to get near the sub. Don't ask any questions of the naval personnel aboard. Mind your business. Fly your airplane, and then leave, and mention to no one what you've carried.

Bagwell heard a chime and studied the gauges. "Fifty thousand," he said quietly, a human confirmation of computer-controlled flight. "We're on our way."

Hughes nodded, not speaking. The feeling in the small of his back, the sight of those hand-held machine guns, all of it unnerved him. All he wanted to do was to get that bunch the hell out of his airplane. The computer blinked its digital message; they had a tail wind. Hughes was grateful for the small favor. The flight would go that much quicker.

Secretary of the Navy Frank Cartwright leaned back in his leather chair in New Washington—sixty miles straight-line distance from the radioactive rubble that had once been the nation's capital—studying the videophone display on his desk. His office was situated four hundred feet beneath the earth's surface, and the space in between was filled with thick percentages of steel and reinforced concrete and permeated throughout with all manner of sensors and detectors and filters and traps. Despite the weight overhead, Cartwright felt no oppressiveness, and claustrophobia was not counted among his problems. He gave his unique positioning only a fleeting thought as he concentrated on the face and voice that came to him through the electronics equipment on his desk.

On his screen, Cartwright saw the man whose

title was Commander, Pacific Ocean. Vice Admiral Timothy Haig was an old friend, and his face showed the need for this direct contact that had been initiated by a call with a coded scrambler priority. They exchanged personal amenities, and then Cartwright, never one to waste time with so few years remaining in his life, went straight to the issue of the call.

"That's an incredible report from Chadwick," he said, opening easily.

In Pearl Harbor, above the surface, Tim Haig nodded, enjoying a breeze gliding through his office. He didn't answer at once, still studying Cartwright's features on his own screen. The navy secretary had been wounded grievously in at least two wars, and the cumulative effects of his personal agonies were stamped on his scarred features. Frank Cartwright in his prime had been a muscular hulk of a man; he still carried his great frame, but now he was like an old and wounded buffalo, moving stiffly and with effort but with all the commanding presence he had known in younger days.

"Yes, sir, it is," Haig said after the pause. "So incredible we can't discount it, as much as I'd like to dismiss the entire affair as so much nonsense."

"I take it you've equated your judgment with action."

Timothy Haig almost laughed at the other man's words. "Yes, sir, I have. I dispatched *Swimmer IV* by air to Amchitka. They'll be in the water about twelve hours from now. Their orders are to duplicate as much as possible Chadwick's mission profile, to try to instigate whatever happened to Chadwick."

"After that point, Tim?"

"They're to keep right on going, sir. All the way to the bottom."

"I've read the full report, Tim." Cartwright

paused for only a moment, weighing his words, keeping it taut. "Do you really believe the Chinese are involved?"

He watched Haig roll an unlit cigar from one side of his mouth to the other. Cartwright detected a shrug that meant "no commitment."

"Sir, their boat was attacked," Haig replied carefully. "I don't know by what or how, really, but there's no way to ignore the event itself."

"Of course not," Cartwright said with a nod. "Sending out the boat was the only thing to do."

"Thank you, sir."

Cartwright leaned forward, an instinctive move bringing him closer to the videophone, as if this might lessen the physical distance between himself and Haig. "Tim, your feelings are important here. Disassociate yourself from your office. I'd like to know your gut reactions. Can you give me any further evaluation of Chadwick's report on the whales?"

Haig shook his head, his expression unhappy. "I wish I could, Frank. But we lack data—and what we do have is, well, it's self-contradictory. Too much conflict involved. We've never known sperms to dive to six thousand feet, and moving in a herd simply is not the same as moving in formation. If I want to be hard-nosed about it, and I have to, then all I *know* is that the minisub was attacked by what Chadwick insists were sperm whales, moving in concert, using audible signals of aggressiveness or attack, and deliberately ramming the boat with Chadwick and Templeton in it. I can't go beyond that. Too many ands, ifs, or buts are involved."

There was nothing else to say, really. Haig had it all in hand. Cartwright was unhappy about their inability to pin down any leads that might involve the Chinese, but precious little could be done about that at this time. "All right, Tim," he said to wrap it up, "keep me informed."

"Yes, sir. If it turns out to be the Chinese instead of the whales—"

"Of course," Cartwright said quickly. "No matter what time of day or night, or where I am. Break in."

"Yes, sir." Haig watched the screen dissolve into the random pattern of the disassociating scrambler code.

The great transport sliced through a thin cirrus cloud deck, the shrill whine of the jet engines at reduced power sounding unusually loud within the aircraft. Clouds flashed by in eye-blinking wisps as the plane descended, and the earth's surface showed through in momentary glimpses. They rocked gently in turbulence and suddenly the world above became the long flat bottom of the cloud deck, creating the impression of an enormous amphitheater below. Water, stretches of islands, mixed sunlight and shadow, and a subdued exclamation, an intake of breath, from Major Bagwell in the copilot seat.

"Jesus Almighty—"

They looked down through the cockpit glass at what had been an island, part of a chain, on which there had once been a large city and a military reservation. *Had* been. Now it was nothing more than a huge crater. Just a large island made up of a high-rimmed crater that contained radioactive glass.

"No one survived that," the navigator said quietly.

"What the hell was there to survive?" Bagwell demanded. "It wasn't even an accurate strike. The goddamned warhead came out of a missile that went wild, and—"

Hughes didn't like the conversation—or the mood it created. The triple-damned war was far behind them, and he preferred to keep it that way. "Get your heads back in the cockpit," the pilot told his men with just enough sharpness to bring them around. "Amchitka's coming up."

Several moments later Bagwell turned to him. He'd been talking with the people on the ground. "We're locked in and number one to land. Straight-in approach."

"Good," Hughes said. "Let's get to work. Start the checklist."

They went in by the numbers, steadily descending toward the expanding concrete ribbon, flaps coming down, gear extending, leading-edge flaps boosting lift, spoilers playing gently out on the wings; they drilled her back to earth as though she were filled with helium, nice and easy and gentle. When they were on the ground they discovered that they were intruders on a naval facility and the navy was running the show. Vehicles with turreted 20-mm cannon rode on either side of them, another was behind, and the familiar Follow Me truck carried a rapid-fire cannon aimed unerringly at their cockpit. Ground control taxied them to a parking site by a dock ramp, and a voice came over their headsets.

"Thank you, gentlemen. Keep your engines running and all your crew at stations. If you'll open the nose hatch we'll unload, and you can be on your way."

They looked at one another and shrugged. Their orders had been explicit. Do *exactly* as they were instructed by Amchitka Control. The nose latches were freed, the great nose cone lifted up and away. They felt the airplane shaking as the submarine and its protective crew vacated the cargo hold.

By the time they were ordered to close the loading hatchway and they could see ahead of them once more, the ramp was deserted—submarine and all.

"It stinks," Captain Sam Duncan, USN, muttered to himself. "It stinks all the way." He stood on the bridge of his catamaran and watched the submarine —he knew it was a submarine because his crew had told him so; you couldn't see anything beneath that canvas covering—being winched to the grapples between his knife-edged hulls. He didn't like the secrecy—not because of the security, but because *he* was the captain of this vessel, and he didn't know what the hell was going on or who was coming aboard. He watched a security crew, armed to the teeth, surrounding four men in strange dark clothing and woolen skullcaps. Definitely not uniforms. Once their sub was secured between the cat hulls, the security team moved back and set up a heavy-fire cordon so that no one else could approach the catamaran. Sam Duncan didn't like that either.

He studied the four men who obviously made up the crew of the long boat that was hugging the catamaran. Three white, one black, all tough, confident, almost contemptuous of everyone around them. They wore name tags on their chests, and he'd already learned their names, as if that told him anything. He had the curious idea that the names might not even be real. The one named Ritter seemed to be the leader, or commanding officer, but Duncan didn't know that for a fact because they wore no other insignia or markings. The other two whites were Tobias and Young, and the black was Sanford. He confirmed Ritter as the leader when his communication came alive.

"A Mr. Ritter to see the captain," his exec told him.

Duncan's eyes narrowed. *Mr.* Ritter?

Several moments later they faced one another, and Duncan was as much put out as before. Ritter was a tough no-nonsense man who spoke in phrases as tightly clipped as his dark beard. He saluted Duncan, who returned the salute in an offhanded manner that betrayed his bristliness. Duncan watched for some clue, anything that might break this strange fog of anonymity. Ritter forced the issue by standing in silence.

"I hope you can tell me what this is all about," Duncan said finally.

The man before him betrayed no expression, showed no discourtesy, but remained beyond his reach. He slipped a folded envelope from a back pants pocket, unfolded it, and presented it to Duncan.

"Your orders, sir," he said.

Duncan held the sealed envelope in one hand and tapped it on his other palm. His eyes narrowed. "That's it? Just this envelope?"

Ritter's face remained a mask. Steel-polite, Duncan would have called it. "My orders were to come aboard this vessel and personally hand you this envelope," Ritter told him.

Duncan showed a flush of anger that he tried immediately to repress. "What's your rank, Ritter? You're no 'mister.' "

"Sir, it's all in that envelope." A split-second hesitation, a decision that was made on the spot: "Captain, I suggest we go to your cabin and you read what's in that envelope."

Duncan's eyes went wide. "*You* suggest that I—"

The steel was out in the open now. "Sir."

Duncan paused at Ritter's word.

Ritter went on. "I could make it an order."

Duncan swallowed it. He knew when to quit. "Come with me," he said, and he walked off. Ritter followed, still expressionless.

They were well at sea, the catamaran prows slicing like knife blades through the water, moving under full speed toward that specific but unmarked site in the ocean where Chadwick and Templeton had been lowered into the depths. Ritter stood slightly behind and to the side of Duncan as both men watched the swiftly darkening sky. Duncan's air was proper but stiff—that of a man who'd been upstaged in a manner he couldn't yet understand. Ritter's voice came to him quietly.

"How much longer?"

Duncan didn't turn. "I estimate zero two hundred."

"Good. We'll have a low moon."

They stood together in silence, and then Ritter left to meet with his crew. When he returned to the bridge, the cat was hove to, rocking gently on a sea that was unusually calm for the Aleutians. The moonlight seemed to cast a baleful glow across the ocean surface. Between the twin hulls, men were working with the submarine. An officer came to the bridge and spoke to Duncan. Curiosity had replaced the captain's pique. He hoped Ritter would let him know something about what was going on.

"Your men report that they're ready," Duncan told Ritter.

"Thank you." That was all he got as Ritter left the bridge to go below.

Duncan followed, leaving his exec in command on the bridge. He watched the men enter the narrow hatchway into the *Swimmer IV*. Tobias was the last in, and his swarthy face broke into a grin as he turned and tossed a salute to the catamaran crew. The hatch clanged shut behind him.

At a signal from the deck officer, the crew winched the sub into the sea, water swirling easily over its rounded flanks. The winches continued releasing cable for another minute, then the cables went slack. Duncan stared at nothingness. They were gone.

Ritter looked up through his port at the shimmering moonlight. The catamaran hulls were distorted pylons seen through moonstruck water, and the sight faded slowly as they fell. Ritter brought in the power gently, feeling her out as he always did when initiating a dive, and the four men went through their drill with practiced, soft-spoken competence. A powerful thrumming grew from far behind them in the bowels of the sub, the shrouded hydrojets increasing their thrust as the throttle beneath Ritter's hand moved forward. The dive angle steepened. The beginning of the dive followed the track of Chadwick and Templeton in their minisub, but this time the scenario played to a different act. *Swimmer IV* had fangs.

Ritter went through the litany they all knew so well. "Commence combat alert. Confirm."

Tobias's voice came back at once, a gentle chanting sound. "Propulsion, electrical grid, all maneuvering thrusters status red."

"Sonar, masers, communications, navigation, auto-computer standby, everything's green." That from Young.

Sanford's voice had the hint of a chuckle. It always did, thought Ritter as he heard the black man join them. "We're hot with fire in the belly, Ritter Baby." It was the sound of a man who had a light but lethal touch, a swift-finger deftness with weaponry.

They went down steadily, four men in two rows of tandem seats, Ritter left front, Tobias to his right, Young behind Ritter, and Sanford, with more space and a wider control panel than the others behind Tobias. They were all in their late twenties and early thirties, tough and trim, combat veterans of a war short-lived, but not that many years back, that had left its impression indelibly in their psyches. Sanford's fingers played lightly across his weapons console like a musician fingering an organ.

"Search torps are in the gate," he said quietly. "Seek-and-destroy fish are stage-three arm."

Sanford grinned as Ritter turned to look at him. "It might be interesting, you know," Sanford said.

"Finding some of those Chinese whales. Know what I mean?"

"Chinese whales." Ritter let the words hang for a moment, glanced at the other men. "Any of you troops believe the sperms really go down six thousand feet?"

"That's a thousand fathoms of fairy tales," Sanford chuckled.

"Made in Peking," added Tobias.

Young hesitated. "I wouldn't be so sure. Old man Chadwick is tops in his business. He doesn't make mistakes."

Sanford's laugh was almost velvety. "He's a civilian. Loves peace above all else. Logic, reality, rationale—none of it counts. Peace at any cost—even if the price is smearing what life is all about. He thinks the world is so flat everything's laid out like the dinner table." The laugh came again and his fingers brushed the deadly keys and buttons beneath his hands. "Man or beast," he added, "it don't matter to what we got."

Ritter's gaze took them all in, one by one, an unblinking meeting of eyes. "I don't want anyone going off half-cocked. This job is more than going downstairs to beat the pulp out of something—whatever that something may be." They laughed lightly at his own hesitant admission. "No matter what any of us thinks here and now, we're guessing. Got it? Just guessing. Chadwick and his assistant may be civilians—sucking lollipops for all we know—but they're good at their job and they *were* here. So we play it cool, we give out our invitation by our presence, and we try to find out what it was that beat that little sub about the head and shoulders. And we bring the story home. All of you understand me?"

He paused and leveled his gaze at Sanford. "And you, Killer, keep off the trigger-happy crap."

Sanford showed a white smile, then screwed up

his face in mock insult. "Team, we got us a nervous turkey for boss-man tonight."

Tobias was ignoring the exchange. Ritter's tone, and his demeanor, had told Tobias something. He turned to the lead man. "You know something we don't, skipper?"

Ritter nodded. "Uh huh. Before we left, after I had my little conversation with the admiral, I went down to S2 and spent some time with friends."

"It pays to have friends in Intelligence," noted Young.

"And?" Tobias pressed.

"There's not a trace of any Chinese boats working the Aleutian Trench," Ritter told them.

Young shrugged. "So maybe they're Russian."

"And maybe," Ritter threw back at him, "Chadwick really knew what he was talking about."

Sanford was openly scornful. "Come off it, man. You're starting with those whales again like—"

A pinging chime interrupted him. Silence clamped a hold on the tight cabin. Silence, except for the background hum of machinery they had long before ignored, broken only by the chime and the increasingly louder pinging sounds. Young bent intently over his scanning displays. He didn't bother to look up.

"Targets bearing two six zero. Range eight hundred yards and they're closing fast."

5

~~~~~~~~~~

"Identify!"

Ritter's voice snapped like a whip. Young was already tapping out data keys on his computer.

"According to the brain, those are sharks coming in," Young said. "But that many of them—" he gestured to take in the ocean beyond their powerful hull, "it just doesn't fit. And not at this depth."

"No sweat," Tobias said to dismiss any threat of danger. "What the hell are they going to do—bite us?"

Ritter ignored Tobias, stayed with Young. "Size, numbers."

"They're big mothers," Young replied. He studied his data displays, and he whistled. "The scan shows them thirty to fifty feet. And the way they're moving, they're aggressive."

The touch of levity wisped away. No one deep in the ocean is very pleased with the unexpected. It can kill you. Then, Young dropped the second hammer. "There's more than a hundred of them out there."

"Where?" Tobias demanded.

"Coming straight at us from all quadrants."

"Jesus."

Ritter's voice hadn't changed a note. "Let's get some light out there."

Sanford's fingers were ready and waiting and they moved swiftly. He depressed keys, stroked controls. They felt the shuddering release of slim torps racing away, fanning out from small ports in the sub hull.

"Twenty seconds," Sanford sang out.

"Four thousand feet," came Young's voice.

"There shouldn't be sharks like that down here." Tobias was more annoyed by the unexpected occurrence than he was apprehensive.

"Five seconds," Sanford said. "Sun's about to come up, man."

They looked through individual ports and scopes. In the distance, on all sides of the *Swimmer IV*, silent explosions of blossoming light sent a ghostly pall through the dark water. A second wave of flare bombs detonated at closer range. The intensity of light relative to the sub went up sharply. Now they could see long shapes rushing toward them.

"Let's have the scenic tour," Ritter ordered.

"Got it," Young answered, working controls.

The liquid crystal sandwiched between the glassite layers in the bow received its electromagnetic current and went from opacity to full transparency. They were "outside" the sub. It was breathtaking—like flying while you're sitting on the leading edge of a wing.

Tobias's voice came through, badly strained this time. "My God . . ."

Young was wide-eyed, sucking in air. "I don't believe it—"

Everything happened with accelerating, blinding speed—with an almost stroboscopic effect of flickering light, swirling water, shockingly swift movement, stark contrasts. A monster shark, perhaps a great white tiger, but unlike any they had ever known before, loomed abruptly from the light-spattered depths, jaws huge and agape, and it slammed into the side of the sub. The view from within the glassite hull was terrifying, the fear instinctive and relentless, for the great teeth had smashed together toward them—and had been stopped only inches away by an invisible wall.

You think of crazy things at a moment like this. The bite of a shark is 26,000 pounds pressure to the square inch, and you know, you absolutely *know,* that nothing transparent can stop those giant piston-like teeth from coming together.

Blood spurted as the jagged blades smashed against the hull and the glassite and then broke off. The men were rocked violently, the world about them a horrendous din of crashing and pounding sounds as shark bodies and teeth slammed against the small sub. Through the uproar they heard Young's voice shouting, a near scream.

"Take her down! *Take her down, goddamn it!*"

Ritter, outwardly impassive, controlling his own primeval fears by using the greatest willpower he had ever exerted in his life, braced himself against the physical mauling and called out the orders. "Toby—full power, emergency dive."

At his own console, Tobias's left hand slammed the throttle into emergency overdrive. The sub controls were like those of a fighter plane—a sidearm right stick and rudder pedals—and he worked them expertly, even frantically, to produce a tremendous howl of energy as the nuclear hydrojets ripped raw power into the jets. The acceleration threw them backward into their seats, yet it wasn't fast enough to prevent the diving sub from slewing about wildly as another beast broke dozens of great teeth against the hull.

Sanford's voice came over the din. "Hang in there—" His fingers flew across his console, relays closed, and a small cloud of torpedoes whipped outward from the hull. The torps didn't go far, just far enough so that their concussion waves wouldn't damage the *Swimmer IV* hull, its systems, or its fragile human cargo.

The torps went off in a crazy staccato pattern. Light reflected garishly from the sudden blasts, and the men were slammed about in their harnesses. Tobias felt blood spray outward from his nose, so violent was the shaking within the sub.

Surcease came with almost as much impact as the attack. One moment they were under furious assault; the next, they felt only the ear-ringing echoes of concussion waves dying away. They sucked in air, looked out through the glassite and through their ports. Young shuddered; a mauled shark, bloody entrails drifting from its ruptured stomach, dragged along the glassite bow and was swept under.

Ritter was half-around in his seat, anger apparent on his face, showing his first open emotion since they'd slipped beneath the surface. He seemed furious enough to strike out at Sanford. "What the hell did you do that for?" he shouted.

Sanford's grin faded slowly, and then his own face turned to a dark stone. "You better take another look out there."

"We didn't need the goddamned torps." Ritter's eyes were accusing. "Damn you—you panicked. The sharks couldn't hurt us, and we could outrun them."

Sanford's eyes narrowed. "They're *sharks*, man. What the hell are you so hot about sharks—"

"I told you to lay off the trigger-happy stuff," Ritter snapped. "And you will *not* fire again unless I give you a direct order. You got that?"

Sanford's bile threatened to spill over and an angry retort started from his throat. Young's voice broke in before Sanford gave speech to his feelings.

"Gentlemen, we have company again."

Tobias shook his head slowly. "You mean those things are still coming at us?"

Young shook his head. "Uh uh, Toby. The computer scan says they're whales." He turned a dial, and sound from a speaker filled the compartment. Sonar pings, unmistakable to their trained ears. Sonar pings *and* the echo ranging of great whales.

Ritter studied his crewman. "No question?"

"They're whales, they're sperms, *and* they're pinging danger signals. At us, I might add," Young said dryly.

"Which is impossible," Tobias said matter-of-factly. "We're past nine hundred fathoms."

Ritter glanced at Sanford, whose eyes were mocking as his fingers rippled the air just above his weapons keys. Ritter turned back to Tobias. "Take her down at eight zero knots. Forty degree dive."

They sat silently for several moments, their body senses judging the acceleration and change of dive angle. Ritter waited, then went back to the business at hand. "All right, troops, we'll just pull away from them. But what we've found out is enough to bring all our attention to this area. Sharks as big as those trying to chew on us, working in concert, almost as if they were controlled—it just doesn't stack right." He let his voice trail away. The sub was down to seven thousand feet, and the sperms were still following, just above, but falling back. Ritter knew the other men had studied the depthometer with him.

"And we all know," Sanford said slowly, "that sperms cannot, repeat, *not*, dive to seven thousand feet—right?"

"Young, get out a message sphere," Ritter ordered. "Put down everything that's happened from all recorders and pop her immediately. I want the people upstairs to have it all down pat."

Tobias turned in his seat, a crooked grin showing on his face. "You make it sound like we might not get back."

Ritter didn't return the smile. "You're right."

They waited in silence as Young prepared the message sphere, worked the release controls. They felt the slight shudder as the sphere ejected from the hull and began its swift rise.

Thousands of feet above them the sphere popped out of the water, settled back, and stabilized. The automatic sequencer extended a long whip antenna, and a transmitter began its high-speed broadcast, repeating the tape each time it went through a complete transmission.

Some miles away, on the bridge of the catamaran, Captain Sam Duncan stared into the darkness. The speaker to his right crackled slightly. "Captain to the radio shack. We have a message from the boat."

Duncan went immediately to the shack. The communications gear translated the signals into meaningful terms. Duncan listened in silence, swore quietly when the tape ended. He stood up, turned to his comm officer. "Comsat transmission at once. Keep sending until you confirm receipt."

Tobias scanned his instruments, relaxed now, the maniacal frenzy of the huge sharks far above and behind them. The crew had eaten, they'd taken high-energy liquids, and they were in top form. "Twenty-four thousand," Tobias announced to his crewmates. "Coming back on power and rate of descent."

Ritter's acknowledgment was usual. "Okay." Ritter turned to Young. "We should have the bottom right beneath us."

He waited, the others remaining quiet, for confirmation from Young. Instead, there was only a sound of air being sucked in. No words.

Ritter showed a touch of impatience. "Damn it, Young, spill it. What's the matter with you?"

Mild confusion had become stark disbelief as Young went through the motions of reconfirming everything his instruments told him. He glanced at Ritter, turned back to his console, looked up again.

"There's no bottom," he announced.

Ritter glanced at Tobias and Sanford; they shrugged. He returned his attention to Young.

"Explain that."

By now Young was so full of tension that his voice was almost breaking. "*There's no bottom,*" he repeated.

The pause that followed was inevitable. Ritter shook it loose. "Spell it out," he said.

Young forced his words through clenched teeth. "There's no bottom, damn it. The sonar just—well, it just empties out. I know the bottom is supposed to be only a thousand feet or so beneath us, but it isn't there."

Ritter loosened his straps to get closer to Young's console. Young pointed to the gauges. "See what I mean? Off to the north, and down here, breaking south, and even behind us—everything's exactly the same as the hydrographic projections. Both on the charts and in the computer."

Ritter pointed to a display panel. "But not below or ahead of us?"

Young shook his head. "I've got a reach of three miles to echo-sound any bottom beneath us. And I can't pick up a thing straight down."

Sanford chimed in from behind them. "Are you telling us you can't find a bottom more than seven miles down?"

"That's right," Young said.

"That's crazy! That's deeper than the Challenger Deep in the Marianas!"

"Get stuffed," Young growled. "My equipment is working fine. *And there's no bottom.*"

Ritter was back in his seat, strapping in tightly. The others followed suit as they saw the grim look on Ritter's face. "Troops," he told them slowly, "this meeting has just ended. This whole dive has been one lunatic binge from the word go."

He took a long breath, studied his gauges, turned again to look at his crew. "You all cinched up? Good. We're going *down.* Young, get out another message ball. Just tell it like it is."

Tobias was openly doubtful of their move. "Skipper, we're taking a hell of a chance. We haven't got any idea of what's down there."

"How right you are," Ritter told him. "Toby, you're about to become a pioneer. Take her down, mister."

They kept their silence as the sub glided deeper, but every man was exquisitely alert, senses and minds tuned to anything that might happen. As the depth changed, they came verbally alive as a team shaped by experience.

"Twenty-six thousand," Young called out.

"Steady as she goes," Ritter said quietly.

Moments later Tobias stiffened, his voice changed pitch. "What's that?" He pointed through the glassite nose.

Before them appeared a long string of undulating lights, a rippling display of color, a fantasy procession floating in nothingness.

"It looks like a bad dream," Sanford said.

Then the lights were gone. The men had no idea what they were. Several minutes later the darkness came alive again, this time with flickering objects that appeared and disappeared, self-illuminating ghosts that tugged at subconscious terrors in the eerie way that an unrecognizable object in an unknown environment can compound a person's fear.

The sea around them went dark again; the ghostly lights vanished as if behind an impenetrable curtain. Young's voice came to them quietly. "Thirty thousand."

"What's the pressure?" The question came from Tobias.

"Thirteen thousand three hundred sixty-two point three zero psi," Young replied.

Sanford's laugh lifted their spirits, backed off the gloom. "I always did like a man who was positive," he cracked.

"I think he was off a pound," Ritter joined in.

"Okay, you clowns," Young said. His words were to be expected but not his tone, and they were alerted when he added, "We're getting a bottom bounce."

"Thank Christ for that," Tobias murmured. "I thought we were going all the way to Africa."

Young ignored him. He was immersed in the incredible readings of his instruments. He looked up, studied each man before speaking. "Nine thousand feet *below* us."

A long pause followed his words. Tobias rolled his eyes. "No one, but no one, is ever going to believe us."

Ritter motioned to Young. "Punch up another message sphere."

"Okay."

They stayed quiet, descending, monitoring every gauge, hair-trigger alert.

Young's voice came through again. "My God . . ."

Angry, nettled by his own impatience, Ritter snapped at Young. "Dump the religious chant, damn it. What is it?"

Young's eyes were wide. "It's a dome. Jesus—I don't believe it but it's a *dome*. It's impossible—"

Ritter came free of his straps, leaned over Young's shoulder. Young pointed to the panel.

"See? It goes on for miles. It's even beyond our scan power. But look at that sonar bounce! It looks—"

"Like what, damn it!" Sanford's question was almost a snarl.

"Like someone *built it*."

Ritter didn't let the situation get away. "Keep those message spheres going. Every ninety seconds with full instrument data, if nothing else. I don't know what the hell's down there, but we're not letting go now. Sanford, you're off your leash. Arm all weapons, stand by to fire on command."

"Yes, sir." There are times not to play games.

"Toby, call 'em off."

"Thirty-six thousand," Tobias answered at once. "The pressure is—uh, skipper—Christ, it's more than eight tons per square inch. We're playing it awfully close."

Ritter ignored the implied protest. "This can will take it."

"Hey, you guys—"

They turned to Young who had remained glued to his console. *"Something's coming up toward us."*

Ritter's voice whipped at him. "Call the range!"

"Just under one thousand feet and closing—"

Sanford broke in. "Can you make out—"

"Shut up," Ritter snapped. "Get some light bombs out there. TV torps. Fire!"

Sanford's hands blurred with movement, his fingers rippling over keys. They felt the shuddering motion of the slim torps bursting away, the sounds of the torp drives coming at them through the hull.

Before them, in the foresection of the cabin, a TV monitor came alive with a signal that was wire-fed from the TV torpedo. The picture was blurred, almost completely dark; then the light bombs began detonating, burning steadily, bringing artificial sun into the sea depths.

"Snakes!" Tobias shouted. "For God's sake, those are snakes out there!"

"We're 36,000 feet down," Young protested. "It's not possible for—"

"*Eels.*" They were startled by the hard flatness of Ritter's voice. "They're eels. Big mothers. Young?"

"Uh, sonar gives—they're, uh—at least a hundred feet in length—"

Sanford's eyes widened as he kept staring at the TV monitor. "*Look!*"

On the screen the impossible had become even more real. Among the sinuous shapes of what Ritter had identified as great eels, moving before the spattering illumination from the burning light bombs, additional shapes came into view. They seemed to have limbs, a vague humanlike form . . .

Sanford's confidence shattered. "We've got to get away!" he yelled. Before anyone could answer him or stop his movement, his fingers were flying over the firing controls.

Too late, Ritter was shouting, "No—*don't!*"

A spread of torpedoes ripped away from the sub. Ritter was half out of his seat; he remained there, frozen in time and space, it seemed, a look of horror on his face, not from what had appeared outside the submarine, but from what Sanford had done. He hung like that for an eternal moment, threw himself back in his seat, turned like a madman to the controls, and threw in emergency override power to the nuclear hydrojets. Power screamed at them, the entire submarine structure groaned from the acceleration at those crushing pressures. But at this depth it took time to accelerate; time to maneuver the hydrojets that turned the boat, changed its momentum, its direction; time to impart to it new speed and new heading. And while all this was happening with agonizing slowness, the TV screen was still alive, the wire still held in spite of their jerk of sudden energy, and on the screen they saw the great eel shapes closing on them.

Screen and vision and submarine shuddered suddenly. The screen went dead as a distant explosion and then another and another smashed the ocean in staccato blasts as the torps detonated.

"*We did it! We got 'em! We*—" Sanford's cry of jubilation ended in mid-sentence, died gurgling in his throat as something crashed against the hull, rattling the boat wildly.

They stared in disbelief and fear through the glassite bow as the great glowing eel shapes hurled themselves against the submarine.

Tobias was frozen where he sat, but his mind was working, and he found hope in the twisting nest of terror. "Thank God for this hull. They can't hurt us inside here—"

"They're—" Ritter had time only for that one word when a tremendous bolt of electricity exploded within the sub and rattled their lives from them. He never did have an additional moment to tell his crew that the shapes out there were those of great electric eels.

6

~~~~~~~~~~~~~~

The dorsal fin cut the sparkling blue water with great speed, rushing toward a beautiful woman in a wet suit who stood waist-deep in the shallows. She remained still, one hand poised above the water, and just when it seemed inevitable that she would be struck by the animal racing at her, her hand cracked sharply against the water.

The sound of her palm still ringing, a bottle-nosed dolphin stabbed upward, balancing on its tail, grinning, almost laughing over the game. Dr. Miko Akasada Stewart shouted and laughed with the porpoise that was now chattering to her. She patted the animal and gestured, and instantly the porpoise was gone. Miko watched carefully for the animal's wide swing back to her, but before she could repeat another hand motion a loudspeaker brought her head up sharply.

"Urgent telephone call for Dr. Stewart. There is an urgent call for Dr. Stewart, please."

Lithe and lovely, she climbed along seawall steps into a building to take the unexpected phone call.

The crippled man emerged slowly from his office, moving with a stiff gait and a cane that betrayed a prosthetic limb that had no bionic advantages. The secretary of the navy disdained the electronic miracles that had helped so many younger men shorn of their limbs; Frank Cartwright was content to be able to walk at all. He left his office, took an escalator down to a small subway car that stood waiting, and let his aide help him to a seat. Pneumatic doors closed, a hiss of expelled air followed, and the single car was whisked swiftly along its side-supporting tracks. It emerged in another underground station, where Cartwright went to an elevator that took him forty stories straight up to a private waiting room. From there he moved slowly along a narrow aisle and stepped through a curving metal doorway into a small four-engine jet aircraft. Several minutes later the machine was climbing out steeply for its long flight westward.

Whirling rotor blades spattered light patterns on the waves as a helicopter lowered itself over the water, slowing its flight as it neared a floating platform. The helicopter circled the platform, talking by radio with a lone figure who was standing there. The pilot waved, turned steeply, and flew directly south to where a flag marker bobbed in the choppy water. Here the pilot brought the helicopter to a hover and winched down a microphone by cable until it descended ten feet below the surface.

Within the sun-washed upper levels of the ocean water, a loud electronic coded chime echoed in all directions. The signal went unnoticed except by one man in a wet suit and pressure face mask who was rushing beneath the surface in a hydrojet-powered mansled. The signal brought a frown to the strong face, forced an unplanned squint to alert eyes. Captain Jerome Manning, U.S. Navy, cursed quietly to himself, swerved the mansled, and eased up to break the surface. He pressed a tongue switch, spoke into a tiny microphone before his lips.

"Sagebrush, Manning here. Go ahead." Manning rested easily, a powerful and intense man in his early thirties, displeased but not really disturbed by this interruption of a planned solo day at sea in the mansled. His earphone crackled gently.

"Sorry to break in, captain. You have a priority one, your eyes only, at base."

"Okay, Sagebrush. I'll come in with the sled."

"Sir, my orders are to bring you in immediately."

"Come get me."

"Yes, sir."

Several minutes later Manning slipped on the harness hoist lowered to him, and he was being lifted up even as the chopper began its run back to the nearby naval base. The chopper settled on a green lawn at San Diego in a blur of flying grass and wind.

Almost at the same moment, another helicopter dropped with a jet roar to the open lawn outside the office of Vice Admiral Timothy Haig in Pearl Harbor. As soon as the blades had quieted, Matthew Chadwick and Larry Templeton emerged and were led to a waiting car. Chadwick was still having some physical difficulty from the battering he had taken in the whale attack against his minisub *Sea Search;* one arm was still supported by a sling.

The car drove off as soon as the two men got in.

Tim Haig hung up his telephone and turned in his seat to look at Navy Secretary Frank Cartwright. They had been drinking coffee, spending several moments in pleasant, personal small talk.

"They're all here except Manning," Haig told Cartwright.

"I don't imagine Jerry was too pleased with his orders to get here."

"I guess not," Haig agreed, "but his feelings don't really matter right now. All I care about is that Manning is the best sub man in the business."

Cartwright sighed quietly. That, Jerry Manning certainly was. And still a relatively young man, who'd distinguished himself brilliantly in and out of war. "Yes," he said aloud, "and *Sea Trench* is the most expensive and the greatest machine of its kind ever built. Manning has been working on his Marianas mission for nearly eight months now."

"Frank, I know all that," Haig said. "Why do you think I spelled out Jerry instead of anyone else? *Sea Trench* and Manning are what we need desperately for this, ah, situation in which we've found ourselves."

"You've upset some applecarts."

"They've been upset before," Haig countered. "I *need* Manning and his new boat. The country needs them."

Cartwright smiled thinly, shifted in his chair. "The word is going around New Washington," he said softly, "that you're the reincarnation of Hyman Rickover."

Haig returned the smile. "Mr. Secretary, I consider that the finest compliment you could pay me."

Cartwright shifted gears so swiftly he almost caught Haig by surprise. "Can you handle Jerry Manning for this mission? No," he said with a gesture, "don't be too quick to answer. Manning is a submariner, but he's also a pilot, the typical aggressive type. He's a genius, but at the same time he's abrasive. He's his own man. He is also, in some ways, politically dangerous. To add to all this, Tim, we've given him free rein in planning for the petroleum search in the Marianas. To pull him away now—" Cartwright shook his head. "He can be ordered, of course," he added carefully, "but in my opinion that would be a mistake. So, before we all meet, I'd like to have an idea of how you plan to overcome just a few of the obstacles that stand in the way of *your* mission?" His face showed a grimace. "I happen to be the secretary of the navy, and I'm not even sure of what has been going on. You're holding a mysterious curtain very high, Tim."

Haig nodded. "I know, I know, and it's all with very good reason. To answer your question, sir, about the Challenger Deep, may I say, without intending any disrespect, that the Pacific is *my* jurisdiction? We can't change long-established plans without attracting undue attention, of course, so a boat will go to the Marianas, and, as far as our government knows and the world will know, that boat will *be the Sea Trench*."

Cartwright held back a chuckle. "That's a rather large-sized lie to swallow, admiral."

"Not," Haig retorted, "if you don't know it's a lie." He smiled at the navy secretary. "Right now, sir, I'd like to thank you for the move you made. It's, ah, the finest vote of confidence you could have given me."

"Let's just say," Cartwright added dryly, "that I'm gambling heavily on you."

"Yes, sir," Haig replied. He picked up a messagegram on his desk and read aloud: *"The United States Navy has announced the discovery of a major petroleum deposit along the eastern flank of the Mid-Atlantic Ridge and—"*

Cartwright gestured; Haig went silent; and Cartwright continued from memory, *"—and a large undersea force has been dispatched for its development."* Cartwright chuckled. "I should know it. I wrote it myself."

Haig, unexpectedly, frowned. "I hope it works. The diversion is important to what we're—"

His words evaporated as a jet fighter thundered low over the building, rattling windows and hammering at their ears. Before they could resume their conversation, the telephone on Haig's desk rang shrilly. Haig grinned at Cartwright as he picked up the phone.

"I know," Haig said. "Captain Manning is landing right now."

He heard a startled "Uh—yes, sir—that's right, he is."

"Thank you," Haig said, hanging up. He looked at the navy secretary. "We can begin the meeting one hour from now." He picked up a folder from his desk, carried it around to Cartwright. "Sir, in here you'll find a brief but concise dossier on the people I've assembled for this meeting. May I recommend you go over it before then? It will help you understand why I've selected these particular people over any others."

Cartwright held the folder in his lap, opened it after a pause. Then he looked up. "Tim, be good enough to have some coffee sent in here. Enough to last me an hour."

There was no avoiding the sense of incompleteness that many of them felt as they sat in the long conference room. Many shared the thought that Admiral Haig was playing something very close to the vest, that he was baiting them along, permitting whatever his message was to emerge slowly, in its own good time, rather than spelling it out neatly and quickly. Dr. Chadwick, Larry Templeton, Haig, Cartwright, Jerry Manning, Miko Stewart, and several technical aides, each with the highest security clearance, were gathered in the room. The doors were locked; armed guards were posted outside; and every electronic and physical link into and out of the room was under maximum surveillance and monitoring.

At this moment Miko's eyes were locked on a movie screen, the others watching intently with her. She turned, as did the others, as Haig's voice sounded behind them.

"This is part of the message sphere sent up by the *Swimmer IV* crew," Haig explained. "It won't need further explanation for the next few moments."

They turned back to the screen, fascinated, awed, not fully understanding, even though what was happening was unmistakable. The film was blurred from camera motion and from vibration, but what they saw was a terrifying attack by great sharks on the four-man submarine. They heard the voices of the men, the shouts of surprise and sudden fear and anger, and even here, in this room where the reality was no more than the sight of flickering images on a flat screen, they recoiled instinctively as the huge animals struck and mauled the sub.

Haig spoke as the film continued. "We had no idea we'd get this sort of test on one of these boats. Negative buoyancy systems certainly seem to be the answer to punishment. Thirteen tons per square inch is the minimum that sub took from a single shark strike. The hull obviously took it all."

Silence followed as the pictures on the screen commanded the group's attention. Miko gestured suddenly, alerted to something. "Admiral—hold the film right there, please."

Haig gestured, and the projectionist locked the frame in place. By then Miko was half out of her seat, pointing. "Look—it's almost too much to believe. Those animals—that's not a frenzy of feeding, or anything else. They *seem* maddened, but they're not. If I didn't know better I'd swear they were being directed to attack that vessel and—"

"What convinces you you're wrong, Dr. Stewart?"

Miko turned to Haig. "Because they have the intelligence level of rats, and although rats can be trained, you can't do that with sharks."

"No one said *trained*. The word you used was *directed*."

"Do you mean to tell me you believe—"

Matthew Chadwick broke in. "*I* believe it, Dr. Stewart. Precisely the same thing happened to myself and Mr. Templeton with the *Sea Search*. In our case the attack was made by sperm whales."

She smiled, her tolerance of his remarks undisguised. "I find that rather difficult to believe," she said quietly.

"And I find your level of disbelief, Dr. Stewart," came the acid response, "as having absolutely no bearing on what happened. You were not there, and you speak only from your past learning and experience, which without sarcasm I remind you have very specific limitations. We were attacked, we were *warned* of the attack, and we were severely damaged during an attempt to destroy us. At your convenience you are welcome to listen to the sonar tapes. Your reputation stands you in good stead. You will recognize at once what I only mention here."

Timothy Haig suppressed a smile, exchanged a significant glance with Frank Cartwright. Things were going quite well indeed, Haig thought. Aloud, he told them, "If you please—hold your discussions for later." He gestured for the film to continue.

The screen was blurred, flickering. They had difficulty making out what they saw. Haig's voice was a help. "What we have here is questionable. This film, and its sound track, came from a message pack ejected by Ritter's crew from deep within the Aleutian Trench. The pack endured heavy damage, and what you see is the best that computer enhancement could salvage."

The screen showed digital readouts of gauges indicating depth, pressure, temperature, movement, other data.

"The digital readouts," Haig went on, "as well as the voice and film, are computer extracted from magnetic-impulse tape. As reliable as is this system, the bizarre nature of the material leaves us no choice but speculative caution."

Cartwright had removed his gaze from the screen to observe Jerry Manning. Haig's voice continued in the background. "According to this particular message pack, Ritter took his boat down to well below 30,000 feet. The tape experts are certain the actual depth exceeds 36,000."

Frank Cartwright jerked his attention away from his study of Manning. Cartwright had believed he'd known the background details of what Tim Haig was going to release tonight, but the old bastard had played from a cold deck. Cartwright coughed at his own unexpected reaction, cleared his throat. "That's preposterous, Admiral Haig. The trench bottoms out at 26,000 feet and—"

"I know," Haig said simply.

Cartwright started to respond, clamped his jaw shut. He wasn't going to let Tim box him in again. He turned back to the screen. The mash and static had become worse. They could distinguish only bits and pieces, but enough came thudding into their brains to freeze them solidly to their seats. A man's voice came through, broken, excited, unbelievable. ". . . looks like a dome . . . goes on . . . miles and miles . . . it's impossible . . ."

They were hypnotized. The film, broken, scratchy, marred with static, absolutely commanded them. Then the scene changed. There was a blur during which nothing could be seen.

Haig's voice came in again. "This last film is from a TV torp using the available light from other flare torps. You know the limitations of light at six thousand fathoms, and only a portion of the message pack survived. I want you to see this in slow motion."

Murky shapes moved against a background of sputtering glows, the static becoming more intense every moment. Finally there was a tremendous burst of electrical noise. The film jerked to a stop, and they saw a frozen shot of a shadowy form silhouetted against a spattering flare, a form that was tantalizingly biped.

The whole thing was crazy.

7

~~~~~~~~~~~

They had retired to a private dining room, sealed off by Haig's security teams, where they might rest from the emotional and visceral impact of what they'd seen and heard. Admiral Haig was determined that his select audience would not be fiercely inundated by the data he had exposed them to. He knew the emotional limitations of cerebral input, and in this case he was determined to control the rate of absorption so that his group would not be overwhelmed. Thus the coffee break, the splitting into spontaneous groups, as personal gravity brought them together in bonds Haig wanted to study. Miko Stewart had sequestered herself with Chadwick and Templeton, and the three were engaged in a pleasant if animated conversation. Then Haig swung his gaze to a far corner of the room where Frank Cartwright leaned on his cane, comfortably talking with Jerry Manning. The submarine commander was intense, smoking fiercely, and yet the two men seemed as comfortable together as old slippers. Very good, mused Haig. Very good, indeed.

"For the first time in many years," Cartwright told Manning, "I'm caught without any fast answers."

"Sir, you're hardly alone. That is the damnedest film—"

"Any conclusions, Jerry?"

Manning nodded slowly. "Yes, sir."

"I am grateful to hear *something* emerge from —well, damn it, man, don't keep me in suspense."

Manning shook his head. "I'm sorry, sir. I—"

"And don't hide behind that *sir*, either."

"Yes, sir." Manning grinned at the secretary. "I just don't want to push it, Frank. The admiral's been right on target the way he's handled this. He hit us with both barrels. We're still in shock from what we've heard and seen. I need to do some digesting."

Cartwright's grimace showed his displeasure.

"All right, Mr. Secretary," Manning said, "then you tell *me* how you add it all up."

Cartwright didn't bother with a smile. "I'm between the proverbial rock and the hard place." He shuffled a bit closer. "Tell me something else, then, Jerry. What do you think of this group Tim has brought together?"

Manning's gaze took in the room. He sucked in deeply on his cigarette and exhaled smoke suddenly. "Tim Haig never does anything without a whole bunch of reasons." His eyes narrowed. "The girl doesn't settle right with me."

"Miko Stewart? If my hunch about Haig is right," Cartwright said, a touch of retort in his voice, "then she's perfect."

Manning was nettled and showed it. "For *what*?"

"You know what happened to Chadwick and Templeton. That thing with the whales? Miko— she really is a doctor of science—is probably the leading scientist in the world in communications work with the whale species. Everything from the small porpoises up to the great blues. She's American, by the way, not Japanese. Third generation. She has some other qualifications—"

He paused, and Manning's hard look prodded him on. "My, you're touchy tonight, Jerry," Cartwright said, smirking. "To answer your question, she's also a specialist in psychological problems relating directly to deep submergence crews in their special environments, and—"

"Oh. One of *those*."

"You needn't say it like it was an obscenity, Jerry."

"Is she civilian or navy?" Manning demanded.

"Do you remember the name of Commander Harold Stewart?" Cartwright's question was oblique, but Manning knew he had to go along.

"I believe so. If he's the one I'm thinking about, he made that wet-suit dive to just over a thousand fathoms. New bionics equipment he was testing. The dive killed him."

"No, it didn't," Cartwright corrected him. "Equipment failure killed him. Anyway, that woman is his widow." Cartwright paused. "She is also a former Olympic gold medal diving champion."

Manning studied her more carefully now, his growing respect obvious. "She seems bigger than life."

"That she is," Cartwright confirmed. "*Now* do you have any idea why Haig brought her here?"

"I'm trying, Frank, I'm trying." Manning watched her for a long time, realizing just how attractive she was, not simply physically or sensually—but there were certain touches. She spelled quality, capability, and more, simply through her movement and speech. At the moment she was bent over a small tape cassette, and Manning saw her look up with surprise at Chadwick.

"Why—you're absolutely right," she was saying to the elderly scientist "I apologize, Dr. Chadwick. Very gladly, I'll admit. Those *are* aggressive sounds. Warning calls to one another, also. The signals they send out when they're going after giant squid at great depths."

It was obvious that Chadwick was enjoying the conversation, in spite of the pain he felt from his slowly healing injury. "I appreciate your candor," he told her. "Thank you. Keep listening, please."

Thumping and crashing sounds came from the tape speaker. "Those are the sounds of the sub being struck by the whales," Templeton said.

She looked up, her face serious. "I don't believe I would have liked being there—"

Templeton laughed nervously. "We didn't believe we'd ever see the sun again." The tape had run out and he shut off the little machine.

Chadwick leaned back, fumbled as he lit his pipe, looked about the room, and then turned back to Miko. "I wonder why we're *here*," he said, mixing statement with question.

"I don't understand," Miko told him.

Chadwick puffed a blue cloud from his pipe. "We were brought here under most pressing circumstances. There's a lot of heavy firepower in this room, Dr. Stewart. The secretary of the navy, for one. But especially Jerry Manning. Why did the admiral bring us all together?"

"He's right, you know," Templeton chimed in. "I don't think, from what I've heard, that any of us had much choice. I mean, the whole thing was given to us as some sort of screaming emergency."

She nodded slowly, thinking about it, really, for the first time. "Yes, it was," she agreed.

"Have you ever heard of *Sea Trench*?"

She looked at Chadwick. "You mean a particular area of the ocean floor?"

"No, no, my dear. I'm referring to a specific name."

"No, I haven't. What is it?"

His face showed regret. "I'm not at liberty to

say." He leaned back in his seat. "But I think you'll know soon enough." He gestured in the direction of Manning. "Do you know him?"

"Not until an hour ago. Should I?"

Chadwick had climbed slowly to his feet. "I do believe you will, and I have the strange but growing feeling, Dr. Stewart, that your life and your future are going to lie in his hands."

Her eyes held those of Manning, then returned to Chadwick. "What a strange thing for you to say, doctor."

Chadwick evaded her response. "I believe the admiral is ready. Shall we go?"

As they returned to the conference room, the movie screen was still fixed with the strange, almost frightening, shadowy humanlike figure. But there were brighter lights on, and Haig held their attention, leaning forward with his arms on the long conference table.

"I want your impressions, your conclusions, your theories on what you've seen and heard in this room, if you please. We'll begin with—" He cut himself short as Miko Stewart raised her hand; he nodded to her.

"My apologies, admiral. But before we proceed any further, may I ask why, in this presentation, we haven't been able to speak with any members of the crew from the *Swimmer IV* submarine?"

A long and hard stare went between Haig and Cartwright. The navy secretary glanced at Manning, who shook his head ever so slightly. Cartwright looked back to Haig in a clear signal, and Haig addressed Miko Stewart directly.

"I thought you understood. They're dead."

The shock on her face spoke more eloquently than any words. Before she could speak, Chadwick was out of his chair, his face showing open anger.

"Dead?"

Haig's expression was stone. "Very much so, I'm afraid."

"Why wasn't I told before now!" Chadwick shouted.

"It wasn't your affair, sir."

Chadwick returned to his seat, tugged gently by Templeton, but he shook a trembling finger at Haig. "You—anything that happens in the deep sea is our affair! You know that—the Scripps Institute is charged with—"

"Forgive my interruption," Haig cut in swiftly. "I prefer not to waste our time in an exchange that serves no purpose. Yours is a civilian agency, Dr. Chadwick. Ritter and his crew were on a military mission."

Chadwick would have gone on except for the shock he saw registered on the face of Frank Cartwright. It seemed that even the secretary of the navy had just heard, for the first time, that the *Swimmer IV* crew had been lost.

"Admiral Haig." Cartwright's voice seemed to rumble from deep in his chest. "These men—what happened? How were they—how did they die?"

"We don't know." Haig's simple honesty was that much harder a blow.

"But you must have some idea," Cartwright protested.

Jerry Manning was leaning back in his seat, fingers quietly drumming the table. No one had expected him to speak, least of all Admiral Haig.

"They were electrocuted," Manning said.

He studied the faces in the room; no one spoke. "More than fifty years ago," Manning went on, "scientists confirmed the existence of deep-sea eels over a hundred feet in length. Perhaps even twice that size. What they didn't know then, and what we didn't know until we saw these message pack reports, is that some of those eels are electric. And any creature of that enormous mass that has an electrical potential—and the ability to discharge it —is *very* lethal."

He looked from Haig to Cartwright. "There's something else." He paused, deeply affected by the thought he was about to give voice to. "Those eels were directed to attack and to destroy that boat. That crew didn't just die. They were killed. Deliberately."

Templeton's voice was a shrill cry of protest. "That's insane! There's no basis for your remarks! You can't—"

"You didn't pay much attention to the small details of that film," Manning said, his criticism restrained. "It was all there as long as you knew where and how to look. That static, the broken magnetic circuitry. Everything points to heavy electrical overload. Those creatures were powerful enough to overcome the grounding systems of the boat. They shorted out all its equipment, including the accessory systems for the nuclear drive. The crew, short and simple, was electrocuted."

The silence turned into a mild uproar. Secretary of the Navy Cartwright had a stunned look on his face that not even his aplomb could disguise. He exchanged a long meaningful look with Haig, then he turned to Miko Stewart, who was on her feet, intense, trying to throw Manning's words back into his lap.

"There's absolutely nothing to *confirm* what you've said," she told him, her anger bringing sharpness to her voice. "It's conjectural. Worse, it's outlandish. That submarine was more than seven miles down, and—"

Manning remained quiet except for one remark. "That's right. More than seven miles down where the bottom is only five miles down. Do go on."

She showed her confusion, but only for a moment, and she swept on. "All we have to go by are the magnetic records, aural and film, and they're broken and unreliable. There's nothing else except —" Her voice trailed off as she looked up at the strangely humanoid shape on the screen.

No one spoke for a while.

"Yes," Manning said finally, "there's that, too, isn't there?"

"There's *what?*" Chadwick broke in. "A shadow on a broken tape?"

Manning shrugged, obviously not interested in debate or argument.

Dr. Chadwick turned to Haig. "Admiral, you've been conducting this meeting like some sort of parlor séance. Would you please get to the point of all this?"

Haig nodded slowly. "All right, doctor. I'll tell you, first, what you're *not* going to do. And that's to hold a public forum, outside of this room or anywhere where there isn't maximum security prevailing, about what you've learned here. I do have specific action in mind, but I will repeat what I said before. What happened to Ritter and his crew happened on a *military* mission."

Templeton had grown more agitated as Haig spoke, and he tugged at Chadwick's arm. Chadwick motioned him to silence, but it was of no use.

"You *can't* invoke some sort of military control to silence us! V 're on the edge of—," Templeton blurted.

"With all due respect, Mr. Templeton, be good enough to sit down until I finish." Haig's look was cold steel, and Templeton sank slowly back in his chair.

"All of you must understand that I am invoking the Military Secrets Act," Haig said flatly. "We are still under a condition of limited martial law since the war, and that act is still on the books."

Chadwick nodded slowly. "All right, admiral. That much I do understand. You have my word, but under protest."

"Any way you like, sir," Haig said amiably. "Does anyone refuse?"

Silence.

"Thank you." Haig went on. "Now, everything that's happened so far—the whales communicating and working together as an aggressive group, their attack against the minisub; the sharks, which I consider to be the greatest surprise of all because of their limited intelligence; and the eels, which seem to stretch our imagination beyond the breaking point."

"Hear, hear," Chadwick murmured nastily.

"I will accept any meaningful contribution, doctor," Haig told him coldly, "but snickering is hardly what we need." He watched the astonishment on Chadwick's face and went on smoothly, "Yet no matter what we surmise or question, there seems no doubt of any kind that Ritter and his men descended miles deeper than the greatest depth we knew to exist in the Aleutian Trench. Before Ritter's dive we knew the trench went to about 26,-000 feet. The *Swimmer IV* went two miles beyond that, and they still weren't on the bottom. They made some strange references to a dome, allegedly miles in length, although numbers are completely beyond our grasp at this point. They were attacked and overcome by animals capable of generating some incredible electrical output. And after all that, we have *this* to confront—"

He gestured to the shadowy form on the screen.

"We don't know any more than we can see. But we can question the obvious. What is a creature of that size doing, moving freely under crushing pressures and cruel temperatures and apparently doing so with little or no effort? *What* is the damned thing? Let me make a concise summary. We have a thousand questions for every possible answer. Those questions are critical. Obviously we're dealing with intelligent direction or control of some kind. It may well be of natural origin within the sea. We don't know, and personally I doubt it. We do know the Chinese have performed miracles with animal control through implantation of electrical devices in the brains and spinal cords of dolphins and whales. How far they've managed to go with other creatures is sheer speculation. They don't share their findings with us."

Haig paused to collect his thoughts. "There's one thing we *must* find out," he said, looking directly at Cartwright. "If the Chinese are involved, we're facing a threat of unknown but dangerous proportion. If the Chinese aren't—" Haig broke off as Chadwick gestured for his attention.

"Excuse me," Chadwick said. "I didn't want you to get away from something. If I may?" He received Haig's nod to continue. "What if all this is natural? What if nature is following its old laws of helping its creatures to survive? What if there's explosive intelligent growth in the sea? What do you do then?"

Haig sighed. "If my aunt had—sorry. Never mind. To answer your questions, Dr. Chadwick, I'd like to remind you—who of all people should remember that nature wiped out 90 percent of all the species of life that ever existed on this planet *before* man ever showed up—well, we're sending Captain Manning to the Aleutian Trench to try to unlock those answers. I asked you people here because," and he couldn't resist a smile, "no matter what acid may have crawled into our conversation, I judge you as the best in the business, and I want you to go with Captain Manning. We could find *anything* down there, and we need the best possible cross section of brain matter on this subject. I consider this project to have absolute priority. We once walked on the moon, although in the long run it seems we did little more than to leave hollow footprints to mock empty space. Man doesn't live on the moon. But we *need* to live within the sea. It's that simple."

He looked again at Cartwright, who remained expressionless, reserving judgment. But Jerry Manning had little inclination to such backseat maneuvering.

"Are you serious?" He was straight up in his chair, showing his disbelief directly to the admiral. "You mean take *Sea Trench* off her assignment? Drop everything to chase these shadows?"

"That," said Haig, pointing to the film still on the screen, "may be shadowy, but it is definitely not a shadow. Neither is the loss of Ritter and his crew, nor the manner in which they were killed."

"But you're destroying two years of special preparations! You know we're supposed to work the Challenger Deep; we've been living hand in pocket with the National Academy of Science for months; and—for Christ's sake, Tim, I've even got two high school kids assigned to my boat, and—"

"I know," Haig said. "They go with you."

Manning appeared thunderstruck. He turned to Cartwright. "Mr. Secretary, with every respect to the admiral, I can hardly accept a recommendation that wipes out what we've been working toward for so long. The petroleum expedition was given its priority to me by yourself, and—"

Cartwright made his first physical move in long minutes. "Captain." His voice was tired, heavy. He had been wrestling to absorb everything he had heard, and it was obvious to them all that he had also arrived at the crossroads decision that this meeting must produce.

"Captain Manning," he repeated, "I believe we should consider something that hasn't yet been spoken of among this group. Very often nature gives us warnings or tries to send us signals, and very often we are so blinded by our own technology that we tend to overlook what is offered us. No one here can question the sequence of events in the Aleutian Trench. Incredulity is the most immediate reaction, but we must be careful not to *reject* what is out of the ordinary.

"Nature follows one law above all: The years have confirmed to me that the only thing we may expect from life is the unexpected. Are you acquainted with the hagfish?"

The sudden question threw them off-balance. "Why, yes, I've heard of it, sir, but I don't see—"

"Forgive my intrusion, Jerry. The hagfish isn't just something unusual. It's a complete refutation of everything normal. It is so abnormal that it makes even such contradictory creatures as the duckbill platypus seem as ordinary as an ear of corn. The point I'm trying to make is that at times nature *warns* us of the unusual: Perhaps there is some other level of intervention, but I don't wish to become philosophical or theological at this time.

"The hagfish," he said quietly, "rejects every biological law we have ever observed. It breathes through its nose instead of through gills, and it *is* a fish. Its method of vision is simply not believable, yet the fact is that the hagfish sees through its *skin*. It is a creature with what appears to be a normal spine column, but it can also literally tie itself into a knot without any ill effects. When it is endangered, it secretes a blob of nauseous jelly about its body that even a shark won't touch. We can't even identify the substance. Wait—there's more. It can live without food for a year, using a biological process of sustenance that absolutely stupefies our best scientists. It also defies basic physiological law by having four hearts, each functioning independently of the others, each pulsing at a separate rhythm, and each controlling the head, tail, muscles, and liver respectively. In conclusion, may I add that this fish has been found most often, as rare as it is, in the area that takes in the Aleutian Trench and the Kamchatka Peninsula off Siberia? That is strikingly within the same area in which we have just encountered another series of biological contradictions."

Cartwright sat stiffly, both hands resting directly before him on his cane. The old man had new steel in his voice. "Admiral Haig, enough of discussion and recommendations. You will be good enough to state your orders to this group."

Haig nodded somberly. He no longer questioned the full support of the secretary of the navy. "*Sea Trench*, under the command of Captain Manning, who will have full authority on this mission, will depart its home port within seventy-two hours. Its destination will be the area of the Aleutian Trench west of Amchitka, and it will make every attempt and use every means at its disposal to seek out and to identify the strange phenomena that have occurred in that area. The people in this room will become part of the crew and staff assigned to Captain Manning. The two students already assigned to *Sea Trench*—owing to unusual circumstances as well as their selection by the National Academy of Science—will be aboard. This is a new world, and we need new and bright minds unencumbered by past convictions."

Haig stood. "You will all retire to your quarters for now to make whatever arrangements are necessary, within the security restrictions imposed on you, to prepare for this assignment. One hour from now, I will be available to anyone or all of you for whatever questions you need answered or assistance you require."

That was all he had to say. No one moved or spoke.

It seemed difficult to break the sudden silence. Behind the standing figure of Admiral Haig, the shadowy biped form on the screen still taunted their grip on reality.

8

The hull was enormous, its size almost beyond comprehension at first sight. Gleaming, powerful rounded flanks swept back in a surge of metallic strength that gave the leviathan sub a sense of motion even as it rested in the huge undersea cavern that was lighted everywhere by batteries of floodlights. Miko Stewart stood on a platform beneath the prow of the U.S.S. *Sea Trench*, overwhelmed by the presence of the incredible shape above her. The air carried messages of around-the-clock preparations, of hundreds of technicians at work: echoing sounds of metal against metal, of voices calling; ear-twitching cries of high-speed drills, of pressures rising and falling from pneumatic and oleo and hydraulic and other systems. There was even the sound of water moving through the drain tubes along the bottom of the cavern that was secreted in the earth's bowels near the great naval base of San Diego. Miko looked up, giddiness touching her, as though the weight of this vessel must crash from its flimsy supports until it crushed everything in its reach. Her sense of unreality was heightened by a thin cry that had no business in this cathedral of technology. Somehow, someone had released a bird —a bird, of all things!—in the enormous chamber, and it flew high overhead, its call reaching her with a Daliesque touch.

Standing beneath the mountainous hull gave her a disquieting feeling of helplessness. She turned instinctively for the comfort of another physical presence. On the metal platform with her was Jerry Manning, sole commander, with full responsibility for this *thing* of such power and mass. She realized at the same moment that Manning was aware of her turmoil, and she fought for words to humanize the moment.

"I—I don't know what to say. I had no idea anything like this was even thought of."

Manning nodded slowly; he understood her feelings, knew the sense of "crush" this moment and place imparted to someone first exposed to the monster submersible. "There's nothing else like *Sea Trench*," he said amiably. "We've needed this boat for a long time, and we've worked on it, oh, I guess ten years by now."

He started walking along the platform. Miko walked by his side, listening intently. She felt as though she'd encountered a person she'd never met before. Certainly he was not the same Captain Manning she'd run into at the meeting in Admiral Haig's office.

"Ten years?" she echoed. "Then, all this," she said with a sweeping gesture, "is long before the war."

"The war had nothing to do with *Sea Trench*," he confirmed. "In all the years we've explored the ocean depths we've never approached the problem on either the right scale or with the proper means at our disposal. *Now* we can. You have to approach the exploration of the deep seas with the same attitude you would have in making a major exploration of another planet. People talk glibly, Miss Stewart, because numbers roll off tongues easily, but numbers have no real meaning. It's the 'in' thing to remark that the earth has 140 million square miles of ocean. That's like saying the sun is big. There are no comparative or relative values. We're not planning to wander about the ocean surface, and it's surely not enough simply to fly over it and look down. Even cruising five hundred or a thousand feet beneath the surface isn't enough. We need to get *down* there and mix it up with what takes place very far from our sight."

He stopped, and she remained by his side as he took a long reflective look at the great vessel of which he was captain. "There's power inside that thing. All kinds of power. Maybe *energy* would be a better word. We've had bathyscaphes and minisubs that could go to the bottom of the ocean, but they were groping blindly. Recently we've put some versatility into the newer boats, but they're small and their endurance is limited. We need true staying power, with the muscle to remain in the deeps, go to work there, and above all to handle problems as they arise. We're going down into a giant, dark bucket, and that's the only way to think of the oceans—330 million cubic miles of bucket. And after all our years of diving, most of it still completely mysterious to us."

"You're using numbers, captain," she said, but there was no sarcasm in her voice.

"So I am," he grinned.

They were walking again along the service ramp and she picked up their conversation. "Would you mind if I asked some more numbers?"

He glanced at her, and the glance was a swift study. Manning kept under wraps his sensitivity on the subject of the submarine. He had tremendous pride in helping to create the boat and an even greater sense of accomplishment in having been assigned as its master. But he had no need to share that pride, and he went through a brief but hard judgment of her sincerity. She felt his scrutiny and was relieved when he answered finally, "What kind of numbers?"

"Oh, what you must consider the usual things," she told him. "They're familiar to you, but to me—" She looked up and shook her head. "I'm overwhelmed, captain, No pun intended, but I feel like a fish out of water."

He laughed. "All right, Miss Stewart, I suppose the vital statistics do have their place. We displace 16,000 tons—which is the same size as a pocket battleship from way back in the Second World War —and everything inside *Sea Trench* is nuclear. We're almost like a huge atom, if you want to think of it that way. Main power and all subsidiary systems run off three reactors. When we leave here we won't need fuel for at least three more years."

"Years?" Damn. She knew she had to stop echoing his words, but even the statistical data shook her.

He nodded. "That's what you need for a true research boat. The ability to get down to what you're after, even if you don't know about it before you get there, and then to stick with the job. Fourteen men, including myself, run *Sea Trench*, and—"

He kept jabbing statements like that at her, and Miko couldn't stop her own blurted interruptions. "Wait, wait—you have a submarine that displaces 16,000 tons, and—how long is this thing?"

He didn't bat an eyelash. "It's 519 feet 11 inches."

"And you need only fourteen men?"

"That's the crew to operate the boat. We can accommodate fifty scientists and researchers if we need to. There are complete labs and facilities for almost any kind of work you might imagine. Four of our men are paramedics. You see, without the need to carry enormous amounts of fuel, like oil, we have room for everything else."

"But—"

"We've got five years' frozen-food storage. We distill all the fresh water we need and we can get all the fresh seafood we want, anytime we want, of course. If we don't want to use the old-fashioned hook, line, and sinker," he grinned, "electric stunners do the job very well for us. What's really important is that every system has three backups, and our shops and labs can fix or even make just about anything we might need."

"But a ship this size—"

"Submarine. Boat. *Not* ship."

She nodded vigorously. "Anything you want to call it. But you operate fourteen men—I mean, you operate twenty-four hours a day with only fourteen men! How can you do that?"

"They're not ordinary men." She couldn't fail to catch the note of pride with this mention of his crew. "And also we've got Neptune. We consider him the fifteenth crew member."

"Neptune?" Would she ever stop echoing?

"Our computer. The superbrain. It's linked into every control system and sensing device of the boat. It hears, feels, sees just about everything. It can even touch through its sensor systems. It also has the most complete memory banks of the oceans and everything known about them. Including," he said dryly, "what we've learned these past few days. Neptune provides the brains, and we make up the determining factor of a mission."

"I don't want to sound silly, but what is the depth capability?"

"The hull takes twenty tons per square inch before it even starts to complain."

"How many propellers? You must need—"

"None. We use hydrojets. Like enormous jet engines, except we can swivel ours. Like an airplane that takes off and lands vertically. In a hydroworld, the hydrojets are much more efficient than screws. We operate in a fluid environment, and, if you can think of the air as a fluid, just like the water, we don't sail or float, Miss Stewart, we *fly*."

She nodded, taking it in, fitting herself mentally into the makeup of this stupendous machinery. "I would imagine, then, you can do at least fifty knots, or sixty or so?"

He laughed, very much at home with what he was doing and sharing. "You're not even halfway there," he said with delight. "*Sea Trench* is a negative buoyancy submarine, Miss Stewart. We're not stuck with a blimp, like the old boats. We're like a fast and heavy jet. If our hydros don't operate, we'll sink to the bottom just as an airplane does when you cut power. So, despite the fact that water is eight hundred times denser than air, our shape, propulsion, and other factors—such as heat rings to eliminate surface body cavitation, just like the porpoise—well, we can exceed 120 knots. This is the first large boat that has been designed with cross section in mind as well as density and cavitation. You have to consider that viscosity also impedes speed, and water is fifty times more viscous than air. You can think of it as a thick oil if you want a good analogy."

He paused, rubbing his chin. "I've got an even better comparison for you. Think of it—when we're deep and we go to full transparency for the bow and you're up front looking out. You will be moving through the sea with the same speed that a sky diver falls through the air."

"That sounds like—" She hesitated, seeking the right word.

"Fun?"

"Well, yes, but I didn't want to say that. Fun, I mean. I didn't want to seem unimpressed. And I *am* impressed."

"Thank you. But you were right. It's many things, and if you think of it that way, then it's as much fun as anything else."

She started to speak, chewed her lip a moment,

then let her thoughts free. "May I ask you something personal?" She didn't wait for his answer but rushed on. "Do you ever think of it as fun, Captain Manning?"

He studied her more closely, openly this time, searching for something he might reject. When the hard lines in his face eased, she knew she had crossed a vital personal barrier. "There hasn't been any time for fun, Miss Stewart. Not for years. Not since—"

Something stopped him and she slipped into the breach. "Were you going to say since the war?"

Coldness came into his voice. "You could say that."

"Captain, I meant no offense." She spoke softly, carefully. "The war's been over for five years."

"For some people. There are all kinds of wars."

There was no mistaking his withdrawal now, and she was frantic to prevent it. She forced the conversation back to safe ground. She pointed upward. "Those rings. Some are marked in yellow, or green, and there, those in red. What are they for?"

"Torpedoes: TV, flare, sonar pickups, assault torps—"

She recognized the hardness in her own voice even as she responded to his explanation. "*Assault* torps? You mean—weapons?"

"Of course." He seemed mildly surprised. "You make it sound like some sort of disease."

"But you said this was a *research* vessel."

There was no stopping the distaste that spilled out now. "Research and exploration, Miss Stewart. It's obvious you find the idea of weapons torps not to your liking."

Well, damn him, she could match him on *this* subject. "I do. Very much so. I imagine I was also mistaken. I wasn't led to believe we were on a military mission."

He stopped again and faced her squarely. "Then

you don't know your history, Miss Stewart," he said icily. "Get your nose out of your books and look at life the way it really is. And don't tell me you've experienced suffering because your husband died on his deep dive. We all get cut up that way sooner or later. No one, *no one,* Miss Stewart, has ever explored a new frontier, and managed to survive, without being heavily armed. Lewis and Clark were wholly and completely a military expedition. So was the voyage of Christopher Columbus. And Marco Polo. And the Vikings. It's a very nasty world out there."

The sound of approaching steps halted him, but only for a moment. "At least we understand one another," he said bluntly. "I appreciate your candor."

"And *I* didn't ask you for compliments about honesty. It happens to be an everyday habit of mine."

He didn't give her the opportunity to reply, but turned to the people joining them. She turned with him, saw a powerfully built black man wearing commander stripes. This was her first look at the executive officer of *Sea Trench,* the second-in-command of the great submarine, Commander William Ryan. He was in his forties, and his authority came through even in the way he moved. She detected a cutting sense of humor in his glance. With him were the two youngsters she'd first heard of in Admiral Haig's office: Richard Castillo and Jessica Ames, the students who had been selected in a nationwide competition to become participants in a research voyage to the Marianas, where they would begin their practical training for careers in oceanographic sciences.

She was impressed at once with both young people. Richard, she would learn, with his breezy air and his self-proclamation as "the new crossbreed of Chicano," was well into the genius IQ class, a mixture of youthful enthusiasm, and an inquisitive mind, and on a par with experienced scientists many years his senior. His strongest interest lay in the field of geology, which had made him especially suited for the Challenger Deep program. For which he still believed he was slated, Miko realized. There were other things to learn about the young man. His infectious grin belied the fact that he was the only survivor of a large family—all of whom had died when he was twelve in the nuclear holocaust that hammered Los Angeles.

And if Richard Castillo earned immediate respect, then Jessica Ames was utterly captivating. She was eighteen, redheaded, doused liberally but attractively with freckles, and she had a smile that never seemed to leave her face. Jessica and Miko were to share an affinity, for the young girl had an astonishing natural rapport with sea life-forms. Their first eye contact established an instant bond between the girl and the woman.

Ryan saluted Manning in a gesture that was simultaneously casual and crisp, and the two men shook hands warmly. "It's good to have you back," Ryan told Manning. "I thought the wahines had captured you."

Ryan's brows went up a fraction as the warmth failed to enter Manning's voice. "We have a change in plans, Mr. Ryan. I'll fill you in later."

Manning turned to the others. "Commander Ryan, this is Miss—"

Two could play his damned game. "Doctor," she said quietly.

"Miko Stewart," he continued without breaking stride. "This is my exec, Commander Ryan."

Jessica pushed forward, her eyes bright above her beaming smile. "You're *the* Dr. Stewart? The woman who talks with whales? Oh, how I've wanted to meet you! I'm Jessie, and this is Richard, and I heard you were coming here, and—and I'm so excited!"

Miko smiled at her, took her hand, and nodded to the boy. She heard Manning talking to Ryan, and she turned to them.

"Chadwick and Templeton are over there," Manning was saying, pointing to the two men who were walking along the service ramp. "Have them brought aboard and assigned to quarters. Everyone is to be briefed immediately on the open and restricted areas of the boat. When you're squared away, come to my quarters."

He walked off without a glance at anyone else, his heels ringing solidly on the metal walkway. Miko watched him for several moments, then she glanced at Ryan.

"I seem to have stepped on his toe."

"Well, doctor, he does have ten of them, you know."

Their laughter broke the sudden tension Manning had left in his wake. Ryan studied her, nodded to himself. "Look, I'd best make several things very clear from the outset," he said. "I don't even know what our new orders are—what the captain called a change in plans. I'll find out soon enough, but there are certain realities that will make life easier for us. Would you mind?"

"Not at all," she said easily.

"Thank you. *Sea Trench* isn't just a superboat, and Jerry Manning its supercaptain. They're a gestalt, a blending of man and machine. That's the best way I can describe it to you. They're part and parcel—you can't talk about the boat without talking about the captain, and it works the other way around as well. Jerry Manning created this submarine. Every inch of it is stamped with his personality. Without him the boat just wouldn't be. One more thing—and this is really the crux of it all, doctor—the navy tells the captain where he takes *Sea Trench*, but that's where it ends. They never tell him how to run the show. It's all his from beginning to end. He has all the marbles, and that includes the responsibilities as well as the failures. If you like, we can forget we ever had this conversation. I—"

He broke off as Chadwick and Templeton came into earshot. He winked at Miko. "Okay. End of speech." He turned to the others. "Dr. Chadwick, Mr. Templeton, I'm Commander Ryan." They shook hands. "It would be best if we didn't wait any longer to board. Please come with me." He started off with Miko at his side, the others trailing behind in a loose group.

Templeton gestured at Ryan, spoke to the others with him. "Well, at least he seems like a pleasant enough fellow. You know what I mean? Not all business and stiff upper lip like the captain."

Castillo glanced at him. "You mean Wild Bill?"

Templeton was surprised. "Wild Bill? Seems rather strange to call him that."

"Why?"

"It's obvious," Templeton replied. "A big man, gentle. You know, well-mannered, that sort of thing."

Castillo's laughter took the others by surprise. "Don't you know who he is? How he got his name? His nickname, I guess. It was from the war. He was a merchant seaman, his ship was torpedoed, and the captain was killed. Ryan was on the bridge and he took the wheel, and even while they were burning —real bad—he rammed the Russian sub. They got all tangled together. Ryan went crazy. He went down a rope ladder to the deck of the sub—it couldn't back off from the ship—and he had a submachine gun with him, and he killed the Russian deck crew. Before anyone knew what was happening, he dropped through the conning tower hatch, firing like a madman. A bunch of men followed him; they all had weapons; and they captured the sub! Ryan took over as captain and helped bring in the sub. I mean, they actually brought it across the ocean to this country. The navy gave him a commission right on the spot."

Castillo chuckled. "That's very funny, man," he said to Templeton.

"I don't see the humor," Templeton frowned.

"You don't? You call this man gentle. Wild Bill Ryan. Of all people." He clapped Templeton on the shoulder.

The light went on suddenly, momentarily blinding Chadwick. He blinked in the mirror flash, heard Ryan's voice at his side.

"Stand quietly, please."

The lights flashed again, this time in a swift multicolored sequence. Chadwick pressed both hands against a metal plate. A buzzer sounded.

"A small green light will flash in five seconds, Dr. Chadwick. When it does, please state your name clearly," Ryan instructed.

As the light blinked Chadwick recited his full name. A door to his left opened and Ryan guided him through.

"Thank you, sir," Ryan said. "As of this moment Neptune has an electronic record of your voiceprint, body mass, fingerprints, retinal pattern, and your specific electrical potential. The computer is now programmed to identify, admit, assist, and protect you." He grinned. "Not necessarily in that order, of course. And Neptune will also take your orders, provided they do not conflict with the prime directive of this mission."

They were seeing both sides of Commander Ryan now: the pleasant smile and modulated voice, the restrained power, and the touch of steel-hard efficiency that lurked behind his every word and movement. Ryan turned from Chadwick to Miko.

"Miss Stewart, if—" He stopped, laughed lightly. "Whoops. That's Dr. Stewart." He gestured with one hand. "If you please, ma'am?"

She stepped into the ID cubicle and smiled at him. "Thank you, commander."

Ryan took them all through the identification process. As they left the area, he handed each of them a magnetized disc to wear about the neck, and he provided each of them with a detailed chart of the boat to help them find their way through the four capacious levels. They followed him along a softly lighted aisle, noting bulkhead and hatch signs and markings. As they walked Ryan continued his briefing.

"You'll notice that everything is both color and symbol coded," he explained. "If you study your charts you'll see the pattern we've set up, and it won't take you long to find your way around. At the end of every aisleway in this boat there's a green phone. Use it anytime for assistance if you get lost."

He stopped by a hatch marked with bright red Warning and Keep Out signs. "Now, your individual ID discs or body codes on record with Neptune won't permit you entry to certain areas. This is the weapons bay, for example. Since there's no purpose served by your presence here, entry is forbidden. Please, for your own sake, never attempt to step through any area you know is on the no-admittance list. You'll receive a nasty charge that will quite effectively render you unconscious, and we don't want that to happen to anyone. Down that way," he pointed, "is one of the nuclear power sections. Admittance to any such area is possible only when you're accompanied by a crew member who is appropriately coded with Neptune."

Dr. Chadwick grimaced. He was tiring quickly of military restrictions and demands, and he failed to conceal the sarcasm in his voice. "That's not very likely, is it?"

Ryan looked at him with a poker face, devoid of any reaction. "The power room? Of course, doctor. In fact, that's next on our list."

Ryan's pleasant response threw Chadwick off-balance. "Sorry," the scientist murmured. "I meant the weapons bay, right here."

"Do you *want* to go in there?"

"Why, uh, no, of course not," Chadwick said defensively.

Ryan glided smoothly through the moment. "Shall we continue, please?"

They moved along a series of aisles, climbed ladders, descended others. Ryan stopped finally by another hatch marked in red. "This is where Neptune lives," he explained.

Templeton edged closer. "I've spent a lot of time with cybernetics systems, commander. Can we—"

Ryan shook his head. "I'm sorry, sir. Only one man can take you through this hatch and that's Captain Manning. I want to warn you very explicitly that a forced entry—an attempted entry, I should say, because you would never make it—will result in lethal action by the computer itself."

Silence. There really wasn't anything to say, and they followed quietly as Ryan led them through another series of hatches into a new aisleway. He talked as they went along. "The nuclear systems of *Sea Trench* come under the control of Commander Matt Matthews. Three of the crew are on console duty around the clock, of course. We can go in here now because, first, the computer is programmed to admit anyone with an ID disc who is in my company; and, second, Commander Matthews has already given permission for your presence."

Standing before another hatch marked with grim warnings and radiation symbols, Ryan looked up into TV scanners that covered the entire area. He placed his right hand on a flat metal plate and inserted his own ID disc into a slot. Lights flickered, and the group saw a scanner move slightly for a better view. Ryan talked, seemingly to thin air. They didn't question that microphones were everywhere.

"Ryan here. Six K Four Niner Sierra Tango."

A concealed speaker responded. "Stand by, please." After a momentary pause the voice came alive again. "Disc identity, please."

They inserted their discs, one by one pressed their hands against the plate. A green glow diffused the area and a chime sounded. Two massive steel doors slid away; another set of steel bars lifted vertically with a pneumatic hiss. The entrance to the power room was now open to them and they followed Ryan inside, stopping on the edge of a small balustrade.

It was nothing like they expected. No pounding noise or driving gears or clanking systems; no vibration, no smell of oil or grease. A deep quiet, a humming sound, the air almost physically charged with energy, something they felt in their bones as much as detected with their ears. Spread out far in front of them were enormous computer-linked consoles and panels with literally hundreds of gauges and flickering light boards. In the distance, seated before one panel wall, was Lieutenant Commander Charles Autry, then on second watch. As they first caught sight of him, his seat began to glide sideways along the deck on concealed tracks, taking him quickly and smoothly to another control section. Autry leaned forward, studied gauges, made several control adjustments, recorded entries in a log, then powered the chair on to another station. He looked up, saw the group, and waved casually.

They followed Ryan down a ladder into the main control room. It was difficult to accept that they were inside a submarine, for the control chamber was akin to a low-vaulted cathedral, with the same awesome effect, heightened by the mild chitterings they now detected as they stood closer to the panels. Ryan stopped before a glassed wall.

"I've already checked with Matthews. He won't be able to spend time with us right now, and you can see that Commander Autry is on watch and can't be disturbed. We can stay briefly and return at another time when conditions allow, but I thought you would enjoy at least seeing our main drive and power facility.

"Commander," Miko queried, "is Commander Matthews also in this section?"

Ryan pointed to a control cubicle with glassed walls. There was a sudden, almost collective intake of breath, for Matthews was a man whose face had been scarred into a grotesque mask. At one time, they knew without explanation, his face had been torn apart and patched together with consummate care—but almost frightening results. One side of his mouth was scar and transplant tissue, and his head seemed stuck at an odd angle to his neck.

Miko let out her breath in a long sigh. She held Ryan's arm, spoke privately to him. "I—apologize."

Ryan showed her a thin smile. "For being startled?"

"Yes," she admitted.

"Then," he said, "you're a very special person to me. Thank you, Dr. Stewart."

"I would be pleased if you would make it just Miko from now on," she told him. He squeezed her hand.

He led them from the nuclear control room through another series of hatches and up ladders, stopping finally before a lemon-yellow hatchway entrance that slid aside. "Foot pressure on the deck," he explained. "It opens automatically. No discs are needed here." They entered a large, comfortable room that was decorated in pleasant colors, the walls alive with paintings of sea creatures and deep-ocean scenes.

"This is our meeting and recreation room. We also hold informal assemblies in here. Now, if you'll forgive me, I'll have to leave you for a while. Down that deck," Ryan said, pointing, "you'll find your individual fo'c'sles, with a name on each hatchway. All your personal requirements will be taken care of entirely in this area."

"Mr. Ryan, when will we be able to visit our laboratories and work areas?"

"Later today," Ryan told Chadwick. "For now, please excuse me." He was leaving the room when Templeton called after him.

"Commander, one more question, please?"

Ryan turned, waiting.

"When do we—uh—leave dry dock? You know —get under way?"

Ryan smiled. "I thought you'd never ask," he said. He crossed the room to a control panel, depressed a switch. The lights faded swiftly, and a large section of the hull became transparent before their eyes. They were looking into the ocean; fish were moving by with startling speed.

"I thought you'd like this," Ryan said, and a twinkle was again in his eyes. "Enjoy the view. We're already 130 miles out to sea."

9

~~~~~~~~~~~~~

Jerry Manning's face was as impassive as if it were carved from marble. Yet there was movement playing across his features, subtle colors reflecting from his eyes and cheekbones, and a single spot on the side of his forehead. For a long time he studied the sprawling control/display panel on the bridge of *Sea Trench*. With him on the main deck were Commander Peter Williams, bridge officer—tall, lithe, sandy-haired, not given to many words; Commander Chris Patterakis, operations officer—dark, curly-haired, stocky, intense; and, Lieutenant Commander Al MacKinney—a large, heavy man whose easygoing countenance belied the fact that he was the boat's weapons officer.

Bridge control, spread before Manning, was a semicircular facility filled with computer banks and controls and a touch of the whimsical—one empty seat marked NEPTUNE. The control officer, when on duty with the hand controls that might override the computer system, was always strapped in, his hands resting lightly on the control stick and throttle, his feet on the rudder pedals. The main power throttle, the slab console, and the stick, with many buttons and switches, allowed power to be played with accordianlike finger speed and quick reaction from small and large hydrojets and thrusters. The man who controlled the U.S. *Sea Trench* was at once a submarine commander, a fighter pilot, and an astronaut.

Behind Manning a hatch slid open. Manning kept his eyes on the data display banks as Bill Ryan came to his side. "We've got company," Manning commented.

Both men directed their gaze to the left and downward. "How long have they been with us?" Ryan queried.

A thin smile touched Manning's face. "Mr. Ryan, I do believe they were ready and waiting."

They continued their study of a darkened area on the bridge where what looked like a phantom fog hovered, almost mystically, over a wide circular platform that was built low over the bridge deck and ringed with optical lenses. Light twisted and bent in weird shifting colors even as they watched, a constant roiling movement.

Ryan broke the brief silence. "You think they've got a handle on us?"

Manning shook his head slightly. "No. Their intelligence knows something's up, but they don't know precisely what it is. So they're playing it cute, waiting for us, tagging along from the start."

As he spoke, the patterns of shifting light before them coalesced. A small phantom submarine—*Sea Trench*—appeared in a phantom ocean. Steadily the ghostly image solidified until they were, literally, watching themselves glide through the deeps in an incredible miniature form.

"Easy enough to outrun them, captain."

"Our speed would be a dead giveaway." Manning paused a moment. "It would tell them too much." He gestured to Williams. "Scale down the holo, please."

The tiny image of *Sea Trench* became even smaller as the scale of viewing changed. Another submarine, well behind, appeared suddenly.

"Oh, ho!" Ryan said with a grin. "I see our friends are closing the gap."

Manning nodded. "Good for their morale. Let them keep coming for a while."

He turned to the other men on the bridge. "Chris, strap in and go to standby."

Patterakis moved to the control seat, secured his harness, and adjusted the controls for instant manual take-over.

"Manual standby ready, sir."

Manning nodded again. "Mac, you ready?"

MacKinney was seated before a board that circled him from left to right with readout presentations, ready lights, keys beneath his fingers. "Yes, sir," he told Manning. "Chop-chop."

"Pete," Manning asked Williams, "how far back is *Albacore?*"

"They'll be coming into holo range any minute. Three minutes to kill range."

"Very good," Manning confirmed. "Chris, be ready for max thrust when I call. Mac, if we have to I want those people—"

He cut off his words as a chime sounded by the entrance hatch. He looked into a TV monitor, surprised as he saw the face of Miko Stewart on the screen.

Ryan glanced at Manning. "In or out, skipper?"

He was surprised by Manning's reply. "Bring her in."

Ryan opened the hatch, brought Miko to Manning's side. Manning didn't turn to look at her. "Miss Stewart, this boat is under a combat alert," he announced suddenly.

Her eyes widened and her lips parted.

"Come closer, please," Manning told her. "I want you to see this for yourself."

She moved closer to the display platform, the magical presentation causing her to stare. "I—I don't understand."

"You're watching a holographic laser projection. Our computer makes it all possible," Manning explained. "Everything picked up by sonar or our green masers is fed into Neptune. The computer has a memory record of us, of course, but also of every submersible craft known in the world. What's fed into the computer is in turn transferred to this system. We are now viewing a three-dimensional laser-transmitted hologram—a holographic projection, if you can think of it that way—of everything that's happening in the sea about us, even including fish passing within our sensor range."

It wasn't quite that simple, and Manning's easy representation was the thinnest gloss over a cake of extraordinary intricacy. For many years the ocean deeps were thought of as placid and quiescent, the quietude a result of crushing pressures that made the depths as thick as the thickest oil. Instead, the men who first ventured into the dark hydroworld crashed into huge waves; they stumbled through a bewildering variety of streams and currents and inversion layers, turbulence severe and unexpected and unpredictable, and myriad other forces that created swirling clouds and mists. There was more than darkness to blind the men who probed this "inner planet" of earth. Mysterious deep-scattering layers were in many ways comparable with the great cloud formations that flooded the gaseous atmosphere men breathe. Astonishingly, it was found that the clouds of the hydroworld rose and fell: They were possessed of intricate movement, they exhibited height and substance, and they affected and were affected by the surrounding medium— which was changing moment by moment.

Human eyes that stare through ocean water know

that everyday taken-for-granted light doesn't exist within this liquid environment. The heaving viscous mass refracts and absorbs light waves and reflects back a weakened and distorted picture. Light bogs down in the miasma of the oceans, and the most powerful beams are swallowed as effectively as water absorbs a pebble tossed idly into its maw.

Thus the men who go deep into the oceans must do as the porpoises, which, strangely enough, have the same poor underwater vision as man. As myopic as his biped human cousin, the porpoise "sees by sound"; optics yield quickly to sonar—sound navigation ranging—known by its other name as echolocation. For a porpoise in search of companions or food, or for sensing creatures dangerous to his own safety, it's much easier than it is for a man because the porpoise does what comes naturally, and man must bring with him elaborate artificial systems.

And sonar vision itself suffers impairment and distortion because temperature and salinity changes in the water bend and twist acoustical signals. Sound beams are swallowed greedily by floating masses, alive or dead, and are subjected to a host of forces yet inexplicable and equally inescapable.

This opacity of the deeps demanded of *Sea Trench* a dazzling variety of artificial senses and devices. TV probes greatly extend vision by taking the transmitter and artificial light to the scene to be studied, but even this device has its limitations because it is a "sourcepoint of vision." Within the depths, man is always the beggar and never the chooser. However, there were other extensions possible through the electronic sorcery of *Sea Trench*. "Liquid radar"—sonar—was used extensively. There were also blue green modified maser beams of monochromatic light that had an astonishing ability to pierce seawater; it was important that masers were pulsed at swift, intermittent intervals, or they had the nasty habit of turning water into steam and mucking up the whole attempt to "see."

Much of the problem lay in trying to interpret visible light, sonar, and maser beams, for these were too often splotchy, distorted, and lent themselves to false images. *Sea Trench*—through its electronic circuitry and the dazzling ability of the computer —had the capability of filtering this mishmash into meaningful presentations. Memory banks, capable of an untold number of crisscrossing comparisons in a thousandth of a second, translated the incoming data into clear picturizations that could be displayed digitally, on flat screens, or in the remarkable laser-transmitted holographic projection that even at this moment was being studied by Manning, Ryan, and Miko Stewart. Whatever came into the computer was sorted out by the memory banks so that each new shred of activity added to memory storage for greater clarification in the future. But there was always a contest between electronic legerdemain and a world of differing temperature layers, of thermoclines that created greenish fog, of wisps ribboning through the seas, of plankton layers, and of vast assemblies of swiftly moving living creatures.

On the display panel of the computer a digital readout began. Williams depressed a key marked VOICE, and the computer vocalized its presentation so that every man on the bridge would know, without taking his eyes from his own controls or displays, what information was being transmitted. A sonorous voice came from concealed speakers: *"Hing Pao, seven thousand tons, forty knots, killer class, eight tubes forward, four astern, present depth seven thousand feet, speed three-six knots forward, closing the range."*

At the extreme edge of the holographic projection there appeared a third submarine, and it was apparent that it was closing the range on *Hing Pao*.

"*Albacore* will get their attention any moment now," Manning said.

"You said—we were under combat alert." Miko's voice was hesitant.

"Look for yourself," Manning urged. "That Chinese boat, *Hing Pao*. She's been stalking us ever since we left San Diego. I imagine her sonar crew is going crazy trying to figure our size."

"But—but that doesn't mean they would try to —I mean, we're not at war with the Chinese."

"Some people really believe what you just said."

Her voice gained strength. "Oh, come now, captain. Aren't you being a bit dramatic about all this?"

Manning showed no reaction to either her words or her attitude. He looked straight ahead when he replied.

"Miss Stewart, I will tell you for the last time that this boat is under a *combat* alert. *Hing Pao* is a killer, and at this moment her captain would like nothing more than to confirm his suspicions about us and then do everything within his power to destroy *Sea Trench*. It would be great face for him."

"But—"

"Commander Ryan, advise Miss Stewart to maintain silence, or remove her immediately from this bridge."

She stared openmouthed at Manning. Disbelief stamped on her face, she turned to Ryan. He caught her eye and nodded slowly, to let her know that Manning meant precisely what he said.

MacKinney's voice came to them. "Sir, we have a coded sonar burst from *Albacore*. They'll make their move in nine zero seconds."

"Very good," Manning said crisply. "Secure. Mr. MacKinney, stand by for screamers. Full spectrum, all torps."

Miko's face went white with the word *torps,* and, as she started to speak, she saw the warning glance from Ryan. She pressed her lips tightly together, her frustration mounting rapidly. She forced her attention to the holographic projection. The third submarine, *Albacore,* was blinking a soft red light.

"Thirty seconds," MacKinney called.

"Confirmed," Manning said. "Control, stand by."

"Control ready." That from Patterakis.

"Ten seconds," MacKinney announced.

"Fire torps on *Albacore* release plus ten seconds," Manning ordered. He turned to Miko. "Grab that handrail and hold on tight."

He did the same, as did Ryan. On the bulkhead directly before them, a digital clock flashed numbers brightly in a grim countdown.

Far behind them the American killer boat fired off a string of torps in step salvo. Slim missiles whipped through the sea.

Aboard *Hing Pao,* the specialist at the sonar board showed alarm on his face. Shrill warbling sounds tore into his headset. He shouted warnings to the control crew, braced himself, felt helplessness wash over him as he heard the torps fanning out swiftly through the water in a radial pattern.

"Torps away from *Albacore,*" MacKinney said.

Manning nodded. "Call them out."

Miko's face was ashen as she lifted her eyes from the hologram to Ryan. He stared back impassively.

Through the hull of their boat, the crew of *Hing Pao* could hear the muted but shrill sounds of approaching missiles.

MacKinney's eyes flicked back and forth along his display panel. A series of rippling red lights appeared, then dull sounds thumped through the control deck. Manning's voice came sharply to MacKinney.

"You may fire, Mr. MacKinney. The works."

MacKinney's fingers rippled along his key studs.

A moan escaped Miko, a quiet sound of despair through anguished lips. "No, no . . . oh, my God . . ."

Even as she murmured, to herself rather than to anyone else, small ports snapped open along the flanks of *Sea Trench,* and slim torps hurtled away from the stern.

The hologram showed tiny shapes trailing glowing lines that radiated away from *Sea Trench,* rushing toward *Hing Pao.*

An insane screaming sound tore through the depths. The hydrophones brought the sound into the bridge, ear stabbing, painful. Manning and Ryan glanced at one another and smiled.

Deep within the ocean three torps suddenly emitted bursts of flame, stopped dead in the water. They sank slowly, trailing tremendous clouds of agitated bubbles that rose steadily above the sinking torps.

"Mr. Patterakis! Take her down, all ahead full."

Sea Trench surged forward with an acceleration felt throughout the great submarine. A deep thrumming from the powerful hydrojets came to them as both sound and vibration.

"Mr. MacKinney, secure from red to standby."

"Standby confirmed, sir."

"Mr. Williams?"

That was question enough for Williams. He hesitated only a moment, nodded to himself. "They've had it, captain."

Manning's sudden relaxation was visible. "Very good, gentlemen. Mr. Ryan, take the bridge, please."

"Yes, sir." He slipped into a wide seat that faced slim monitoring panels. His voice was unusually formal. "You are relieved from the bridge, captain."

There was no more holding back the anger within Miko. She faced Manning squarely, eyes blazing. "Damn your orders for silence, I—"

"Please speak freely," he interrupted. "We are off alert."

She was struggling for control, breathing hard, hating the thin, knowing smile on Manning's face. "You and this band of cutthroats have *murdered* the entire crew of that Chinese submarine! And without warning, of any kind, to people with whom we're not at war, who never fired a shot at us!"

"Is that all, Miss Stewart?"

She hated him totally, completely, shock naked on her face. "Is that *all?* My God, don't you have any *feeling* for what you've done? I cannot believe—" She sucked in air, fighting for control, gaining it swiftly. All of a sudden she was cold, her voice clear, explicit. "You know you'll never be able to keep me quiet about this. I could never be a party to mass killing, and—"

"We haven't killed anyone."

"I just saw the whole whole thing!"

"Miss Stewart." His iciness was a perfect standoff to her fury. He spoke her name, watched her clamp down on her lips, then he continued. "I told you *Hing Pao* was a killer boat that had been lying in wait for us. At the same time, we have known of its mission, we've known where it's been all the time, and we were prepared for its moves. Just as *Hing Pao* trailed us, so *Albacore* trailed the enemy. When—"

"You keep saying *enemy!* We're not fighting these—"

"If you interrupt me again, we have nothing further to say to one another, now, or for the rest of this mission."

Bill Ryan thought that her eyes were close to producing real sparks. He watched her nails digging into her palms, and he listened to the tightly controlled "I apologize" she forced out to Manning.

Manning, for his part, went on as smooth as silk. "*Albacore's* torpedoes were spaced to detonate in a perfect circle about *Hing Pao*." He paused, locked his eyes on hers in a steely glare. "They were also spaced to detonate at least one thousand yards from that Chinese boat. When they exploded, it was extremely clear to *Hing Pao* that *Albacore* could just as easily have driven those torps straight in."

He looked at her with less steel, knowing the turmoil that must be charging through her. "Are you with me so far, Miss Stewart?"

She shook her head in confusion. "But—but *you*, I mean, *we*, this submarine, also fired torpedoes. I heard you give the order, I know we—"

He waited as she faltered, then he picked it up, his voice gentle but unquestionably in command. "Our first torps, Miss Stewart, were screamers, intended to give the Chinese a very bad headache. On their particular sonic frequency they have quite effectively destroyed the sonar tracking systems of *Hing Pao*. They did absolutely no other damage. The second brace of torps set up a thick screen of air bubbles that made hash of any sonar tracking that might have survived *Albacore*'s blast waves *or* our screamers. So, all we gave the Chinese was a severe headache and no small confusion, and in that process, without harming a single hair of any precious Chinese head, we have vanished completely."

10

Behind Manning, the bridge hatchway opened. They turned to watch Commander Syd Prentiss approach them. The barest trace of a smile came to Manning's face. Syd had timed it perfectly.

"Miss Stewart," Manning said, "I'm sure you're anxious to see your laboratory facilities. This is Commander Prentiss, and he will escort you there and provide whatever assistance you may require."

Prentiss took her hand; he was a self-contained package of personality, charm, good looks, and intelligence. "Dr. Stewart, my pleasure. I'm familiar with your work, and I believe you'll be most pleased with the lab setup we've arranged for you and the science party. Would you come with me, please?"

She nodded, turning to speak to Manning. Confusion crossed her features. Manning wasn't there. She looked up at Prentiss. "Of course. Thank you."

When she was gone from the bridge, the watch crew looked at one another, grinning. "The old man's still got the touch," MacKinney said.

"You'd better believe it," Ryan murmured. "Okay, troops, back to bearding the denizens of the deeps, shall we?"

The hydrophones brought the sea to life. *Sea Trench* glided forward with minimum thrust, her hydrojets on "position depth" maneuvering so that they generated a minimum of sonic disturbance in the sea. Commander Prentiss had sent out slow torps with hydrophone pickups that transmitted back to the submarine by wire the sounds that generated deep within the water. When the "listening devices" were turned to maximum gain, it took a trained ear or even the computer to distinguish sounds among the cacophony of ocean racket, for under these conditions even a rumble from afar, a whisper or a sigh, could be increased to a horrendous liquid jungle of sound. The quiet depths, once your "ears" were sufficiently sensitive, roared and hissed, crackled and thundered. The sea was filled with croaks and chittering and twitters and groaning cries and soprano shrieks, thrumming and snapping, and it was often difficult to pinpoint the source if any distance were involved because the ocean was splintered with strange thermal ducts that could carry noises halfway around the planet. Sound in the ocean depths was a mind-boggling phantom that became distorted, bent, twisted, doubled back upon itself, and was often much louder far from where it originated.

Deep ocean sounds weren't restricted to the creatures that moved beneath the crushing pressures. Sonic viols came from ambient acoustics, waves marching across and within the ocean, currents and streams that clashed, whirlpools with strange sucking noises, even liquid slobberings and upward wellings of air bubbles from creatures no one had ever identified or even imagined. Mysterious grating noises carried for hundreds of miles. Gas pockets exploded along the sea bottom; lava pushed into frigid water and exploded with subterranean thunder that produced odd reverberations, echo bouncing off echo. There were quakes that toppled entire mountains, and these caused their own thunder of tumbling land masses and sent sound waves crashing through the ocean floor like huge gongs tolling worldwide. Geysers were particularly ear dazzling; they hissed and cried with rasping boilerlike screams.

There were screams of whales, cries of life and death, animals snarling to the kill—and all this was mixed with the orchestration of man's devices. Ships' screws pounded and churned and rumbled. Explosive blasts accidental and deliberate caused booming pockets of sound to burst outward in all directions and then, caught by unpredictable thermal ducts, to reappear hundreds or thousands of miles away. Ships and dredges and probes and offshore drilling, great bubbles of oil and gas gurgling upward. A million pipes and drains discharged the sputum of industrial and biological sewage, burbling and rumbling from along the shorelines. Sometimes ships sank, and their acoustical signature was unmistakable, for a ship dies in a frothing foam of trapped air bubbles breaking free explosively and rushing upward, followed by a thumping groan as the hapless vessel settles to the bottom.

There were unpredictable sounds: A meteorite weighing a million tons or more might smash into the ocean, creating ripping shock waves, turning millions of tons of water into steam at the point of impact, sending concussions through the water to bounce off the bottom and echo up again until everything roiled together in an acoustical headache. The sea wasn't always that way, of course, but it could often be, and the moments of quiescence that lulled the unwary were liable to be punctuated with nerve-rattling dinosaurlike cries.

In the science laboratories of *Sea Trench* at this moment, sound was a subject of attention. One of the observation chambers held Dr. Chadwick and

Larry Templeton, accompanied by Richard Castillo and Commander Prentiss. The chamber was completely dark, for the four men were looking through the glassite wall that formed part of the side of the submarine hull. The effect was much the same as if they were completely exposed to the deep ocean; marine life drifted or sped by on the other side of the transparent hull. In the darkness, the sound of drums came and went, at times barely audible, then increasing abruptly in volume until the chamber thundered with the hammering of drumbeats. Chadwick leaned forward, his eyes guided by glowing crystal dots that, unless viewed from directly head on, showed no light. He slid a lever down to lower the suddenly painful level of sound.

"Drumfish," he said idly to the others as they passed a huge swarm of the creatures coming into view as the sub's side floodlights struck them. "I've never seen so many at one time."

"That sound," Castillo complained, rubbing his ear. "It was like a bass fiddle, but with a higher pitch. It *hurt*."

Chadwick nodded. He well knew that aggravating sound.

"Doctor," Castillo went on, "just how do they do that anyway?"

Chadwick turned a dial that brought a pale greenish light into the chamber. He wanted to smoke his pipe. One of the oddities of the human mind is that smoking—when you can't *see* the smoke—loses most of its flavor. He sucked on his pipestem, savored the taste, let the smoke drift idly from his nostrils. "They have bladders that are filled with air," he told the boy, "and they use a vibrating muscle to slap against the bladders. The sound is amazing. As you say, if you're near a large number of them and you're listening either in the ocean itself or through the hydrophones, it can hurt."

Prentiss laughed. "Well, ten thousand of the damned things do have their effect."

Templeton nodded to Castillo. "The drumfish really aren't that bad, you know. The croakers are really the worst. They turn the sea into a jungle nightmare."

"You mean they're worse than what we're hearing now?"

"Oh, very much so. They can sound like several thousand people beating great sticks against hollow logs."

"It's a staccato sort of sound," Chadwick added. "Very unnerving. It gets to you after a while. There's really a whole list of those bloody things out there. Groupers, pompano, toadfish, crabs, lobsters—the lot of them make up the worst."

"Don't forget the sea lions," Prentiss threw in.

"That's mammal. I thought the whales were the loudest, especially the humpbacks," Templeton remarked.

"Whales are whales," Chadwick said, "and they can sing and cry and the rest of it. But the sea lions actually roar. I don't know how they manage it this far down, or at any depth, really, but they just open their mouths and sound like lions starving for food. The four-legged variety, I mean."

Castillo shook his head. "Well, it's weird. Maybe it's some form of communication, but it's weird."

Prentiss laughed, clapping the boy's shoulder gently. "I'm not too sure about that, Richard. You weren't around when a whole generation was raised on acid rock."

"They're just talking," Jessica said. "You know, just fun talk." She looked sharply at Miko Stewart. "I'm right, aren't I?"

Miko glanced up from her close attention to a tape-machine speaker. They had been listening to groaning bass sounds, squeaks like doors opening on rusty hinges, loud and long cries, and eerie warbles. Miko turned down the volume of the machine and nodded. "You're right. Fun talk. That's what we were hearing. No danger or warning signals there."

She leaned back, settled herself comfortably. "Jessica, how did you know the whales were just talking? They have danger, mating, assembly— many different calls—and I've spent most of my life working with them. But you're so young—"

"I don't know, really. I just, well, you know, I just *feel* it. I know, inside me, what they mean when they're calling one another."

"You've been right almost all the time." Miko smiled. "I haven't told you, but I'd already heard about you, Jessie."

Jessie blushed. "It's nice—I mean, to hear *you* say that."

"I mean it, young lady. For some time now, in my field, we've heard about a young girl who talks to porpoises, who makes friends even with killer whales in the wild."

"They're really not killers," Jessica said, rising to the defense of orca. "They kill only when they have to feed, and they're so very smart, and—"

"You don't have to convince *me*," Miko broke in with a laugh.

"I didn't mean to, well, you know—"

Miko nodded. "Can you really understand them, Jessie?"

Her eyes brightened. "Oh, *yes*. I don't know how it started, but I was scuba diving once, and I saw some dolphins come by and I heard them, you know, their sonar pings, and I took out my mouthpiece and made sounds. I really didn't know what I was saying—it just seemed the right thing to do —and the next thing I knew, they were rubbing gently against me. They came back to shore with me, and when I went out again the next day they were *waiting* for me. I stayed in the shallows, and we played together, and I'd take a deep breath and go underwater and make sounds, and I always seemed to know what they wanted me to understand, and they understood me—" Her voice trailed away and she seemed embarrassed. She shook her head, her hair tossing about her pretty young face.

"Jessica, I want to ask you something." Miko's tone was serious, almost somber. "It's personal, and you may not want to answer. I don't want to pry, and—"

"Oh, Miko, you can ask me anything."

Miko fumbled for the words. "I was asking about you, Jessie. Trying to find out about this talent of yours. It's more than curiosity on my part. What you have, what you're able to do, can be so important for us, and, well, I haven't been able to find out a thing about you—about when you were much younger, I mean."

Jessica brought her hands together, fingers intertwining until her knuckles were white. It was obvious that the girl wasn't sure whether she wanted to move back into a part of her past where wounds might still lie open. Miko waited.

"It's—it's strange," Jessica said at last. "You know I'm not American, don't you?"

Miko shook her head. "I didn't know that or anything else. I've been asking these questions because no one has ever said a word about your family, or where you're from, or how you happened to get into the advanced school and were picked for this program, or, well—Jessie, I want to understand so we can work better as a team."

"My family—I suppose you would call them gypsies," Jessica said, faltering. "I understand they were from Hungary, or maybe it was Romania. No one is sure."

"Then how—"

"How did I get here? Into the United States?"

Miko nodded.

"I don't even remember. Not in detail. Just generalities."

"Those would be fine," Miko assured her.

"We were very poor. I remember that. Also that my parents and my two sisters were running. Or I think we were running. Momma, as much as I can remember, said that poppa was afraid of the war and that we were right in the path of the Russian army in case war broke out. So we sold everything, and we got on a ship of some kind. I know they wanted to fly, but that wasn't possible, and it was an old ship, a freighter of some kind that would take us to South America. I had never seen the ocean before and I was crazy about it. The sea and the smell and the wind—it was so marvelous! Anyway, we were somewhere off the coast of South America, I'm pretty sure that was it, when the war started. I guess we were lucky, but—" Her face went pale, then she regained her color. "We saw the night turn into day—and the lights were terrible, and everyone was talking about hydrogen bombs, and it was the middle of the night when the wave came."

"The wave?"

"A tidal wave, I think. It was supposed to have come from the Panama Canal."

Miko nodded. "That would be right. The canal was destroyed by a hydrogen bomb."

"I don't know much about it, except that it was hot and I was sleeping on deck, and there was a terrible roar. I remember this part very clearly because the moon was full and the water was like a giant wall, foaming green and glowing, and it hit the ship without warning. And that was all I knew because the ship, well, I don't know what happened to it, but suddenly I was in the water and I suppose I was screaming. I never saw the ship or anyone on it again, but someone was holding me up. I was just a little girl, and I felt these warm bodies against mine, keeping me above the water. I knew how to swim, I had done a lot of that in a river near my home, but this was different, and all night they kept me above the water, and I even slept a couple of times, I guess. When the day came the sea was quiet, and I couldn't see anyone, and then I saw these great fins in the water, and—"

"Sharks?"

"Oh, no. These were *friendly*."

"How did you know that, Jessie?" Miko looked at her closely.

"Well—they had held me above water all night. They were the gladiators. You know, Miko, the gladiator orcas, the big killer whales, although they're really not that at all, and—"

"You mean *they* were the ones that kept you above water all night?"

"Oh, yes. It was wonderful. I should have been mad with fear, I suppose; I mean, I knew by then that my family and everyone else on that ship must be dead, but I had no fear, and the orcas stayed with me and I rested on one of the animals—he was *huge*—and somewhere about the middle of the day, I suppose, I saw a small boat coming toward me. There were some fishermen in the boat, and they were frightened silly because some of the orcas had been pushing the boat toward me. The whales waited around until the people in the boat took me aboard. The people, there were three men and two women, looked at me like I wasn't real. They took good care of me because the orcas stayed with us until we reached a small town, and when I went ashore I saw the big one lift out of the water, and I waved, and then they were gone. I was taken to a hospital, I guess it was that, where a lot of people asked me questions day after day, and then some strange people came there and took me aboard a plane and flew me to a place I never even knew existed. It was filled with people in uniforms and—"

"I know the rest," Miko said, her voice subdued. "That was the Markinson Institute."

"That's right. But how did you know?"

"I have your records from there. They say a great deal about you, Jessica, but very little about what happened to you before you arrived there. You were given foster-parents about a month after you arrived, weren't you?"

Jessica nodded. "Bill and Emily Ames. They were —they are—wonderful people. They were like real parents to me. They let me go to a special school, and, well—it was like a dream—I had the chance to work with animals and study sea science and, well, I guess you know the rest."

Miko did, indeed. From the moment the story of the strange girl had reached the American consul in the small Central American country where Jessica had been "directed" by the great killer whales, Washington had moved mountains to bring her into the U.S. For it was recognized that whatever talent this child had, it could and should be developed, and every move was made to give the girl a normal home and upbringing. Apparently it had worked.

"Jessie, how do you explain your understanding of the animals?"

"It's like ESP, you know." She added lamely, "I guess," not too certain of proposing that particular explanation.

"I understand," Miko said to ease her concern.

"Do you? I mean, *really*?"

"Yes, I do," Miko said with confidence. "Try to remember that I've spent most of my life working with porpoises. I only wish," she sighed, and the wistfulness in her voice was honest, "I had your incredible touch with them."

"If you want me to show you, I would."

"I'd love that." Miko paused and frowned. "It might even help me to get through to—to—"

Jessica laughed, almost squealing. "Captain Manning?"

Miko sighed heavily and nodded. "That man has a wall around him that—well, every time I think I understand him, he does something that makes me hate him, and then—" Her voice trailed away.

"Then you find out he really knew what he was doing all the time, and he's always right, isn't he?"

"Always?" Miko said in defense.

"It ends up that way," Jessica said with a laugh. "He's the most fascinating person I ever met. I mean, without him this submarine wouldn't even *exist*. Miko, he's so busy, and he has so many responsibilities, but the first time Richard and I met him he went out of his way for hours to explain things to us, to make us feel comfortable." She drew up her knees, hugging them tightly. "I'm crazy about him," she said with conviction. "I really am."

She peered carefully at Miko. "I think that if you let down your wall just a bit, you might feel the same way about him."

Miko stared at the girl. "Well, never mind that for now. Let's listen to more of the tapes."

The circular black object seemed to hang suspended in midair, and a gloved hand smashed it hard against a court wall. All about Jerry Manning and Bill Ryan were walls—the front and back a dazzling white; the sidewalls, ceiling, and floor different pastel shades. The two men, in gym shorts and sneakers, played a tight, hard game of handball. It was their best way of "cutting free" of the otherwise constant responsibility of the great sub.

Ryan returned the smash, concentrating on his play, talking as he moved. "Think we shook the Chinks?"

Manning paused, got in a return. "For now, anyway," he said, grunting. "But they might figure us for the Aleutians."

"What about *Albacore*?"

Manning went back, hit the ball high. "They'll stay with the Chinese all the way home, worry at them."

"What about your other little problem?"

Manning didn't answer immediately. He delivered a killer smash and took the point. He recovered the ball and stopped, breathing hard. He studied Ryan. "You're playing word games with me, baby."

Ryan grinned. "You're dodging pretty good."

"You mean Miko?"

"*Miko*, is it?"

"She's a pain," Manning told him. "Smart, sharp, and a pain."

"Best-looking one I've seen in a long time."

"Why don't you have a crack at it, then?"

Ryan shrugged easily. "One never knows, but a man's got to be careful. Them angled, glossy black eyes. I might start to get serious—and then where would I be?"

He ducked as Manning threw the ball at him. They laughed and went back to no-nonsense playing.

"Cook should be shot."

They looked up across the table at the brutally scarred face of Matthews. For some reason he was wearing his thick glasses instead of contact lenses, and the room lights reflected in the glasses in bright points. Matthews grunted and went to a wall panel, tapped a series of buttons. "The food stinks," he said after a pause, making sure to glare at Larry Templeton as he spoke.

"I don't understand," Templeton told him.

"Man, do you know how long it's been since I've had a decent mulligan stew?"

"Well, no, of course I don't."

"Too damned long," Matthews snapped. The pastel plasticized wall before him, glowing with lights and push buttons, chimed softly, and a tray issued slowly from a slot. He picked up the tray, gesturing. "Got to eat this tripe, instead."

On the tray was a beautiful sirloin steak, a steaming baked potato, vegetables, apple pie. Behind Templeton, the others were grinning.

"I still don't understand," Templeton said. "Your food looks excellent, and mine has been delicious. I—"

"You're too young to know what good food is. You and the bloody cook." He stalked off, limping slightly, a battered hulk dragging old pains with him. He sat down heavily at a table, placed his dishes before him.

At another table, watching it all, Miko Stewart, Jessica Ames, Chuck Autry, and Syd Prentiss ate their dinner meal. Autry grinned wolfishly at the others. "Old Matt's sure been pulling Templeton's string."

Jessica sniffed. "You mean he's picking on him?"

"Well," Autry shrugged, "maybe just a little. But you've got to admit, little one, Templeton's perfect for it. Besides, it makes the chief feel better, and that makes *me* feel better."

"I don't understand," Miko broke in. "I mean, he complained about the food, but," she glanced at her own tray of swordfish steak, "this is heavenly. If Matthews really wants that—what did he call it?"

"Mulligan stew," Prentiss said.

"Then why," Miko asked, "doesn't he just tell the cook to make it up for him?"

Prentiss and Autry exchanged glances, broke into smiles. "Miko, would you like to meet our cook?"

"Why—of course."

"You already have." He paused. "It's Neptune."

"That's asking me to believe a great deal of a *computer*."

"I—we," he said with a glance at Autry, "thought you already knew. Every meal on this boat is prepared by the computer. Oh, we can whip something up if we like, but all our requests for particular specialties were fed into Neptune's memory banks long ago, and the frozen-food stores were stocked that way. Think about it. How does your food always come to you just the way you like it?"

Miko's eyes widened, and she nodded slowly. "I—well—I never even thought about it. But— you're right! Everything has always been just the way I like it."

"When you order your food," Prentiss added, "Neptune picks up your ID, of course, from your disc. It has an amazing record of you, much of it supplied without your knowing about it. So now, when you tap in your selection, Neptune checks back through its memory and cooks your meal just as if you'd ordered it from a chef."

Miko glanced from him to her food, then across to Matthews at his table. "Then—Commander Matthews could have his mulligan stew, or whatever it is, if he wanted it, couldn't he?"

"Sure could," Autry said affably.

"Then why doesn't he—"

"He hates mulligan stew," Autry broke in.

"But he told Larry—"

Autry gestured, grinning. "Look, Dr. Stewart, it's just that Templeton is such a virgin. The chief can't resist the needle."

She couldn't help it. She giggled.

Commander Williams held his hand over a lever, gripped it gently but securely, and pulled it back slowly. "Hover speed, sir," he told Manning.

The captain nodded from the bridge command seat. "Very good. Mr. Sparco?"

"Sir?"

"Away with the combat receiver, please."

The communications duty officer worked the controls; a red light blinked on.

Along the exterior hull a hatch snapped open. Metal gleamed as a sphere rose steadily, trailing a thin wire.

In the bridge the confirmation lights flashed. "On its way, sir," Sparco announced. "Standing by to receive."

They waited until the sphere reached the surface. Far above them the sphere bobbed, stabilized, and made clicking sounds as its automatic sequencer went into action. A long antenna extended upward, and moments later the sphere was active, receiving signals from a communications satellite, transmitting the data by wire down to the submarine.

On the bridge, Sparco punched in the tape recorder, watched his dial readings, and turned to Manning. "It's ready, captain."

Manning nodded. "Get rid of it, please."

High above them light flashed as a small explosive charge shattered the sphere, sending it beneath the waves as sinking junk. By the time it fell to where it had been launched, the great submarine would be miles away.

Manning and Ryan left the bridge together, went to the radio shack—a term left from the old days, now describing the computerized communications center—and read the digital display of the message.

"We're clean," Manning said slowly. "No reports of any other subs working this part of the Aleutians."

"But plenty of them in the south Atlantic."

"The admiral still knows how to call the shots. Everybody's tracking our boats down there trying to get first dibs on that petroleum find."

They returned to the bridge and looked down at the holographic projection display. Manning keyed the system to navigation scan. Before their eyes, light wavered in the familiar swirling distortion of the lasers coming alive, then snapped into a clear picture, a three-dimensional projection of the north Pacific, with longitude and latitude lines superimposed over the scene. *Sea Trench* showed as a tiny sliver of soft pulsating light.

They watched in silence. The display always intrigued these men, for one's automatic visualization of the "sea bottom" was of a *floor*—flat and vast. But the ocean bottom had more ups and downs than a mountainous area as rough as Colorado. The true "edges" of the ocean were the steep continental slopes that formed the walls of what was in reality the ocean basin. Now Manning and Ryan were seeing another demonstration of that reality. In northern Canada the Aleutian Trench began, a fissure splitting the ocean bottom, one side higher than the other, forming a magnificent wall that rose vertically for thousands of feet. The trench wound its way along, following a curving line that was revealed above the surface by the pattern of the Aleutian Islands. Just before the trench reached the mainland of Asia, there rose from the sea floor, running south, a great wall known as the Emperor Seamounts. This was the first gross feature to interfere with the clifflike march of the higher wall of the Aleutian Trench proper. As Manning and Ryan observed the scene, they might have been in space looking down on an ocean floor from which all water had been stripped away. Their attention was drawn to a soft white dot that began to blink on the holographic projection.

"That's the spot, captain," Ryan commented. "Exactly 253 miles west of Amchitka."

"Eleven hours from now," Manning confirmed. "Be sure to have our passengers meet in the bow observation center one hour before that time."

"Yes, sir." Ryan looked at Manning. "You seem disturbed," he said.

Manning nodded. "I'm not all that pleased with the report from the admiral. In fact, Bill, I want you to take the bridge yourself until we arrive at our initial destination. Maintain full red alert all sensors, and I want MacKinney *in* his seat."

"You feel something crawling along your neck, Jerry?"

"Yes."

They filed into the bow observation center one by one. This was their first time in the forwardmost part of the submarine, and they were somewhat awed by the expansiveness of the space. The seats were arranged almost as in a small theater, in a half-moon layout, facing their direction of travel. The seats were cushioned for comfort, with armchair-type controls for sound, communications, and other signaling purposes. The center two seats were lower, separated from the others, with full control panels on their armrests. Each seat had retracting seat belt and shoulder harness equipment; these would be worn only when a light signal appeared on each armrest console. Between the two front seats and the circular arrangement aft of them was another holographic projection platform. As the group entered the room that was appropriately named OB or Observation Deck, to Miko Stewart's surprise, Manning directed her to the seat at his right, the second of the two command seats.

Manning leaned forward, adjusted his armrest controls, and the hologram sprang into life, showing the three-dimensional view of the ocean bottom off the Aleutian Trench. He tapped several controls, and another display console and control panel extended from his seat so that he had full access to every part of the sub. He swung his chair about abruptly to face the others. It took Miko several moments to do the same. Now the hologram projection was between them and the other people in the room. Manning flicked his gaze over the people who were studying him and waiting for word as to what would happen next.

"We'll be at our deep-dive start position in several minutes," he said without preamble. "I'll be brief. Our computer has been programmed to duplicate the descent profile made first by Chadwick and Templeton in *Sea Search*, and then by Ritter and his crew in *Swimmer IV*. You all know that *Swimmer IV* was lost, and I want you to understand that we're trying to recreate the events that took place during Ritter's dive. It's impossible, of course, in the literal sense. We don't control lifeforms; and the variations of salinity, current, temperature, and other elements are unpredictable except on a broad-base consideration. If we're fortunate, this boat will attract the attention of whatever it was that went after Dr. Chadwick's submersible—and of what struck the *Swimmer IV*."

He swung his chair about abruptly, facing forward again, and worked his control console. Miko followed him, swiveling in her chair. Above and before them, a large flat TV screen snapped into life. "The TV monitor you're watching is carrying the images seen by our remote probes," Manning explained.

They watched brilliant light beams stabbing dark water. Different creatures came into focus and vanished—fish, several seals, a ghostly great shark. Manning's voice went on. "The probe is twelve hundred yards in front of us, and we're receiving a picture through masers that are operating at maximum range. Beyond that the signal breaks up, but at least we have this optical sensing to that distance. Now, look at the hologram."

They watched *Sea Trench* in the sea. "Our sonar signals are computed into the holographic projection. This time we can have an accurate picture of whatever sea life moves within our clarity range." He swung his chair around again. "Miss Stewart is seated with me because of her expertise with such large animals as the sperm whale." He glanced from one person to the next. "Any questions?"

Chadwick gestured. "Can we listen to sonar search? If we do get, ah, company, it might be enlightening to hear them."

"Very good," Manning said. "We'll let you hear anything we pick up. You can use the earplug receiver on the left side of your chairs, and if you feel it's necessary we'll go to loudspeakers."

"Excuse me," Templeton said. "What about our hydrojets, captain? Won't their noise block out the frequencies of echo ranging from any whales?"

"Excellent point, Mr. Templeton. As you know, this boat is negative buoyant, so we can descend at desired rates with the main jets on standby. The small jets produce minimal and noninterfering noise factors. In any event, they won't bother the whales we'll encounter."

Miko turned to him, her brows raised. "You expect them?"

"I expect anything," Manning said, deliberately noncommittal.

"But it sounds as if you're seeking them out."

He nodded. "In a way," he admitted. "But only passively. We are not attempting to arouse anything in this ocean except by our presence, and that is not even remotely aggressive. But whales did attack Dr. Chadwick's boat, and they tried the same with Ritter. Obviously that doesn't fit into any normal scheme of things. There may be whales among us, or a Chinese submarine, or animals directly under their control, or even bionics systems to make us believe they are whales when they're not. We just don't know. So all we're doing is retracing the dives of two boats that preceded us." He glanced at his gauges. "Four thousand feet. We're into the area now."

He turned his seat again to face forward, and Miko did the same. She studied her panel. They were coming into 4,400 feet, with a sink rate of 465 feet per minute, the pressure at 1,958 psi. As she glanced up she saw Manning bringing the TV screen back into life.

Above the screen was a digital readout that gave the constantly changing distance of the maser probes from the sub. The glowing numbers read 1,050 yards, and almost at the same moment a great shape, indistinguishable in the murk, moved past the probe. Then they heard it—loud pinging sonar sounds. Manning had turned on the main speakers in the observation deck.

Chadwick listened intently. "It's big—whatever it is."

Commander Prentiss responded at once. "Squid, by the echo pattern."

Chadwick looked at him with surprise and open pleasure. "You're right. Very good, commander. That was fast."

A moment later a new sound overwhelmed the rhythm of sonar pings. It was startling, a sudden barrage of sound—like the uproar of thousands of frying pans in which bacon and eggs sizzled and crackled with a terrible clamor. It was also reminiscent of the sound of electrical static, or millions of dry twigs breaking, or millions of long fingernails snapping one against the other.

Jessica's eyes widened. *"Shrimp!"* she cried. She knew the sound: pincers snapping together with varying speeds and intensities.

Castillo looked at her as if she'd gone mad. "Shrimp? Jessie, you're crazy. That's some kind of radio static. It's—"

"You stick to your silly rocks," she shot at him. "Those are shrimp."

"If they're shrimp, then I'm—"

Chadwick leaned forward to touch him gently on the arm. "Don't say it, son, because you'll eat your words."

He turned, disbelieving. "You're serious?"

Chadwick nodded. "I'm afraid the young lady is right, Richard. Those are shrimp, beyond any question."

Castillo looked at him suspiciously, angered by Jessica's smirk. Then Chadwick pointed to the screen. The remote beam reflected its floodlight garishly across a thick heaving layer in the sea.

Templeton's voice rang out. "Good God! There must be millions of them!"

"Make that billions," Jessica corrected.

"And we have no idea of how thick the layer might be. It's like a living mattress that goes on for mile after mile. And as far as our sonar is concerned it's a solid wall that—" His voice fell away as he saw Manning staring hard at him.

"Say that again," Manning ordered.

Prentiss was taken aback by the sharpness in Manning's voice. "The shrimp layer, sir. It could be inches thick or a few hundred feet. Either way it'll soak up the sonar or bounce it back and—"

Before Prentiss could finish, Manning was cursing under his breath, whipping around again, his hand darting across his controls. There was a slight tremor as two slim torpedoes whipped away from *Sea Trench,* racing toward the glowing, heaving layers of shrimp. The noise from the speakers became a chaotic mixture of the creatures' sounds and the whiplike drive of the torps.

Manning was speaking urgently into the boom mike before his lips. "Captain to the bridge. Away two sonar torps."

Eddie Holvak was at bridge control, Bill Ryan standing behind him, when Manning's voice cracked to them. MacKinney was at his weapons station; Larry Urback at navigation hydronamics; and Autry at propulsion.

Manning's voice came again. "Able One alert immediately."

As quickly as his words were spoken, red and amber lights flashed on and warning chimes sounded.

Again they heard Manning. "Ordnance ready standby, no firing except on my command."

MacKinney glanced at Ryan. "What the hell is going on?"

"When the old man's ready," Ryan said with a thin smile, "he'll let you in. Five to one we got company just below that shrimp layer. The sonar torps will let us know. All the shrimp in the ocean can't stop wire transmission."

The TV screens throughout the boat showed the remote TV torpedo lights plunging into the mass of shrimp. At the same instant two slim shapes raced past the lights and vanished into the heaving layer of living creatures. Almost at once a new sound pounded from the speakers.

The unmistakable sonar signals of great sperm whales.

Without thinking, Miko's hand shot out to grasp Manning's arm. "They're—they're warning us away!"

Behind them Jessica's voice called out with its own urgency. "Captain Manning, she's right. That's their—it's their danger call. All the whales in the area will be listening, coming as fast as they can—"

She stopped.

Templeton's voice was quiet, almost slashing with his icy tone. "They're going to do it again. They're coming in to attack us."

By his side, Chadwick nodded grimly.

They heard MacKinney's voice from the bridge. "Fire control to the captain. No question, sir. They're converging. Two hundred yards for the closest one, and the others are coming in as fast as they can."

"Bridge, maintain course, slant angle, present descent. Mr. Holvak, floodlights on full."

Miko's face was twisted. "We can run away from them! Order full speed. Please!"

"Captain, from fire control."

"Go ahead, Mr. MacKinney."

"Sir, I consider us under attack. Impact imminent. I believe we should—"

"Stand by your orders, Mr. MacKinney."

Miko fought for control. "Captain, *please*—"

11

The prow angled steeply downward through the thick mass of glowing shrimp, as if *Sea Trench* were a huge dirigible diving through a translucent fog. It was a scene beyond anything ever known before in the oceans, a vessel virtually unstoppable, the movement of its mountainous bulk as satiny as it was enormous. Steadily, shedding fiercely glowing creatures that sparkled brilliantly as they tumbled away, *Sea Trench* came back into open water, still shoving aside the thick layer of life. Floodlights from the submarine reflected garishly among creatures that were glowing with their own life; but the murky depths extended immediately beyond, as if the light had been stopped by an invisible wall.

Here were the great animals who saw optically when light was available, and, when there was none, they saw through sound, through the echo ranging of their biological sonar. Here were the powerful and aggressive sperm whales, largest-toothed creatures of the entire planet. It was impossible to tell how many whales there were, but they were all beneath the layered mass of shrimp, answering the call, responding to a summons, the nature of which the human beings in *Sea Trench* could only guess. The great mammals hammered the water with their flukes, muscled thunder growing ever louder.

The slim torps raced away from the submarine, carrying eye-stabbing flare bombs that exploded silently in the depths. TV torps went with them, slightly lagging, the glass lenses sending images back through trailing wires to present clear pictures on the TV monitors within the sub. And now the last doubt was gone, the last question vanished, as the lights sputtered and flared and the cameras caught it all and relayed the incredible sight back to the awed human observers.

The sperms came rushing in, eyes reflecting light, the great lower jaws partially agape, showing their spiked teeth. Their own pinging sounds—their sightless vision—grew even louder. It was a scene out of some liquid hell where madness reigned; a swirl of brute strength and explosively imminent danger, all of it amidst a weird, crashing cacophony.

Jerry Manning watched from one screen to another, seeing from all flanks and rounded sides of his submarine. Until this moment he had limited his audience's view to tiny windows of sound and TV screening. Now his finger hit the stud over which it had been poised, and the stunned viewers in the observation deck watched as the entire prow of *Sea Trench* went transparent.

Exactly at that instant, the first sperm hurled his body headlong at the prow of the descending submarine, looming horrific and unbelievably gargantuan to the tiny human figures. The whale thundered against the glassite; and through the dense water, through the structure of the submarine hull, could be heard the terrible screaming cry of rage as the jaw was pounded aside and bones broke, teeth cracked, and bloody froth boiled out, rushing along the rounded glassite. The broken body, writhing in pain, slid away and behind.

Yet it was only the first, and now the whales came, faster and faster, more and more of them, suicidal in their ramming plunges, the sonar cries an insane medley as they crashed into the submarine, the huge boat trembling from the blows. Then the other sounds—Jessica sobbing, a strangled sound from the throat of Templeton. Chadwick stared in hypnotized silence; and, alongside Manning, Miko's hands trickled blood as her nails dug deeply into her own skin, unfelt, unknowingly.

Then, Manning's voice. "Bridge from the captain. Full power ahead five minutes, then come back to drift descent. Confirm."

He sat impassively as Holvak's voice sounded in his earplug and was heard by the others through the speakers, "Bridge confirms, sir."

They felt the thrust, heard the powerful hydrojets ramming the boat faster, downward. Manning sat quietly another minute, making sure there were no more impacts, no more sounds and screams. No more whales. He nodded to himself, removed his earplug, and slowly and deliberately placed it on the armrest. He sighed, looked up. He worked the armrest controls and the glassite prow went opaque as it closed off the ocean.

Behind him, the group was coming out of shock. Castillo held the quietly sobbing Jessica. Templeton had withdrawn into a brooding silence, and Chadwick was deep in thought. Prentiss seemed lost in his own disbelief and shock. Miko Stewart struggled for speech, her face white and contorted, hatred naked in her eyes as she looked at Manning.

"You bastard. You filthy rotten bastard."

His reaction was impassive indifference. That

was all she saw. And his controlled coolness was all the more infuriating to her. "You must have some good reason for saying that," he told her.

"Reason! There was no *reason* to—to kill those animals!"

"Agreed."

She gaped at him.

"That is why," he said slowly, "we made certain not to kill any."

Her disbelief gripped her so wildly that she began to tremble. "Didn't—you saw what you did! You saw them die, heard them!"

He sat like stone. "We remained passive, Miss Stewart, and I'll thank you to remember that. *Passive.* We sustained a steady descent, a steady course; we threatened nothing in the sea. We were attacked by the whales."

"Attacked by animals reacting by instinct, you mean!"

"I can understand your emotion, Miss Stewart, but not your stupidity. Any child would know that a group attack, unprovoked, by sperm whales, at this depth or any other, was motivated. How or by what I don't know, but beyond any question instinct had nothing to do with it."

She started to reply, then faltered. He didn't give her the chance to pick up her stumbling thoughts.

"I don't know how it all happened, or even why, but we were attacked by dangerous creatures where concerted effort and directed intelligence was involved. What took place was beyond the boundary of everything we have ever known about these animals. Only the orca attacks in this fashion, and never with deliberate suicide, and they do not make group attacks below four thousand feet."

She fought desperately for stronger ground. "You knew they couldn't hurt this submarine.

Damn you, you could have pulled away from them and prevented that slaughter."

"And in the process learned nothing." He was building to an open show of contempt for her. "Has it occurred to you *yet* that this boat is on a mission to discover the answers to certain mysteries? To learn why we're the third submarine to be attacked? To learn why four men died and a boat was lost forever? To find out," he added with the first open touch of anger, "just what the hell is going on down here in the sea, and to do something about it?"

He had finished and he was half out of his seat when she stopped him. "Those animals are intelligent, Captain Manning. We—*you*—are supposed to have the greater intelligence, which imposes on you some responsibility to protect them. We've slaughtered those creatures for so many years that—"

His anger came through unstopped, and the look on his face brought her to silence as he stood over her.

"You will remember, woman, you will remember now, and in the future, that *I* haven't slaughtered anything. Your principles ring untrue to me. Your words are questionable, and your accusations obscene. And *whatever* you do, don't prattle to me, ever, about saving intelligent life."

He stood ramrod straight. "My primary concern is with the intelligent life that lives on the surface of this planet, and you will do well to remember that—now and in the future. I find nothing inviting or noble in sacrificing myself or other human beings to save *any* animal, whether it be a whale or a chicken."

He turned on his heel and walked from the deck. She stared at where he had been standing, still trying to see him. What stared back at her were digital numbers; and a part of her brain she couldn't control noted that they were at 8,000 feet, outside pressure at 3,564 psi, and their rate of descent was slowing to 625 feet per minute. She barely felt Prentiss leading her away.

12

~~~~~~~~~~

Miko and Bill Ryan were secluded in one of the side observation rooms of the sub, the glassite wall before them transparent to the sea, all lights in the room turned off. They sat in silence, Miko tormented by her thoughts, drawing strength from the man with her, who shared and respected whatever troubled her. They looked through the glassite in utter darkness, and then lights appeared, as sometimes happened in these deeps. Nightmarish dreams come to life: self-glowing caricatures of higher-level barracuda; although the barracuda in the sun-drenched levels were minnows compared to these monsters. The creatures were gone as quickly as they had appeared, turning off their bioluminescence as they pondered the enigma of the great submarine.

Another of these creatures glowed into visibility. Obviously it had no natural enemy down here, and not even the sensed mass of the U.S.S. *Sea Trench* disturbed its instinctive invincibility. It could be described, in human terms, only as hideous—a huge jaw fully extended, within the savage mouth multiple rows of razored fangs. The teeth differed from those of any upper-ocean barracuda, bent sharply back into the throat so that any prey once snared could never escape. Nightmare in the great depths begets nightmare. Beneath the gleaming mouth bayonets, surrealism went wild. From the fangs, there stretched a long and slender filament, twice the creature's body size, drifting downward perhaps thirty or forty feet, there was no way to tell. Blue and red lights glowed brighter at the end of the filament, so that it seemed to belong to another creature. It was nature's compensation for eternal natural darkness. Ryan and Miko watched, mystified and awed, as the thing drifted away, its speed undeterminable because of the steady motion of the submarine.

Ryan reached out in the darkness and brought a soft glow back to their chamber. He leaned forward to look directly at Miko. "I think it's time you talked it out."

"You don't understand," she said, shaking her head. "If you had only *heard* him—"

"I know the man. I didn't have to hear him," Ryan said quietly. "What it amounts to is that you had your feelings stepped on. You've survived more than that, Miko."

His words seemed to clear her thoughts. "Feelings be damned, Bill. That's never been the issue. I can still see those animals destroying themselves against the hull, and—"

He gestured, interrupting her. "Hold it. Hold it right there. I want you to ask yourself a question, and then answer it aloud for me. Why were those creatures so all-fired bent on destroying *us*?"

She was surprised by his question. "But they couldn't do that."

"Damn it, that's not the issue," he said with exasperation. "*They tried.* And if they could have done what they tried to do, we'd all be wreckage and dead bodies ourselves right now. *That's* the whole point of all this. They tried to destroy us. *Why?* What motivated that? What *controlled them?*"

"I—I don't know, Bill."

Ryan leaned back in his seat. He let out a long sigh, calmed his voice. "That's what Jerry was talking about. You shot off your face without anything hard-knuckled to back it up."

"Oh, I know, Bill. *I know*. But everything was so twisted up inside me, I—Christ, there's got to be a better way."

"Oh? Don't mind my sarcasm, then. If there is a better way, you let me know and I give you my word we'll try it. And then—"

He stopped as someone knocked on the outer door of the chamber. Ryan got to his feet to open the hatch.

Matt Matthews stood there. "Excuse me," he said. "May I talk to Dr. Stewart?"

She stood. "Of course. What is it?"

"If I am correct, doctor, your specialty is intelligent life in the sea?"

She was taken aback by his rasping, quiet voice, the scarred visage changed by the soft lights. "Why, yes, but—"

"Then you're about to have a rare opportunity, madam. At this particular moment the pressure against our hull is more than five tons to the square inch. We're some 23,000 feet deep. And I believe we've found what Ritter and his crew also found—to their unhappy demise, I suggest we keep in mind."

"Matt," Ryan said, "what the hell are you talking about?"

A crooked smile slowly appeared on the scarred face. "At this depth the bottom should be less than four thousand feet beneath us." He chuckled deep in his throat, as though he would find humor in Hell itself. "Would you believe it isn't there?"

"I don't understand," Miko said.

"*There's no bottom*. It just falls away, and clearly that is impossible. Our sonar man is tearing out his hair. That is where you come in, by the way. Some sort of life. It's large, there's quite a bit of it, it's moving in what seems to be a definite pattern, and I would bet my mother's own spectacles, and she's near to blind without them, bless her, that surely it's not friendly. I just thought you might like to enter your petition to save it, too."

Ryan shoved forward, anger showing. "Matt, damn you—"

He got no further. An alert light came on, a chime sounded from the bulkhead, and they heard Holvak's voice on the speaker.

"Bridge here. All personnel report at once to their stations. Captain, contact with the bridge. Captain, contact with the bridge."

They assembled again in the forward observation deck, seated as they had been, Miko beside Manning again. She took her seat warily, but he nodded to her, gave no sign that they had ever exchanged a harsh word. She turned her seat to study the holographic projection. Before them was the navigational grid, the sliver of light they had come to know as *Sea Trench* itself. Miko glanced at the digital readout; they were slicing through 26,000 feet, and the outside pressure showed at 11,580 pounds to every square inch of their hull. But there was something terribly wrong with the hologram. The "living three-dimensional map" showed the bottom—no—*there was no bottom beneath the light sliver*.

Manning talked without taking his eyes from the hologram. "The thing is impossible. And yet, there it is. We know the Aleutian Trench bottoms out at 26,000 feet. But we're there now and—nothing." He shrugged and spoke into his mike. "Bridge, have Neptune give us an overlay of the bottom as the memory banks have it."

Another layer appeared on the hologram. The

"old chart" showed as a thin glowing layer, and *Sea Trench* was already below the bottom shown on the old chart.

"A very interesting paradox," Chadwick said slowly.

Templeton spoke up. "Captain, do we get any bottom return at all from sonar?"

Manning shook his head. "Something soaks it up. We send down the signal, but it doesn't come back. We don't know why." Manning turned to Castillo. "Richard, plate tectonics—the whole bottom of this bucket—is your specialty. Any ideas?"

Before replying, the youngster stared intently at the hologram. "We're not getting a skip from an inversion layer?"

"Down here? No way, son."

"Well, sir, it could be an embolism effect—you know, the kind of air-bubble wall you used with that Chinese sub—or it could be a layer of some creatures like the shrimp we went through. But I don't believe either of those possibilities."

"Neither do I," Manning told him.

"This may sound crazy, sir." Castillo was clearly hesitant.

"Nothing's crazy anymore. Let's hear it," Manning urged.

"Well, from what I heard and saw, you know, on the tapes from Ritter's crew, and from what's happening now, I think we're going to find that same dome they talked about."

Jessica turned to him. "But what does that have to do with not getting any sonar return?"

"Because," Castillo said, choosing his words with care, "we're using search sonar right now. Survey mode. And it won't pick up what's alive, and—"

"You mean the *dome*?" Manning broke in.

Castillo looked stubborn. "Yes, sir," he said finally.

"That, Richard, is a tough one to buy." Manning shrugged again. "But so are a lot of things." He turned to Miko. "Do you have any ideas on those creatures, or whatever they are, we've picked up?"

"No, I don't. It just doesn't fit. I mean, starfish, flounder, shrimp, other animals live even as far down as the Challenger Deep. That's seven miles. But there's nothing known that would answer to what sonar has reported."

Manning nodded slowly. "Everybody relax. We'll wait this one out. We'll keep on going down, slow and easy."

They were at 32,100 feet, pressure 14,370 psi, sink rate 420 feet per minute, when MacKinney's voice came to them from the bridge. "Captain, sonar contact with those—whatever those things are, sir. More of them—and coming toward us. But there's something strange. They've been keeping their distance, some of them staying with us, and more still coming up from below."

Templeton swore quietly. "Jesus Christ, it can't be. We're past 32,000 feet, and there are animals still coming up from *beneath* us?"

Manning glanced at him. "Neptune tells no tall tales, Mr. Templeton." Then, into his mike, "Mac, call the range."

"Approximately one thousand yards, sir."

"Pipe it into the holo," Manning ordered.

The holographic projection blurred as the computer added in the sonar returns. Thin shapes appeared on all sides of the submarine. As they watched, the pattern became clearer. The shapes were converging, but holding a minimum distance.

Manning made a sudden decision. "Bridge, one-third ahead."

Holvak confirmed. "One-third ahead."

"Bridge, Able One alert status. MacKinney, bring 'em all alive, stand by full spectrum all torps."

"Confirm," MacKinney said.

Manning turned to the others on the observation deck. "Strap in, please. Seat belts and shoulder harnesses."

They adjusted their seats, tugged the straps securely. Miko tightened her belt, looked to Manning. "Can you tell us what you expect?"

He nodded to her, then turned to Jessica. "Jessie, I want you to do something for me."

"Yes, sir."

"Tell me what your feelings are. Not what you think. What you *feel*."

They all turned to the girl. Undefinable emotion showed on her face as she concentrated. Then she closed her eyes, relaxed, opened to something only she could discern.

"I—I can feel—" Her voice was barely a whisper, and suddenly her eyes flew open. She was frightened. "Danger," she murmured. "I—I don't understand, but a feeling—almost alive, some kind of danger—"

Manning watched her, his own face grim. He keyed his mike. "Mr. Matthews!"

Matthews's voice came back at once. "Here, sir."

"Rig for electrical repulsion."

"Captain, I've been anticipating your orders. We've been set for some time."

Manning nodded. "Very good." He glanced at the digital readout. Depth. 33,700 feet. The crush on the sub was at 15,009 psi. Manning came to another decision, keyed his mike.

"Captain to all hands. Extinguish all external lights. Seal off all lighted areas from external view. Comply immediately."

In the observation deck, lights faded until the holographic projection was the only glow. Manning turned a dial on his armrest console, and they were in absolute darkness. They heard a thin humming sound. Manning's voice came to them in the solid night surrounding them. "We're going to transparency for the bow."

For a while all they could see were the after-images on their own retinas. Absolutely nothing was visible. No one spoke. They felt a touch of nausea, for they had no visual frame of reference, and instinctively they held their armrests for security.

Somewhere in the distance the faintest spattering appeared. It was the barest scratch of light in eternal gloom. Then more light appeared and, as their eyes became accustomed to the optical blackout, the scratch gained slowly in intensity. They began to see other lights, how distant or large they could not tell. They waited, and soon, where there should only have been absolute dark, eerie, mystifying lights drifted closer, weaving slowly. The display increased as the mesmerizing lights moved in curves, flashed brighter in a wide spectrum of colors, then faded. Then there was a sudden glow, like a dull starshell bursting silently in some thick black fog.

More light out there—a rippling effect beginning to make itself evident. It was impossible to tell whether the lights were getting brighter or coming closer. There was no depth perception, but conviction led to the idea that the lights were approaching, the dim coruscations gaining slowly in intensity.

Manning's voice cut through gloom. "Sonar, call the range."

"Just under two hundred yards, sir, and still closing."

Manning spoke aloud, but it was clear that he was simply confirming his own thoughts. *"That's what came after Ritter and his men."*

Then, to the bridge, "Mr. MacKinney, stand by."
"Yes, *sir*."

No question any longer. Long shapes, alive with
light, the glow rippling along enormous bodies.
Eels, averaging at least a hundred feet in length.
Maybe more. It was hard to tell, although sonar was
getting better returns now. The creatures kept
coming in slowly, made visible by their own incredible light. Great heads, huge teeth, powerful
bodies appeared.

It was like being on another planet . . .

"Captain to the bridge. Mr. Williams, release a
message sphere with full data up to this moment. Immediate release. Continue to release the
message packs every sixty seconds, all data and
film mag tape, with continuing updates. Set for
emergency comsat pickup, scrambler code."

"Aye, sir."

The people in the observation deck emerged
slowly from their stupor, trying to come to grips
with the unreal. "It's—the only word is incredible,"
Chadwick said, the first among them to break silence.

"I never dreamed anything like this could be
possible." Miko's voice was a murmur, almost a
deferral of the ultimate acceptance.

"Look at them!" Templeton exclaimed, his
voice strained, almost hoarse with tension. "They
must generate enough electrical output to—I
couldn't even begin to guess!"

Manning's voice was a source of strength. He had
no doubts, and exclamations of the bizarre seemed
not to touch him at all. "You don't need to guess,
Mr. Templeton. They're putting out enough amps
to overcome a small boat. That, out there, is
what killed Ritter and his men."

Jessica's voice quavered with fear. "They're—
dangerous. They're going to—to hurt us."

Manning was straight in his seat. "All right," he said loudly, "let's see how they like a dose of real light down here.

"Mr. MacKinney! Full spectrum flare strobes, all quadrants, *fire!*"

They could feel the torps punching away from the sub.

Moments later, hell erupted all around them. The flare torps exploded silently in the midst of the monster eels closing on *Sea Trench*. Rapid-fire detonations of light ripped through the ocean. In the observation deck they drew back instinctively, their minds already numb with what had been happening.

The nightmare went to insanity as the eels were struck blind, confused, tumbling violently in sudden optical shock.

Manning's voice came through. "MacKinney! Screamers away!"

More small torps whipped out, and the shrieking howl of the screamer torps, a sound never before heard in the deeps, smashed outward in all directions like constantly exploding bombs. Pounding through the terrible pressures outside the hull, the screamers seemed to render the eels mad: Seemingly terrorized, they flung themselves about in pain-stricken paroxysms.

But not all of them. Jessica's cry of fright came like a tiny knife blade of sound as one of the eels hurled itself against the side of the sub prow, and new light flashed, a great burst of half-blinding electrical energy.

Deep within the boat, at his control board, Matthews smiled grimly as needles jerked violently. "You've come to the wrong place to play, me buckoes," he murmured, and his hand shoved a lever full forward. Instantly a deep thrumming sound—a visceral cry of energy groaned through the submarine.

In the prow they watched, frozen, as the eel was hurled violently away from the hull, raw electricity jerking through its body, tearing it open. Moments later the eel went limp, its colors fading almost at once.

"It works." Manning's voice was a hard call of triumph. "They can generate enough electricity to kill, but only through special organs. Their own bodies can't withstand a real blast."

Electrical repulsion systems activated by Matthews had rendered the outside surface of *Sea Trench* lethal to any creature who touched it. Several more eels crashed against the hull, the roar of electricity followed, and the creatures were flung away, broken and dead.

Manning brought control lights back on in the observation deck and activated the holographic projection. They heard him talking to the bridge. "Mr. Williams, send out a message pack. Make it clear that this boat will continue its descent." He glanced at the digital display. "We are currently passing through 36,000 feet, pressure on the hull at eight tons per square inch, and we are entering what I am now officially naming the Ritter Deeps."

In the bridge the men grinned hugely at one another as Manning's words came to them. Ryan held up a fist in joyous agreement.

They continued their descent, moving ahead slowly without seeing any further sign of life. Well ahead of the submarine, two remote torps paced their movement, powerful floodlights bruising aside the blackness. But the wire-transmitted pictures of the accompanying TV torps showed nothing but water. Then, watching the TV screens, all hands stiffened. Complete blackness had yielded to a barely perceptible greenish tinge. The glowing digital displays showed the depth at 38,600 feet and the hull pressure at 17,000 psi.

Chadwick found his voice. "If I use the word *incredible* again in my life . . ." He looked up at Manning. "But how do you describe all of this? We're already more than two thousand feet deeper than the Marianas Trench, and we're *still* going down."

Miko Stewart had been forced, like the others, to cast off now threadbare convictions. "Everything we've ever believed about the deeps—this makes a mockery of so many things that—"

A chime interrupted her. The glowing hologram demanded attention. For the first time the computer gave indications that their descent would not go on forever.

Williams's voice came through the speakers. "Captain, we have bottom contact."

Manning might have been sitting in his living room at home for all the excitement he indicated in his voice. "So I see," he told Williams. "Have you range?"

"I wouldn't trust the bounce at this pressure, sir, but the best we can make out is approximately 1,800 yards."

"Steady as she goes," Manning called to the bridge.

Several minutes later the greenish tinge was unquestioned. The TV torps, riding with the brilliant floodlights, revealed a strange, broken green surface. Manning ignored the sudden murmuring and exclamations and concentrated on the issue at hand.

He gestured to Prentiss. "Take direct control of the torps from here. Place them a thousand yards to port and starboard in line position, and send out another set directly ahead of us."

"Aye, sir."

"Bridge, scale down the holo until we get a complete computer extrapolation of that—whatever it is, beneath us. MacKinney, if anything so much as blinks an eye at us, let them have the full spectrum, and that includes seek-and-kill torps."

"Ready, sir."

They watched, knowing once more that feeling of magic as the holographic projection blurred before their eyes, expanding the computer-enhanced picturization. And then they knew what Ritter and his men had seen, just as they had reported from *Swimmer IV*.

The U.S.S. *Sea Trench* moved ahead slowly, maintaining the same depth, gliding on her hydrojets just above an astonishing surface. There was no calling what lay below a bottom, for clearly it was something other than the floor of the ocean. Green—textured green; smooth, yet not even: an incredible substance that went on for mile after mile. It had a consistency that might be described as loose green fur, the way a shag rug might look if it were flowing under a gentle current of water.

Manning took the sub down slowly, very slowly, until the boat's rounded belly touched the green material, and the substance yielded ever so softly, swaying. There was no resistance as it gave way to the mass of the vessel.

"It's *alive*," Chadwick said in awe.

"Just like Richard told us it would be," Manning reminded him.

"It's an algae," Templeton added. "It looks like an algae." Under the direct lights of the powerful beams from their own hull they could clearly see the swaying surface.

"I can't understand how it can even exist," Miko said. "We're nearly eight miles down. There's no light, no photosynthesis. It can't be plant life. Not as we know it."

Manning couldn't help the short laugh that came to his lips. "You'd all better throw away the word *impossible*. It can't exist—and there it is. It can't grow—and it does. It can't be alive—and it is." The laugh was gone. "And I don't like any of it."

He keyed the mike. "Bridge, have we gotten a reading on the thickness of that stuff below us?"

Ryan's voice came back immediately. "Sir, the sonar just mushes out. The returns break up and we can't give you anything definite."

Manning nodded to himself. "What about Neptune? Or is the computer also biting its nails?"

He smiled at Ryan's laugh. "We're getting some sensor readings, captain. We put some probes into the stuff. Neptune shows some form of algae, although the composition and chemistry don't match up with anything in the memory banks."

"I could have bet on that one," Manning said.

"Captain, this is Urback."

"Go ahead."

"Sir, I recommended we lift above this stuff. We can't even get through with the masers. If what I'm reading makes any sense, it looks like it's at least six hundred feet thick, and according to the computer there are some sort of rigid supports all the way through. First readouts show they're spaced about a hundred yards apart."

Manning looked at the green mass moving beneath the glassite bow and again studied the holographic projection. The fuzzy, distorted lines didn't please him. "Bridge, take her up to one hundred yards above this goo. Slow to hover."

Holvak's voice confirmed his orders. Soon they were poised above the green mass, looking down, still mystified.

Miko looked at Manning. "What happens now?"

He nodded to her instead of answering directly; she knew his next words were intended for her as well as for the bridge. "Mr. Ryan, ready *Seeker I* for immediate launch."

He turned to Miko. "We're not taking this boat down there. It's too risky. We're too large, for one thing. And we can't see in that stuff, we might not be able to maneuver, and we could be trapped by—well, I'd hate to use nukes to blast our way out. We just can't sit here on our hands, so the next best thing is to take one of the armored subs and— no pun intended—get our feet wet."

"You're going *down*? Into that—algae?" She forced herself to think for a moment. "I understand. Of course. It's the only thing to do. But I'm going with you, Captain Manning. It's my job as much as yours."

"Don't be too quick to climb aboard," he cautioned her, his words heard by the others. "You have no requirement to expose yourselves to any unknown or unnecessary dangers. Make no mistake about what I'm saying to you. What's below us is a complete unknown. We've been attacked by—well, you were all here and you know what's happened up to now. Something or someone is working very hard to keep us away from whatever is below us, even if they have to kill us to do so. Richard's right; that dome is alive, and there's got to be something beneath it that can answer questions. But whatever is there can also be lethal."

He glanced at all of them. "Do you understand what I'm saying? In this boat you're safe. Down there—" He shrugged.

Miko stood. "I hope our differences have no place in your decision as to who goes."

He met her gaze, held it. "They don't."

"Then my position on this mission calls for me to go with you."

"I don't care who goes," he told her. "There's room for three more beside myself. Make that decision among yourselves."

"There's room for *two* more," she told the others.

"There's little choice, really," Chadwick said quickly. "I must go, obviously. The only question is who has the fourth and last seat."

The others clamored immediately to be chosen for the small sub. Chadwick motioned for silence. "There's no use arguing about any of this," he told them. "Captain Manning has told us the decision lies among us. My position is chief scientist. I'm going. Dr. Stewart is going." He rested a hand on Castillo's shoulder. "This young man has already demonstrated great perception, and despite his age he is the expert in our group on hydrographics. If anything, he should—"

Manning was already moving from the room. They followed, rushing to catch up.

13

~~~~~~~~~~

The interior of the *Seeker I*, despite its long and sleek appearance, was cramped, the available space for the crew of four jammed amidst controls and instruments. Four cushioned seats were arranged two in front and two in back, with Manning at the controls in the forward left seat and Miko Stewart to his right; Chadwick sat behind Manning, Castillo behind Stewart. They strapped in carefully, belts and harnesses, and hooked up to the communications system so they could speak directly among each other or listen to communications between the small armored sub and *Sea Trench*. That contact would last only as long as the wire reeling out behind *Seeker I* remained unbroken. The wire had a length of five miles, beyond which it would snap and they would be on their own. But no one had any hopes that contact would remain for long—not in that mysterious algae.

They were almost ready when Bill Ryan leaned into the top hatch, his anger undisguised. Protocol had vanished. "Goddamn it, this isn't your job," he snapped at Manning. "You belong—"

Manning cut him short. "Mr. Ryan, you have command."

They stared at one another, and the angry scowl

on Ryan's face faded slowly. Finally he nodded, a twitch of a smile at the corner of his mouth.

"Yeah," he said softly. "Keep your socks dry, hear?"

"Seal the hatch, Mr. Ryan."

They heard the clamps taking hold, the hatch spinning closed. Out of sight now, Ryan sealed the hatch to the flooding chamber, stepped through another lock, and sealed another hatch. He stopped in a control room, Autry by his side watching every move as a safety backup. Ryan worked bulkhead controls, and the scream of air receding before the massive water pressure sliced through the metal with astonishing effect. Through the observation ports, Ryan and Autry confirmed that the smaller boat was completely in water at outside pressure. A green light came on, Ryan released the bottom bulkheads, and *Seeker I* began to drop away gently beneath the giant sub.

When they were free, Manning brought in the hydrojets. Lights flashed on from prow floods, and Manning went to full transparency of a wide section of the cabin, as if they were looking through the windshield of a Jet Liner.

They went down slowly, without conversation, until the boat touched the algal mass, which yielded before them. Manning slowed their descent, and then they were enclosed completely by living green. They were surrounded by a ghostly luminescence, yet their powerful floodlights helped little, if any, to provide forward vision. Sonar was mush within the green mass, and they were reduced to blind probing. The automatic systems flashed data through the trailing wire to the big sub. Then the *Seeker I* rocked as it brushed against an unseen obstruction, and a red light came on.

"That tears the link," Manning said quietly. "The wire's broken. We're on our own now."

Behind him, Dr. Chadwick was experiencing

utter fascination, almost open joy. He cared not a whit for whatever danger might wait for them; he was a scientist in the glory of pure exploration, punching into an unknown the likes of which he had never dreamed. To discover that his own cherished idea of reality had been severely threatened and then to have the means to enter a world beyond his knowledge and explore it fully, was enough to make a man, even of Chadwick's reserve, drunk with the moment. Chadwick kept a tape running steadily in order to record every word they spoke; it would lend a sense of immediacy that might never again be captured, and a time-hack recording of their commentary could later be compared to the data recorded by the instruments, so they could always correlate every detail of what happened *when* it happened.

Chadwick peered through the bow glassite, his eyes going back and forth from visual study to what the probes and sensors of the small submarine told him. "It's alive . . ." His words were spoken in awe, and he gave full release to his emotions. "I can hardly believe it, but it's alive all right. What's more," he mused as much to himself as to the others, "it does not live on oxygen that drifts down from the surface. I don't know what it uses instead of photosynthesis, but the instruments—it seems to produce not only oxygen but a whole variety of other gases, and from first guess it seems able to break down sugar and protein. I can't understand how it does all this under the incredible pressure—"

Manning nodded in agreement, adding his own thoughts. "The pressure is relative, doctor. Compared to what's around us now, the earth's atmospheric surface is hard vacuum. But compared to what exists on the moon's surface, our gaseous atmosphere on earth is an ocean just as dense and viscous as the water around us."

"I think we'd all better throw away our rule books," Miko added. "But what are we going to use for a yardstick? It's so easy to forget that, in our own ocean of air, the albatross is a billion times heavier than the gnat, and they both fly." She sighed, as awed as the others.

Castillo leaned forward. "Captain Manning?"

Manning glanced at him, and Castillo pointed to a panel of guages. "Sir, the temperature. Outside, I mean. *It's going up.*"

There was no answer to that one. It was another impossibility. The temperature at the ocean bottom is always slightly higher than the water above because of compression effects, but the percentage is minuscule. Now they looked at a temperature gauge that was rising steadily, and there simply was no known phenomenon to cause that.

"Look at the pressure!" Miko exclaimed. *"It's dropping!"*

The odds for that happening were about equal to those for finding a herd of mastodons chewing purple flowers on the moon.

"It's getting crazier every moment," Manning murmured, and even his steel-hard composure was taking a beating.

Castillo motioned again, his excitement forcing his words out in staccato fashion. "Look—it's getting—lighter—in front of us."

They watched in wonder as the green gloom began to yield to an increasing brightness from all directions. Now the floodlights pierced a greater distance through the algal mass, reflecting back less light, turning the world into a glowing green cloud. In moments the strange illumination became much like a thick fog. Manning cut the floodlights; now it was possible to see without them. It was one more astonishing fact heaped upon others, and the brightness kept increasing so that the light streaming through the glassite to the interior of the submarine was great enough to reflect about them.

Still the temperature climbed, more rapidly now, but all eyes were on the most impossible aspect of all.

"The pressure . . ." Miko's voice was strained. "My God, look at it—it's falling right out of the guage." The digital display was almost a blur as the pressure kept decreasing before their eyes.

"The sonar—" Manning's voice intruded as they stared blankly at the pressure gauge. "It's coming alive. The signals are getting through."

Miko glanced at him. "This green—this algae is only some sort of covering, a growth over something else." She looked at the others, who waited for her to continue. "All this—," she said with a sudden sweeping gesture, "it's clear now. All this is a single network, laced together like some incredible roots joined for mile after mile. It's porous—"

"But how could that be?" Castillo said in protest. "The pressure just above us would crush everything."

Miko shook her head. "No, Richard. It only seems that way. That's how fish can survive at any depth. It's not the pressure that matters but the relative pressures—the differences in pressure. In fish, the internal pressure of tissues, permeated as they are with water, remains the same as the pressure where the creature lives. And this structure is, well, it's like a weightless environment, and it's got enough strength to bear up on any loads above it, and—"

She shrieked suddenly as the sub lurched sharply. The expanse of green seemed to fall away beneath them. They went through a series of severe rocking motions, pitching up and down unexpectedly. The thick green mass, still increasing its light with amazing speed, suddenly disappeared in a spray of bubbles that covered their entire view. Manning's hands worked the controls swiftly. He slammed the power lever forward, trying to regain control, going to automatic dampers after their sudden yawing motions. The small sub surged ahead and the bubble froth about them trailed away. They gaped.

They were in clear, brilliantly illuminated water, as if they were moving only scant feet beneath a sun-drenched ocean surface. The same one that lay nearly ten miles above them . . .

Disbelief had numbed into a steady state of shock. At this point they could handle anything. There had been so much stunning input that their senses could scarcely take in more, and their minds automatically compensated. They simply absorbed, at least for now, what was happening, and rather than continuing to be overwhelmed, they each made a subconscious adjustment to accept whatever events slammed at them.

At this moment, mere realization of what they were seeing would have been enough to unhinge most minds having their level of comprehension of the physical world of the sea. Nearly ten miles down, beneath a living dome, they looked out through a clear liquid world that went on for uncountable miles before it blurred in the distance.

Then they looked *down*, and again they fought a silent battle within themselves to handle mentally what was thrust into their vision and deeper into their minds.

They were gliding high above a vast lighted valley. Dazed, bewildered, nearly overcome, they looked down a thousand feet, perhaps even more, where giant kelp and other growth lofted upward from giant boulders or emerged from thick verdant forests of unknown flora that covered the final bottom of the ocean. Strange plants swayed in invisible currents, keeping tune to the beat of liquid eddying; and the growth, they saw with only their first long look, extended from filamentlike grasses of unknown length to dazzling flowers with enormous multihued petals and fronds.

Far beyond they saw hills, small domelike structures, and features they could not yet identify. They recognized at once, however, several of the eels they had encountered in so devastating an assault; but now the creatures moved slowly, no threat indicated in their presence, accompanied by smaller creatures too far away to be discernible.

The details blurred, and there was a single overwhelming crash through all their minds that they were in the midst of a magnificent underwater world where there existed order rather than randomness or chaos; that *everything* they had ever known or believed of the deep ocean had to be cast aside. And they knew, even as their eyes took in one unbelievable sight after the other, that too many things were happening too quickly for them to be able to understand the most important or the most obvious elements of what they had encountered.

Miko had been trying to talk, almost frantic with the urge, but for several moments only a strangling sound had issued from her nearly paralyzed vocal cords. Finally she found her voice, and she said aloud what she had been silently repeating. "My God, I don't believe this—*look over there!*"

Her hand extended with such rigidity that she trembled, and the others swept their glances from whatever sights were astonishing each of them individually to see what had precipitated her shout.

There was no mistake. Vast fields were arrayed with lines and patterns. The implications were staggering.

Chadwick's voice came through as a hoarse whisper. "We're seeing cultivation," he said, breathing heavily. "It's inconceivable—*those are farms of some kind.*"

No one said anything. If you come face-to-face with God, you don't need words.

When you discover unmistakable signs of living intelligence ten miles below the surface of the ocean you suffer that moment in silence.

Jerry Manning was the first to verbalize what they had all known instinctively from the moment they dropped beneath the algae dome. He gestured to take in the valley. "The light," he said slowly. "The light. It comes from all around us—*it's alive.*"

What is shockingly obvious can often escape acceptance by the mind. It was obvious that there could be no light here from the sun; such light had been swallowed completely many miles above them; and yet they were bathed in light from all sides, strange light, eddying with the water. Now they saw that there were different sourcepoints; the light did indeed come from everywhere, it seemed, above and below and behind, everywhere. Which again defied everything they knew, demanding instant adjustment.

At such moments the mind rushes back to its memory banks. Therefore, they reviewed, almost frantically, what they knew of bioluminescence within the abyssal deeps. Self-created light is as much a reality in the depths as are great currents and upwellings; and many thousands of different beasts produce sparkling, glowing, spattering, intermittent, and other varieties of light in a place where the sun since time began has been banished.

There are crimson worms that float gently in blackness, their glowing coats a signature of their own doom as they are seized and eaten by shrimps who wear coats of dazzling scarlet. Copepods of red, reddish orange, and a variety of related hues drift through waters that have no knowledge of stars in the sky. Jet black fish appear, burst silently into light, and as quickly lure beasts of prey to them. There are creatures that issue explosive blasts of liquid fire, and many of these include varieties of shrimp and prawn; their red is a bloody stream, and when frightened they hurl from their bodies clouds of what seem like billions of fireflies.

A product of some insane imagination would have to be the ten-armed *Vampyroteuthis infernalis*, a heaving beast that nature should have obliterated millions of years ago. These hideous beasts, varying in size from one foot to seventy feet, are at times explosively luminescent, and their bulbous shapes can eject forcefully a strange slime that on contact with seawater, erupts into a startlingly bright cloud of luminous blue.

This nightmare of a creature is distantly related to the squid and, of all the creatures known to man, the squid has always been the undisputed master of liquid pyrotechnics. Like the octopus, many squid have their own systems of color-changing communication. The most common colors of the animals are creamy white, mottled Vandyke brown, maroon, or even bluish gray. They can change body colors in astounding fashion, operating through a central nervous system that controls slim muscle fibers which work on chromatophores, rendering full color control to the animal. And it is not only the range of color that is astonishing—it is also the rate of change, for a giant squid can go through complete color changes *in less than one second*. There is no other creature anywhere in the known animal kingdom that comes even remotely close to having this extraordinary control. The animal can send continuous waves of color rushing across its skin in shifting shades and stripes at the rate of thirty color pulses *per second*.

In marvelous ways do the giant squid use their color, for they can also direct beams of light from their bodies, as a man would project beams from a searchlight with different-colored lenses. They actually activate reflectors along their rubbery hulls to focus the glow; they intensify the beam; and then they direct it in the manner of a searchlight. How the squid so utilize their critical chemical, luciferin, is still a mystery—but nowhere nearly as astonishing as what the four people in the tiny submarine now experienced.

They became witness to the result of hundreds or even thousands of years of intelligently directed development of bioluminescent creatures. Just as men have produced hybrid strains of wheat—or heftier cattle from scrawnier ancestors—whatever creatures dominated this great undersea valley had wrought genetic changes that gave them living light, producing intense illumination when and how they so desired.

There was a dominant form of living light, and this became evident immediately as great clusters of globular creatures appeared—whether plant or animal the newcomers could not yet determine—drifting at different elevations, glowing with a brilliance one might expect from powerful globes of artificial light. These were actually individual bioluminescent creatures grouped together, and these clusters seemed to be spaced at planned intervals, at different levels, extending as far as the eye could see.

Castillo tore his gaze from a nearby light cluster, his eyes wide as he pointed downward. "Down there, see? A little to the right. More of those things."

Along the ground surface, there were enormous glowing pools of light, deep-hued reds and oranges. "They're different," Castillo said. "That's volcanic of some sort. You can tell it's a heat source. See the thermal rippling? You don't get that from those— well, whatever they are, floating around us." He shook his head slowly. "I'd like to know how they control volcanic activity to do that—"

His voice trailed away. The *they* was haunting to their ears.

Chadwick had been successfully struggling to marshal his thoughts coherently. "We're facing so many contradictions," he said, forcing himself to talk slowly, "that it would be dangerous to draw conclusions. Certain gross assumptions, however," he added dryly, "can hardly be ignored. The dome above us, to begin with. It's a living organism, like a coral reef. Maybe it's structured along some line of intelligence such as we find in ants. I don't know, except that it's alive, and serving its purpose, and that means it must be capable of reproduction, of rebuilding damage or failure. It may also be an organic structure, producing oxygen and other gases that drift down into this valley, for no matter how this place is set up, there are embolistic effects, an exchange of gases. The flora make that unquestionable, as well as the signs of fauna we've seen."

Chadwick took a deep breath and pointed into the distance. "And those fields down there—that's cultivation, and that means intelligence of a high order."

Castillo stared at him. "What does—*high* mean?"

"At the least, equal to human."

Not a sound met his words, although Manning was nodding slowly in agreement.

Chadwick went on, his words quickening. "There's just no question," he emphasized, "there is social order, social structure here. I have only to look at those things giving off light to *know* we're witnessing controlled biology. Perhaps even some incredibly advanced form of genetic engineering. I don't care how impossible it all seems, but if we walked on Mars and found an artificial structure, it would give us vast amounts of information with only a single glance. Here we've had that single glance a thousand times over, and I think it would be wise for us to anticipate *anything*. Look," he pointed, "those eels, or whatever they are, in the distance."

They watched the great creatures swimming slowly, posing no danger or threat to the smaller animals swimming alongside them.

"Notice how there's not a sign of aggressiveness now. So they also must be controlled," Chadwick stressed. "I don't know how—or by whom—or even by what. And the pressure outside our hull! Have you looked at the gauges lately?"

He saw the startled look on Miko's face. "That's right," Chadwick confirmed. "It's down to 200 psi, and that's what we encounter only 500 feet beneath the ocean surface. In some way there's environmental control here of a fantastic degree. The weight of a planet is over us, and there is not only control of pressure, but of what's obviously a desired ratio of gases."

Miko Stewart had collected her wits. "It's all symbiotic," she announced suddenly, as if Chadwick's words had galvanized her own thoughts. "There's a sense of—harmony all about us. The plants and the animals, and everything Dr. Chadwick's said—like him, I don't know what the controlling factor is. The bioluminescence may include strong ultraviolet. I'm sure there are chemical reactions entirely foreign to us, and—*look there! To the left!*"

They saw it, then. Cliffs rising from the bottom with entrances precisely cut into their flanks. Miko gasped, "That couldn't exist without *tools* of some kind! Do you know what that *means*? It—"

She never finished the sentence. Something crashed against the side of the sub with an impact that rocked them wildly. They were saved from injury only by their belts and harnesses, but even then their heads snapped back and forth from the sudden violent movement. As quickly as the shock came, it disappeared, and they looked at one another with blank stares.

Miko suddenly clapped her hands to her ears, wincing in agony. The others, a split second later, heard and felt the savage high-pitched sound that tore through the hull and into the submarine. It rose steadily in frequency, digging into their ears and brains, an assault they knew dimly must be ultrasonic. Moments later they were writhing in pain. Chadwick fainted first, Castillo immediately afterward, eyes rolling back in his head. Manning fought grimly to find something against which to strike back. He had a glimpse through pain-filled eyes of Miko, mouth open and gasping, slumping unconscious.

He was stronger than the others; he lasted longer, fought harder, but the world wavered crazily before and inside his eyes, and he knew he was slipping into darkness. There was a final moment of unbearable agony, a moment for a last clear look through the glassite bow. He felt he had gone mad.

Three green human faces, gills in the sides of their necks, with mixed expressions of determination and curiosity, stared back at him.

14

~~~~~~~~~~

They emerged slowly from their stupor, vision still blurred; it was as though all blacks and whites were reversed on their retinas. They heard one another groan, for their muscles and tendons had been pulled during the convulsions they experienced. Ultrasonic hammering is never pleasant, either during the assault or when crawling out of its effects. Jerry Manning was the first to regain competence for purposeful coordination, and he grabbed a medical kit to pass pain-killers and water among them.

"Don't talk for a while," he cautioned. "Go slow. Sip. That's it. Take it slow and easy." He turned his attention to the view of the ocean through the glassite bow. Darkness. Damn. He switched on the floodlights. He had been through enough recently to feel that nothing in the world would ever again catch him by surprise, and so there was no visible reaction when he noticed that the *Seeker I* was now above the green dome. He carefully scanned the instrument panel, studying each gauge separately, taking stock of the boat and its equipment. All systems were functional. He let his eyes rest on a blinking light in the navigational grid. The cabin speakers gave forth a faint but persistent booming sound that echoed through the ocean.

"Homing signal," he said aloud to the others. "From *Sea Trench*."

There are certain instinctive patterns that never seem to change. Miko blinked rapidly, regaining focus. "Where are we?" she murmured.

"In the ocean," Manning told her; then, seeing that the joke went by without effect, he said quickly, "We're above the dome. I don't know how we got here, but," he shrugged, "outside of some aches and pains, I guess we came out of what happened clean as a whistle."

He held off conversation for several moments, working the controls to put the boat on automatic pilot, locked onto the homing signal that would take them back to the mother submarine. They were quiet most of the way, shaking off physical and mental effects, almost as if they had made some unspoken agreement not to push matters until they were safely aboard the great sub. They watched in silence as Manning eased into the belly hold of *Sea Trench*. The grapples locked onto their hull, the outer doors closed, and, with a powerful shriek, compressed air forced the immense pressure from the lock.

They were still in the chamber lock when Manning established their communications link with Ryan. "Bill, get Sawbones down here with some help. We're all going to need complete check-outs in sick bay."

"What the hell happened?" Ryan was fairly clawing through metal and glass to get to them.

"Later, later," Manning said, suddenly weary. "Tell John we've gone through what I guess almost certainly to be ultrasonic scanning under near-lethal intensities."

"*Ultrasonic?* Jesus—"

When they opened the hatches, Dr. John Simmonds was there with Matthews and Williams. They removed Miko first, white and groggy and trembling almost uncontrollably. A quick study was

enough for Simmonds. He snapped orders to the
other men. "Get them to sick bay immediately. Hold
your questions for later."

They were supporting Manning beneath his arms.
"No— wait a moment," Manning told Ryan. "Get
the tapes from the sub. Process them right away."

"Goddamn it!" Simmonds was shouting. "Get
them to sick bay *now!*"

Manning was starting to slide to the deck, and
only the support of the others kept him from falling.
"Do as . . . I said," he told Ryan. "Process tapes, put
them under . . . security. Don't open . . . without direct orders . . . from me, and . . ."

He slumped unconscious.

Bill Ryan stood alongside the doctor in the sick
bay. The four who had been aboard the *Seeker I*
were sleeping soundly, at peace for the first time in
hours. "They'll be out at least six hours," Simmonds
told Ryan. "God knows their bodies, as well as their
minds, need the rest."

Ryan's face was grim. "All right, doc. I've played
nurse for two hours now without opening my mouth.
Time to spill things. What the hell happened to them?"

Simmonds shrugged, but he wasn't putting off the
query. "You heard the skipper," he said quietly.

"Ultrasonics? How the hell could that happen
down here?"

"I have no idea, Bill. But it happened. Every one
of them shows all the signs of ultrasonics—well, I
hate to use the word, but you can think of it as a
severe and very dangerous internal massage. The
organs and everything else."

"But it's crazy, John! You don't get ultrasonic frequencies in water at eight tons to the square inch!"

"Sure," the doctor said amiably. "But it happened."

"Haven't you any idea *how?*"

"Bill, I'm a doctor, not a hydrographics expert."

"Then," Ryan said, "spell out what you've learned from all that probing you did."

Simmonds nodded. "They all have almost complete spatial disorientation. Vertigo, if you wish. The semicircular canals and the otoliths have been vibrated beyond the point of endurable pain, and the inevitable result was—"

"I know, I know," Ryan broke in. "First the vertigo and then unconsciousness. Damn. That meant they were as helpless as babies."

"Worse," Simmonds told him. "They were close to death."

Ryan walked past the beds, studying the four sleeping figures. His face showed twisting emotions. Looking down rather than at Simmonds, his words came out slowly, ominously. "Then someone—something—tried to kill them."

His head snapped around with Simmonds's reply. "You're wrong, Bill."

"Wrong! How the hell can you say that? They were completely helpless, they were tortured by an ultrasonic beam that's impossible to begin with, and you—" His voice trailed away as he began to understand just what the doctor had meant.

"That's right," Simmonds said, confirming Ryan's sudden realization. "They were unconscious and they were helpless. If whoever or whatever had wanted to kill them, why didn't they? It was easy enough."

"Maybe," Ryan said, his face sour, "they did try."

Simmonds shook his head. "No way, Bill. No way. Another thirty seconds of that treatment would have been fatal. So whatever hit them was stopped, deliberately, before any permanent damage took place."

The anger drained from Ryan's face. "You mean they had them buried and let them go?" Ryan full well understood the doctor's words, but he insisted on verbal confirmation.

"That's right," Simmonds said. "They let them go."

Ryan nodded, and he came to a major conclusion. "Well, doc, I'm coming to some answers. I don't know what the hell happened in that boat, and we won't know until the captain is awake, but he told me to run this boat and that's precisely what I'm going to do. I don't like my people being toyed with. I don't think it's amusing. And anything that even comes near us," he held up a powerful fist, crashed it into his hand, "is going to get zapped but good."

He stalked from the sick bay and returned to the bridge. *Sea Trench* went on full combat alert, weapons poised for unleashing. But the long hours passed in utter silence, the submarine undisturbed. Ryan's impatience grew. Finally, Manning stirred from his deep drug-induced sleep. A hot shower, a solid meal, and what seemed like a half gallon of coffee later, and Manning was back in shape.

It was time to review the films.

They gathered in the main recreation room; the atmosphere was quiet and grim. They appeared reluctant to converse, preferring to wait until the automatic tapes and films from *Seeker I* were ready for study. Manning had told no one of that last incredible sight before he was hammered into unconsciousness, and he was the only person in the viewing room who wasn't stunned when the picture appeared on the screen of three green forms swimming directly at the camera, coming right up to the glassite bow, and peering inside.

"Hold the film there," he ordered, and the scene before them came to a grinding halt, three humanoid faces frozen in motion. The people in the room could hardly speak. *They were looking at humanoids.* All the mythical nonsense about grotesque creatures abiding in the deeps was shattered in that single instant. These figures on the screen were obviously technical, scientific, curious, investigative, philosophical, open to input—and all of it was right there.

The throat gills were clear, and they noticed that the gills—which Chadwick mentioned later he would have expected to find on the high sides of the chest, beneath the arms—had a sort of skin overlay that would permit not only closing, but complete sealing of the body. Muscular development was evident, but in a world in which weightlessness was common, suppleness came through strongly. The greenish hues of the bodies were more evident in the still scene than had been obvious in motion, and without discussion, there was no question but that this skin, and any external surfaces, were entirely comfortable and suited to the saline liquid that would have brought on severe breakdown of the observers' own tissues. They expected the webbing structure in the hands and feet, and although the quality of the picture left much to be desired, no question remained of genetic adaptation to supple movement within the sea.

There were other items of intense interest—biology notwithstanding. A single glance spelled reams of information, for two of the three figures held in their hands strange projectors with gunlike muzzles, composed of ceramic rather than metallic material. On reversing the film it became obvious that from a distance these two figures had pointed the projectors directly at the small submarine, just as in the closeup shots taken by the autocamera system the weapons were no longer being used. Two of the green humanoids wore straplike garments with what appeared to be pouches, or pockets, with locking flaps, such as might be found on a handbag. The viewers could only guess at the material: It could have been woven seaweed or kelp, or even animal material, like sharkskin, although there was a definite impression of fibers.

That these creatures were not wholly practical became clear with only a glance at the touches of shell or other similar material in their straps—unquestionably in the realm of decoration, either cosmetic or symbolic of status or rank. The third individual, the one without any weapon, was clearly much older than his two companions, and his garment was distinguished by a larger number of symbols that were more intricately designed.

None of the three appeared angry or frightened, and their expressions seemed to convey determination more than any other emotion. The eldest seemed almost unconcerned, as if what was happening was inevitable, and its immediate outcome—the rendering helpless of the submarine occupants—beyond any question.

Manning's voice broke into their reverie. "Lights, please," he called out.

The screen remained alive with the frozen scene as the room lights brightened across Manning's face. "I wanted the film stopped here for a particular purpose," he said, looking around the long table at Miko, Chadwick, Templeton, Jessica, Castillo, Bill Ryan, and Syd Prentiss. "None of us, and that includes myself, has seen what comes next. I want us to watch it together. But before we do I think it's best to consider that we've been flooded, even drowned, with new information and stimuli, and we need this break. It will also give us a chance to throw some ideas out in the open, and to share opinions and first judgments. I want to appraise what's happened up to this moment."

Throughout the submarine the rest of the crew watched and listened over the TV links piping the meeting to their stations. Hal Sparco was off duty in his fo'c'sle, wearing shorts, reclining on his bunk and studying his screen. Lieutenant Thomas Baker, also off watch, studied his screen from an easy chair. Holvak was in the captain's seat on the bridge, where Pete Williams, Patterakis, and MacKinney also had the watch. James Peck and Larry Urback were in the engineering workshop, tools forgotten on the tables before them; and Dr. Simmonds, sitting cross-legged on a bed, watched a wall-mounted screen. They heard Manning pick up his instructions to the others.

"I want to make something else clear before we start," Manning cautioned his audience. "This isn't a discussion. You've all had time to think over everything you've learned so far. Certain conclusions, right or wrong, have solidified in your minds. You've been asked to key into Neptune, along with your ID codes, how you interpret what you've experienced up to this moment. I want you to do that again, to update your notes and thoughts on the computer input panels in front of each of you. No discussion, please. Keep it tight; you can do all the editing you want to later. When we're through with this session," he concluded, "we'll be able to get the computer's own assessment, and that will be a key bridge to where we go from there."

By his stopwatch, Manning noted, eighteen minutes went by before they all sat back, finished with tapping into Neptune what they had assimilated, judged, or concluded. That would also help to clear their minds, open them all to new prospects. Manning scanned the group again, then nodded to Miko Stewart.

"Miko, if you please."

It was the first time he had ever addressed her by her first name—a moment she would not recall until later.

For now she took a deep breath, intent completely on the issue before them. "It's so—difficult to put into words," she said carefully. "One thing, however, overshadows everything else. We can't do anything sensible until we admit, and accept, openly, one fact."

She paused, looked around at the others, and returned her unblinking gaze to Jerry Manning.

"We have discovered another race. Our own species, really, but a genetic breakaway that makes them distinct from us." She closed her eyes, breathing deeply, then started again slowly. She was almost quivering.

"Those people," she paused to flick her eyes at the screen for a moment before looking back to the others at the table, "are *not* another species. It's so terribly important for us to keep that in mind. They are human beings like ourselves, and whatever is alien about them is genetic adaptation. Saying they're not human is like saying a dwarf and a man seven feet tall—with hundreds of pounds difference between them, different skin color and shape of eyes and, oh, all the rest of it—aren't both human beings. This," she paused again, "is an intelligent *human* race, fully adapted to living in the sea. I venture that our physiological processes are essentially the same. I—well, I have much more to say, captain, but I'm trying to keep my remarks essential, as you asked."

Manning studied her carefully for several moments, nodded slowly, and with an abrupt motion turned to his left. "Dr. Chadwick?"

The older scientist sighed. He was in full control of himself, but anyone who knew him would have recognized the great effort he made to remain casual. "Dr. Stewart is right, of course. But I want to add something."

"Please," Manning said quickly.

"It's the pressure beneath the dome. It's vital to any conclusions we draw now or will arrive at later. Two hundred pounds per square inch doesn't assure us that these are deep-sea creatures. Are they restricted to the dome? To their valley? Can they venture into the terrible pressures just beyond the dome? If they can—and I have thrown out almost every biological rule I've ever known—then we may discover that this particular race returned to the sea in the same manner as the family of whales and the porpoise: land animals that came from the sea to the land and, for some terrible reason, perhaps an ice age, they returned to the sea. The same may be true in this case. One of the most intriguing aspects is that they retained the basic biped form. They adapted to the sea, but not so drastically as the whales. The social, agricultural, engineering—mechanical and biological—evidence we saw in the valley leads me to concur with Dr. Stewart. We are dealing with a most extraordinary—*human*—race."

Manning left no wasted moments. "Mr. Templeton?"

"I would extrapolate on what you have already heard," Templeton said. "I agree. If I would add something specific, it would be with regard to their means of communication. They've developed, obviously, a means of talking or communicating within water as effectively as we do under atmospheric pressure."

Manning stirred in his seat. "Forgive me, Mr. Templeton. What you've said just now—it tends to be ambiguous. Could you be even more specific?"

There was a flash of resentment on Templeton's part, then he dismissed it and was completely earnest in his response. "I see what you mean," he answered. "My point, captain, is that they *must* have a written language of some sort. The implications may be staggering in a way we haven't thought of. Any historical language means a record going back, well, we have no way of knowing numbers yet, but I'll bet their history could fill in huge gaps in *our* history and evolution. It could open incredible doors."

"Very good," Manning commended. "I hadn't even thought in that direction yet." He turned again. "Jessica?"

The young girl was bursting with excitement, still wide-eyed and irrepressible. "*They're lovely.* I mean, they're the most beautiful people." She gestured to the screen. "They remind me of warmth and intelligence. Just *look* at them. When I look at the face of that elder, the one on the right, there, I think of old Japanese prints. There's understanding and compassion there. I mean, you can tell this, you can *feel* it."

Templeton gestured before breaking in. "Those same people attacked us, Jessica. Tried to kill us."

She shook her head suddenly, her hair flying, her nostrils suddenly wide. "You don't know that yet, and, even if it's true, you don't know *why* they did that, or why they may have thought they had to do it. *I'm* not a killer, Mr. Templeton, and neither is Richard, here, or Miko, or you, for that matter. Yet *we* Americans, used hydrogen bombs in a war, didn't we? There's a word and I can't remember it—"

Miko touched her arm. "I think you mean dichotomy, Jessie."

Jessica Ames nodded fiercely. "Even that doesn't matter. We'll find out all those answers when we can talk with them. I don't want to say the science of all this isn't important, but if we don't *feel* for them, or them for us—" She shrugged, feeling further words on the subject were unnecessary.

Manning's smile was warm. "Your feelings, Jessie, are as important, if not more so, than any scientific judgment. Do you want to add to what you've said?"

She twisted in her seat, nodding. "Yes, sir. You see, it's even more than—well, you saw those great eels, and the films of the luminescent things, and don't you see what all this means? These people have a complete symbiosis with their environment! They're in harmony with life all around them—like we talk about what we should be doing on the surface of the earth, only this is their way of living, every day!"

Manning answered her with an unblinking stare. "We'll see, Jessica. You're basing a lot on a brief look, and that's led to some interesting mistakes in the past. However, you may also be right. Now, Richard?"

Castillo was hesitant. "I was—well, you know, I was paying more attention to other things."

"That's what I hoped you would do, son. Go ahead."

"Well, it's like Dr. Chadwick said. About a structured society? I was looking at the way they were channeling volcanic heat. What I could see—and it wasn't much, of course—well, it told me a lot. I saw those structures, the places that had entrances. They were carved, or made, and the way I see it, having the pressure they do, in gas and temperature, it means they also would have air caverns where they could develop things like ceramics. Just as we, where we live, worked out how to process metal and alloys. They could have the same kind of technology with ceramics. They'd be just as advanced as we are, only in a different way. And there's something else, Captain Manning."

Manning studied him carefully, ignoring the others. He nodded, spoke quietly to the boy. "Go ahead, Richard. Any way you want to say it."

Castillo's words went off like a bombshell.

"They're air breathers."

Silence leaped between them with the youngster's remark, until Prentiss, who had been sitting quietly through the entire session, leaned back in his seat, both hands on the table, and broke the pause. "My God, he's right. He's *got* to be right!"

He looked around the table and then he straightened in his seat, his excitement growing. "We've got a race of beings here, homo sapiens just like ourselves, with the same genetic pattern that determines life everywhere in the world—yet these people have been as far removed from our atmospheric life on the earth's surface as we ourselves have been removed from the ammonia or methane of Jupiter, *and they have stayed men.*"

He laughed—coughing, without amusement. "Every human embryo goes through a phase when gills develop in the body. We all know that, and we know the gills are absorbed because the instructions locked in the genetic code issue those orders—in the same way that we've stopped growing tails. But the rudiments are there, and they've been there for millions of years, and we—here and now—represent a rung on an evolutionary ladder that's been determined by cause and effect on the earth's surface. We lost gills because we didn't need to extract oxygen from water. But men can be adapted surgically or bionically to live underwater and get their oxygen from seawater *because the ability has always been there.*"

Prentiss's eyes seemed alight. "Our bodies are made up mostly of water, the same water found in the seas. Concentrated chloride and sodium and potassium. The key is that the salts in the bloodstream aren't the same as in the sea today. We carry in ourselves the oceans as they were hundreds of millions, even billions of years ago, and our chemical structure has got to be the same as that of those people in the sea."

Dr. Chadwick had found comfort in his pipe, and smoke curled from his mouth as he spoke. He nodded to Prentiss. "You're right, of course. The genetic code of every creature on this planet traces back to the primordial. The mightiest all have the same humble beginnings. The essential difference is that we—and our, ah, cousins in the sea—are the winners of the evolutionary struggle. We're built of cells that learned how to eat other cells. That means growth and—but we don't need biological rudiments here. However, there's a basic rule. *We're still changing.* The shark hasn't changed for millions of years, and, although it's a natural predator, it can't change its environment. The hagfish, the lamprey, certain octopuses—they haven't changed for four hundred million years. They've survived, but that's all. The key to our development occurred, as I mentioned, when certain cells learned how to feed on other cells. In the long process of death and replication and evolution, man rides the top of the ladder because he's capable of exercising greater control over his environment than any other creature. This other man, deep within the sea, under horrendously more difficult conditions, has done the same thing in his own way. But under his green skin and our white and black, or whatever color, we're creatures of the same ilk."

Miko was almost beside herself. She waited impatiently for a break in Chadwick's conversation. "Dr. Chadwick, you said before that man has become the dominant creature on this planet because he exercises greater control—environmental control—than any other creature."

She waited as he nodded, then she turned to Manning. "This is terribly important because we may just be finding a lodestone on which to make further assumptions of these people."

Manning played his role, remaining cryptic. "How?"

"Well, when we step back in time, we reach a point in evolution where two creatures were of almost parallel development—man and porpoise. Man has always been, ever since his appearance, the most intelligent creature on the surface of the planet. We know that the dolphin, or the class he comes from, such as orca, has always been the most intelligent creature in the sea; and both men and porpoises descended from the same mammalian ancestors, perhaps sixty or seventy million years ago. But the dolphin has managed to do only one thing all this time—*survive*; he can't control his environment. We've always believed that our mutual ancestors who went from the land back to the sea doomed the dolphin to his permanent role. Now it turns out that men have developed both above and within the sea."

She leaned back in her seat. "All my life," she barely whispered, "I've communicated with these creatures, had empathy with them, held them in esteem as the lords and masters of the oceans. And I've been *wrong . . .*"

Chadwick blew out a cloud of smoke, a sudden unplanned exhalation. "Wait —if these people are air breathers, good Lord, this just struck me—if they can function from seawater to air, and back again, that means—that means that, if they are in air caverns, *they can have a spoken language based on pressure acoustics precisely the same as we do.*"

Prentiss held up a hand. "You're assuming vocal cord functions and development such as ours, aren't you?"

"Look at the picture! That's a man, not a fish!"

"We can communicate with them," Miko said in agreement.

The sudden babble in the room ran uncontrolled for several moments. Manning chose not to interfere, waiting out the exchanges. Slowly the others sensed his position and ended their discussions. They saw Manning watching Bill Ryan, who leaned back in his chair, shaking his head slowly, a strange smile on his strong dark face.

"All right," Manning said dryly to Ryan. "Let's have it."

Puzzled, they looked from one man to the other; it seemed as if the two were holding an exchange from which the others had been excluded.

Ryan held his eyes directly on Manning. "You know that old saw about not being able to see the forest because of all the trees?"

Chadwick had been trying to get into their conversation even as it started. "I don't understand," he said to Ryan.

"Obviously," Ryan said, and his sarcasm, although

not directed personally was inescapable. "None of you do. You've all missed it. You've been so busy adding up facts and figures and saline percentages and comparisons with dolphins and the rest of all that tripe that you've been blinded to what's right under our air-breathing noses."

Jessica fidgeted uncomfortably. "Mr. Ryan— you're making fun of us." She didn't disguise her hurt.

"No, no, little one," he responded quickly. "Fun? Not at all, honey. But you've got to listen to the words as well as the music going on in this room." He swept his eyes over them all. "Don't any of you understand? You've talked about these sea beings as people, but you haven't *accepted* them as human beings, as homo sapiens in your own class. You haven't even imagined that they might even be superior to us. Not in weaponry or technology, but in how to live. *They're green.* That makes them different in a psychological way. They've got gills, and that's another difference. They've got expandable webs between fingers and toes, and they can breathe oxygen from water. All those things are different, and you've been concentrating on details for your notebooks, so you've missed the most important part of all of this."

He laughed aloud, a sound of sincere mirth, but as much with pathos in his voice as any other emotion. "Miko started it when she compared man and the dolphin. Man controls his environment to some extent, the dolphin doesn't; ergo, man is the superior creature. And on the basis of environmental control, well, maybe he is. He's stronger and smarter and a hell of a lot more dangerous, but maybe he's not *better* at all. Nature doesn't seem to give a damn, of course. Muscle counts in all ways, right?"

Manning started to break in. "Bill, I—"

"No, hold it, captain. With all due respect—"

Manning's eyes were hooded, but he nodded agreement.

"Maybe," Ryan said slowly, "it's because I can recognize a soul brother easier than you people. I've found the secret ingredient. Think about that for a moment."

They waited him out, and he leaned forward, resting his powerful forearms on the table, the smile now gone from his face, a feeling of loneliness coming through, and they detected a strain in his voice they hadn't known before.

"They've been *testing* us."

His eyes stared into every face in the room. "Don't you see? They *have* been communicating with us! They've given us a crystal-clear demonstration that they'd rather talk than fight, that no matter what happened before, despite the loss of *Swimmer IV* and its crew, they've never meant us harm, they've wanted to establish contact."

Templeton reacted first. "You're assuming a hell of a lot, commander."

"Damn your blindness—the proof is right here. Manning, Stewart, Chadwick, and Castillo."

Someone started to protest, but Ryan angrily waved aside the interruption. "These four people are alive!" he shouted. "The sea men had them cold turkey, damn it. Absolutely helpless. Unconscious. They could have killed our people anytime they wanted to! Instead, they knocked them out, and when they had them laid out for the kill, they moved the boat above the dome. *They set them free.*"

He laughed harshly. "And I'll tell you something else. It's a guess. Maybe it's crazy, but it's so crazy I've got to be right on the money. One will get you a hundred they understand the *English language.*"

They gaped at him in stark disbelief, and Ryan stabbed a finger at Templeton. "What do you say, bright boy? You're the archaeologist in this crowd. You're the linguistic expert. You speak fourteen languages and you did code work in the navy before you became a highdome. So this is your specialty. Do you think they can understand English?"

Templeton was flustered, and his words tumbled together as he spoke. "But—that's *crazy*. You're right, it's mad. There's no exchange, there never has been. There's no possible way for them to be able to—"

"You're dead wrong. Do you know how many of our ships and planes have gone down in these waters? With ships' almanacs, with books, with pictures, with mechanics' and engineers' and electricians' manuals and God knows what else? They've had years to put it all together and—" He cut himself short, turning to Manning. "Put it to the test, skipper. I think it's time you ran the rest of the film and," he paused dramatically, "we get the rest of the message."

Manning held Ryan's gaze. Finally, Manning nodded, and the film started rolling.

The film started jerkily from the frozen tableau of the three humanoids staring into the small submarine. The sound track gave only water movement sounds coming in through the external hydrophones, and there were blurred moments in the film itself. But there was no mistaking the three great electric eels that glided into view behind the humanoid figures.

Jessica's voice rang out in the room. "Look! Around their necks—some kind of collars—"

She was right; as the eels drifted closer a band or an identifying symbol became visible around the neck of each creature. One of the humanoids gestured, and the creatures held their position, flanks rippling with power. The eels were easily a hundred feet or more in length.

Chadwick's voice came out choked. "Those eels—they're docile. Like pets—"

"They may be just that," Prentiss said. "Not only that—"

His voice stopped abruptly as several other humanoids swam into focus accompanied by great globes that pulsated with light—living things with beautiful wavy hairlike tendrils. Then the light steadied and the picture became brighter. One of the humanoids was wearing what looked like a mother-of-pearl garment, apparently representing a high station among the group. Older than the others, he carried a small staff, intricately carved or assembled, glistening when it caught light at different angles. Floating easily, he half turned, gesturing. Several globes drifted closer, and the light increased until the humanoid was bathed in the glow. The viewers on *Sea Trench* watched the movement of his gills, his complete body control in the water; and then an incredible moment came.

No one doubted that he understood what a camera was and what function it served, for the human occupants of the submarine before which he floated were obviously unconscious. What he did could only be performed for the benefit of a recording device.

He looked directly into the glassite hull—directly into the camera, in effect—and he smiled. It was a facial expression of utter warmth, of beauty.

Jessica began to cry softly.

The figure before them on the screen spread his arms fully wide. He looked from side to side at his hands and opened them outward, palms flat, upward.

"Damn!" Ryan cried. "He knows that we have some way of looking back to this moment. Jesus— oh, Jesus Khee-rhist!"

Manning's voice cut in sharply. "Hold it—"

The humanoid drew his arms together, gestured again, and another figure swam to his side, passing him a large flat object. It shone as if it were mother-of-pearl or some form of slate, and the man brought the flat surface closer to the camera.

There was no sound in the recreation room. They were stunned as they looked at a perfect circle and two sets of figures. One set was in a language unknown, with strange markings. But the other set, directly beneath the alien language, was written in carefully executed Arabic numerals: **3.14159**

Chadwick's voice came through with almost a sob. "Never in my life would I believe this could ever happen—"

The ring in Ryan's voice was triumphant. "You'd damned well better believe it. *Look at him!* He's smiling because he can figure the kind of reaction this would get!"

Miko turned to him. "But *how?*" She fought for the words. "That's the sign for *pi*—it's not simply numbers—it's higher math and—oh, God . . ."

Manning's hand clasped hers tightly, as if he would transfer strength to her. "You're right," Manning said to her and the others. "We're looking at people who live underwater and have never seen the sky or the sun or the moon or the stars, who may not even know the wheel exists because they have no need for it, and yet they've worked out the ratio of the circumference to the diameter of a circle. It's as much philosophic as it is scientific. But I'll be damned if I can understand how—"

He stopped talking as another humanoid in the film swam up and passed an object to the elderly figure. Again there was that marvelous smile, and the figure swam with all the elegance and flow of a dolphin until he was close to the submarine bow. He held what looked like a clear plastic or translucent case. It filled the screen, and it answered all their questions.

Ryan was right.

Within the transparent material was a navigational almanac and reference book. On the cover they made out the words clearly: **PROPERTY U.S. NAVY 1982.**

Ryan's great hand crashed against the table. "I knew it! Goddamnit, *I knew it!*"

The humanoid figure backed off easily, and the scene began to fade somewhat as a larger group approached the submarine, several great eels with them. In a blur of motion, of bubbles and froth, there was a glimpse of a huge woven net being moved over the glassite bow of the *Seeker I.* The images on the screen became jerky and the green mass of the dome came into view. The film ended at that moment.

The recreation room lights came on. The people assembled at the table found themselves staring at each other, awed, dumbfounded. Miko noticed how tightly, even painfullly, Manning had been holding her hand. Red-faced suddenly, she withdrew. He didn't seem to notice. Jessica was weeping quietly, Prentiss holding her in his arms. No one seemed able to speak. Manning climbed slowly to his feet, looked at them, his hands flat and strong on the table. He looked directly at Ryan, waiting for him to speak. Ryan had understood it all while they still groped.

"It's something, isn't it," Ryan said quietly. "We've been to the moon and we've taken pictures of Mercury and sent our probes through the corona of the sun. Oh, we've done it all, looking for life, for *anything* out there. Our robots have landed on Mars and Venus, and we've played tag with bacteria; we've even landed probes on Jupiter's moons, and we've gone through the rings of Saturn. We've even sent five ships *beyond* the solar system, and we thought we were so goddamned smart. And all the time, all the goddamned time, the other intelligence we've been trying to find has been right here, right inside our ocean, and while we looked for alien life-forms, we just discovered that the race of man has his brother in his own sea. How stinking stupid blind we've been."

15

~~~~~~~~~~~~~~

The gleaming hull of *Sea Trench* broke the ocean surface, a strong spray faintly phosphorescent in the darkness, blowing across the rounded flanks of the sub. Far down in the bridge, the watch crew scanned radar, sonar, laser sweep, and other detection systems.

Ryan nodded. "Pass the word topside. We're clean."

Moments later a hatch in the great submarine conning tower or sail opened, and several figures emerged onto a long, narrow platform that extended out to the side of the sail. They wore life jackets and clung tightly to the cable that formed a safety rail. Looking toward the sky, Prentiss listened to the headphones in his helmet; he pointed to the east from where a deep waspish cry could be heard above the hiss of wind and spray. Moments later, the sound of jet turbines screamed down at them and dull red lights blinked on. Locked in with guidance radar, the helicopter hovered smoothly despite gusts beating across the sea and a cage was lowered to the platform. Jerry Manning helped Miko Stewart into the cage, snapped her safety clasp, and followed her in. The chopper brought up the cage, lifting away from the sub at the same time. Behind them *Sea Trench* vanished into the dark ocean.

Thirty-five minutes later Manning and Miko transferred from the jet chopper to a small plane that was waiting for them. The crew sealed the door, spooled up to power, and raced into the dark skies with wings swept forward. The wings rotated back, and they were still climbing when they went through the Mach. At 63,000 feet the air force jet raced to the southeast at better than fifteen hundred miles an hour.

Manning and the woman by his side were asleep when the jet rolled into a long final approach to a military airstrip in the Virginia countryside. The plane landed with a hard thump, screamed its reversers, and turned off the landing strip and rolled smoothly into a cavernous hangar. Doors rumbled closed behind them as the jets wound down. The engines were still turning as Manning and Stewart emerged, met by a man in a dark suit who led them to an elevator.

They stood quietly as they dropped twenty stories beneath the ground. The doors hissed open and they emerged from the elevator and crossed a steel floor to a bullet-shaped passenger vehicle. Inside, they strapped in and waited. A curving door slid down, compressed air shrieked briefly, and the tubular shape rolled smoothly but swiftly into a darkened tunnel. No conversation passed between them. Dimly, through heavy soundproofing they heard the deep cry of air sucking away from the tunnel before them. The car accelerated with surprising force through the vacuum tube, and a surrealistic blur of lights flashed by as quickly as the eye could define what it was. Manning and Stewart remained quiet, content to let any turmoil within them operate on a mental back burner. It was a good way to settle disturbing and conflicting concepts.

A voice came from a concealed speaker. "Arrival in thirty seconds. Have your ID sensors ready, please."

The car hissed to a stop, the doors slid open silently, and they found themselves in an area that bristled with warning signs, armed men, and hidden defense systems of which they would never know. Their guide led them to a security computer panel, held a flat card that was on a chain around his neck, and inserted it into the proper slot.

Seconds later, a green light came on, a digital code blurred swiftly on another display, and a mechanical voice sounded: *"Vance Gardener cleared to Block One."*

A sliding door of steel bars opened, and without a glance at the armed men Gardener stepped through. At that moment the bars closed again to separate them from Gardener. "Please go ahead, Dr. Stewart," he told her. Miko stepped forward hesitantly and repeated the sequence she had seen Gardener follow. The computer cleared her into the next security block and she waited with Gardener as Manning repeated the sequence.

The computer voice came to them again: *Thank you. Please face the orange wall. Place your right palm flat against the wall for three seconds. Then state your name.*

Miko glanced at Manning. He squeezed her hand and nodded. They followed the procedures in order.

"Vance Gardener, Security 66K71928."

"Dr. Miko Stewart, ah, no number, I think." She shrugged.

Manning grinned at her and she returned a wan smile. He went to the wall and spoke crisply, "Captain Jerome Myron Manning, United States Navy, DOD 92518214. Open this stinking door," he added with a grin.

The bars slid noiselessly aside, and they began

walking along a featureless corridor. "Why did you say that?" Miko asked. "To the security system, I mean."

"Telling it to open the stinking door?"

She nodded, and Gardener glanced at him, curious.

"It bugs me to let computers have the last word. And if no one tells them off, how are they ever going to learn humility? A little character building never hurts."

The impudence of his remark brought a chuckle from Gardener. "Most people are afraid of computers," he said to Manning.

"That's because they never made friends with them." Manning left Gardener to ponder that one on his own.

They approached a thick glass door. Even as they hesitated, the doors slid open to an office where a young woman, dressed smartly in a tunic, greeted them.

"Dr. Stewart, Captain Manning, our pleasure. Please come in." They entered the office. By the time they turned around, Gardener had vanished.

"I'm Ms. Younger. The president is waiting for you. This way, please."

Miko stood rooted to the floor, staring at Manning. "The president?" she finally managed.

"Uh huh."

"You never said anything about our seeing the *president*."

"And you never asked."

She looked around. "I know this is a silly question, but where are we?"

"New Washington," Manning replied. "We're 680 feet straight down beneath the steel armor and concrete."

The other woman smiled at Miko. "There's no need to be frightened, Dr. Stewart. A lot of people become upset down here. It has something to do with the great pressure above us."

Miko and Manning burst into laughter. Ms. Younger looked puzzled. "Is—something wrong?"

Manning shook his head, still humored by the moment. "No, no, not at all. A private joke." He turned to Miko. "Anyway, we're going topside. Another elevator ride."

They went through a doorway into an elevator and began the swift ride straight up. "There's no other way to get into the private camp on the surface," Manning explained. "All defenses are automatic. Even something flying overhead would be cut down by lasers. The president has full working facilities down here, but he uses this place only when we get a combat alert. He doesn't like it underground. Says the world has enough of a mole mentality as it is."

"I agree with that," Miko said emphatically.

Manning grinned at her. "I thought you would."

The doors opened and two marine guards were waiting to escort them to the presidential office. Miko was astonished by the startling change in their surroundings. Through floor-to-ceiling plate glass she saw thickly wooded hills. A pastoral atmosphere was the last thing she expected. Then she recalled Manning's explanation. Trying to get into this area from above the surface would mean instant destruction.

Another surprise awaited her in the presidential office. She had expected to find her long-standing convictions of the trappings that went with power— a grim and foreboding office, maps across all the walls. A command-center hookup with computers, the infamous red telephone. Instead, she walked into a room richly furnished in natural wood, the seats comfortably padded and leathered, the decor that she would expect to find in a ski lodge. At the far end of the room, his desk catching a beam of sunlight, President Hillary Church stood to greet them. Miko's impressions were of necessity swift, but she was a practiced observer. As they approached the other end of the room, she saw how well he filled his dark business suit; he was slender but broad chested, and immensely strong in his presence.

Not until they were well into the room did she see the easy chair to their left, where sat Navy Secretary Frank Cartwright, his cane resting on the floor, both hands atop its grip. He nodded and favored her with a smile. From another chair, Vice Admiral Timothy Haig watched them and stood up as they approached.

"Jerry! I can't tell you how excited we've been— and Miko, my dear, it's so very good to see you again." Haig clasped Manning's hand, embraced Miko, and turned, holding her gently by the arm.

"Mr. President, may I present Dr. Miko Stewart. You're well acquainted with the role she's playing in this situation."

Church came from behind his desk, taking both her hands. "Dr. Stewart, I'm honored."

She was flustered and she stammered out something she couldn't later remember. She felt relief as the president turned to Manning. "It's been a long time, Jerry," he said, taking Manning's grip.

"Thank you, sir."

Manning walked to Cartwright's chair. The navy secretary climbed to his feet. Whatever pain he had endured before had worsened, and what he suffered showed, if not in his words or expressions, in his eyes. He nodded to Miko. "My dear, you have done well by all of us. Thank you."

He coughed suddenly, and Manning helped him back into his seat. "Sit down, sit down," Cartwright urged them. "We have much to discuss."

When they were seated, the president nodded to them. "I regret not being able to spend more time with you." A smile appeared briefly. "We have a unique problem on our hands."

Haig was fairly beaming as he looked at them. "It seems we're in a storm at the U.N. China is demanding international sharing rights to the, ah, enormous petroleum find in the southern mid-Atlantic ridge."

Manning shook his head in mild disbelief. "You're not going to tell me it really worked?"

"It worked like a charm," Haig affirmed. "Ever since we set our red herring loose in the south Atlantic, the Chinese have been raising six kinds of hell to get their share of the loot that's supposed to be down there."

"Jerry," the president said, "the admiral is a madman. He even went so far as to have a convoy of submarine oil barges towed to the new discovery, and then he opened the valves."

"Which was very convincing proof," Haig added, "that we really were working crude down there." He sighed. "However, that isn't the issue here, and the president's time is limited." Haig looked to Cartwright, passing the moment to him.

"We have everything you sent by satellite," the navy secretary began. "All three of us have reveiwed it. The film, the data tapes, your impressions and first conclusions. There is no way any human being can overestimate the enormity of your discovery." He coughed, rested a moment. "I believe I speak across the broad spectrum—science, humanity, history. Our future, as well. There's no question that we will apply every effort to communicate with, to be friends with, to join with these people. That," he said solemnly, "will be the responsibility of all of you who make up the crew and the science team of *Sea Trench.*"

Miko waited, then realized that Cartwright was ready for their response. "Mr. Secretary, you can't imagine how much your words move me. May I ask a question?"

"All you have, Dr. Stewart."

"We will be working, I hope, with those organizations best equipped to help us, won't we?"

"Be specific, please."

"I mean the Scripps Institute—the Franklin team that's been doing so much in deep-sea work, and—even the Office of Naval Research. We'll need all the help we can get from the anthropologists, and—"

Cartwright's voice had unexpected strength. "*No.* Absolutely not."

She didn't hide her surprise. "For heaven's sake, *why not?* This is an effort to which we should apply every element of our science, and—"

"And *guarantee* the utter destruction of these people," Cartwright said, his voice grave and utterly commanding, "just as we have destroyed every other group like them on the surface of this planet."

The president saw her consternation and stepped in quickly. "I'm afraid he's right, Dr. Stewart. Please believe that we've spent much time on this matter. But reality isn't to be suspended, I'm afraid, and if word ever gets out about this strange race of man—and all of us here accept them as men—there will be an invasion by every major power in the world. You can call it research, or study, or even humanism, anything you want, but their destruction would be inevitable. It doesn't matter what anyone in the world—public or private—says. If any government even suspects that these sea people have something that would help gain an advantage in the power play of international politics, it would be the end of their underwater world. Would you wish to make yourself a party to such a catastrophe?"

Dismay showed on her face, and the president softened his tone. "Dr. Stewart, you're the kind of humanitarian the world has always needed. You have dedicated your life to trying to protect intelligent life in the sea. You are renowned for your communications work with whales. Now the other dominant form of intelligent life—man—appears afflicted by a strange destructive madness.

"We have listened to the tapes when you first reviewed the films, and this point was discussed among you then. So I must ask you know: How successful have you been in saving the whales and the seals? A world out there is hungry and hurt and fearful, and they have little room for humanitarian feelings when their bellies are growling. Food is food. The chain is inexorable. To live you must eat, and in the world we know—the only world, as it were—to eat you must kill. It so happens, doctor, that I agree totally with your concepts. So do the other people in this room. So do millions of people throughout the world. But many in power do *not* agree, and there is wanton slaughter and bloodletting of intelligent and compassionate creatures. Life demands its pound of flesh, doctor, and there are periods in history when that demand is unrelenting."

She nodded slowly stricken by his words, but unable to argue.

"We have several immediate priorities to discuss," President Church said to the group. "Jerry, you and Dr. Stewart will accept what I tell you now as your orders."

Manning nodded. "Yes, sir."

"Of—of course," Miko said quickly.

"Admiral Haig will continue to have complete control of all activities," the president went on. "The project started with him, and it will remain under his direction. I will support him to the full, and his orders will be, in effect, the same as mine." Church turned to Haig. "Admiral?"

"You know your first priority," Haig told Manning and Miko Stewart. "Absolute secrecy. Whatever you need that lies beyond your immediate capabilities you will communicate to me by a new code that has already been incorporated into the Neptune system aboard *Sea Trench.* Your boat, Jerry, in effect, is now a total command and science center for this effort."

Haig looked at the president and then back to Manning and Stewart. "Beyond that immediate security issue, your most critical need is to establish communication on a basis of both languages. Ours *and* theirs. One-way understanding is not acceptable. Everything else proceeds from that point."

Haig shifted his attention to Miko. "Your husband Harold died six thousand feet beneath the ocean surface in a free dive. What killed him?"

She didn't like the question, and her stiffened body made that clear. "You know what killed him," she said coldly.

He was unruffled by the ice in her voice. "Your own words, please," he insisted.

"Equipment failure. His death was as stupid as it was tragic. Why do you insist on bringing it up now?"

Haig kept swinging the hammer in his own way. "What's the status of your liquid-lung program? The effort to adapt men to breathe seawater and extract oxygen without external equipment."

"It also died," she said, "but the cause was financial anemia."

"If you had the money and the facilities for a major research effort, could you develop a method of breathing seawater with only bionic implant assistance?"

"Absolutely," she snapped, more severely than she intended. But if she thought she had nettled Haig she was wrong.

"Then that, doctor, is your assignment. As I understand the problem, it's coming *out* of the deepwater breathing that's been the killer."

"That's true," she confirmed. "We've been using a bionic second kidney, and it can be fitted externally or implanted, to remove blood impurities when water breathing. But when a man emerges from extreme pressures, removing the liquid from the alveolar areas of the lungs and restoring internal air pressure quickly, that's—"

Haig held up a hand to interrupt her. "And do you think that working with another race, a *human* race that's been water breathing for thousands of years, might just reveal the answers to those problems?"

16

~~~~~~~~~~~~~~~~

Her eyes grew wider as Haig's words began to sink in. A terrible part of her life, a memory that she had encased in emotional scar tissue, had been ripped open, but now there was no pain, only a hope she had forsaken. Her voice was little more than a whisper when she answered, "My God—admiral, we could do almost anything we wanted."

The president's voice came to her unexpectedly. "That's right, Dr. Stewart. Your program could lead to our ability to live in the sea as well as we live on the land. I'm sure this is a great oversimplification of the issue, but the problems seem to be within our grasp. And if such a thing becomes a success, it would be the same as finding several new planets."

"Yes, sir." She didn't know what else to say.

Frank Cartwright joined in. "Captain Manning, you know we have a very special need for Dr. Chadwick. He's one of the world's leading experts in farming the sea for food—what we call the science of mariculture." He shook his head, coughing. They waited.

Cartwright wiped his lips with a handkerchief before going on. "Unfortunately, sea farming has so far been virtually a complete disaster. That nasty little war we had did more than just kill a billion people. It wrecked most of the world's agricultural systems. You all know how hard we've tried to make up for land failures by increasing our catch from the sea."

"Yes, sir," Manning told him and then caught them all by surprise. "And it won't ever work. At least not the way we've been going at it."

President Church leaned forward, alert, a sharply questioning look in his eyes. "You're going against the grain, Captain Manning."

"Yes, sir, I am."

"But you've done that before, and you've always come out on top, if I recall," Church added.

"Thank you, sir."

"Now tell me why it won't work, Jerry."

"People talk glibly of fish, Mr. President, but they forget to specify that what they really mean is edible fish," Manning said. "And when we talk about edible fish we're talking about the creatures on the highest levels of the seafood chain, the protein animals. Unfortunately, the fish we need to eat are tremendously wasteful of their own food supply. I've gone over this at length with Dr. Chadwick, and he and I are in complete agreement. We know it's a problem that can't be answered simply by talking about numbers of animals. Sir, many people have argued that eating beef is wasteful of the agricultural system. In some ways it may be, but in other ways it's tremendously efficient. For example, many critics say that you've got to expend ten tons of fodder—grain, if you wish —to produce only one ton of beef."

"True enough," the president said crisply.

"Yes, sir, it is, but it's not wasteful compared to our attempts to obtain high-protein animals from the sea. To get one ton of fish like tuna, you've got to consume about ten thousand tons of sea vegetation. That's why the huge fish catches we talk about don't work. The waste is staggering."

Miko stared in disbelief as Manning talked. She

had not even an inkling of his knowledge in this area. She watched the president mulling over what he'd heard; then Church came back at Manning.

"But Dr. Chadwick isn't going on those lines, is he?"

"No, sir. He knows better than that. The thing to understand, really, is that nature squanders life in the sea. It's as wasteful of its creatures as it is in sperm transference from male to female. May I use some examples?"

"By all means," Church murmured.

"We've found that during mating season," Manning continued, "as many as one billion squid will fill a cubic space of only four hundred feet in diameter and one hundred feet deep. That's a billion, I want to emphasize. On a different level, we've estimated that as many as one billion mackerel will produce sixty-four *trillion* eggs. But of every million eggs laid among these creatures, only one to a hundred, never more, survive to maturity. That's a mortality rate about as close as you can get to 100 percent and still remain in existence."

He looked to Haig, who nodded for him to stay with it. "What complicates everything," Manning said, more slowly now, "is that even the slightest interference with the natural processes of fertilization can wreck everything. There are still trillions of shrimp in the seas—we encountered one of the living layers ourselves—but the shrimp population is still only a fraction of what it was before the last war. What happens, sir, if fertilization is disrupted, as occurred when shock waves cracked through the oceans, is that at that critical moment, most of the female shrimp reabsorbed their eggs just prior to fertilization. The loss is estimated as high as 90 percent of the shrimp population in all the oceans.

"There's more to tell, but I think this gives some idea of the enormity of the problem of living off the sea. It's fine for a small population, but when you're talking about billions of people, it just doesn't work."

President Church went directly to the heart of the matter. "Now tell me something else. *Can* it work? Provided the right elements are involved?"

"Yes, sir."

"You're more encouraging now, captain. Go on."

"Dr. Chadwick works with mariculture. This is somewhat different from the popular picture of aquiculture. Mariculture in its most efficient form establishes a chain of different species of sea animals. Each order feeds off the wastes of the order below it. The Chinese use this system, and it's the only reason they haven't had widespread famine, despite the tremendous radioactive fallout they suffered."

President Church turned to Miko Stewart. "Doctor, didn't you—or perhaps it was that youngster, Jessica—make much of the symbiotic relationship the sea people have with their environment, both fauna and flora?"

"Oh, yes," Miko said quickly, "but it is Jessie who deserves the credit. She's extremely sensitive about such things."

"Then these sea people could teach us that, as well?"

Manning answered for her. "Much more, sir. We've already seen huge areas of cultivated sea vegetation, and we have no idea of what was growing. Dr. Chadwick was both dumbfounded and elated by the possibilities of such food production."

The president spent several moments considering what he had heard.

Manning turned to Haig. "Excuse me, admiral, but just before we left the boat, Templeton seemed pretty close to finding what he felt was a key to understanding what might be the spoken language of the sea people. We've never heard them talk directly, but the computer picked out some voice exchanges we caught on our hydrophones when we were inside the valley. Templeton claims, and the rest of us agree, that they understand our language, for all the reasons you've already heard. But Templeton was asking for additional information from the master computer here in Washington. Have you got any more on that?"

Haig deferred to Cartwright.

The old man chuckled. "Your boy, captain, is driving the cryptographic computer people quite mad with his research. He has some wild idea that the language of the sea people is somehow linked to an ancient language used by an Indian tribe. The Cherokee, I believe. That's all we know so far. If we hear more before you leave, you'll have the information to take with you."

"Yes, sir. When will that be?"

Cartwright's eyes were unblinking. "You and Dr. Stewart leave in six hours, captain." Cartwright chuckled. "Don't be so surprised, you two. When you leave here there are teams of experts waiting to brief you on special projects. Also, we consider it critical that we establish a working communication with these people in the shortest possible time. Aside from everything else, Captain Manning, and I don't mean fish or food, it looks as if we may desperately need the assistance of these people."

"I don't understand, sir," Manning told him.

"You'll be told at the right time, Jerry. I assure you it's of the utmost concern for this nation."

The president intervened. "I have only a little more time to spend with you. As the saying goes, the world continues to turn and grind out its problems. Is there anything else, Captain Manning, Dr. Stewart, I may do directly for you?"

Miko gestured. She seemed hesitant, as if she might keep silent; then, encouraged by an inner decision, she went on. "Mr. President—a question, if I may?"

"Of course."

"Please believe me when I say I'm not trying to be difficult, but I still cannot accept everything I heard before. I mean, all this is so important to the entire human race, and—," she blurted, "must we keep it secret even from other scientists?"

The president favored her with a warm smile. "You are indeed diplomatic, doctor. Aren't you really asking why I believe *we* can be relied on to deal fairly and humanely with these people, more than anyone else?"

Miko's face reddened. She pressed her lips tightly. "Yes, sir. Please forgive me if I have offended you, but—"

"May I call you Miko? Thank you. I want to leave with you a story that was told to me by my father, who fought in the Second World War. When that war ended, our country—yours and mine, Miko—undertook the greatest gamble in world history. I know it sounds incredible now, but in 1945 and for some years afterward we were the only nation to possess the atomic bomb—as well as the means to deliver it anywhere in the world. For those years the United States had what is known as the absolute weapon. In effect, the entire planet lay at our mercy. We had, with our allies, just destroyed the war machine of the Germans and the Japanese, and on our horizon we saw communism as perhaps an even greater danger."

He paused, as if he had slipped back in time, his words having had almost a hypnotic effect on himself as well as his audience. Abruptly he shook himself free and smiled again at Miko.

"I wish every American then, and every one of us today, could understand what truly happened. We believed we had the power to stop the growth of world communism right at its inception. By using the atomic bomb in great force, when there was no defense for it, we could have assured American domination of the entire planet.

"But we didn't. We judged ourselves, Miko, and we judged that were we to do such a horrendous thing we would be no better than the enemies we had just destroyed. And so the people who led our government in those days, and we had an irascible man for president, gambled the existence of our nation and all its people. We placed our hopes squarely with the rest of mankind. And it is my humble opinion that that was, and remains, one of the more splendid moments in the history of this race. So my answer to you is yes, I believe we are best entrusted with this secret. There will surely come a time when the secret will be shared by the entire world, but that time is not yet here."

President Hillary Church sighed, almost regretting the time he had taken. "I'm not especially religious, but all this has given me pause to wonder. Why was it we who had the bomb? We were the legions of Rome a thousand times over, and we—well, there it is. We have come to another of destiny's crossroads. I intend that we tread very carefully."

Miko felt her eyes misting. "Thank you—for everything you have just said to me. It will be much easier now."

She heard an alarming cough at her side, and she turned to see Cartwright wiping blood from the corner of his mouth. Manning went to his aid but was waved off.

"Stop it, Jerry. I'll be fine. I want to add something to what Hillary said. You see, I can call him Hillary. He once served under my command, and I will confirm that he is definitely not a religious man. However, I am. And I'm also drawn back in time to another parallel with today."

They waited as coughs racked his worn body. "I am old, as any fool can plainly see, and there are things that puzzle other men, but give me great comfort. I address what I am going to say to Hillary and to the rest of you as well. You are all well versed in history, and you are all aware that one of the great mysteries of the past has been the ancient civilization of Sumer. As we understand civilization, these people were the first. They led the way. Four thousand years before the birth of Christ, it seems they were thrust overnight into a new era. They were simple folk living near the water, no more advanced than any of the tribes of their time. They—" Again the coughing spasm, the flecks of blood.

Haig was on his feet. "Damn it, Frank—"

"Be quiet, Tim. This is important. The old legends say that in ancient times, on the shores of the Persian Gulf—I believe it was near the Sumerian town of Eridu—a being called Oannes came out of the water to talk to the people of Sumer. This is thousands of years before the time even of the Babylonians. The legend says that Oannes walked out of the Persian Gulf, and he spoke to the Sumerians of science and farming and law and many other things. He also warned of a terrible danger, that a great flood would sweep all the lands of the world. And then he returned to the sea."

Cartwright brooded for several moments, a weathered relic of a stormy period of recent history. When he looked up again, he radiated a new warmth.

"I do not know if all this is true. But this race beneath the sea—well, the coincidence is truly most extraordinary; and I am not one to believe that extraordinary coincidences are accidental. You will forgive an old man, but I am convinced all this was destined to happen, at this time, and this place."

His smile had the dust of years on it. "I am only sorry I shall not be here to see it all."

Miko was alarmed. "Why do you say that?"

"Because, my child," he said in a voice ever more grave, "some years past I took a severe dose of atomic radiation, and there is a cancer that will not be denied. That sort of clock does not run forever. But I have lived, I believe, just long enough.

A month from now, when these two races are joined beneath the sea, I shall be dead."

He looked at them all, a strange love on his face and in his eyes.

"I am going to take the liberty of naming this mission. We shall call it Aquarius. It will be a journey for which we can have only hope, rather than answers, at this time.

"A long time ago other men set out on an expedition to new lands. We are here now because of what they did then. And in the language of their time, the last words spoken to them were *vaya con dios*. I say them to you now."

BOOK

II

17

Excerpt from the Historical Record, THE AQUARIUS MISSION, prepared by the Documentation Branch, United States Navy, in conjunction with Dr. Vern Renaud of the Scripps Oceanography Institute:

The old man who coughed blood and carried in his body the wasting knife blades of radioactive exposure was right. One month to the day after the fateful meeting in the office of the president, Secretary of the Navy Frank Cartwright was dead. But his was a prophesy to be fulfilled. Even as his mortal remains were consumed and his ashes cast widely over the oceans he loved so well, the crew and staff of the huge submarine U.S.S. Sea Trench had made first contact with the sea race that came to be known as the Ikians.

The contact was inevitable, and after the first encounter—even if it was only on film—the sea people waited for the reaction of the other race who came from an atmosphere that to them was as sparse and deadly as the cold near-vacuum of Mars is to us.

It was a confrontation that went slowly and painstakingly, a single careful step at a time, the interface between the two races of man—so much the same and yet so crucially different—kept deliberately slow, cautious, even painfully courteous; neither side was willing to commit what might be construed as a serious breach, affront, or danger to the other.

It is fortunate indeed that Captain Jerome M. Manning, USN, brought to his command both discipline and deep understanding. For he deemed it essential to consider the point of view of the Ikians, who for the first time were to confront the "other race" they knew to be warlike, destructive, and even, at times, hopelessly cruel. Yet the confrontation must take place, and with minimum friction. It should be recorded that there were those among the Ikian group of rulers who did not welcome the presence of the Americans, and resentment ran so strong that proposals were made to defend encroachment through the living dome that formed the upper reaches of the Great Valley. One man, Hydrea, was bitterly opposed to the welcome proffered by his peers, and this man especially had to be considered, for the ritual history of the Ikian society held that dreadful horrors would result from any contact with the race that lived on the surface of the planet—theologically a point of intense interest, since it was the belief of the sea people that the earth's surface represented the equivalent of what Christian civilization calls Hades.

Yet not even Hydrea, or his fear of the surface people, or his thundering denouncements of the Ikians violating their sacred scripts, could deny the inevitable. When the U.S.S. Sea Trench returned to the crushing depths nearly ten miles beneath the ocean surface, the crew discovered that a homing signal had been set out to aid their approach. No member of the sea people was to be found yet above the dome, but a long line of "living light globes" had been emplaced along the ocean floor, leading directly to what can best be described as a living air lock.

Captain Manning and his crew had considered long and hard just how they might breach the thick dome protecting the Great Valley without endangering the security of that structure against the tremendous sea pressure just above it. The Ikians themselves had anticipated the problem, as well, and, during the absence of Sea Trench, they had prepared a huge tunnel shape emerging from their dome. The lights emplaced on the ocean floor directed the submarine to this point, and Sea Trench was moved into the tunnel with great care. There it lay on the bottom for a week while the dome was rebuilt and strengthened.

The submarine crew knew that all was well, and that they were welcome, when they saw that the dome structure directly before them had been opened, that the pressure outside their hull was down to two hundred pounds per square inch, and that several of the sea people swam before the transparent bow, beckoning clearly for the submarine to move in their direction. The sub was brought to an area of gentle hills on the floor of the valley, where a resting trough had been prepared. What could not be communicated with words between two races meeting for the first time was understood fully through both high intelligence and common sense.

Another sixty days would pass before Captain Manning and his staff considered the all-critical "first stage" of the contact to have been accomplished. The embittered resentment of the dissenters notwithstanding, the Council of Elders, led by Gella, had accomplished on their part what Captain Manning and his team had attempted on theirs.

The two races were no longer strangers, and they were more than friendly aliens.

18

~~~~~~~~~~~~~~~~

"It's almost as if she were a new person. Like some-one we knew before, but not really." Miko shook her head in wonder, her eyes shining. "I know I don't make much sense, Jerry, but just look at her! Is that the same girl with the grin and the freckles?"

It was true; the Jessica Ames they had known had slipped quietly into a memory: freckled, grin-ning impishly, exquisitely sensitive to the living creatures of the oceans. She was still Jessica, of course, but she had blossomed overnight, it seemed, into a young and beautiful woman, and now she was as much water nymph as if she had been born to the sea.

Jerry Manning and Miko stood together in the glassite bow on the bottom of the sea valley. Fair-skinned Jessica wore a beautiful one-piece mother-of-pearl shell that seemed impossibly resilient as it molded to her lithe body, glistening among the liv-ing light globes, gliding through the crystalline water. An Ikian youth named Arnom swam by her side. Arnom moved effortlessly, as supple as a dolphin; his warm, friendly smile might have been found on a river raft straight out of Mark Twain.

To any observer who came upon the moment without foreknowledge, the sight of the young girl would have been staggering. Jessica moved through the water with beauty and flowing grace without any artificial breathing apparatus. People do dive in the sea and manage quite well by holding their breath for as long as they're underwater, but Jessica had been swimming in the pristine waters of the valley for more than an hour, and she suffered no lack of oxygen. Moreover, she could remain in that water another day or even longer without difficulty. Her skin, which would normally have been subject to severe effects after prolonged exposure, had been treated with an oil native to the Great Valley, and it coated her body with an invisible film that protected her completely from the salt water.

The fact was that Jessica had been the first of their group to be adapted surgically—in the bionic sense—to being capable of moving water through her lungs and of extracting her necessary oxygen from that water and expelling her waste gases and other products. To Jessica, breathing water or air had become equally natural and equally functional. A bionic unit had been implanted in her lungs; and from this unit, flowing outward through her circulatory system and back to the bionic system, sped the oxygen she needed for life. Jessica no longer needed to breathe a gas in order to receive oxygen. If she were in atmosphere, the system functioned as a flow-through unit without being activated. If she were in water, as at this moment, the water taken in through her nose or her mouth went into the bionic unit where the oxygen was extracted, and only that oxygen was sent on through her body via her natural circulation.

It was more than simply efficient or convenient. Jessica swam *without breathing a gas*. This meant that she had been set free from the problems of nitrogen bubbles collecting in her system, massing in her joints, and bringing on the dreaded bends with its agony and too often fatal results. In addition, she would escape becoming a victim of nitrogen narcosis, or the so-called rapture of the deep, where a sense of euphoria leads a diver to ever-increasing depth and an inescapable lack of air. Jessica, not breathing air, was as free in the water as any fish.

With the bionic unit, she surpassed any mammal in the ocean in terms of capability of living within the sea. No seal or porpoise, or even the deep-sounding sperm whale, could remotely approach the freedom Jessica now enjoyed. All mammals in the sea sustain themselves, whether for five minutes or five hours, on stored oxygen and drastically modified metabolism. The Ikians were the only mammals in the oceans who breathed water *or* air, but who never *needed* their oxygen in the form of a gas.

The bionic unit, however, no matter how efficient or flexible, was only a mechanical device, a convenient implant, and it suffered from the problems of all such devices. Sooner or later they malfunction, and in the interim they are in need of servicing. Jessica could remain underwater—or within water, in effect—for several days at a time, but she would have to replace the oxygenated fluid unit and the carbon dioxide absorbent every seventy-two hours.

In the meantime, she experienced a freedom and litheness in the sea that no surface human had ever known, and had Miko and Manning not been aware of the bionic implant, only the skin color of the girl and the boy, as seen from a distance, could have defined the fact that they were two separate races of man swimming together.

There was yet another phenomenon that Miko and Manning did not miss. Jessica and Arnom could talk underwater. It was not the free-and-easy speech of atmospheric conversation, for talking in a medium eight hundred times more dense than air leaves much to be desired in the way of elocution. Yet speech was effective, and not even the water could disguise the most beautiful sound of all—Jessica laughing with delight.

The *Sea Trench* hydrophones picked up that delight and carried it through speakers in the glassite bow. Miko stiffened suddenly and grabbed Manning's arm as a deep rumble, the growl of an enormous beast, carried heavily through the water. They could hear the water itself being swept away as a massive form approached Jessica and Arnom. The two youngsters turned, but instead of fear, the girl showed excitement.

"Arnom! Look!" she called, her words warbled but still understandable through the sub's speakers.

The boy laughed. *"Grektor!"* he shouted. *"Na loo, na loo!"*

Miko and Manning stared in wonder as Jessica's legs propelled her toward the monster eel, directly to the great head with its gleaming teeth as long and sharp as bayonets. Arnom slipped along behind her, and it seemed he too was mystified by Jessica's inexplicable rapport with this deadly fighting animal. The Americans had learned quickly that the great eels were something much less than pets, as they understood that term on the surface. There was a close relationship that had been established for untold years, and the two species—underwater man and the eels—functioned more or less as a team, if not quite on equal terms.

Yet here was Jessica, placing total trust in the killer that stretched more than a hundred feet from its saberlike teeth to its flat hard-as-iron tail. Jessica swam up to the head, the eye on her side rolling in its socket to follow her moves. Of a sudden the eel drifted, the muscles rippling almost quietly along its body as it waited for whatever move the girl might make. Each of the great eels, shortly after birth, was fitted with an expandable neck collar; these collars were marked by symbol and color so that the creature would always be identified. Jessica swam upward, behind the head, patting the thickly corded neck and talking quietly and steadily to the beast. It half turned its head, watching her, until it felt her body pressure against its neck. Then the great head turned forward, as if the animal were waiting. Jessica grasped the collar and braced herself, and just before Arnom reached her she cried out to the eel and slapped its neck.

The water boiled. The eel moved so swiftly it seemed that froth exploded outward along its great flanks, and in an instant it had shot ahead under the bidding of the young girl. Arnom shouted after her, but Jessica's laughter was fading swiftly as the green-skinned youth was left behind. He gave up the chase, drifting idly, waiting, and soon they saw the disturbance in the water as the eel came speeding back, Jessica's legs straddling the powerful neck, guiding the monster with easy pressure. Her hair streamed out behind her in the water, and she rode the animal with the practiced ease one might expect from a girl on a horse.

The eel came to an almost abrupt stop in response to another imperceptible signal from Jessica, and she eased down from the neck, swimming to the side of the head, stroking the nose of the animal. The jaws yawned wide, and Miko and Manning shuddered again at the sight of those savage teeth no more than inches from the girl.

Even Arnom was impressed, and they saw him shaking his head as he swam to her side. The boy and girl talked easily with one another, and Jessica pointed at something and began swimming, Arnom by her side. The eel followed without bidding, an incredible "guard dog," that had remained within sight of Jessica ever since their first encounter.

Miko sighed. "She's uncanny. I still can't get over how natural Jessie seems down here." She glanced at Manning. "She's the best thing that could have happened. Her adaptability to the sea, her affinity with those animals—they seem to *know* she's a friend—it's all worked so well in our favor. Jerry, do you think they'll go through with the surgery for her?"

Manning, enjoying Miko's comments as she ran on enthusiastically, nodded slowly. "I believe so. The bionic unit is really a test. Not of the equipment, but of us."

"If they can transform her breathing system to be the same as theirs—" Miko let it hang. She knew Manning was fully aware of the implications of the Ikian surgery. They would be able to render Jessica almost capable of living within the sea, of breathing air without the need for any artificial device. And if that happened, there would be a link between the two races that would bind them more tightly than any government agreements could ever hope to do.

"Somehow," Manning said slowly, "I get the feeling that our little girl has finally come home. Or that she's finally found what she would consider to be home."

Miko laughed with delight. "Jerry, there are times when you absolutely amaze me. Do you realize what you just said? 'Our little girl . . .' You sound like a father!"

She regretted her words instantly. Manning stared straight ahead, his expression frozen.

"Once—a long time ago. Her name was Dawn. Where they lived, she—Dawn and her mother. It was a direct hit."

Agony lined Miko's face. She reached out to caress his face. "Jerry, I didn't know. I'm—so very sorry."

His arm slipped about her shoulders and he drew her closer. He held her tightly, still looking through the glassite into the sea. "It's all right, Miko. Sometimes it catches me by surprise. The past has a way of hiding from you and then catching you smack in the mouth."

He pointed ahead of them. "What counts now is out there. You know what Jessie is? Tomorrow—and the time after that. She's hope and life, for all of us."

"Do you think she and Arnom will, uh, I mean, they might—"

"Mate?" He nodded. "Yes, I believe so. The boy is crazy about her."

A frown crossed Miko's face. "We might be going too fast. I know that Hydrea is extremely upset over their relationship."

Manning shook his head. "Hydrea doesn't like *any* of us. If he had his way he'd ship the boat and all of us away from the valley and make sure we never returned. Yet the old man, tough as he is, speaks with honest feelings, and we've got to tread pretty easy there." He led her to a wide couch and they sat together, the sea still visible through the glassite. "I've already spoken to Gella about all this. Since he's the man who leads their Council of Elders, his word carries the greatest weight. Even Hydrea, according to their system of rule, must go along with what Gella decides. Only a unanimous vote against Gella by the entire council would be considered tantamount to overruling him, and I understand that's never happened. They understand, as we do, that we both come from the same genetic stock."

He paused, thinking before he spoke again. "You know, one of the best things that's happened is that they consider themselves fortunate that we, instead of the Chinese or the Russians, made this contact. They were able to make some pretty good judgments on how different nationalities might react down here, and they knew contact was inevitable. We didn't exactly come up roses—"

"But we're the least of the evils?" Miko broke in.

"According to Hydrea," Manning said with a grimace, "even the least is too much. But there's more to it than that. Gella and most of the council know they're in much the same predicament as we are on the earth's surface, even if the causes aren't the same. There's that old rule of nature that one must grow, must continue to evolve and develop, or the only place to go is backwards. These people fear they've reached that point. I don't think they question that their importance to us is matched by ours to them."

"And we haven't helped before now, have we?" Manning looked at her. "We?"

"Oh, I don't mean us directly. Personally, that is. Or even any one nation. I'm talking about the entire race. Our wars, the radioactivity we've poured into the sea. The pollution, the destruction of one species after another."

He had a sour look. "On that subject, Miko, I usually take a stand opposite yours, but right now I can't. I have to agree. I was talking with Gella a while ago. Hydrea was there also, and they were sort of being evasive about some danger they face down here. A recent mutation of some natural enemy they've had as long as anyone can remember."

"Mutation? The way you say that," Miko observed, "it spells trouble."

"You'd better believe it. It all started with radioactive wastes," Manning explained. "Whatever this devilish thing is, and it's a primitive but tremendously adaptive form of life, the Ikians have always been able to handle it. Like wolves circling the fort. Only now the mutative form is far more dangerous, and—"

"And the wolves—these sea things—are getting through the dome?"

"That's the gist of it," Manning confirmed. "It's more dangerous than it ever was, and it seems to be mutating with tremendous speed."

She thought for a while, then spoke. "Hydrea. It's got to move around him. He blames it on us, doesn't he?"

"On the men from the surface," Manning noted. "The evil ones. Only he's got good enough reason from his point of view because it's all true, damn it. I would add that—"

A bell chimed and a light flashed on.

"That should be Matthews and Castillo in the pressure room," Manning said. "Let's go."

They went back through a long corridor and entered a room where there was a fireman's pole with sliding squeezegrips and footpads. It was a neat and efficient way of getting to the lower deck in a hurry, and Miko and Manning emerged into a large chamber where a strange echo effect carried back and forth between the bulkheads, the deck, and the overhead. Glass and metal sweated from the high humidity the cooling system was never really able to carry away. As they came into the chamber, Manning glanced at the pressure gauge: 220 psi. They stopped for a moment to clear their ears, then went to a circular opening in the bottom of the chamber. Sudden movement held their attention, and Matthews appeared on the ladder leading upward into the chamber, water streaming from his body. As soon as he cleared the ladder, Castillo came up right behind him.

Both men wore flippers on their feet and brightly colored wet suits. They wore bionic backpacks, although these were far less sophisticated than the implant carried within the body of Jessica. Their packs were compact, flattened and curved to their bodies, with thin flexmetal cabling running to and from their bubble-shaped helmets. The glassite helmets, with self-adapting crystal layers for changing exterior light conditions, were fully equipped with radio mikes and headsets, and they screwed on and off in the same manner as astronaut helmets.

Manning eased Matthews's helmet off, and the scarred face looked up at him with a lopsided grin. "I must be getting old. Or maybe I've got hardening of the ears." He tapped his skull. "This sort of pressure change unhinges me." He jerked a thumb at Castillo. "And as for young nibs over there, all he talks about day and night is getting the same stuff in his belly as Jessica."

Castillo had his helmet off, and he nodded vigorously. "He's right. I hate wearing this stupid helmet."

"You won't have to much longer," Miko told him. "The Ikians are convinced the implant works so well with Jessie that any of us can have the operation done."

Castillo brightened. "You mean it? I can really go to direct water breathing?"

"Whenever you're ready."

"Hey, that'll be great!"

Manning was on to another subject. "What did you find?" he asked Matthews.

Matthews by way of answer gestured to the chamber door behind him. "You want to wait with me through decompression?"

"Sure."

"Is it all right if I go back out?" Castillo asked. "Jessie said she and Arnom would take me to one of the volcanic areas. I want to get a good look at the upwelling there."

"It's all yours," Manning told him.

Miko screwed on his helmet, checked his gauges,

gave him a fast equipment check. She tapped him on the shoulder and nodded. Castillo grinned, stepped off into the open space, and disappeared in a spray of bubbles.

They went into another chamber, sealed the hatch, and made themselves comfortable while Matthews slowly came down from the higher pressure he'd worked under for the past several hours. A motion caught Manning's eye; he looked up to see a small TV scanner swiveling in his direction. At the same moment the wall speaker crackled.

"Captain, Sparco here in the bridge. Do you want a recording of the briefing?"

Manning enjoyed the comment. His crew were staying razor-sharp all the time down here, always anticipating. And Sparco was right; best to record Matthews's comments and have them for later reference if his memory sagged. "Good idea," Manning said, his voice picked up by mikes in the chamber. "When we're finished, pass it on through comsat."

Manning saw Sparco nod on the small bulkhead screen. "Yes, sir."

Miko had gone to a small equipment console, and she brought a cup of steaming broth for Matthews.

"Ah, thanks, lassie." He sipped slowly, nodded to Manning, and began to talk. "Well, there's no doubt I can speak their language." He noticed Manning's raised brows. "Oh, I don't mean stumble through it, like I've been doing for a while. I'm getting down to subtleties. It's as though I've gone through a final wall. That Templeton may be an ass sometimes, but he bloody well knows his linguistics. And how he ever knew my family, despite my name," he added dryly, "was full-blooded Cherokee, and that I could still speak the tongue, rusty as I am, is beyond me."

Manning nodded. "It's in the computer."

"So. I forget sometimes I'm on record down to my navel."

Manning ignored the side talk. "What happened out there?"

Matthews took a deep breath. "Well. Templeton has been wanting me to speak fully in their language, as you know. The idioms and nuances and the rest of it. Literal translations can be dangerous. They don't speak Cherokee any more than I speak Ikian—or we didn't before, anyway—yet the similarities, once you're into it, become all the more remarkable. It helps that we both speak English. I still can't get over how fluent they are in that language."

"Matt, they've been practicing for ten years."

"I know, I know. But without someone who grew up with the tongue, not even practice would do the trick. Today I found how and why they're so good at it."

Manning gave him a sour look. "Never mind the buildup. Get with it."

Matthews was almost smirking. "There's always a key, a Rosetta stone of some kind. That's just for deciphering or translating. We know they've had books and pictures and the like from the ships and planes that sank to the bottom. But about ten or eleven years ago one of those ships was still pressure-sealed inside. Ellev told me—"

"Ellev?" Miko said.

Matthews turned to Miko. "She's one of their historians. Heavy in language. Smart as hell, also. Anyway, the power systems of this sunken ship were still working, and they'd learned enough from earlier wrecks to have figured out how to use the power. They brought the equipment into one of their air caverns, and in the stuff were tape recorders and film cassettes. Loads of them, apparently, and they got the stuff to work."

Manning nodded slowly. "So they could actually listen to us."

"More than that," Matthews said. "They could watch and listen at the same time. Mannerisms of speech, dress, walking, talking, all sorts of stuff. A hell of a lot more than speech. They worked out how we handled electricity, what we did with it. At first they used only the long-life battery packs. Then they learned how to work generators and recharge the things, so they could run the films over and over again."

"It all figures in," Miko observed. "They've had *the* Rosetta stone."

"Matt, let me ask you something," Manning said abruptly. "Aside from all the technicalities, what do these people think of us? Deep inside, gut feelings."

"Well—you know it's not all roses."

"The war history again?"

"Not again, skipper. Always."

"It sounds like the old sins-of-the-father bit."

Matthews snorted with disdain. "I can't buy that," he said sharply, "and I'm not trying to defend either the Ikians or us. But I can see things more clearly from their side now, and when you cut it to the bone, captain, it comes out that if you were them and you knew about us and the things we've done wouldn't you be suspicious that the entire race was afflicted with a sort of madness?"

"It makes for a strong argument," Miko yielded.

"Is that what they really think of us?" Manning insisted.

"Not all of them," Matthews came back. "Gella is an understanding soul. Hydrea, for his part, believes implicitly in their ancient scriptures, which warn against manlike creatures from the surface. The point is he *believes*. Another thing to consider, and it's almost theological, is that symbiotic relationships with nature to these people are their *way of life*, deriving from their history, right up to this instant, and involving their foreseeable future. Skipper, if it came to a vote, Gella and his people would prevail—but Hydrea isn't alone in his thinking."

Manning thought over what he'd heard. "What if Hydrea were in control?"

Matthews laughed, but there was no humor in the sound. "We would be told flatly we were not welcome here, and we would be asked to leave—pronto."

"Do they believe we would?"

"That's the rub. Not even Gella would want to put it to the test. If they judge by our history and our antics on the surface, they doubt it."

Miko shuddered. "In other words, they suspect we'd take the role of a dominant power."

"That's right," Matthews said. "It's a current that underlies everything about us, and they can't ignore it. Now, don't let me mislead you. I'm making judgments in a good part of what I've said to you because you asked me to do just that. In some areas I might be wrong. Gella and most of the people with him are honest, warm, and friendly, and they want nothing more than to have an open relationship with us. But the pot's stirring, no matter what."

"One more thing, Matt," Manning hesitated, "do you recommend anything on our part?"

Matthews held his gaze. "Honesty. Scrupulous honesty. They recognize that we've been that so far."

Matthews grunted. "You just said the magic words. 'So far.' See what I mean? That's Hydrea's argument. The first shoe to drop is our history. He claims the second one is only a matter of time."

He stood up, nodding with satisfaction at the pressure gauge readings. "I'm ready now. Need to get to my quarters. Got personal things to do." He rubbed his stubbled chin and grinned his crooked grin at them. "Never thought I'd see the day when I'd be shaving for dinner eight miles beneath the ocean."

Manning was surprised. "Dinner? You? Shaving?"

"Consider it my present to you two. We've been invited to share the sumptuous goodies of the deeps. With Gella, no less." Matthews showed a look of pride. "It's the first time, skipper. And apparently Gella is going to have a whole bunch of his top people there tonight."

"But—but where, Matt?" Miko asked.

"It's an air cavern, lassie, the likes of which you won't believe until you see it. I'd rather not tell either of you more than that. I don't want to spoil your fun."

"When, you idiot?" Manning growled at him. "What time?"

Matthews looked at a timer across the room. "By that dingus on the bulkhead, two hours from now."

He started for the hatch, stopped, and turned, a questioning frown on his face. "Miko, tell me something. It never occurred to me until this minute. These people, they've never seen sun or moon or stars; the earth's rotation can't mean a thing to them; and the tidal effects this far down are meaningless—how the devil did they ever establish a system for keeping time?"

Miko's smile was almost radiant. "The power of the woman, Matt," she answered.

He stared at her.

"When you're in darkness, Matt, there's only one thing to count on, no matter what else. It's eternal."

"Miko, what the hell are you talking about?"

Matthews and Manning were confused, and they showed it.

She looked steadily at both men. "This entire world, down here, runs on the reality of the female. They first told time, and they still do, by the menstrual cycle." She paused to relish the moment. "That's why the Ikian calendar has thirteen months in every year made up of our twelve months. Incredible, isn't it? Thirteen months in a year of 364 days—almost *exactly* like ours."

19

~~~~~~~~~~

They swam slowly through water that rippled with light from either side as the living globes moved ahead of and alongside them. The Great Valley was aglow. Soft radiance and distant points of sharp, hard light came to them shimmering and beautiful. Swimming with little effort, their flippers making the journey a pleasure, they had time to enjoy the moment. Matthews led the way; then came Manning, Miko by his side, followed by Dr. Simmonds and Syd Prentiss. Alongside Matthews was an Ikian they did not recognize who clearly had become a friend of Matthews. Several more Ikians followed at a distance, and there were still more far off to one side acting as their escort.

Their sense of wonder, long since overwhelmed in this incredible undersea world, was again brought to its fullest. They moved along an area they had not seen before, about five hundred feet above the floor of the valley. Their movement was surface humans: to be able to float; to levitate in itself a realization of a deep-rooted dream of all without effort high above the ground; to fly by no more power than the will to do so and the slightest effort of one's limbs. In their own atmospheric world, floating at this height without hard support would have brought instant fear to them. But there was no falling here, no sense of everything dropping away beneath them. They were birds in the slowest of motion, and, unlike any feathered creature with wings, they were not in need of movement through air, or rising thermals, to support them. Every move was sheer enjoyment for its own sake. By comparison, scuba diving was sorely limited, for now they were within a world of warmly beckoning living light rather than of increasing gloom and unseen predators.

Far and away to their left stretched cultivated fields, between which ran row after row of bioluminescent radiation that contained a miraculous ultraviolet effect from living creatures. What could not be obtained from the sun directly, nature provided through an elaborate chain in the form of life specially adapted to this world of the deeps.

Nothing remained constant, and, for the visitors, this took some psychological adaptation. In the surface ocean of air, clouds moved through the sky, but mountains and forests remained still, and birds were only fleeting specks and animals chained by gravity to the hard surface. Not in the Great Valley, where swaying and movement was a part of every moment. Schools of fish beyond counting were brought together like vast glittering sheets or drapes hundreds of feet high, moving purposefully, beyond doubt herded by the Ikians and the great eels. The manner of control—whether color or sound or movement—remained on the visitors' list of unknowns still to be spelled out. Tonight, at this dinner—more ceremonial than any other step they had yet taken—the real walls might start coming down.

They swam perhaps thirty or forty minutes, flowing over the great farmlands—strange areas of chaotic surface they recognized as volcanic in origin. Deep, glowing light came into view, and through the rippling water they could tell, even without detail, that this was an area where some sort of industrial process was under way. Long tubular structures and domes against the bottom made that evident and posed questions that would be answered only when the proper time had come.

The guide with Matthews signaled for them to start their descent. They went down slowly at a long slanting angle, until the sight before them captured their attention. The first high hills rose before them; their guide led them past the flanks of a steeply rising formation and took them around its side.

A great cliff loomed from the valley surface, and it was evident that the Ikians had chiseled and grooved a solid rock formation into a structure of beautiful design and function. There were terraces and platforms and balconies; most of the surfaces were covered with a rich but carefully tended flowing of flowers and strange plants, the entire structure seemingly alive as the growth wafted back and forth in the gentle currents.

They followed their guide downward to a great curving arch of shining stone, its surface glowing. By now they knew that tiny versions of the living light globes must be used for this purpose—"welded" together as would be a coral reef, alive, casting a glow that seemed part of the structure itself. The effect was breathtaking. As they came close to the arch, more detail became evident, and they saw that it had been fashioned with much the same exquisite artistry as adorned the ramparts and statuary of ancient Greece and Rome. The bas-relief features were startling in their clarity, depicting sea animals familiar and unknown to the surface people.

They swam slowly through the archway into a wide tunnel that formed a continuing arch. The walls around them glowed in bands and patterns, and now they saw that the light came from within the stone; that the stone had been shaved almost to a transparent thinness; and that the luminescent animals were amassed behind the stone so that their light would glow through. It was an effect to shame the heart of an artist who worked with oil and canvas.

Manning appreciated the beauty of what lay about him on every side, yet somehow he also expected to find something crafted for harsh utility rather than sheer aesthetic effect—and coming around a bend in the tunnel, he saw what he knew, sooner or later, must exist in this underworld paradise.

At the top of the chambered tunnel, most of it concealed, was a massive gate. It was obviously to be lowered into the tunnel proper, to seal the tunnel off completely in order to separate what lay inside from the valley itself. There was time for only that fleeting glimpse, and they swam on.

The lights above them began to grow in intensity, and the tunnel floor sloped sharply upward, widening as it did so. Now the surface beneath them appeared in the form of steps, and they saw that the water surface was only scant feet above their heads. The Ikian guide turned to Matthews, gestured for him and the others to follow, and then they saw only his legs moving upward along the steps. One by one they followed, to emerge in a high-domed chamber that seemed made of glowing marble and a material strongly resembling mother-of-pearl, but of shifting colors and degrees of translucence.

Several Ikians awaited their arrival and helped them remove their underwater breathing gear, their helmets, and their flippers, placing the equipment on shelves cut into the stone walls. No more than a minute had gone by when another Ikian entered the domed chamber, and they turned to greet the leader of the valley, Gella.

They had never seen the Ikian leader in what

they knew at once was ceremonial dress. His woven garment, of a material still unknown to them, reflected light with subtle and shifting tones, as if it were alive. It hung from Gella's strongly supple frame by crossed straps, and it had a loose belt they could only liken to velvet. The top garment hung several inches below his waist, and his trousers—strangely resembling clam-diggers—were skintight, of the same material, but fitted with pockets and loops for holding objects. Crisscrossing straps about his feet and ankles, up to the calf, were obviously for style rather than need.

There was no way to tell how an Ikian—man, woman, or child—would dress, and they would as often be found naked in the sea as wearing clothes. The Ikians' physiological makeup seemed to attend to their needs of temperature control, so that whatever garments they wore served functional poses or, at this moment, were ceremonial in nature. In a world where symbiosis with nature was a way of life, false modesty had not yet gained entrance. The Americans understood these things, fortunately: A missionary attitude would have insulted and angered these sea people. The proclivity of the Ikians to appear unclothed had actually proven a blessing in disguise, permitting immediate visual observations as well as hidden-camera recordings that told the visitors even more of the sea people than would have been otherwise attainable without subjecting these people to detailed physiological examination. That point had not yet been reached, and Manning had judged, with the agreement of the others, that when it happened it would be with an equal exchange—a male and female from each race—so that there would be no bent dignity as to subjecting either side to guinea-pig status.

Direct observation had established by now that the Ikian skin was impervious to the effects of salinity that would have irritated and begun to destroy human (surface human, that is) skin tissue. Whether this defense system was a gland secretion or an epidermis structure was yet to be determined; all they knew, really, was that salt water had no untoward effects on the Ikians. The sea people grew their hair—and it was, at least visually, strikingly similar to the surface people's own hair—to whatever length seemed to please them, and they adopted whatever hairstyles met the immediate moment. Again, the exception was one of utility rather than fashion. Long hair when working in the open water could be a disadvantage in eddies or swirling currents, and it was often tied or pig-tailed or bobbed.

Other adaptations were more fascinating, in both the personal and medical sense. No Ikian had ever been seen circumcised; and it would have appeared foolhardy under their environment to deliberately expose the glan penis to saline elements when the foreskin provided such excellent protection. Similarly, when an Ikian woman entered the water, her nipples, no matter what the size of her breasts, withdrew by some autonomic function, so that in effect the skin of the breast that closed over the nipple served the same function as the male foreskin.

Thus, the attire of Gella and the accompanying Ikians at this moment of ceremony told them much, as well as pleasing the eye. People who place great store in such moments and prepare carefully for them invariably do so as a sign of respect and welcome; it was a form of language that told even more than words.

Gella walked across the room, slow but proud, supple and smooth, his movement similar to the liquid grace of a big cat. He smiled broadly as he stood before Manning, and he placed both hands on Manning's shoulders.

"It is good to welcome you, Manning Captain. As you would say in your language, you do us all proud to accept our invitation."

Gella turned to the others, and by now they had come to know him well enough to recognize a touch of friendly tongue in cheek.

"It is—I try to remember from your inscribed words—warm for us to have you with us."

Matthews moved forward from where he had been standing and looked directly at the Ikian leader. *"Gratoom; naya harn chibra. Loo sengri; ahn mayanet son?"*

Gella threw back his head and laughed heartily. He turned to Matthews, clapped him heartily on the shoulder, then looked back to Manning and the others.

"He asks," Gella said with what could only have been a twinkle in his eye, "if I speak your tongue better than he speaks ours. The answer must be yes. He does very well, but we have spoken your language for more than—than ten?"

Matthews nodded, encouraging him to go on.

"Ah. Than ten of your years," Gella said, "and you will not then mind my mistakes. Please, all of you. Come with me."

He led them from the chamber along another curving tunnel that opened into a beautifully decorated high-vaulted room that was filled with glowing creatures in tanks along the walls. The walls glowed as well, as had the tunnels they moved through, but the fishlike creatures were stunningly beautiful in their unpredictable color and light-intensity changes. In the center of the room there was a wide oval table of a pale beige color, around which were placed sculpted seats that accepted their bodies with an incredible sense of *right*. The Americans were directed to seats on one side of the table, the Ikians took the other side. At one end of the table, two seats were vacant. The guests had a moment to look around. For the first time they saw what appeared to be drapes, but it was impossible to tell if these were fabricated or of some living substance; the material glowed softly, strange living-color gossamer veils along one wall.

Miko's eyes opened wide and she started to lift out of her seat.

Matthews gestured immediately for her to remain where she was. "Don't be alarmed if the seat seems to move beneath you, lassie. It's perfectly all right," he explained for her as well as for the rest of his group. "The seat is alive. I mean it; it's a living seat. Some sort of genetically controlled sponge, I would imagine. It senses the heat and pressure points of the body, and it adjusts to the most comfortable contours. Just relax; the seat will take care of you."

He made a show of snuggling downward. "We could take these home and make a bloody fortune with them. Think of it, now. A chair that's alive and loves you."

They laughed, and it was the beginning of the sense of heavy formality fading away. For several minutes they engaged in conversation, enjoying the informality of not having to be careful of the intricacies of opposite languages. Then, at a hand signal from Gella, several Ikians entered the chamber, placing servings of unfamiliar food on the table. And with a shift in mood, ceremonious to its extreme, young women placed two goblets before each person seated at the table, the five Americans and the four Ikians.

Gella sat straight in his seat, his mood changing, his attempts to commit no language errors painfully clear. "I am Gella," he said slowly and carefully, "and my people, whom you know as the Ikians, have chosen me as their—"

He came to a sudden halt and turned to Matthews. "I must ask from you the help, my friend. I try but I am not sure."

Gella turned to the others. "He knows our words and he can place words in our thoughts." He nodded to Matthews.

"The people of the Great Valley," Matthews said with the same serious demeanor he had seen in Gella, "which we would call by its closest name in our language, Amphibus, are governed—and that's as close as I can come to the intent of the word in English—by their Council of Elders. Gella speaks for the council, although they all have the same—again be careful that I might be in error with some of the nuances—the same authority. For our purposes, because they have placed him in this position, he *does* speak for the others. But as a representative who expresses their thoughts and feelings."

Matthews paused to sift through his own thoughts, then continued. "Like us, they also have differences among them. Yet, on this subject and at this moment, he wishes us to understand there is complete agreement. So, now, if we may spend a few moments of your time, we have made special arrangements."

He glanced at Gella, and the Ikian nodded. "Time is good," Gella said quietly.

"I agree," Matthews answered.

Gella motioned to the woman at his side. This was their first occasion to meet—or even to understand who she was—Gella's life-companion, or mate. Luna was striking, sensual in a startling way, her green hues subtly different from the men. She wore a gleaming slim headband about her forehead and a necklace pendant hung between full breasts. Her garment was almost iridescent: a banded body-contour covering of shells and mother-of-pearl with the suppleness of the softest satin. Her every movement was a glide, without a trace of abruptness. She rose to her feet, presented a dazzling, warm smile, and without a word left the chamber. They remained in silence until she returned, holding a bottle in one hand and a strange flask in the other. She placed these on the table before Gella and resumed her seat, still without speaking.

"Gella and I planned this together," Matthews told the group. "It seems appropriate enough. I had sent over a bottle of our finest wine and Gella personally selected the contents of that flask to match our offering. It's an Ikian wine. Rather remarkable, when you think of it. The grape of the sun and the grape of the sea."

Gella handed the flask to Miko and the wine bottle to Luna. At his gesture they poured into the goblets. Gella reached for his and held it aloft.

"Matthews has told me how to do this. It is a good ceremony. Two races of men, now, join."

They sipped of the green wine.

"It's—marvelous," Prentiss said slowly.

"That it is," Matthews said with more heartiness. "And who would ever believe this is fermented sea cucumber? Now for ours, please."

They exchanged goblets, held up the red wine. Matthews nodded to Jerry Manning; there was no need for any words between them.

Manning extended his goblet to Gella. "To our people, and yours, Gella, who have waited the long history of mankind for this moment."

They drank and returned the glasses to the table. Gella raised his right arm. "Manning Captain. Before we—"

"Break bread together," Matthews said.

"Ah, thank you," Gella responded. "Before we do this, we have a sharing moment. It is most important, and we do not wish to offend. It is much easier to understand big things, and the heart is very—," he paused and concentrated, then added, "fragile."

He took a deep breath. "Matthews has explained to me your custom of marriage, of words like *mate,* or *husband and wife.* Our word, most like yours, he has told me, would be *companion-for-life.* Like myself and Luna. In our world, our young people need never ask of any man to become such a companion. Such a thing has happened now, but it is both old and it is new. For a first time. Because our races come only now to each other, it is needed that we join our minds on this matter."

He was struggling, and he turned to Matthews once again for assistance.

"I've explained to Gella," Matthews said, "what we would mean by legal age, but it's an alien concept to them, and—"

Miko could no longer restrain herself. Her eyes were bright as she broke in, "It's Jessica—you're talking about Jessie!"

Matthews smiled and nodded. "Yes, that I am."

"But—where is she, and what, I mean—"

They laughed at her confused and excited outburst. Matthews motioned for her to wait. "Just a few minutes longer, Miko."

Matthews nodded; Gella in turn gestured to an attendant who left the chamber, returning immediately, followed by Jessica and Arnom.

There were no further questions nor a need for them. The manner in which the two held hands, the touch of shyness, their expressions—all spoke an age-old story. Around the neck of each youth hung a slim wire necklace, and from each was suspended a glorious glowing blue jewel. Jessica, wearing garments similar to those of Luna, smiled timidly at her friends at the table.

Manning broke the awkward silence. "Jessie—"

"Yes, sir?" Her voice was barely audible, and they saw her hand clench tightly around that of Arnom.

"I suppose," Manning said slowly, "I should make a speech or something like that, but I don't need to ask you what this is all about; besides, I believe I'm too happy for you to express it in words."

Jessica stood just a bit closer to Arnom. A tear glistened on one cheek.

"Thank you," she whispered. "Thank you so very, very much. For the first time in my life I feel—at home."

Manning reached for the goblet of Ikian wine. "Then we toast your joy and happiness with Arnom, Jessie."

They raised their goblets.

The joining had begun.

20

~~~~~~~~~~~

The young couple slipped into a world of their own, most of it Ikian, with a subdued element of the newcomer adapting to conditions that might have been found on another planet. Were Venus a watery world rather than a hellish desert—to the eternal woe of fantasy writers—the happiness and love of Jessica and Arnom would be perfect grist for an interplanetary mill.

Yet, adaptation is a matter of attitude, and Jessica's words to the assembly of her own people and the Ikians had expressed it perfectly: "For the first time in my life I feel— at home."

And home was something that did not come in a manner familiar to Jessica. To her great pleasure, Arnom made the selection of their living place a matter of mutual choice, and Jessica immediately opted for a private or individual structure rather than one of the cliff apartments she had come to know. She felt much like one of the pioneer women when the western lands of America were being settled.

About two miles, as she could judge the distance, from the main structures of the Ikians, were a series of small rolling hills, rounded knobs and upthrustings covered with luxuriant vegetation. Here

many of the young couples of the valley had chosen
to live, and she and Arnom decided to do the same.
It would afford them privacy in a small but ade-
quate dwelling, and they would also be among others
of their own age.

The house was astonishing to her, and she found
hidden pleasures at every turn. Their furniture
would be simplicity itself; their seats and chairs,
low-slung couches, and their bed would be formed
from the same genetically controlled sponge material that Matthews had described so well as the
"chair that's alive and loves you." Arnom's friends
worked with them, and Jessie was able to select
colors—to her surprise and further delight—to suit
her ideas for decoration. It was a house without
windows as she knew them, for the lower half of
the dwelling would remain always in water, and the
upper half would remain under the high air pressure that would keep the upstairs section snug and
dry and water tight. The bottom section of the
dwelling, which was in the form of a great rounded
pumpkin, was their liquid entrance and their storage area, and the upper—or air half—was where
they would live. The situation also solved the problem of Jessica's need to change her bionic breathing
apparatus in plenty of time to avoid overextend-
ing the useful lifetime of the system.

Upstairs was composed of their bedroom; a room
used as a sitting room or a parlor or a den; their
dining room, where food was also prepared (with
supplies "downstairs" in the liquid part of the structure); and their bathroom. The bathroom was another revelation in ecosystem living. The Ikians
did not dump their wastes into the very environment that made up their world, yet individual
homes lacked the sewage and plumbing systems so
familiar to Jessica on the surface.

Symbiosis was the answer, of course. So advanced
was Ikian life that every structure had an enclosed

system of bacterial control that attacked waste products and, within hours, reduced such material to full purity levels. It was swift, efficient, and a full-circle system, and it had definite possibilities for application in the surface world, where energy and water-supply systems had suffered grievously and were in critical demand.

There was no electricity in the little house, and this was perhaps the single most radical departure for Jessica from the world she had known. Yet the rooms were filled with light—walls that glowed as well as pools of light in globes within their water level and in their air home as well. Living light, of course, such as she had found elsewhere. She toyed with the idea of bringing in electricity—a simple matter for the submarine crew to accomplish—but she decided against such a move, for it would sharply violate her acceptance of her new world. The Ikians produced light of all intensities and colors and moods, and to abuse this natural gift with what she came to look upon as harsh (albeit necessary) mechanical light, she would not do.

There were personal touches, of course. She had an overwhelming urge to be able to look out from the upper level of their dome quarters, and for this purpose the *Sea Trench* crew produced several portholes that were encased by the living coral structure of the house. There were other "upper world" touches. Jessica wanted and needed to read, and shelves were sculpted for books and personal items.

Cooking Ikian-style demanded sharp departure from her past life. Much of their food was available in quantity from the vast agricultural lands of the valley, as well as from what grew wild, and there was no shortage of fish or lobster—or creatures that looked and tasted like lobster, anyway—in the valley. Without electricity or fire, she wondered—but Arnom had those answers before she could voice the questions. He showed her containers into which different chemicals were placed. One simply closed the container, and within a few minutes' time (or faster, depending on the chemical concentration) the container was as hot as a fiery stove; it could also be kept to a medium temperature for slow simmering. Although the technology was totally different, the intents and means were similar. After all, man's wants and needs may change in style but rarely in substance.

Metal containers were unknown, as was metallurgy, but the Ikians were deft and skilled masters in ceramics and a porcelainlike material. Their own technology had produced, along with controlled heat (without fire, they had heat even in water), a remarkable artistry and science in ceramics, and there was scarcely an artifact in the valley for which Jessica did not have some identifying comparison in her "old" world.

People—green hued or otherwise—desire pleasure and escape, and life beneath the sea showed differences only in content and style. One surface habit was entirely absent here; no Ikian ever smoked an object, tobacco or otherwise, and the reasons were many. Yet the Ikians did have substances that provided a feeling of intoxication and a sense of well-being. They had fermented plants to produce various types of wines, and they had other brews more wicked to the senses. They bowed to the sensory demands of taste by producing a wide variety of spices. As in the surface world, there was no end to their ingenuity and diversity of lifestyle.

Young women came and spirited Jessica away from Arnom to arrange her new clothes and small articles dear to a girl's heart. There was so much to learn! How to attend to garments that were woven of sea fibers or treated to glistening maillike material, adjusting them to individual taste and size. They sewed here as they did on the surface, and they ran looms as well, not with electrical power but with astonishing animal-mechanical systems where trained fish and other strange creatures turned wheels that operated looms, weavers, and other devices.

Life is not all swimming, or homemaking, or tending the farms and creatures. Arnom was young and bright, and just as a new world opened to Jessica so Arnom was selected by the Council of Elders to be one of those who would learn the ways of the power and machinery and science and technology of the surface world, to determine how it might be adapted for the Ikians. In this he had the extraordinary help of Jessica, of course, for whenever he did not fully comprehend something in his work with the crew of *Sea Trench,* he obtained assistance from his mate in their home. Just as Jessica became a link between the two races, so did Arnom, and the advantages of the situation were not missed by either race.

Yet even science palled; and Arnom's curiosity, whetted by countless questions from his friends, prompted search and discovery in other areas. Card playing brought astonishment to him, for he had never thought of the surface-worlders in terms of play, and yet—he could hardly wait to show Jessica the slim cards made of a flat pearly material with which the Ikians played their games of numbers and colors in their own fierce competitions.

Culture matures in every race. Where the Ikians knew nothing of photography, they were masters in ceramics and sculpture. The crew of *Sea Trench* sought eagerly the figures they would take with them (to remain restricted, known about only by a select group, for years to come) and promised to exchange with statuary, paintings, and other objects to be carried down beneath the sea.

And so it went, a meeting, a blending, a learning. Through these two bright, lovely beings, the two races began to fuse their history into a single path into the future.

But it could not be done without solving certain problems, thus far alien to the people who lived beneath the sea.

High above the land, the night sky grew angry. Above the low-hanging clouds a squall line had moved into the area, and the rain increased steadily in intensity. The hammering downfall began to hiss as it sliced the air. Abruptly the night flashed with the violence of lightning spearing darkness. Navy Secretary Timothy Haig and his aide, Captain Arnold Switek, stood motionless for the moment. The harsh lightning was gone by the time the booming thunder cracked over them.

The two men stood on a water-soaked grass pathway; trees studded gentle slopes all about them. Dim lamps every hundred yards barely lighted the way, but they both knew this area well enough without the lights. Both men were also in civilian clothes, raincoats and hats providing some protection against the hissing downpour. Another flash of lightning held long enough for them to glance up to where the nearest hill revealed long rows of small white crosses. The men walked slowly, not speaking. Switek took a small flashlight from his pocket and held its beam on one of the white crosses. A small bronze plaque, glistening wet, reflected the light.

A memorial to Frank Cartwright.

Haig stared at the plaque and the raindrops reflecting the flashlight. "Frank's death was too much of a price to pay for this stinking job," he said to his aide.

Switek spoke to Haig, but Haig's eyes remained locked on the ground. "I can't buy that, admiral," he said slowly. "You knew you had to step into his shoes. We all knew he was going. And the way that man was holding up under his pain. He—"

Haig gestured suddenly, turning finally to face the other man. "I know, I know, Arnie," he said. "I'm just sorry the old man isn't here now. I don't like being the secretary of the navy. Not this way. I wanted Frank to know the miracles going on down there in the Aleutian—in the Ritter Trench." He paused for self-reflection, his craggy features revealed again by the lightning. "I'm glad Jerry did that. Ritter was a good man."

He turned and started along the walk. Switek switched off the light, walked by his side. Haig stopped, turned back for a last farewell to a departed friend. A long shudder wracked his body, then he continued walking. Rain poured against them and all the world around. They walked past the dim reflections of the lamps along the path. After a while Haig started to talk.

"Arnie, I think we've got to send Morgan down there."

Switek took the words carefully. "Into the trench?"

Haig nodded. "Yes. He can meet with Manning in the sub. We need to do it that way."

"Is it really that bad, sir?"

"You know, Jerry Manning had an expression he used a lot. When things didn't work out, no matter if they were trifling or if they were very bad, he would say everything's not coming up roses. Well, it's not, Arnie. It's worse than we thought."

"When did you find out, sir?"

"We received confirmation this afternoon." Haig stepped into a puddle, stopped, ignored the water in his shoes as he walked. "If we don't break up what the Chinese have all set," he went on, "they're going to have us with our necks right on the chopping block."

He stopped, looked Switek closely in the eyes. "Arnie, they could take out half the United States without firing a single missile."

Switek's expression showed mingled dismay and anger. "God*damn* it, sir, we could have stopped them. Why the hell didn't we—"

"Easy, easy, son," Haig broke in, holding up his hand. "We didn't stop them because it's a very old and familiar story. The Congress and the Senate are tighter than a frog's ass at fifty fathoms when you even mention military confrontation. By the time we were able to convince them of the true danger, it was too late. Oh, they've given us complete freedom *now*, but—the Chinese have the ships in place, right where they want them, and the guillotine is sharp, and it's ready."

Switek couldn't push away the bitterness welling up in him. "And a preemptory missile strike by us isn't in the cards, is it?"

"Arnie, I'm an old war dog, and I don't think I'd like to be responsible for starting that business again. We lost a billion souls the last time, and another billion are suffering from disease and radiation and famine and God knows what else. Would you want to push that button?"

"No. Of course not."

"And yet—" Switek saw his own bitterness reflected in the tormented eyes of Haig. "And yet," Haig continued, "the Chinese seem willing to test *us* all the way. So we've got to get down there, under the sea, on the ocean floor. But if we do—"

"We may trigger the bombs ourselves."

"That's right. And if we don't try to remove it, then we live with the blade over our heads every minute of the day and the night, while the Chinese start taking bigger and bigger risks because they'll always get away with the chances they just finished taking."

They started walking again, silent until Switek spoke. "What's the answer, Mr. Secretary?"

"Well, the president is backing me all the way," Haig answered, "and that's a big help. I want

Morgan out of here in no more than eight hours for a surface rendezvous with one of the smaller boats from *Trench*. He goes all the way down, he briefs Manning, and he turns the whole damned thing over to Jerry. It's in Manning's hands then."

Switek whistled softly. "That's a tough one."

Haig's voice had a touch of sharpness. "Got a better idea?"

Switek pushed aside the thrust. "Sir, I'll get started with Morgan right away."

Haig nodded. "Go ahead." He looked back along the path through the hissing rain. "I'll be along shortly."

Switek tried unsuccessfully to conceal his concern. Haig's reaction was mixed anger and gratitude. "Oh, get the hell out of here, Arnie, and leave an old man alone for a while with his ghosts."

"Yes, sir," Switek said, and Haig watched him walking away in the enclosing rainfall. He looked until Arnie was gone, and he wondered how it was possible for a man to put love for another man into words like yes, sir.

21

~~~~~~~~~

They had never imagined anything like this: a deep sculpted bowl, tiered from the top to a stage at the center of the bowl. It was an underwater auditorium where the audience could sit, recline, or float, linked to woven strands or hammocks to keep them from drifting away. The tiers were seats or cupolas or small grottoes from where the Ikians either looked down on, studied from eye level, or looked upward at the performers. Since the viewing possibilities were so varied, those who attended the nude swimming dances would come several times to see the same performance from severely changed points of view, depending on the level of the tier. Each performance was also enhanced and altered by moving globes of light.

The first time the Americans witnessed a performance they were almost mesmerized by the stunning grace of the Ikian dancers. It was literally a liquid ballet with a fluidity of expression the new audience could never have preconceived—and almost every man and woman aboard *Sea Trench* was an excellent if not a superb swimmer. The Ikians, of course, were bred to move within the sea, as well as genetically adapted to breathing effortlessly, and they gained additional control through

their webbed feet and hands. They emphasized
their movements with subtle flowing costumes,
some of which contained luminescent creatures that
were placed between layers of woven cloth, so that
the performers themselves were enveloped in deli-
cately shifting hues.

But of all he saw, it was what he heard that most
caught the attention and the imagination of Jerry
Manning. Until they were invited to this theatrical
performance, he had never consciously considered what kind of music—if any—might be part of
the Ikian culture. There had been so much to see
and do and learn, and they had made their moves
so carefully, that part of his thinking, at least in
terms of art, seemed to have been inhibited. But
what he finally heard was haunting, melodic, with
a unique—actually liquid—quality to it. It was
like nothing he had ever heard in his own world,
until Bill Ryan astonished him with a rejection of
that claim.

"It's not that different," Ryan told him. "If you
had ever listened to music, other than engine
sounds, you wouldn't be so surprised."

Manning shook his head. "Give me the link," he
said finally.

"Do you remember the name Mike Oldfield?"

Manning looked at him blankly.

"He goes back to the 1970s. He was a smash hit.
His first work—he often wrote and played his own
material—was a gut-ripper. A lot of people might
never have heard of it except that it was used as
the theme for a movie, and it lowered theater temperatures by at least ten degrees." He grinned at
Manning. "The picture was called *The Exorcist,* and
the music was *Tubular Bells.* When that thing
played you could feel demons coming out of the
woodwork."

"Demons? You're relating that to the Ikian music?"

Ryan laughed. "No. Later, Oldfield did another piece, I think it was his third, called *Ommadawn*. It's haunting, moody, fluid, and I'll tell you one thing—it'll reach the Ikians. It will flat get to them."

Manning thought about it. He looked suspiciously at Ryan. "You've got a pretty good music library with you?"

"The best. I do go beyond old-time minstrels, skipper."

Manning made a sour face. "You thinking of letting the Ikians hear that piece? It may be a pretty good idea. We haven't made that bridge to them yet, and our music might just be something to tumble down some walls we haven't touched yet."

To his surprise, Ryan shook his head. "Not yet. I have something better in mind. More power. A hell of a lot more power, in fact. I think I could rig up an underwater sound system in that auditorium —that bowl of theirs. But I'd like to set it up differently. I'd place the listeners in dead center and rig the speakers—I can adapt to underwater acoustics through the computer, by the way—so that they get a full-dimension effect. From all sides."

"I assume you have the music already selected?"

"Right down their alley, skipper. And from right down our alley, I might add."

"What is it?"

"Trust me. I want you to hear it yourself, *with* them. That way you'll react with them, you'll be more sensitive to what they feel or show. And I'm curious. Especially with what I have in mind."

Manning accepted the inevitable. "Any hints?"

"Would Hovhaness mean anything to you?"

"No."

"Then relax and wait to enjoy it."

With meticulous care, Bill Ryan ran insulated cables the entire distance from the submarine to the amphitheater. The speakers were something else again, modified to withstand the high pressure in the valley, resistant to salt water, the speaker fronts carefully altered so as not to produce sonic disturbance as the sound waves moved outward from the various speaker elements. He tinkered and tested for a week, studying oscilloscopes and other instruments that he suspended across the auditorium. And he prevailed on Gella to gather a select audience to assemble in the center of the auditorium so that the speakers would be directed precisely at them. With the Ikians sat Manning and Miko, who were aware that, whatever they heard, the Ikians would hear with greater clarity and depth, across a broader sonic spectrum.

Ryan was more than an enthusiastic buff with his sound systems; he was in his own way a brilliant innovator, and he adopted the Ikian idea of a presentation of lights, although now the lights were powered from the submarine and linked by computer to follow the mood of the music, running the full visible spectrum, with undulating effects because of the water.

When it was done and all was ready, Ryan stayed to one side and watched and listened and smiled.

In the early 1970s, Alan Hovhaness, in a burst of inspired genius, intertwined his own mastery of mood music of the sea—every facet from stormy surface to gliding depths—with recordings of the oceans' greatest creatures, the whales.

Alan Hovhaness called his stunning work *And God Created Great Whales* and turned it over to Kostelanetz to bring to life. What had been recorded those decades ago, frozen in sonic time by the miracle of electronics, now came to new life nearly ten miles beneath the ocean.

The reaction of the Ikians was almost pure shock —the music captured them; it was magical and hypnotic and overwhelming. For the first time, as a musical crescendo mixed with the cry of the great beasts of the depths, the visitors saw an Ikian weep with joy and love.

The doors opened wider.

Jerry Manning swam slowly, gently finning through the softly illuminated tunnel.

By Manning's side was Gella, and leading the group was another Ikian—Nema—a middle-aged woman who was beautiful in a way amazing for her age. Her lithesome grace made a mockery of the number of years she had lived.

Nema's most prominent traits were those of her office. Which they had yet to learn. This woman, green hued or otherwise, was clearly a person of high intelligence.

Manning heard Ikian voices coming to him in the water. Almost at the same time Matthews moved to his side and pointed upward; there, the tunnel was starting to bend in that direction. Manning turned back to Matthews. He seemed startled with what he saw.

Christ . . . I completely forgot. . . . This is all so natural now I wasn't paying any attention. It's so damned incredible. It feels like I've been breathing water all my life.

He looked harder at Matthews, concentrating. The Ikians had been able to adapt the bionic system used with Jessica; it functioned in much the same manner but it was not a permanent adaptation to the body. The surface men were able to breathe water in through their nostrils; against their noses and into their throats, the Ikians had inserted flexmetal tubing. Body-contour power packs ran the equipment. Before the water passed into their lungs it was tremendously enriched in oxygen content, so that they had a high saturation effect within the bloodstream. The difference from Jessica's equipment was that she was free to swim unhindered through the water, replacing her bionic system only once every three days. Manning, Miko, and Matthews had to be powered all the time, and when they emerged from the water they were required to remove the flexline leading into their nose and throat areas. At first it had been extremely uncomfortable, but that lasted only during the initial few hours of adaptation. The Ikians had learned swiftly from their work with Jessica; in weeks, they had advanced the science of underwater breathing to what—in the surface world—would have been considered miracle levels.

The group swam along the rising tunnel into a circular area, emerging from the water into one of the high-air-pressure caverns they were coming to know from experience. They sat there, out of water from the waist up.

Matthews looked at them with a wide grin. "I'm out of my mind with this equipment," he chortled. "*Water breathing*. It's hard to take. The idea of all that water going into my lungs, and there's no choking and it doesn't hurt, and I feel—just incredible."

Gella observed him carefully. "You feel no—ills?"

Matthews shook his head, deferred the question to Manning.

"None," Manning said. "Not a bit. I'm just as amazed as he is. I've tried this sort of equipment before, but—" He shrugged. "What I mean, Gella, is that we've tested this kind of breathing apparatus before, but our tests never seemed to work. We always felt like we were choking or gagging. But not anymore."

Matthews was removing his tubes. They had plugs that could be left in place for weeks at a time, and the tubes were easily inserted and removed. "Well, you know the key now," he said. "When you come into air from the water, you're fine just so long as the air pressure is equal to or greater than the water pressure. We've still got to decompress if we go to lower air pressures."

Miko nodded in agreement. "Or you may drown, even in the air," she said, "from residual liquid. Can you imagine, though—as great as this is—the freedom Jessie has now?"

"How long," Matthews asked, "does the return to normal pressure, to fourteen psi, say, take?"

"Two hours. That's what I consider the greatest part of all this. Just two hours, because of the saturation effects, and everything is back to normal."

Manning, his tubes removed, breathing air normally now, looked about him with growing interest. "Nema was talking to you in Ikian before," he said. "Why didn't you tell us what it was about?"

Matthews grimaced. "Because when *I* talk underwater I sound like Donald Duck." He was beginning to show signs of exasperation. "Damn it, skipper, your excitement level must be as low as your feet." He gestured to take in the chamber. "Do you have any idea where you are at this moment?"

Manning looked around, Miko following his gaze. Gella had a knowing smile on his face. Manning turned back to Matthews. "If you don't spill it, you're going to burst," Manning said. "And no," he answered the question, "I have no idea what this is all about."

Manning went to one of the near walls and examined it closely. For the first time he saw that the wall was honeycombed, a feature he had never noticed before in any of the undersea structures.

Matthews grinned. "Then, captain, I suggest you get yourself a hat and hang onto it tightly. You're inside a computer."

"A what?" Manning said.

"Inside?" Miko echoed.

A chuckle greeted their tones of incredulity. "That's where you've been for the last ten minutes," Matthews explained. "Gella and I were discussing computer systems, and he'd seen references to them in the literature that came down with ships and aircraft, but we were so far apart where equipment was concerned that neither of us had any idea we were talking about the same thing. You see, the Ikians don't build their computers. They *grow* them."

Manning's eyes were wide as he scanned the walls and ceiling, trying to form a mental picture of what lay beyond. "You mean," he said slowly, "this whole system—" He gestured to complete the query. "This whole thing—*is alive?*"

Gella smiled. "Yes, Manning Captain. To us this is *mlen*. What Matthews has told me your people call *computer*."

Gella looked about with pride. Obviously he had learned the crucial role computers played in that strange and frightening society so far above his own world, and he had come to understand, through Matthews, just what a marvel he and his people had wrought with their own system. His pride was enhanced by the astonishment of the surface people.

"This *mlen*," Gella went on carefully, "is older than any of us can remember. It goes back through many generations."

"In other words," Matthews broke in with Gella's willing acceptance, "they've had the computer far longer than our own culture has. We built the first cybernetics system in 1947 with Norbert Wiener. That's fifty-two years ago. They've had the equivalent of a highly advanced computer system for hundreds of years; and it helps to explain how the Ikians, without much of the technology we depend on, have been able to accomplish so much, when at first appearances they seem more agriculturally oriented. In their own way, these people are on a technological par with us. I've been stunned by the entire affair since I first came in here." Matthews gestured about him. "Welcome to the other world of the Ikians."

"Do you have any definite idea," Manning asked, "just how long they've had this—"

"*Mlen,*" Matthews said.

"How far back it goes?"

"My best guess, and we'll work it out closer, perhaps, is between five and eight hundred years."

Miko had kept silent through their exchange. She was familiar with computer systems, and her own astonishment had clenched her tongue. She stirred to life from her quiet study of her surroundings.

"Matt, how can it work? No, no, I mean, how does it work?"

"Well, I'm a bit more accustomed to it by now," Matthews said. "You know how we build up our computer systems with bits and pieces—diodes, printed circuits, magnetic memory fields, matrix foci, electron fields—stuff like that. And we have the whole complicated goo of switching points, readout systems, feedout and feedback, and the rest of it. Well, we don't need a lesson in cybernetics mechanics. The *mlen* does everything our computers do, but the Ikians don't build their systems. As I said before, they *grow* them. This substance is a sort of silicate or coral, and the electrical current and sensitivity—it's electrochemical in origin, just like our own bodies, but the potential is ten thousand times greater, or more than that—well, then you've got to understand the molecular structure and—"

He brought himself up short, realizing he was trying to cram too much into too few words, and suddenly he snapped his fingers. "Look, you're familiar with the flatworm, right? It's got a strange molecular memory. Every molecule in its body is a memory bank as if it were part of a brain. If you train one flatworm, chop him up, and feed him to other flatworms, they gain his memories in the process of ingesting their hacked-up buddy. Well, this silicate coral, or whatever it is, does exactly the same thing. And Nema, here," he gestured to the Ikian woman who had made no comment, "is known as the Mother. We'd call her a programmer or custodian, but that is terribly short of the actual; her relationship—you'd better think of it as symbiotic—goes much further than that because every cell in here, and there are trillions of them, well, *they know her*. It is as if these cells, individually and collectively, have memorized her voice, her sound, her presence, her chemical-electrical output, her life radiance. And since all life functions on electricity, this computer works as fast as anything we've ever built. It's also able to keep an enormous storage of electrical power, just as we would keep generator banks in reserve."

Manning's face was screwed up in intense concentration. Finally he nodded, then looked slowly at Matthews. "Matt, there's something here we never dreamed of."

Matthews grunted. "Skipper, I certainly couldn't have come up with this, even in a happy nightmare."

Manning was showing sudden impatience. "Didn't you tell me, when you were talking before with Hydrea," he asked sharply, "that the plate structure of this valley is extraordinarily sensitive to any disturbance?"

"For sure, captain. Some of our distant bomb tests in the sea, for example—"

"Never mind those," Manning said. "What about earth tremors? Quakes, landslides, undersea volcanic eruptions, that sort of thing?"

Gella motioned. "I will answer. It is yes. The earth moves beneath us. We know that well. Every time the earth has moved for hundreds of years past is inside *mlen*. I believe this is what you want to know."

"Then," Manning said carefully, "can you also predict when there will be—more earth moving?"

Gella smiled. "Yes, of course. With what you would say is great—"

He was searching for the word; Manning filled it in. "With great accuracy?"

Gella pondered the word, nodded. "Yes. Accuracy."

Manning held Miko's arm as he looked at Matthews. "For Christ's sake, Matt! With the records this system has, this *mlen*, we could make a quantum jump forward in quake prediction alone! I'll bet Gella's scientists, like Nema, here, could teach us things we can't even imagine about seismic structuring and faults—"

"The San Andreas fault—" Miko said, not needing to add to what Manning and Matthews already knew so well. The San Andreas was on the point of cataclysmic disaster; another ten or twenty years could wreck much of the south California coast beyond saving. Miko turned to Gella, speaking as much to Nema as to the Ikian leader.

"Do you understand our problem, Gella? About earthquakes? I mean, as we would experience them on the earth's surface, above the water?"

Gella frowned, and a moment later they realized that Nema, instead of standing by without comprehension, understood English about as well as did Gella. Which, had they thought of it, they should have expected from someone who masterminded the Ikian computer system.

"It is—difficult," Nema said at last. "Never any water—to breathe." Nema turned to Matthews, and there was a swift exchange in the Ikian tongue. Matthews turned from her to the others.

"The answer is yes," he confirmed. "On a quick

observation I'd say they were a century or two ahead of us in understanding plate tectonics, crustal movements—well, the whole of it."

"Gella, will your scientists work with our people if we bring them here?"

"I see many ways, Manning Captain, we learn from each other."

The long pause that followed his remark contained even more promise than his words. Gella stood, a smile brightening his face. "Now. A new experience, a surprise. What Matthews calls a sym—sym—"

"Symbiotic relationship," Matthews added quickly.

"Yes," Gella said. "You have wanted to see what Dr. Chadwick says he is interested in, what he calls aquiculture and mariculture." He laughed. "I have practiced those words, so they come easy. Dr. Chadwick has explained to me what happens about food from your war."

Gella frowned, and the smile was completely gone as he concentrated. "We do not understand," Gella went on. "We learn from your papers and your books. So many different people, so many different ways to talk language. This is not like Amphibus. You know this to be so. Here in the great valley we are all of one tongue. But Chadwick, he says many people on surface side are without to eat; they are hungry; there are bad problems of food. He says that what we know of growing things can help."

"Most certainly it can, Gella," Manning said.

"Then we go," Gella announced. "This time we ride. Matthews say this is damnedest sled he ever knows."

Laughing at their expressions, he turned to Nema, continuing to speak in English. "Please. Have them bring *yren*."

"*Yren*?" Miko repeated the word, searching for familiarity, not finding it.

Matthews chuckled. "You'll see, lass. Let's go. We follow Gella."

After replacing their breathing gear they slipped into the water, returned along the same tunnel, and emerged again into the open valley underwater, where a group of Ikians waited for them. With the most incredible device they had ever seen or even imagined.

It was a framework made up of a rigid coral structure and ceramics arranged in the form of tubing. There were places for three people atop each structure. The passengers would lie in a semiprone but comfortable position, their heads higher than their feet. The feet were pressed against stirrup-rests, and the arms were placed in contoured spaces so the fingers could grasp—and this left the visitors with heads shaking—reins instead of rigid controls. The framework was arranged in the form of a teardrop, with a large clear plastic shield across the bow. They noticed two separate *yren;* and a number of Ikians were in attendance, working about the sleds.

Using hand motions, Gella directed the Americans into the semiprone positions. Gella took the center seat of one *yren,* Manning and Miko at his sides. Matthews and another Ikian, Tia, settled in the second sled. The Ikians checked their passengers carefully. The three visitors were able, despite acoustic distortion in the water, to understand Gella's words; but being able to judge his motions and signals was as much a part of communicating as hearing his speech.

Gella nodded with satisfaction. "Good," he said, his words muffled. "You will not fall away when we go."

Manning started to tell the Ikian leader they were secure, but he had not yet mastered the knack of underwater speech, and his words came out garbled.

Gella laughed, then leaned closer to him. "*Yren* is alive," Gella said, speaking slowly and distinctly so they would understand him. "What you call sea sled is framework. Inside are squid, but none like you know. Our men of science for many years change growth of these animals. Matthews teach me this is to modify. These squid are powerful muscle with contraction and expansion systems, very special. You understand?"

Manning nodded, tried again to speak, sent bubbles frothing lightly from his mouth.

Gella laughed. "Like Matthews say—hang on!"

Beneath them, responding to Gella's tugs on the reins and stirrups, stirred a huge squid that had short, bunched tentacles and a large body that was a pure concentration of rippling muscle. They glanced down through the framework, saw the sharp eyes and hooked beak, as well as the pulsating water being drawn into the animal's front orifice. Not until they made this observation did they understand that each *yren* contained two of the mighty creatures harnessed to the sled framework.

Gella snapped the reins and the *yren* jerked forward with astonishing acceleration. Water swirled swiftly around the curved prow directly before them. Faster and faster, they were climbing steadily above the valley floor, and as they moved, as powerfully as any man-made submarine, they were aware of a pulsating, low-keyed rhythm that they could feel as much as they could hear: It was the contraction and expansion of the musculature of the two squid, taking in water with enormous flow, constricting the liquid, and ejecting it with powerful jet thrusts.

Jerry Manning was overwhelmed by the idea of this adaptation of living systems to the need for fast underwater propulsion; he had never conceived of an arrangement such as now bore them through the waters of the Great Valley with powerful speed and sure control. He forced himself to realize that at this moment he was part and parcel of a living, breathing, liquid-jet propulsion system of unparalleled efficiency.

They continued their swift rising movement until the sleds leveled off above the ocean bottom, their speed undiminished. Ahead, the sea floor changed from general flatness to gently rolling hills, and as their progress continued they caught sight of strange domelike structures floating in the water, tethered at different heights. Far below them, anchored to the bottom, were other similar structures.

Manning glanced at Gella, the question clear on his face, but the Ikian chose not to bother with answers at this moment. He gestured ahead of them. Below, but much closer now, were vast fields of cultivated sea vegetation: wondrous stalks swaying in the eddying currents; sea cucumbers; wheatlike plants; fruits; some bulbous, others long and slender. Glowing lifelights were spaced along the fields, moving slowly. Small figures could be seen within the cultivated areas, obviously Ikians working the fields, and among them were the *yren* sleds of overseers. Several of the great eels were visible, although they seemed to be doing no particular work. Then, off to one side, there loomed an astonishing sight.

They saw a living mountain of fish, most likely numbering in the millions, all of them moving in an area that obviously must be determined by an invisible but effective boundary line that the fish never crossed, veering slowly away from whatever force or control kept them inside of their penned area. The number of the creatures was staggering. There was no real way to count or even to estimate true numbers, for the front ranks were so thick they might have concealed behind them miles of fish.

The *yren* sleds went beyond the great schools of controlled animals and eased into a long curving descent, slowing as they approached one of the tethered domes. The *yren* came to a stop; Gella released himself from his straps, watching Manning and Miko emulating him. He motioned them to follow as he swam into an opening at the base of the

dome. Moments later Manning understood. The
dome was kept under high air pressure, and the
water rose only several feet into the structure. Inside were steps and ledges, and tier upon tier of
seats that were reached by spiraling stairways.

They emerged from the water, climbed to the third
tier, removed their breathing tubes, and sat and
waited until Matthews and Tia joined them.

"Gella—these domes," Miko asked, able to talk at
last in an air pressure environment. "We saw many
of them. What purpose do they serve?"

Gella frowned, not answering for a while. He
glanced at Matthews, then turned back to Miko.
"The garm cannot enter here."

"Garm? I'm sorry. I've never heard that expression before, Gella. I don't understand."

Gella nodded. "Hydrea spoke with Manning Captain of these. Also with Matthews. When they come,
our people go quickly to these—what you call domes
—and also into our buildings."

At that moment Manning recalled the gates in the
tunnels, and he finally understood something that
had been puzzling him. The gates—and what Gella
called the *garm*— all came together. "The garm that
Hydrea spoke about. They're a type of jellyfish, aren't
they? Or maybe that's not strong enough a word,"
he said to Gella.

Matthews answered for Gella. "Aye, skipper.
They're far more than that. They have a jellyfish
shape, but even that's misleading. To us they *look*
like jellyfish, but that's where all resemblance ends.
They move under their own volition, not just floating or pulsating their way about blindly. They have
volition control and a lot of it. They're also capable
of ingesting large amounts of animal tissue." The
look on his face was grim. "Or human flesh, for
that matter." He saw the look of horror on Miko's
face. "They're most dangerous because of some sort
of acid they exude. They can direct it in streams as

well as simply fill an area around themselves for many yards. The acid, if that's what it is, eats away just about anything it touches, except the material for these domes and the granitelike stone of the cliff buildings, and—"

He stopped as Manning gestured to interrupt. "Hold on, Matt. Is that the reason for the heavy gates we've seen in the tunnels?"

Matthews nodded. "It is. Somehow those damned things can eat or burn their way through the great dome that surrounds this valley. The structure just yields when they excrete that acid. Fortunately, the dome is alive, as you know, and it seals itself afterward, but in the meantime these devils get through."

Gella looked at them somberly. "It is true. Until several years before now, the *grektor*—how you call the great eels—they stop the garm, kill them, with electric shock. Then—"

He stopped again, his face growing darker. "Then, something happens. The garm change. They are terrible. When the *grektor* attack with their teeth, the *garm* are torn apart. But they do not die like before. They—" He was struggling for words and Matthews motioned to him.

"Gella, may I?"

Gella nodded, and Matthews picked it up. "That's what Hydrea has been talking about, what's behind his tremendous resistance to us. During the war, there was tremendous radioactivity released into the sea. Bombs, wastes—so much of it. And the Chinese haven't helped. They've built so many fission plants along their coastline to run off the heat from fuel-processing systems, and they've been pouring a steady stream of radioactivity into the water all along the Asian coast. Well, the garm are apparently a very ancient and basic form of life, adapted only for survival and nothing else. As such, they react swiftly to environmental changes, and all this radio-active mess has accelerated a strange form of mutation. They're about impossible to kill, and it seems to get worse all the time. Hydrea is especially bitter because he feels that the Ikian defenses are failing them now and that their time here is doomed."

Manning's face was like stone. More than ever he understood the feelings of the tough old man whose dislike for them was close to hatred. "What about the eels?" Manning asked Matthews. "That electric shock. It was enough to destroy one of our subs, if you recall."

"It's their main defense, and it's also failing. I said the garm were incredibly adaptive, captain. The shock that used to kill them now only seems to stun them for a while. Apparently those bloody creatures are evolving faster than anything biology says is possible. You're going back hundreds of millions of years on the evolutionary scale. I don't know. All my yardsticks have been wiped out ever since we got down here. The main issue is that even if the eels tear these things apart, each part remains alive, like a giant cell splitting in half; but each cell becomes just as bad as the larger unit it came from."

Miko shuddered. "Matt, you make it sound as if they're indestructible."

"That could well be," Matthews told her.

An awkward pause followed. Manning stepped into the breach. "We just might have something that would do them in," he said quietly.

Gella's interest was instant. "Matthews has spoken before of a—a weapon."

Manning nodded. "Yes. I know you have ultrasonics, of course, but you haven't even mentioned them in helping to fight these garm."

"They work—sometimes."

"And you've got great fighting power with the *grektor*, as well as their electrical shock," Manning reviewed. "None of them work anymore."

"Not only that," Matthews broke in, "but explosives won't work either. The shock waves would probably kill these people faster than it would the garm. And you'd only be making matters worse by splitting each animal apart. You really wouldn't be killing them. Either way, it won't do."

"The masers," Manning said quietly.

"By God!" Matthews exclaimed."Of course—"

Miko was quick to interrupt. "You two had better consider the cultural shock."

Gella's face showed bewilderment. "I do not understand."

She turned to the Ikian, speaking carefully. "Gella, you know that in many ways our people differ from each other. You know we are, well, a warlike race. Our history and what we have done offends many of your people. Hydrea is just one voice among others. And in many ways he is right. We have fought during all of our history. Nothing like that exists down here. We do not even think alike, in many ways. The masers that Captain Manning speaks about are very powerful. They may do your people more harm than good. If—"

Matthews's expression was sour. "Damn it, it can't hurt them if they're being killed off by these garm! Either way, you end up very, very dead."

"I know, Matt, but—"

"We'll talk about it later," Manning said. "With Gella, of course," he added directly to the Ikian leader. "Right now we've got company."

They looked down to see Chadwick and Templeton emerging into the dome from the water.

Chadwick waved cheerily. "Ah! Glad you're here, captain. Have you seen what these people do with their farming?" He climbed the steps to join them, his excitement clear. "Good Lord, if we adapted their methods and their know-how to the first hundred feet below the surface, or even deeper, we could feed the world population five times over!"

"And it *will* adapt," Templeton added with a breathless rush. "We're already made our tests. It'll work, captain!"

Manning couldn't repress his smile. The staid scientist and his uptight assistant were like children turned loose in a world of new miracles. "I've never seen you two so excited," he observed.

"Excited?" Chadwick echoed. "We've got good reason to be, sir! If the bellies of the world are full, people won't be so eager to fight. And we could feed the entire world this way. Oh, not by giving them food, for all the reasons we know won't work, but by having all seashore and even lake countries producing food as they do here, but on a mass basis." Chadwick took a deep breath, became a bit formal. "Captain Manning, for the record, I would like to return as soon as possible to New Washington. This is so crucial to the planet that I believe I should bring my report personally to the president."

Manning nodded his agreement. "All right. It's your field and no one knows better than you. It's extraordinary news, of course. I'll go ahead with whatever you recommend, and you can begin your plans immediately."

"Marvelous, marvelous! If you have the time, captain, I'd like to take you and Miko through one area especially. It's—" He broke off as an Ikian swam upward into the dome and spoke rapidly with Gella.

Gella turned to Matthews, who had listened to the Ikian conversation.

"Sir, you've got a code red message for you at the boat," Matthews explained to Manning.

They exchanged a long silent glance. Miko's concern was evident; she knew no reason for a code red, but it was obviously crucial.

Manning turned to Gella. "I'm sorry. We must return right away to the submarine."

"There is a—problem?"

Manning hesitated, made a sudden decision.

"There could be. Gella, we have been completely open with each other, and I do not wish to have secrets from you."

"Secrets?"

"We promised we would never do anything here in your land that you did not know about. No matter what it is. Will you come with me to the submarine so you will know everything, even as I do?"

A smile widened on Gella's face. He nodded. "Yes. It is—good. Thank you."

22

~~~~~~~~

Aboard the *yren*, they went swiftly through the valley watching the distant *Sea Trench* assume its enormous shape as they approached. The *yren* slowed by the belly entranceway, the submarine dominating the world all about them. Manning swam to the ladder that led up into the pressure chamber, the others, including Gella, directly behind him. Inside the chamber, they removed their fins and disconnected their breathing tubes. They looked up as a side hatch to the chamber opened and Dr. John Simmonds entered.

"This is still pretty new to us, captain," the doctor said, "and I want to become a lot more familiar with that equipment. You're going to need a couple of hours to work any residual liquids from your system. You, and the others. I'm staying here to monitor the whole show."

Manning looked at Simmonds with open disbelief. "A couple of *hours*—for Christ's sake, John, there's a code red I've got to—"

"You don't go anywhere until I say so."

"All right, damn you," Manning ground out. "I'll handle it from here."

He crossed the chamber to an angled bulkhead console, sat before the controls, and activated the system. A TV monitor blinked on with a test pattern as Manning spoke into a microphone.

"Bridge, the captain here."

The TV monitor came into focus, showing Bill Ryan in the bridge command seat.

"Captain, it sounds hot," Ryan said without preamble. "We got a code one through the buoy on station just above the dome."

"Let's have it," Manning said tersely.

Ryan glanced at a paper before him. "Yes, sir. The word is from Secretary Haig directly. He's sending a Captain Morgan to us for rendezvous and pickup."

"Here?"

"That's right, captain. We've already sent one of the boats to pick him up. We have confirmation they're on the way back."

Manning rubbed his chin, thinking hard. "If Tim Haig is sending someone for a face-to-face session instead of using code—"

"I was thinking the same thing," Ryan said.

"All right, Bill," Manning said. "When he gets here, keep him on ice for a while. Sawbones here," he glanced at John Simmonds, "insists on decompression for at least two hours."

On the screen Ryan nodded. "He's right. What's the use of sending you home in a seaweed coffin?"

Manning could hardly conceal his sarcasm. "When did *you* start baby-sitting?" he asked with a raised eyebrow.

Ryan smirked. "Consider it a weak moment. Besides—oops; hold on, boss."

On the TV monitor Manning watched Ryan studying another panel. Ryan turned back, looked directly into the screen. "Contact with the boat. Morgan will be on board within fifteen minutes."

"Very good. Let him know what's—"

His words stopped suddenly as a deep resonating boom, like an enormous muffled clang, came to them once, then repeated two more times. Everyone showed surprise—*except* Gella. The Ikian looked up sharply, shock and alarm on his face as the signal boomed again.

In the midst of the towering plants in the great cultivated fields, Chadwick and Templeton looked up with surprise as the booming signal thundered through the open water, striking their ears painfully. The Ikians about them froze in mid-motion, fear on their faces, then began tugging frantically at the two Americans to follow them as fast as possible.

In the great cliff buildings, Luna and several other women felt, more than heard, the clanging booms through walls and floor and looked at one another in dismay. They ran from the room.

Within the honeycombed tunnels of the age-old computer, Nema's hand flew to her mouth when she heard the booming cry. All about her the living cells of the computer pulsated with the alarm signal.

Jessica and Arnom were swimming through tall swaying flower beds, the great eel with them. The huge body of the eel stiffened as the alarm boomed through the valley. Jessica showed her confusion as the animal bared its gleaming teeth. Arnom grabbed her wrist and shouted for her to follow him as fast as she could.

Richard Castillo and several young Ikians were swimming in gently roiling water near some volcanic upwellings. The landscape consisted of grotesque but beautiful frozen lava flows and glow stone, and water currents swirled about them like twisting veils. The alarm thundered through the water and the Ikians froze, then pointed, urging Castillo to hurry with them.

In the pressure chamber aboard the submarine, they stared at Gella's face as fear and concern twisted his handsome features. He looked straight ahead, as if he could see through steel and water, far beyond the hull of *Sea Trench*. "It is the—garm. They are here. Very bad. The three-time signal. It is a dangerous breakthrough."

He rushed to the water entrance, stopped, and turned sharply to look directly at Jerry Manning. His face seemed tortured.

"You spoke of weapons," he said. "If you can help, Manning Captain, then—*please*."

A moment later he was gone.

They looked at one another in the chamber, startled, confused, trying to gather their thoughts. Then the alarm came again, the muffled booms ringing through the hull. Manning closed off all doubts, made his commitment. He spun about on his heel and hit a wall switch. The pressure decrease stopped at that instant and started to build again.

"For God's sake, don't!" The cry came from Dr. Simmonds, but it had no effect.

"Shut up, John," Manning snapped. "We're going out again, and *now*. Miko, Matt, get into your gear at once."

He turned to another switch, pulled away a cover, slammed down his hand on the button marked GENERAL QUARTERS. Instantly the alarm clamored throughout the great submarine. Manning turned back to the video mike.

"Ryan! All hands, general quarters. Ryan, you stay on the bridge, Sparco in the drive room. MacKinney, you reading me?"

"Go, sir."

"Combat status, Mr. MacKinney, *at once*. Patterakis, you there?"

On the bridge they pushed aside their questions in response to the alarm and to the mood that was clear in Manning's tone. Patterakis rushed across the bridge to his seat, punched in his video scanner. "Go ahead, sir."

"Chris, release four mantorps right away. I want two maser rifles with each one. Everyone who goes outside is to use his helmet; I want close-in radio or maser communications. Chris, bring the mantorps directly ahead of the bow. Move it. Ryan!"

"Here."

"Bill, notify the *Seeker* not to open their hatches for transfer. Keep Morgan aboard, and have the crew stand by, full weapon status, and be on the alert for attack by some kind of jellyfish. It'll be—," he paused, took a deep breath.

"All hands from the captain. Under no conditions will any man use explosive weapons against these creatures, these jellyfish. I repeat, under no conditions will explosives be used." He paused, then went on, "Prentiss!"

"Here, sir." Prentiss's face came onto the monitor.

"Syd, get cracking with Simmonds. We don't know what we're going to run into, but you'd better set up the pressure area here as a sick bay. Bring all medikits down here and be ready for anything. Got it?"

"Yes, sir."

"All right," Manning concluded, speaking on all channels, "everybody get the lead out."

Behind him, Miko and Matthews were already into their helmets and breathing gear. Simmonds waited to assist Manning into his own equipment. They checked each other over carefully, and Manning went to open line on his communications.

"Okay. You two read me? Miko?"

"Five by five."

"Clear, captain," Matthews said.

"Let's go," Manning said sharply. "Miko, you're to stay close by me from now on."

He turned without another word and went into
the water feet first, disappearing in a froth of bubbles
and swirling foam. Miko went behind him, Matthews following her.

In the bridge, Ryan half ran from his seat at control. He looked across the conn to the nearest officer.

"Holvak! Take the conn," Ryan told him. "I'm going outside."

The other man hesitated, uncertainty crossing his
features. "But—but the captain said for you to—"

Ryan's voice bellowed through the bridge. "Holvak, that's a goddamned *order!* Take the conn!"

Ryan didn't wait for a response but took off at a
dead run through the far hatchway. Still running, he
grabbed a sliding pole, dropped down the circular
tube. He emerged in a long chamber that contained
torpedo vehicles. These torps had powerful hydrojets
at the stern and smaller hydrojets in the bow for
tight control. Each mantorp revealed two open sad-
dlelike seats with belts and rigid stirrups, protected
by curving flanges for the occupants. Ryan slipped
from his jump suit and grabbed his wet suit from
the locker bearing his name, dressing as fast as he
could. He turned at the sound of steps.

"Turn around," he heard Autry's voice. "I'll check
out your gear." Moments later Autry was screwing
on Ryan's helmet and tapping him on the shoulder.
"You're all set. But would you tell me what the hell
this is all about? I heard the skipper—"

Ryan turned to him. "Cool it." He looked at the
others in the chamber staring at him. "Damn it, you
forget how to move? You people ready? Get those
damned masers in your hands and set them on full
power!"

His voice came to them through their helmet comsets. Urback tossed a maser rifle to Ryan, who
snatched it expertly in midair and turned the power
to FULL. The maser rifle was sleek, with a regular
metal-frame stock, but an open-hole sight along the

barrel. Where there would have been a recoil firing mechanism and a clip there was a small but enormously powerful electronic system that fired in pulsed phases.

Ryan gestured impatiently. "I'll take the first torp. You people bring the others." He signaled. "Let's go."

Autry went through a final gesture of confusion, pushed it from his mind, and signaled Pete Williams who was watching through a thick glass control-room window. Williams nodded and activated the flooding system. Red lights blinked, and there was a tremendous scream of air pressure bleeding away as water poured into the chamber from all sides.

Three minutes later they were in the mantorps, Ryan in the lead torp, Autry riding the second, Williams the third, and Urback and Patterakis riding together in the fourth. A section of the hull slid open to the valley. Ryan eased his torp from the chamber, swung away from the hull of the submarine, and headed for the bow, the others following. Moments later he saw three figures in the water, recognized Miko pointing. He heard her voice on open channel.

"They're coming."

"And not a moment too soon," Matthews added, glancing behind him. In the distance there was an indication of furious activity: tiny forms streaming for cover; others moving with the great eels; still others on the squid-powered *yren* racing for distant positions.

Manning stared at Ryan as the lead torp eased to a stop. "Damn you, I told you to—"

"I heard all about it," Ryan broke in. "You want to talk now or save it for later?"

Manning gestured angrily. "I'll take this torp with Miko. You and Matthews ride with the others."

Manning took the first seat, Miko directly behind him, as Autry brought them their maser rifles. They wasted no more time, accelerating steadily in a loose line-abreast formation with Manning and Miko leading, Ryan and Matthews second, Patterakis and Urback third, Autry and Williams taking up the last torp.

"All right," Manning said finally, coming through on their comsets, "we're into it but good now. We don't really know what we're up against, but from what we've heard, those garm—the jellyfish, or whatever the hell they are—are nasties. Whatever happens don't let them get to contact with you, or you've flat bought it."

Ryan's voice came to them all. "How many of our people are out there?"

"A bunch," Manning said. "Chadwick and Templeton were in the farm area. I don't know where Richard or Jessica went."

"Skipper, what's with the no-explosives order?" Urback queried.

"From what Gella told us, these things are way down on the evolutionary scale. But they're tremendously adaptive. You can think of them as giant amoeba. Cut them in half and both halves are just as dangerous as the original."

"Jesus—"

That was all Williams could say when Patterakis's voice broke in. "Hey, off to our right—all hell is breaking loose over there!"

Manning veered in the new direction, the others following in a loose swarm. Even above the sound of their hydrojets and the water rushing by their helmets, the Great Valley carried the shrill and deeper sounds of what seemed to be terrible fighting.

They rushed closer and froze in their seats as the body of an Ikian twisted slowly, falling directly in their path. As the body sank lower, moving past them, flopping limply, they saw half the face eaten away revealing white bone beneath, teeth glaring, skeleton-fashion, and only a thin trail of blood following. The corpse rolled slowly and they saw the rib structure. Parts of the body appeared to have been drained or sucked away.

Miko's voice was a strangled gasp. "I— I think I'm going to be sick."

Manning half turned. "Goddamn it, not now—and not in that helmet. Hang on to yourself," he snapped at her.

She swallowed hard, fought down the nausea. Barely. "It's—it's all right. I'll make it."

"It's not going to get any better, Miko," Ryan's voice came to her.

They were approaching what appeared to be a defense line of Ikians who were swimming freely about several *yren* sleds, and with them were a large number of the huge eels.

Even as they watched, one of the eels, pulsating with instinctive anger, hurled itself at the garm— the first one the Americans had seen. The creatures were about seven feet in diameter; of a bewildering and constantly changing band of colors; ringed with luminescent patches; and having whiplike tentacles that seemed as strong as steel cords and moved with unbelievable control, always seeming to be seeking prey. Instead of recoiling before the screaming eel, the garm moved *toward* their attacker, and the eel slammed its huge form against several of the enemy. An enormous flash of light raced out, and the water crackled with the electrical pulse.

Autry's voice rang triumphantly in their comsets. "That ought to take care of those things! He got them dead on!"

"They're just stunned," Manning warned. "They—"

"Watch out!" Williams cried. "There's a bunch above and to our right, closing in—"

An eruption followed. Great crackling bolts of electricity came from the eels, their screams primal as they attacked, and now came the additional sound of ultrasonic generators being fired steadily by the Ikians. The water seemed to boil with furious activity. The mantorp riders turned to the approaching garm, Williams swinging his maser around first, not yet firing.

Manning turned back to the scene of attack. The eel had left several garm stunned, drifting helplessly; then it tore into another of the jellyfish, slashing at the creature's inner body with its spikelike teeth. Several great swipes of the animal's powerful head ripped apart the garm, tearing it into chunks; but the scattering chunks stirred, sent out new tentacles, came alive with new force of their own. By now the nearest garm were swarming against the eel.

"Did you see that?" Miko gasped. "Those things came to life again!"

"Some Ikians coming this way." That was Autry's voice. "They've got those ultrasonic projectors—"

"Look at the damn eel!" Patterakis shouted.

A scream tore at them, vibrating their glassite helmets. They watched the eel twisting violently through its entire length, writhing in a terrible agony as tentacles found the body, instantly curled around the powerful form, locking as by adhesive into place. They saw a whitish secretion from the tentacles. Wherever it touched the flesh of the animal the flesh seemed to burn away as if plunged into acid. Naked muscle and coiled bone came into sight, and the garm moved closer. Now the shorter, stubbier tentacles nearer to the central body of the jellyfish became visible as fluids were sucked away from the writhing eel. The eel gave several last convulsive shudders, and suddenly went limp, its jaw and teeth showing through its slack head.

"Jesus Christ—"

"Below us!" Manning shouted. *"Below us! There's the kid down there!"*

In the distance, well below them, Richard Castillo

was in the midst of a group of young Ikians, all of them firing their ultrasonic generators. The water thrummed to the sound of the short-range weapons in waves that actually hurt as they brushed along the bodies of the humans. But all the ultrasonics did, even at close range, was to temporarily stun the garm.

"He's trapped!" Miko cried out, watching Richard. "Faster!"

They went down under full hydrojet power as a gathering horde of the garm closed in from all sides against Castillo and the group of Ikians. Manning's torp was there before the others, and with the foot controls he backed off on power, the maser rifle in his hands as he aimed carefully. He fired, a dazzling bolt of green light flashed brilliantly through the water, and the maser cracked loudly with a sound of tearing cloth. The maser pulsed, and he fired again.

The green light shot away, absolutely straight, undistorted by the density of the water. The beam arrowed into the nearest garm.

The effects were instantly visible. The tremendous heat of the pulsed maser beam punched through the central body of the jellyfish, severing tentacles as it burned through. A mist seemed to erupt as steam swirled violently through the pulsating semitransparent body. The heat was so tremendous that the garm was literally boiling, the animal tissue being steamed away. What remained was charred or melted tissue, but little matter.

It was dead.

"By the great horned toad, it works! *It works!*" Matthews exulted. His own maser cracked suddenly. "All of you, get in there!" he shouted.

They left the mantorps, fanning out, firing steadily, protecting themselves as well as blazing away at the horde of garm. The effects of the masers were instantly visible, as one after the other of the lifeless garm, boiled and shredded, began to drift downward. The masers added to the wild din within the water, but it was a sound of success. Within several minutes nearly a hundred of the hellish creatures had been killed, but so many had appeared that any progress to rescue the Ikians and Castillo was painfully slow.

"Cover me!" Matthews called. "I've got to get in closer."

Manning shouted for him to wait. "Hold back!" he ordered. "We'll go in together, blast our way—"

But Matthews was already driving downward as fast as he could swim, his finned feet moving in a blur, the maser firing steadily. The ultrasonics of the Ikian group had delayed, but only briefly, the full force of the garm closing against them. Matthews began to pick off the closest jellyfish, killing one after the other, but it was a race against time in which the winner was yet to be decided. Immediately behind him came the others, firing steadily.

They were too late and the garm too many, and several Ikians were brushed, held by the tentacles, instantly covered with patches of the white acidlike substance. The youngsters screamed in sudden paroxysms of agony, and, directly before the eyes of the maddened Matthews, died hellishly. This close he saw there was no lapse, no slow eating away of flesh; it was almost as if invisible fangs ripped at the flesh. The tentacles drew in the writhing forms, the stubby, sharp tubes stabbed into the bodies, and the young Ikians went limp as tremendous suction ended their lives.

"Hold on! Hold on, boy!" Matthews's voice was frantic as he drove in closer, still firing. "I'm almost there!" He shouted as if the youth could hear him, but Castillo's face was white with fear as he and the Ikians stayed close to each other, firing their pitiful weapons. Then he looked up in astonishment as Matthews's body appeared between them and the garm, the maser snapping out its lethal flashes of green light.

Matthews motioned furiously for them to leave, and Manning and the others heard him on the comsets, shouting, "It's clear, you damn fools! Get the hell out of here!"

Castillo and the Ikians were swimming for their lives, away from the garm, toward Manning and the others, now nearly upon them.

Ryan's voice burst in Matthews's comset. "Matt! Behind you, for God's sake, *behind you!*"

Maser beams split the water about Matthews as he twisted in his own length, feet flailing to meet the sudden threat. He looked up, his mouth opening in wordless horror as tentacles curled around his neck. His maser spit green killing light and several garm upon him died in boiling froth, but there were too many. Another tentacle curled about an ankle, sending pain ripping through his foot. He gasped, and agony smashed into his chest as acid cut through his wet suit into his ribs.

They were firing their weapons, but they could only watch the dying of their friend, a terrible agony enacting itself with a horror of timelessness, seeing Matt's skin dissolving before their eyes, his body jerking in mindless convulsions, his mouth open but only strangling noises coming through, the maser rifle in his hand still firing but now by jerking reflex instead of control. His back arched wildly, and abruptly he went limp, the final pain stamped into his gaping eyes and mouth. He fell slowly past them, his head attached to his body only by blood-leaking skin.

23

~~~~~~~~

They fired in concert, forming a small circle, the masers blazing almost steadily, and with every passing minute the numbers of dead garm increased. Now there were only a few left alive, and these were being boiled and steamed by the masers without letup. Ryan signaled to Manning, pointing down where Matthews's lifeless form fell slowly, trailing a thin scarlet ribbon of blood. "I'm going after his body," he said to Manning through his comset.

"No. There isn't time," Manning said tersely. "Look over there, to your left. They need us. Everybody! Back to the torps. Follow me, and give it everything you've got. This thing is a long way from finished."

They moved out under full speed toward a milling throng of Ikians, many of them crowded about the *yren* sleds, from which they fired large ultrasonic projectors. All they could do was to stun, to slow the encroaching movement of the jellyfish, trying to buy enough time to get into the protective domes and the buildings where they could close the gates in the tunnels.

Manning saw Gella on one of the *yren*. Beneath the sled several garm swarmed upward with surprising speed, and Manning saw that the squid under the sled no longer answered Gella's urging. In a sudden decision Gella unstrapped and swam almost frantically from the sled, rising at an angle. He was just in time, for even as he moved to safety several of the jellyfish reached the shackled squid in the sled. Long tentacles snaked in through the framework and the imprisoned creatures went mad with pain and fear as they were literally eaten alive. The sled jerked madly, snapping forward, lunging in gyrations. Several garm were torn loose by the violent motions, but they were already effective in their attacks; the squid would die within seconds or, because of their tremendous strength, in minutes at the most.

Gella looked about wildly as a blinding shaft of green snapped past him. He saw Manning and the others firing, and he turned to watch the maser beams spearing into the garm. The water boiled furiously, the ripping sound of the masers cutting through water a cry of killing. He stared at the boiling beasts, steam hissing from the bodies as the animals turned gray and died.

The Ikians swam away from the jellyfish, no longer firing their own weapons, getting out of harm's way as the seven Americans continued to snap out maser shots at the milling garm. It was no longer a battle. The closest garm were killed with a single strike of the masers, and now, experienced with what they were doing, Manning and his crew went at destroying the jellyfish in a steady, concerted effort.

Within five minutes the entire local area was safe; dead garm settled slowly. Gella swam to Manning's side, hope and disbelief and wonder all showing in his expression. He grasped Manning's arm, pointed urgently to the east, where in the distance there were signs of great activity and fighting.

They returned to the mantorps, Gella taking

Matthews's seat, and went under full power. A huge cloud of the garm had assembled about one of the large tethered domes that seemed to have developed a gaping tear along one side. The mantorps passed the first group of mangled and torn bodies of Ikians, but they sped forward until they were within maser range.

"Open fire!" Manning called. "Fire steadily!"

The scene was a repetition of before. Manning was grateful for the nuclear fuel cells in the masers; any other weapons would long since have exhausted their power. Again and again the green lights hissed through the water, and the jellyfish were being killed with every successive burst. Ikians streamed past them, trying frantically to escape, and the garm, fortunately, kept concentrating on the dome where they sensed their prey was trapped. The moment could not have been better for the maser-equipped team from the submarine; they had their targets concentrated in a single area. They swam slowly about the dome, firing again and again.

Manning's vision was blurred, his muscles aching, when he felt Ryan's hand on his shoulder. He turned to Ryan, saw Gella immediately behind. "It's over, Jerry," Ryan said quietly. "It's over. We've got them all in this area. I think we'd better sweep the valley, just in case."

Manning nodded, gestured to the mantorps holding level under autopilot. "Let's go," he said.

They returned to *Sea Trench* red-eyed, exhausted, stumbling as they climbed from the mantorps into the decompression chamber. They were helped to contoured chairs and ordered by Dr. Simmonds to rest as he went from one to the other. He stood next to Miko and turned to Manning. "She's exhausted. Completely. She's got to sleep or she'll collapse."

Manning nodded. "Whatever you say, John."

Manning's mumbled words were enough to tell them all just how wiped out he was.

Simmonds studied Manning, his eyes narrowing as he said, "You don't look in much better shape yourself."

Manning gestured offhandedly. "No arguments." He leaned back, closing his eyes.

Simmonds looked around the chamber. "Where's Matthews?"

Manning's eyes flickered open. He had forgotten that Simmonds had no way of knowing what had happened. "He's dead."

He waited, knowing the shock his words must have given the doctor. "So is Williams," Manning said in a voice flat and toneless.

Simmonds rallied his own strength. "All right. What about the others?"

"We don't know. Gella will get us word as fast as he can."

"Jessica? Do we know about—"

"I said we don't know, goddamn it!"

Simmonds backed off. "All right, sir." He paused. "Is it over—out there?"

"For now, anyway." Manning rubbed his eyes. "I never knew such things could exist."

Simmonds made his decision. "Let it wait, captain. It can all wait until later. MacKinney is staying on general quarters for the boat. It's all under control. But you and the others who were outside, well, under this kind of pressure, the energy you've burned from your systems—"

Manning lifted a hand, let it drop wearily. "Whatever, doc, whatever."

Simmonds went quickly among the group that had returned, slipped a needle into the left arm of each. "You'll sleep now. You'll all—"

He stopped speaking as an air-lock hatch opened and a stranger stepped into the chamber. Simmonds read the jump suit nameplate: STEVE MORGAN, USN. Morgan's face showed disbelief at the sight of the bodies sprawled about the chamber.

"What the hell happened to everyone?"

Ryan was nearly out. He struggled to one elbow, fighting his own exhaustion and the drug in his system. He managed a feeble smile. "Well, look who's here. Welcome aboard, Morgan. You were almost in time—for the—party—"

He fell asleep even as he was talking.

They slept for fourteen hours. Simmonds was with them when they came out of it. Muscles aching, still weary, they were no longer beaten as they had been. Simmonds had high-energy meals ready for them, and after they ate he put them all through whirlpool baths and checked them over. "You'll do," he announced to the group when he was through. "But I wouldn't try to swim any four-minute miles for a while."

Manning didn't answer. His mind was on certain other critical affairs. He went to the ordnance block of the submarine, Ryan and some others with him. Gella and several Ikians had been there for the last hour. When Manning came into the block he saw MacKinney holding a training maser rifle, teaching Gella how to use the weapon. Manning watched for a few minutes as the Ikians, one by one, went through the drill. MacKinney picked up a weapon from a sealed compartment, handing it to Manning.

"We've checked them out, sir. They're all ready to go, but you're the only one who can—"

"Right, Mac. Good work." Manning turned to Gella. "We have thirty of these for you. The others who need training are to come here as soon as you can bring them. We want each man who will be given one of these weapons to know it perfectly. Now, they're yours."

He handed the maser rifle to Gella, who hefted the weapon in his hands, studying it from all sides before he looked up at Manning.

"It is strange," Gella said slowly, "how a thing like this can mean life."

"It *is* life, where your people are concerned," Manning agreed. "With enough of these masers available, you'll be able to solve the problem of the garm yourself." He turned to Morgan. "Did that priority get through?"

Morgan nodded. "Yes, sir. Coded for Secretary Haig directly. One thousand maser rifles, and power units and spares for twice that number." He looked at the Ikian leader. "Sir, they'll be on their way tonight."

Gella looked from Morgan to Manning. "We are grateful."

Manning exchanged looks with Morgan, and Manning nodded for him to continue with what they had agreed on before.

"I have been told," Morgan began carefully, "that I may speak to you with no need to hide any words."

Gella tried to judge what he was hearing, and he turned to Manning for help.

Manning said, "It is just as we have been since our first meeting, Gella. Nothing is to be hidden. Mr. Morgan needs to talk with you on a matter of great importance to us."

Morgan spoke to Gella. "I have explained to Captain Manning why I had to come here, personally, to your valley. He has told me that you understand about such things as large ships that move on the surface of the water, and—and about other weapons. I am referring to hydrogen bombs."

Gella's distaste showed briefly. "Yes. I understand," he said haltingly. "What I do not know, Manning Captain will explain to me."

"Thank you," Morgan told him. "I understand that I may not be able to make everything clear in words, but I believe we might have a better way to explain. Will you come with us, please?"

Manning led the way to the bridge. Gella looked around him, overwhelmed by the complexity of control systems and panels. He already knew the crew aboard *Sea Trench,* at one time or another having met each of the men and the science team. Manning stopped at the holographic projection platform and took the controls himself. Gella had never experienced the three-dimensional laser projection, and he blinked several times as the empty space blurred before his eyes; then a living section of the Pacific Ocean snapped into existence. They gave him time to become accustomed to what he was observing. Gella had sufficient association with maps and globes of the planet to understand the landmass of the world, as well as the depths and contours of the hydrospace made up by the oceans.

Morgan used a glowing dot to pinpoint specific areas, and the dot moved down the western coastline of North America, then eased slightly to the west. "Here, Gella, is where we are most concerned. The area is the central Pacific Ocean, but the point of interest—as shown by the light—is only two hundred miles off the West Coast of our country. On the floor of the ocean."

Morgan nodded to Manning. "The full scan, sir."

Manning worked the controls, and a complete projection of the Pacific Ocean floor snapped into life. The scale was perfect, down to an accurate presentation of the true curvature of the earth. The glowing dot moved again. Gella watched intently.

"This is the Aleutian Trench," Morgan went on, "where we are. Your valley, Amphibus, is—here." The dot moved along a small area, then drifted away under Morgan's control. "And the western coastline of our land is—here. I thought it was important that you could see the distances from one area to another."

Gella nodded.

"Increase the scale, please," Morgan requested. The picture shimmered, hurt their eyes with its twisting distortion, and settled down again to show a greater detail of the western coast of the United States. "About two hundred miles off our coastline," Morgan went on, "just about here, in some ten thousand feet of water, the Chinese have sunk two large merchant ships. They are, um, one is right here, and the other is—there. We have good photographs of them on the bottom, and—"

"How'd you manage that?" Manning broke in. "From what I understand you didn't dare go near any of them with any sort of propulsion system. The vibrations would detonate the mechanisms."

Morgan nodded. "We didn't, sir. We sent in dolphins—oh, about a hundred miles upstream of some carefully charted currents. The animals released floating cameras that went down to within two hundred feet of the bottom, using a drift touch wire for depth control. They set off automatic lights and cameras to get the photos, and, well—"

Manning nodded, working the holographic controls. "The ship to the south," Morgan said as the picture was changing, "is lying on its side."

They looked at a perfect three-dimensional view of a merchant ship resting on a rocky bottom.

"And the one to the north, west of San Francisco," Morgan went on, "is still upright."

The hologram roiled within itself, and then they were looking—from an oblique angle—at a second ship on the bottom. The holographic view continued to shrink, as though they were gaining altitude; and then they were at altitude, in the visual sense, looking down on both ships through a "transparent" ocean.

"Each vessel," Morgan said slowly to Gella, "is a complete hydrogen bomb. We will explain whenever you need to ask more questions. Forgive me if I use numbers or terms that are still foreign to you. They will mean more later. The power of these weapons," he gestured at the holographic projection, "is in what we call the gigaton yield. Each bomb, or ship is equal to many billions of tons of high explosives. Think of a thousand—or a million volcanoes exploding all at the same instant in the same small space."

Gella stared, struggling to believe. "Each ship—is like this?"

Morgan nodded. "Yes, sir, it is. Each one. And if one bomb goes off, the detonation will set off the other bomb as well. If that happens, my country— my people—face a terrible disaster."

"Gella," Manning broke in, "we estimate a wave, a tidal wave, about twelve hundred feet high, moving at a thousand miles an hour—"

He saw Gella's eyes widening, saw the sense of horror seeping into the Ikian's face as he realized the implications of what he was hearing.

"That tidal wave," Manning intoned, "will hit the West Coast of my country and will carry everything away that is aboveground, from the coast to the great mountains we call the Sierra Nevada. That wave will turn into a fog, a mist, and it will be terribly radioactive, and it will cover most of my land, moving before the wind."

Gella turned away, closed his eyes, stood with his fists tight, knuckles white, struggling wildly for better comprehension. He turned back finally, his cheek muscle showing a tic Manning had never seen before. "These other people from the surface, whom you call the Chinese. They would do this?"

Morgan stepped forward. "They sank the ships there. Then they told us about them. It was their warning. They said that if we tried to make the bombs harmless, they would go off."

"It would be—as you call it—insane," Gella protested.

"It is insane," Manning admitted. "We have all suffered from that kind of insanity. But many of us are struggling to prevent it from ever happening again. To anyone."

Morgan stuck to the moment; he had come here on a specific mission and there was no letting go. "In the meantime, sir, they threaten us in other ways. You understand the working of governments—political, military, economic, and—"

"Stop, stop," Gella pleaded. "You ask me to understand too much. I do not know of such things. Oh, yes, the words, but not the meaning. There is no such thing in Amphibus as you would call the military. I have tried to understand from your books."

His eyes pleaded with Manning for the American to know how hard he was trying. "I must think in our words," Gella went on. "Maybe the best saying is—you live under threat of—of garm beyond all number, suddenly about you."

Manning showed his respect. "You have said that very well, Gella."

"But not enough. You live with such garm, but—but *without*—maser rifles to help."

"It is true," Manning replied.

Gella endured his self-tortures several moments more, struggled his way free as he looked directly at Manning.

"We can—help?"

Manning and Morgan exchanged looks. "Yes," Manning told the Ikian leader, "you can help. We need that help as you received ours with the garm. Miko—"

"Your woman; yes."

Manning hesitated only a moment. "Miko has told me your people can go into the open sea at great depths. Even with the pressure as great as it is just beyond the dome of Amphibus. That they are not harmed."

"That is so."

Morgan's disbelief fairly exploded as he listened

to the exchange. "Under eight tons to the square inch? It would crush them like eggshells under a tank!"

Gella turned to him. "No. That is not true. Ikian system is very different. You do not understand. Miko talk long with me on this matter, with our—"

"Doctors?" Manning offered.

"Yes. As your woman explain this to us there are animals that can stay underwater for many hours. They breathe air, but they stop breathing for hours. They can dive to many thousands of feet. She calls this—I find trouble with the words, but try to remember—adaptive biology. Weddell seal is one animal like this. Also sperm whales. But they cannot breathe water and so they can be hurt. Not so with Ikians. We can breathe both. Miko tells us in her words that our lungs—"

Manning picked up the explanation after a studied glance from Gella. "There's a total saturation of the lungs and organs. The entire body," he explained to Morgan, "undergoes a drastic change, but the need isn't so much to conserve oxygen as it is to use it fully. The Weddell seal collapses its lungs, just like the sperm whale and other animals. That doesn't happen with the Ikians. They fill their systems with seawater, so there's an equalization of pressure. Inside and out. In effect, the Ikians function as warm-blooded fish. Because of equalizing the pressure—and their internal systems undergo a change that would drive some of our biologists right over the wall—they don't suffer any ill effects. There's an autonomic compensation for temperature as well."

"But—wouldn't that work only for a few hours? At the most?" Morgan was honestly taken aback by what he had heard. "They couldn't survive long enough, not for what we need—"

"Morgan, damn it, will you get it through your head that the Ikians *breathe water?*"

It began to sink in finally, as radical a departure

as it was from everything Morgan had ever known about sea and mammal biology. "My God—*then it would work.*" His voice was a hoarse expression of found hope where there had been none.

"Yes," Manning said, "it'll work."

The momentary elation fled, and bitterness showed on Morgan's face. "Damn me, I let my emotions run away with me," he said aloud. "I forgot. We can talk forever about living in the sea, but those ships are thousands of miles from here, and it would take mechanical movement to get to them. And the moment the Chinese pick that up, they're liable to take the plunge and—" He let it hang.

To his astonishment, Manning laughed. "You underestimate the Ikians, Morgan. We could bring them to within two or three hundred miles of the ship and leave the rest to them. They can handle it. Their scientists, in their own way, are as good as ours. They can be taught the mechanics of the operation with no problems."

"What the hell are they going to do?" Morgan demanded. "Swim a couple of hundred miles at a depth of ten thousand feet, carrying what they'll need in their arms?"

"You've never seen a *yren,* have you?"

"*Yren?* I don't think I can even pronounce it."

"It's a living sea sled."

"Living—"

"We'll arrange a demonstration for you. Then you'll know. But getting there from here and back again, without mechanical propulsion, simply isn't a problem. You can set Secretary Haig's mind at ease on that issue."

"Jesus, I wish it were that easy." Morgan showed his agitation. "I mean, captain, you just can't gloss over these things. They—"

"You sound like you're making your problems, Morgan."

"Well, damn it, sir, I'm not. The thing is, if *anything* goes wrong, it can, well, you know what would happen."

"If you've got better ideas," Manning said, "I suggest you lay them out. Right here and now."

"I'm not trying to raise walls," Morgan protested, "but all possible problems must be discussed. Those people are going to be in the open seas, right? They're going through waters that may be infested with sharks. If they run into the big whites, especially—hell, you know those animals always bite first and wonder what it was all about later. We can't allow weapons to be used. Not even the masers. Anything the Chinese detection systems pick up that isn't alive would probably set off the bombs. So how do Gella's people protect themselves? They—"

"*Grektor.*"

Morgan stared at Gella. "What?"

"He said *grektor*," Manning told him.

"Look, you're using words that are Greek to me. What the hell is a *grektor*?"

Manning exchanged a smile with Gella. "I think it's best if we show him."

Gella nodded. "Yes. Good."

Manning turned and motioned to Holvak. "Call the outer chamber, Eddie. Two suits with helmets. One for Captain Morgan and one for myself. We're going outside with Gella."

They explained no more to Morgan and went directly through the air lock to the pressure chamber. They suited up, had their gear checked by Prentiss.

"All set," he told them. "You need anything else, skipper?"

"Uh, no, but you'd better stand by," Manning told him. "We may be coming back unexpectedly. We want to introduce Captain Morgan to, ah, *grektor*."

Prentiss pursed his lips. "I see." He glanced at Morgan. "He's charming. Different, sort of."

Manning led Morgan to the open hatch leading into the sea. "Gella, you first, We'll follow."

They went into the water, swimming slowly beneath the great prow of the submarine. Gella looked at Manning and nodded.

Manning spoke by comset to Morgan. "He'll call him now."

"*Grektor?*"

"Uh huh."

Gella took a whistle from a pocket, brought it to his lips, and blew two short blasts. The sound came to them muffled, but still piercing.

Morgan looked about him. "I, uh, don't see anything."

Manning smiled. "Uh, Steve, we've got company."

"*Grektor?*"

"Right you are. Turn around slowly. He's just behind you."

Morgan twisted to look behind him, and his face went slack with sudden shock. His eyes went wide at the sight of the enormous head of the eel, no more than several feet away, the body seemingly endless, the great teeth shining like chrome spikes. There was a strangled sound in Manning's comset, and Morgan slumped unconscious.

Laughing with Gella, Manning brought the limp form back to the chamber entrance beneath the sub. He didn't think Morgan would have any more questions about the Ikians protecting themselves in the open sea.

24

Jessica and Arnom, hand in hand, emerged from the water and climbed stone steps into a wide high-ceilinged chamber. Across the room Luna and Miko turned to watch the approach of the youngsters. Jessica broke loose from Arnom's grasp and ran to Miko.

"There's wonderful news! Just wonderful!" she cried. She threw her arms around Miko, drenching her where their bodies met. "I—I just spoke with Commander Ryan," Jessica rushed on, nearly breathless. "They've been in touch with—with—" She drew in great gasps of air.

Miko laughed and held her at arm's length. "Easy, easy, Jessie. Take some deep breaths. That's it. Get your wind back."

Jessica shook her head, waiting several moments to regain her breathing control. She started again, the words rushing from her as she looked from Miko to Luna. "They've been in touch with New Washington, Miko, and—and they think they've located the place!"

"*What*, Jessie?"

"The spawning grounds of the garm! Where they breed!"

Miko exchanged a swift glance with Luna. The Ikian woman knew something of great import had happened, but the words had flowed too fast for her limited grasp of English. "I do not know what all this—means," she said with hesitation.

Miko took her hand. "Oh, Luna, it could mean *everything* to this valley. Captain Manning and the others were talking about it. They knew that if we could find where the garm gather to breed, to reproduce—they believe it's somewhere off a place we call the Marianas Trench—then they could go there in special submarines and destroy the garm."

Luna's eyes widened. "If that can happen, then— no more garm—here?"

"That's right!" Jessica said, half shouting with delight. "Oh, Miko, wouldn't that be a marvelous thing for us to do for our friends?"

"Yes. Of course it would," Miko replied. She thought of the incredible attack, the way both the Ikians and the others had died, and a shudder went through her body. To know that her people could smash the breeding grounds and free the Ikians from that horrible danger—a black cloud seemed to lift from her mind, a terrible weight alleviated, for Miko had never been able to forget for an instant that the radiation loosed into the sea by the race living on the surface had done more than simply despoil the ocean. It had changed a threat into a horror that could destroy the delicate balance under which the Ikians had lived for so many thousands of years.

Jessica stepped back suddenly, studying Miko as if she were seeing her for the first time. "I—I never noticed," Jessica said slowly. "You're wearing an Ikian dress! It's—beautiful, Miko. You're beautiful!"

Again she was in Miko's arms, hugging her tightly for joy. Her face was against Miko's shoulder. "Oh, I'd love for it to happen to you, too. You know, like me and Arnom."

Miko stroked her glistening wet hair. "You never know, Jessie. You just never know." She smiled. "It does seem to be a time for miracles, doesn't it?"

Luna touched her arm gently. "You are talking about Manning Captain."

Miko averted her eyes, nodded.

"These things are the same everywhere," Luna said quietly. "It will be."

Miko's feelings showed in her face, "Perhaps. That's all the promise I can give myself. At least it will do for now." She laughed, her eyes bright. "Anyway, maybe it will happen by the time we return."

The room went silent. Jessica's strained voice broke the heavy air. "*Return?*" she forced out.

Luna reached out to take Miko's hand. "You, Manning Captain, the others—you are leaving us?"

Miko held Luna's hand with both hands. "Not all of us, Luna. Templeton will remain here, but Dr. Chadwick must speak to our—president. He will come back. Commander MacKinney and two other men are staying to work with your people so they will be able to use the maser rifles if necessary. And there are projects to generate electricity, and, well, many other things." Miko looked fondly at Jessica. "And she, of course, is home now."

Luna did not smile. "When will this happen?"

"Tomorrow, perhaps the day after," Miko answered. "But we'll all be back soon. Don't look so unhappy, Luna! It's only for a short while. Anyway, we're not leaving until Captain Manning is back from a trip. He's going to the surface in one of the small submarines. With Gella."

Luna held her hand over her mouth, her eyes wide and staring. She seemed to have been struck a physical blow.

"Gella! To the other—world?"

"Yes. It will be a visit when it is night." Miko

turned to Arnom. "Captain Manning wants you to be at the big submarine this afternoon."

Arnom didn't speak but pointed a finger at himself, his face questioning.

"That's right," Miko smiled. "You are to go with them."

Jessica spoke for Arnom. "But where are they going?"

"I believe it's to—" Miko shook her head. "Captain Manning will explain it to him."

They assembled in the main pressure chamber with one of the four-man submarines ready for launching. Manning, Ryan, Simmonds, Prentiss, and Autry were present, joined by Gella and Arnom. Several more Ikians were expected to arrive shortly to witness the event and departure. Throughout the chamber, special pressure suits had been hung on racks, and the shelves and floor were virtually littered with equipment. Manning and Simmonds were deep in conversation, Gella standing by their side listening intently.

"Then it's a reverse process," Manning said slowly to the doctor. "The Ikian body can withstand greater pressure, but only a restricted reduction—in other words, it's dangerous for them to move into an area of *low* pressure—either water or air."

Simmonds nodded. "That's how I see it. I've spent hours with their medical people. We're in agreement. Gella?"

The Ikian leader spoke. "That is right. We have never done a thing like that. It is too dangerous. Even the air rooms always have more pressure than the Great Valley."

"It's easy enough to understand," Simmonds said. "You and I," he nodded to Manning, "live our lives under normal air pressure of about fourteen to fifteen pounds per square inch. We can go into the sea, or even into a pressurized compartment like this with a few hundred pounds per square inch without any ill effects, just as long as we take proper precautions and follow time procedures. We can take reduced pressure also, like flying in unpressurized aircraft, or increasing oxygen content. We can make it on three to five psi without trouble if we're under 100 percent oxygen. But we do reach a limit: We just can't step out of a ship on the moon—"

"Without a pressure suit to carry a bit of local environment with us," Manning added.

"Precisely. So the thing to keep in mind," Simmonds said, "is that *our* normal pressure would be like a vacuum to Gella and his people. They'd go through the same kind of explosive decompression we would experience if we moved from sea level pressure to, oh, say seventy or eighty thousand feet up. It would kill them."

"Okay so far," Manning said. "So the nut of all this is that if they're wearing a suit to about 150 psi, they could make it fine in our atmosphere, right?"

"Just like our people did when they walked on the moon or moved around outside their orbiting ships," Simmonds agreed.

Manning turned to Prentiss. "Syd, what's the pressure limit on those suits?"

"It's 240 psi, captain."

"So we've got a safety factor of ninety psi, then," Manning said.

A knowing look dawned on Simmonds's face. "Hey, wait a minute. I thought this was some sort of intellectual exercise, skipper. You don't intend to take Gella to the surface?"

"I do. And he wants to go. We're also taking the boy, Arnom." Manning gestured to the other crewmen. "Bring those suits here. Give Gella and Arnom a hand. Do it slow and do it by the numbers, and check it out every step of the way."

Manning walked to a wall comset and punched the transmit button. "Manning here. Ryan, you ready?"

Bill Ryan was already in the control seat of the small four-man sub. His voice rang clearly from the bulkhead speakers. "We're all set, captain."

"Very good, Bill. Bring the systems up to full activate."

"Right."

Manning hesitated, spoke again. "Bill, be sure to set the suit pressure exactly at two two zero."

"Got it," Ryan confirmed.

They spent the next thirty minutes assisting Gella and Arnom into their suits, explaining how the equipment functioned, how to increase internal pressure if the sub-supplied systems failed.

Simmonds watched every move closely. For a long time he kept silent, then he motioned to Manning. "Captain, would you mind spelling out just what this is all about?"

"It's obvious, isn't it? We're going topside in the small boat."

"But you're taking a hell of a risk! Do you know what will happen if something goes wrong and Gella is hurt badly, or dies? You'd wreck everything we've done down here!"

"It's worth the risk, John."

"How the hell can you say that?" Simmonds demanded. "What's so bloody important that you've got to take this kind of chance!"

Manning locked his eyes with those of the doctor. When he spoke, his voice was quiet, confident. "John, have you ever seen the stars?"

"What?"

"You heard me."

"Of—of course I've seen them. I don't understand what you're getting at."

"Gella is breaking tradition. He's working with us. A lot of people down here in this valley can't even begin to comprehend what the sky looks like. I want Gella and that kid to see the stars. Just to see them. Even through their helmets. It'll say more than all the words we know a thousand times over. *Just one look*. That's all."

He turned away from the doctor. Gella and Arnom stood clumsily in their heavy suits, barely able to move without assistance. It was more than satisfactory. They would be seated in the submarine. There'd be no need for them to move about. When they were on the surface—and Manning and Ryan would decompress slowly through the long ascent—the Ikians would still be subjected to the same pressure they felt at this moment.

A journey to the surface—to another world.

For one look at the stars.

Enough to change a man's life—and to bring two races closer together.

Manning studied the two Ikians, hooked up now with snap-in communication plugs. Through the glassite helmets Gella managed a weak smile. He spoke into the small microphone in the glassite before his lips. "You can hear me, Manning Captain?"

"Yes. Very clear. How about yourself, Gella?"

He nodded inside the helmet. "It is all very strange."

Manning smiled at him. "That's how we felt when you taught us to breathe water."

"Yes. I understand." Gella's voice came through with a faint mechanical tinge. "It is also, as you say —I cannot remember the word."

"Exciting?"

"That is it."

Manning turned to the others. "Are we ready?"

Prentiss nodded. "All set, captain. They're ready to board."

Gella strained to lift a gloved hand. "We must wait."

Manning turned slowly. "I don't understand.

"I have promised—the council. They are to be here before we leave. Never before has such a thing happened to our people. It is necessary."

Manning frowned. He wished Gella had mentioned this earlier, but . . .

"Of course. When will they be here?"

"They are coming now. They will have—"

A warning chime sounded and the bridge came through on the speakers. "A group of Ikians, sir, waiting to come into the chamber."

The belly hatch was well lighted, and the water swirled as the seven members of the council came into the chamber. Dressed in ceremonial attire, they moved solemnly, as if heavy weights were attached to their bodies. For several moments they stared at Gella and Arnom in their suits.

Hydrea stepped forward, stiff and formal. He nodded to Manning.

"Manning Captain," he said, and his voice was icy, almost trembling, as he went through the necessary protocol.

"I greet you, Hydrea, and welcome you," Manning replied in the same manner.

"We would speak with Gella."

"He can hear you."

"We must speak also to his eyes. It is necessary."

Manning nodded. "Remove their helmets," he said to his crew. They waited while the pressure helmets were unscrewed and taken from the suits of Gella and Arnom.

Gella's face was impassive. None of the Americans questioned that they were on the edge of a possible dangerous breach in their relationship with the Ikians.

"The council speaks through me," Hydrea said, and it was a sign of respect that he forced out his words in English rather than in their own tongue.

Gella nodded. "I listen."

Hydrea drew himself up straight; there was anger and distrust in his eyes. "The council speaks through me," he repeated, "and we ask you also to listen, Manning Captain."

"I am listening," Manning said, maintaining the formal exchange.

Hydrea turned back to Gella. "It is not good. The council speaks through me. You and the boy are not to visit the other world. It is not to be permitted."

The room went deathly silent. Manning, expecting Gella to protest, was caught completely unaware when Gella nodded his assent. "I listen," Gella said finally. "What the council decides will be done."

Again the long, awkward pause until Manning broke the silence. "We will—we will accede to your wishes, of course," he told Gella. Then, to Hydrea, "And to the council. We do not wish to offend. But may I ask why you have decided this way?"

Gella answered for him. "It is to be maybe later," he said. "I understand. They have met, and they have talked about what you would call our scriptures. The holy book."

"We must not go against the Father," Hydrea added.

"I do not understand," Manning said to him. "I listen, and I hear, but I am confused. Will you help us to understand?"

For the first time the strain eased in Hydrea's face. There could have been confrontation here. His worst fears were being bled away. These were the men who had brought poison to the great waters, who had created the garm as they were now. No matter that they had helped to fight them, that now they could destroy the garm forever. These were the men who had brought evil—long before they themselves appeared—to the Great Valley. The council had studied and spoken long among themselves, going over the scriptures that every Ikian learned from childhood. There was violation here of the Old Laws. Laws could change, but these were not yet to be broken.

The scriptures had never been wrong, and they warned of disaster.

"Manning Captain, I will try," Hydrea said, his words halting, spoken with difficulty in the alien language of English. "Matthews friend, he understood. He can speak best, but he is gone for us. We have made friends with your people. I have not agreed with this, but the council spoke, and I have listened to their words. Now Gella must also listen and he must obey. Your people, and our people, are learning much together. As you helped us with the garm, so we will help you with the ships in the far ocean."

Hydrea took a deep breath, looked back to the council members. They nodded for him to continue.

"No Ikian may leave the world in which we have been given the blessings to live," Hydrea said. "It is dangerous."

Manning shook his head. "We would not permit any harm to come to them, Hydrea."

"Not to them," Hydrea corrected Manning's interpretation. "To our race."

He stood proudly and his eyes seemed to go vacant, as if he were looking elsewhere. "I will speak of our scriptures." His voice took on an almost hypnotic tone, and it was obvious that he believed implicitly in every word he spoke.

"In the beginning the world was barren," Hydrea began slowly. "The holy scriptures tell us that waters go forever about whole world. Then Father of All placed His hand beneath the waters and . . . and He pulled up land. Here where there is no water there is no life. But where the Father's finger touch . . . there became a mountain. Still it is dead. Then the Father breathe on land and there is fire. From land and fire, and from water that the Father now bring to mix with the land and fire, there is *Iki*.

"This means . . . man. Iki is the first man. The Father grows living plants, and from a flower he creates *Hava*. This means woman. And the man and the woman were taken by the Father to what is called shore. This is so they can live where there is both land and water.

"Iki and Hava they . . . mate. Out of them rose the People. But they live only on dry land. Iki and Hava walk among the children they bring to the land. Many generations pass, and there are many more people, and they grow old and they die even as children born to them. But not Iki and Hava. They are . . . different, they can live on the land and they can live in the water, as the Father made them. But the land people forget the Father, and they scorn Iki and Hava."

Hydrea stopped, breathing deeply, for he was struggling to relate in this alien language what he had known by heart since he was a child who had completed his First Learning. Gella looked at him without expression, waiting. Hydrea went on, more slowly now.

"There is no place for Iki and Hava. They leave the land and go deeper into the water. They swim very deep. One day they find the Great Valley. They live there, under dome, helping it to grow. They live in water as the Father of All meant man to live. They begat many children who also breathe water or air, like them. Finally the Father of All say it is time for them to rest. So Iki and Hava die and return to the True Father of all things that swim in the sea. Life is good to sea people of Great Valley. It is true home."

Hydrea's face seemed to take on a hardness. "It is not so on the land, where the people forget the Father of All. A madness comes to them. They kill one another and they destroy the home where they live. It is bad. Poison is everywhere and one day the poisons come into the sea. The sea people know this and they make the great dome ever stronger. And the Father told the sons of Iki and Hava never to venture above the waters, never to go to the land where there is madness, for they would be destroyed. And what happen to them will happen to the Great Valley.

"This is . . . scripture," Hydrea concluded. "It is holy law. Gella and Arnom must not break. They must not go to the land. Evil will fall upon us."

Gella moved forward slowly until he stood face-to-face with Hydrea. He did not speak for a long time. Finally he nodded.

"I say two things to the council," he said. "First, we will obey the council. It is always so and must be so."

Murmurs of assent and approval came from the elder Ikians until Gella held up his hand, a strenuous effort in the pressure suit he was still wearing. Silence met his gesture.

"But more is to be spoken. Hydrea does not tell all the scriptures." Gella turned from the council to face Manning. "The scriptures say more. They say there will come time when men not of evil will be led by the Father of All back to the sea. When this happen, then all men would again be as they were at the Beginning."

Hydrea's anger flared. "This time not here yet!"

"I do not know," Gella told him calmly. "You do not know."

Manning had been listening carefully. Now he spoke. "We will not go against the council," he said. "But you are wrong, Hydrea. We believe the time has come for men to join. All men."

"Evil is here," Hydrea said darkly.

"There is evil everywhere," Gella said. "But this is not for us to say with new friends. We must talk ourselves." He gestured to the Americans. "Please." They helped him and Arnom from the pressure suits.

Gella stood tall and proud. "The scriptures say more. They say sea people, like all people, must obey the law of the Father of All. There must be no fear of the future. We have fear. Hydrea is a good man. He fears for us. That is good. But we must learn to understand. Just as Iki and Hava were driven away once, so we must not be driven to hiding forever. Manning Captain has taught me much of time, of a time for growing. If there is no growing, there must be a dying."

Gella looked at the council. They met his gaze, nodded slowly. "Good. We agree. You leave Great Valley, when?" he said to Manning.

"One day from now."

"We wish you to return soon."

Manning flicked his eyes from Gella to the other Ikians. "Is that the wish of the council also?"

They nodded. "It is," said one Ikian who was wearing a deep blue suit. Manning recognized him. He was known as the Keeper of the Law. His voice went a long way. Manning was pleased; it wasn't as bad as it had started out to be.

"While you are gone," Gella said slowly, "we would like to make the girl of us."

The operation. Jessica would be able to breathe air or water as freely as the Ikians. Without bionic or any other implants. It was also a test, for the surface people would leave her totally at the mercy of the Ikians.

"The girl wishes this to be so," Manning said. "She has chosen Arnom as her life-companion."

"It is true," Gella said.

He turned again to the Ikian elders, but his words were meant for Manning. "When you return, much will have been spoken here. Much will be decided. The girl Jessica is to become one of us. She will then be of both of us. There will be no evil, for none is meant."

"That is true," Manning said.

"When you return, it will be the time," Gella went on. "As the girl becomes of us, so we must start to become of you. It will be then, when you are here again and the races are joined, that I will rise with you to the top of the water world."

Murmuring spread among the Ikians. Gella surprised them all with the sudden authority in his voice.

"It is time for the crossing," Gella said.

He looked from one face to another until he had met the gaze of every man in the chamber.

"It is time for an Ikian to see where lives the Father of All.

"And that is beyond this world. It must be so. It is time."

Manning turned to face the Ikian he had come to know as a friend. He reached out to grip Gella's arm.

"We will be back, and you will make that crossing, if it is to be so. I leave you with a promise, Gella."

"Speak, Manning Captain."

"We will be back, and the stars will be waiting for you."

ABOUT THE AUTHOR

MARTIN CAIDIN, a prolific and versatile writer with more than eighty books to his credit, is also a commercial and military pilot, a stunt flyer, parachutist and a recognized authority in the field of aviation and astronautics. From 1950 to 1954 Martin Caidin served as nuclear warfare specialist for the state of New York. He analyzed the effects of nuclear and other weapons on potential targets in the United States. As a commercial multi-engine pilot, Mr. Caidin flies his own plane all over the country. He has flown two-engine and four-engine bombers to Europe. For a time he flew his own World War II Messerschmitt in Europe and the United States. Martin Caidin's first novel, *Marooned*, a thrilling account of a space rescue, became a major motion picture, and *Devil Take All, No Man's World* and *Almost Midnight* were all bought for films. *Cyborg*, published in 1972, is now the highly popular ABC-TV series "The Six Million Dollar Man." Mr. Caidin is the author of an impressive list of authoritative books on military air history. Many of them, including *Samurai!, Zero!* and *The Ragged, Rugged Warriors*, are considered classics in their field. Martin Caidin is a charter member of the Aviation Hall of Fame, a Fellow of the British Interplanetary Society and a founder of the American Astronautical Society. Although he and his wife, Isobel, live within sight of the launching towers at Cape Kennedy, Martin Caidin is giving much of his attention these days to the problems we have fashioned for ourselves with nuclear weapons.

Turn the page for an exciting Special Preview of another book.

JAWS 2

CHAPTER ONE

Bantam is pleased to bring you this bonus preview. It's the exciting opening chapter of the completely new novel based on characters created in Jaws. Read on...

JAWS 2

CHAPTER ONE

A flattened, blood-red sun rose dead ahead.

The white Hatteras powerboat, *Miss Carriage* out of Sag Harbor, slithered around Montauk Point. She emerged from Long Island Sound and rose to the swell of open ocean. The two half-suited Scuba divers high on her flying bridge took wider stances.

The taller of the two, an obstetrician from Astoria General on Long Island, flicked off the running lights. The shorter was a Manhattan attorney for Union Carbide. The two had little in common except an interest in diving, diminishing as they aged, and a partnership in the boat. They almost never met except on summer weekends.

Years ago the doctor had decided that his little partner was a Jewish pinko, and simply accepted it. The lawyer sensed bigotry but ignored it. Friends or not, each had some $30,000 in the boat, and there was the security of a known companion. Each was sure that the other was a steadier diver than himself.

Every year, the physician dreaded the first few scallop dives of spring. Equipment always felt strange at first. The water would be cold and cloudy. And here, off Amity Township, lurked a ghost.

The beast was dead. The doctor had all but forgotten the stories in the *Long Island Press*. The Manhattan lawyer seldom thought of the pictures in the *Times*. But a secret half-tone specter swam in the subconscious of each.

The doctor was suddenly cold. He glanced at the recording fathometer tracing the depth. They were searching for a clump of bottom-rocks they knew, but the graph on the instrument was still flat as the trace of a terminal patient in Intensive Care. The doctor pictured mud below, and silt.

He shivered and swung down the flying-bridge ladder. He tugged his neoprene upper-suit from behind a tank-rack in the cockpit, and squirmed into it. He had put on weight.

Even after he smoothed it on, he was still shivering. He stepped into the cabin. He had not got his sealegs yet. Crossing to the stainless galley stove behind the service bar, he lurched into a rattan barstool and knocked it over. He swore softly and set it up. Then he moved behind the counter and took two cups from a rack. He poured a double slug of Old Grandad into his cup and a single into his partner's, then filled the cups with coffee from the stove. He started out, remembered that it was impossible to carry two cups up the ladder to the flying bridge, and sat down at the lower steering-station to sip the stronger one below.

The groundswell, which was making him queasy, told him that they were paralleling the beach too closely offshore. He gazed for a moment, through binoculars, out the starboard window. The gray summer cottages of Napeague, Amagansett, East Hampton and Sagaponack slumbered less than half a mile away. In them, early tenants would be awakening to the gut-growl of the boat's twin Chryslers. A child poked along the tide-flats, teased to run by a huge woolly dog. The doctor found a strange comfort in the cottages and decided after all not to ask his partner to move further out.

The sound of the engines suddenly diminished to a quiet chortle. Obviously, the first trace of the fathometer had sprung to life.

The doctor slipped down from the lower helmsman's seat. He hesitated, then slugged down the drink he had intended for the man topside. He went forward and dangled a stainless Danforth anchor until he felt the bottom some 30 feet below. As his partner backed slowly, he paid off chain and line. Finally he snubbed the line on a bow-cleat, and signaled his partner that the hook was properly set.

Sidling aft along the narrow deck outboard of the cabin, he glanced at the shoreline. All the shoulder-to-shoulder communities lining Long Island dunes had always looked the same to him, but he was pretty sure he had anchored on the doorstep of Amity.

The Great White swam south, 20 feet below the surface, leaving Block Island to her right. She came left, dead on course for Montauk Point.

She was gravid with young in both uteri and her hunger was overwhelming. She had fed last night off Nantucket on a school of cod and all night long she had held course southwest along the coast of Rhode Island. She had swept into Newport Bay and found nothing, banked gracefully like a cargo plane, and resumed her track south. Her six-foot high tail propelled her bulk with stiff, purposeful power.

Before her, an invisible cone of fear swept the sea clean, from bottom to surface. For a full mile ahead the ocean was emptying of life. Seals, porpoises, whales, squid, all fled. All had sensors—electromagnetic, aural, vibratory, or psychic—which were heralding her coming. As she passed, the Atlantic refilled in her wake.

Man would have ignored such sensors, if he still

had them, in favor of intelligence. But man was not her normal prey.

To overcome the clairvoyance of her quarry, she was ordinarily swifter than whatever animal she pursued. Her food included almost any creature of worthwhile size that swam, floated, or crawled in the ocean. But she had become so large, near term, that her speed was down.

She grew more ravenous with every mile that passed.

Halfway down the anchor-line the doctor paused. His panting, amplified in his regulator, was ear-splitting. He was sure his partner, descending in a green flowering of bubbles 10 feet below him, could hear every gasp. Clinging to the half-inch rope, he tried to relax.

Hyperventilation in the first dive was normal. But if he could not slow his breathing he would be out of air and forced to surface in ten or fifteen minutes. There was pride involved. Despite his size and greater metabolic requirements, his tank always outlasted the smaller man's. He could not understand the apprehension that was making him pant.

When his respiration eased, his ears began to ache. He jammed his mask tightly against his face, wheezed air through his nose, and cleared his Eustachian tubes.

He resumed his descent. Visibility was better than he had expected—15 feet or more—but he had already lost his partner. When he reached the bottom, he followed the anchor line along the sand until it became chain. Fifteen feet further he found the lawyer in a cloud of silt, trying to bury the Danforth against the outgoing tide. He assisted in this and finally they had the anchor-flukes buried.

The lawyer glanced at his wrist compass,

jerked his thumb toward the north, and began to swim back along the track they had taken, searching for the clump of rocks. The doctor followed, cruising five feet above the bottom and off his partner's left hip. He began to feel at home again. His heart had stopped hammering. His three-shot breakfast was working through his system, calming him wonderfully.

Swimming along, he glanced at his partner and found himself smiling. The little attorney was burdened with all the equipment that money could buy. His mask was prescription-ground so that he needed no glasses. He wore a pressure-equalizing vest. This was its maiden voyage, and he kept climbing and descending as he tried to regulate it.

On the lawyer's left wrist was the compass, and on his right an underwater watch to give him bottom time. From his neck dangled a Nikonos underwater camera. They had used it last year and found the light below too weak, so now it had a strobe.

Strapped to the lawyer's left calf was a Buck diving knife; on his right leg was an aluminum scallop-iron for their prey.

He looked, thought the doctor, like Dustin Hoffman in *The Graduate*, hiding from the festivities at the bottom of his parents' swimming pool.

Dawn had begun to shimmer faintly down to her as she passed Montauk. Her eyes were black, flat, and unblinking, giving her an air of profound wisdom. Her pupils were mirror-polished inside, so she had excellent vision even in this dim light. But she continued to navigate as before, blindly and mindlessly as a computer would, using the electro-receptor *ampullae* which covered her head to sense the orientation of the earth's magnetic field.

Two years before, not far from here, she had been hit by a male not much smaller than she. Grasping her dorsal in his jaws, he had somehow borne her, despite her superior strength, to the muddy bottom. There, passive and supine, she had received both of his yard-long, salami-shaped claspers into her twin vents.

Her back, though her skin was composed of thousands of tiny teeth itself, was still scarred from his grip.

Even before her pregnancy she had outweighed her passing mate and any creature in the seas except for some cetaceans and her own harmless relatives, the basking and whale-shark.

At 30 feet and almost two tons, she was longer than a killer whale and heavier by half.

Now, near term, her girth was enormous. In her left uterus squirmed three young. In her right lived five, three females and two males. The smallest was a little over three feet long and weighed only 22 pounds. He was, nevertheless, a fully functional being. He had survived *in utero* for almost two years, eating thousands of unfertilized eggs and, with his remaining brother and sisters, some 30 weaker siblings.

He himself was not out of danger yet, especially from his sisters, who were uniformly larger than males. If the mother hunted successfully for the next few weeks, her egg production would satisfy his siblings and he would probably live.

If he successfully fought off his sisters, he would be born at the top of the oceanic feeding triangle.

Already, he feared no kind but his own.

The lawyer slowed and the doctor almost overran him. His partner was pointing to the left. The doctor turned his head. He saw a shape, tinged darker green than the pale water through which they swam. It was not the clump of rocks they had dived last year. It was abrupt, angular, man-made.

Excitedly, his partner swam toward it. The doctor followed. The stern of a wrecked fishing boat, bigger and heavier than their own, loomed from the murk. Green shards of light played on her barnacle-covered transom. She was an immensely rugged old craft. The growth on her twisted planks told them that she had been here for some time.

The doctor spotted a heavy hawser lying along the sand. It led below the half-buried quarter of the hulk. He pulled himself along it, jerked at the line, could not move it. He rounded the stern to see where it led on the other side. The lawyer porpoised along beside him, trying to adjust his buoyancy.

The doctor found the other end of the rope. Secured to it by a giant shackle, a 55-gallon iron drum bumped restlessly against the hull. It was crushed and dented, but the remains of yellow paint showed that it had once been meant as a float.

The current swept it suddenly against the hulk with a mournful clang. The Old Grandad left the doctor's veins in a rush. He was very cold.

The lawyer had swum aft. He was rubbing at the seagrass whiskers growing on the stern. He suddenly yanked his scallop-iron from its scabbard and chiseled loose a half-dozen barnacles, loosening a mist of mud. When the water cleared, the doctor could read, in faint orange letters, the name *Orca*, home port *Narragansatt*. The name chorded some deep memory. He looked at his partner.

Behind the lawyer's face-plate, enlarged by the prescription lenses, he saw his companion's gray eyes crinkle in thought. Suddenly the lawyer jammed a fist into a palm, remembering something. Excitedly, he began to grunt, their signal for something out of the ordinary. He waved toward the orange letters. Then he took both hands, fingers clawed like teeth, and swept them through the motion of huge jaws closing.

He pointed again at the name on the shattered stern. The doctor understood.

The half-forgotten news story of a shark-fisherman, a tank-town police chief, and some oceanographic expert or other, read long ago in the *Long Island Press*, surfaced in his mind.

He discovered that he did not like it here. They were after scallop, not wrecks, and anything of souvenir value must have been salvaged by other divers long ago. He found, in fact, that he was no longer even interested in the scallops. His breath was rasping again and his heart hammering, and he felt the first indications of low tank pressure.

He pointed to the surface, but his companion shook his head, tapped the camera, and drew him to a position by the stern. He planted him under the overhang of the sternboards. Then the lawyer backed off, camera-to-faceplate.

The doctor pointed obediently at the letters on the transom, smiling idiotically around his mouthpiece. His partner, trying to stand erect on the bottom, seemed to take forever.

The doctor had suddenly to urinate. The strange apprehension he had felt all morning gripped his bladder and squeezed it tight. When he could wait no longer he simply voided into his wet-suit pants. The warmth of it was good along his side, but did not help the chill in his gut.

He heard the *clunk* of the steel barrel against the hulk, and felt it through his glove where he held to the plank. He could hear his own hoarse gasping and his companion's breath as well.

The strobe light fired, turning everything momentarily white. All at once he heard a sound like a subway train, fast approaching from his rear. His partner, dancing on sand as he tried to balance in the current, wound his camera, then stopped. He stared at something approaching from above and behind the doctor. His mouthpiece fell from his face.

The doctor, startled, began to turn but instinctively hunkered down instead, clinging to a broken plank. His eyes were riveted on his companion. A great bubble soared from his partner's mouth. The lawyer threw up an arm to protect himself. The camera strap fouled and the strobe fired again, illuminating everything and making the doctor feel naked.

The green surface light faded. An enormous bulk, descending like a gliding jet, swept by, a foot above the doctor's head, blotting out the dancing sunlight. It seemed to pass forever. The last of the shape became a tail, towering taller than himself. It swished once, almost sweeping him loose and blotting his view of his partner in a cloud of bottom-silt and mud.

There was silence. The barrel clanged.

The doctor clung to the splintered plank, peering into the settling murk. He could hear only his own tortured breathing. He was terrified at the loudness of it, and of his bubbles, beckoning whatever it was back to the spot. But he could not quiet the panting, and he could not budge from the stern.

One of his partner's diving fins bounced past, heading to sea on the tidal current. He could have reached out and touched it. He made no move.

It was fear that finally drove him from shelter. He became more frightened of dying where he was with an empty tank than of discovery. Tentatively, he moved a few feet from the stern and waited. Nothing happened. In a burst of courage, he kicked off.

He remembered to rise no faster than his bubbles,

remembered to kick slowly and steadily without panic—for whatever it was would be attuned to panic—remembered, as the depths turned from dark green to shimmering jade, to breathe and breathe again, so that the expanding air in his lungs would not burst them—though the noise of his breathing terrified him. He remembered, when he surfaced into golden sunlight, to shift his mouth from regulator to snorkel. He remembered to drop his weight belt for easier swimming. And he remembered, for a while, to kick with a careful, pedaling motion so as not to splash the surface with his fins.

He eased his head from the water. The Hatteras slapped at anchor hardly a hundred feet away. His fear diminished. A rush of joy that it was he who had survived, a flow of ecstasy almost sexual, warmed his veins.

Carefully, he slithered toward the boat. He hardly broke the water. Once he stopped and glided, gazing straight down. He saw nothing but shafts of emerald light lancing the depths below.

He raised his head. A thousand yards beyond the boat slept the houses by the dunes. Two tiny figures raced along the tide line. It seemed an eternity since he had seen them from the cabin, but it was the same child, same woolly dog. He could hear the dog barking.

He shivered suddenly. Deep in his soul he felt another onrush of terror. He quickened the beat of his fins. One of them plopped loudly, and then the other, but he had less than 30 feet to go. He could no longer stand the dragging pace.

With 20 feet to go, he was sprinting, thrashing recklessly, breathing in enormous chest-searing gulps.

All at once, 10 feet from the boat, he felt a bump and a firm, decisive grasp on his left femur, some three inches above his knee. It was surprising, but not at all violent. His first thought was that his partner had somehow survived, caught up with him from below, and plucked his thigh for attention. He dipped his mask, looking down.

He was amazed to see half a human leg, swathed in neoprene, tumbling into the depths. He observed that, though fully detached from the upper femur at the *superpatellar bursa*, it exhibited little bleeding from its own portion of the femoral artery, though a cloud of blood from somewhere else was forming quickly. Whoever had amputated had performed neatly: the skin along the incision was scalpel-clean.

He was filled with sudden lassitude. He floated, fascinated by the leg spinning into the depths. He had the sense of something vast moving below the limb, out of his zone of visibility, but he was strangely giddy and somehow did not care. The leg rose as if bumped, and disappeared.

His left side was weak. He wondered if he had had a heart attack or even a stroke. He was getting too old to dive. He might even sell his share in the boat. He began feebly to swim again.

He heard the faint subway roar. He did not care. He stopped moving. He was too tired to fight his sleepiness, though the boat was only three strokes away. He would doze awhile like a basking seal, and swim the last few feet later.

Then he was borne aloft. He sensed that his ribs, lungs, spleen, kidneys, bowels, duodenum, were being squeezed firmly together as if in a giant hydraulic press.

He felt no pain at all.

And the great white shark moves on, gliding silently and undetected underwater, still in desperate search for food.

On land, Chief of Police Martin Brody, his wife Ellen and their two sons are unaware of the dangers in store for them once again. In fact, the town is just recovering from the disaster caused by one shark four summers ago.

JAWS 2

an all-new novel, contains many of the pulse-pounding elements of Jaws, as well as new people, new situations and intimate knowledge of diving and the sea life—all of which make this totally new book an edge-of-the-seat reading experience.

Amity, four years later. The terror continues.

JAWS 2

A novel by Hank Searls. Based on the screenplay by Howard Sackler and Dorothy Tristan. From the characters created by Peter Benchley.

JAWS 2 THE BOOK

APRIL 19 Read the complete Bantam Book.

On sale wherever paperbacks are sold.

JAWS 2 THE MOVIE

JUNE 16 See the Universal Release.

At theaters across the country.

ROY SCHEIDER LORRAINE GARY

JAWS 2

A ZANUCK/BROWN PRODUCTION

Also Starring

MURRAY HAMILTON

Screenplay by CARL GOTTLIEB • Screen Story by HOWARD SACKLER and DOROTHY TRISTAN • Directed by JEANNOT SZWARC • Based Upon Characters Created by PETER BENCHLEY • Music by JOHN WILLIAMS • Produced by RICHARD D. ZANUCK and DAVID BROWN • A UNIVERSAL PICTURE • Color by Technicolor • Filmed in Panavision

DON'T MISS
THESE CURRENT
Bantam Bestsellers

☐	11001	**DR. ATKINS DIET REVOLUTION**	$2.25
☐	11580	**THE CASTLE MADE FOR LOVE** Barbara Cartland	$1.50
☐	10970	**HOW TO SPEAK SOUTHERN** Mitchell & Rawls	$1.25
☐	10077	**TRINITY** Leon Uris	$2.75
☐	10759	**ALL CREATURES GREAT AND SMALL** James Herriot	$2.25
☐	11770	**ONCE IS NOT ENOUGH** Jacqueline Susann	$2.25
☐	11699	**THE LAST CHANCE DIET** Dr. Robert Linn	$2.25
☐	10422	**THE DEEP** Peter Benchley	$2.25
☐	10306	**PASSAGES** Gail Sheehy	$2.50
☐	11255	**THE GUINNESS BOOK OF WORLD RECORDS** 16th Ed. McWhirters	$2.25
☐	10080	**LIFE AFTER LIFE** Raymond Moody, Jr.	$1.95
☐	11917	**LINDA GOODMAN'S SUN SIGNS**	$2.25
☐	2600	**RAGTIME** E. L. Doctorow	$2.25
☐	10888	**RAISE THE TITANIC!** Clive Cussler	$2.25
☐	2491	**ASPEN** Burt Hirschfeld	$1.95
☐	2300	**THE MONEYCHANGERS** Arthur Hailey	$1.95
☐	2222	**HELTER SKELTER** Vincent Bugliosi	$1.95

Buy them at your local bookstore or use this handy coupon for ordering:

Bantam Books Inc., Dept. FB, 414 East Golf Road, Des Plaines, Ill. 60016

Please send me the books I have checked above. I am enclosing $_____ (please add 50¢ to cover postage and handling). Send check or money order—no cash or C.O.D.'s please.

Mr/Mrs/Miss_____

Address_____

City_____State/Zip_____

FB-3/78

Please allow four weeks for delivery. This offer expires 9/78.

RELAX!
SIT DOWN
and Catch Up On Your Reading!

☐	10077	**TRINITY** by Leon Uris	$2.75
☐	2300	**THE MONEYCHANGERS** by Arthur Hailey	$1.95
☐	2424	**THE GREAT TRAIN ROBBERY** by Michael Crichton	$1.95
☐	2500	**THE EAGLE HAS LANDED** by Jack Higgins	$1.95
☐	2600	**RAGTIME** by E. L. Doctorow	$2.25
☐	10360	**CONFLICT OF INTEREST** by Les Whitten	$1.95
☐	10092	**THE SWISS ACCOUNT** by Leslie Waller	$1.95
☐	2964	**THE ODESSA FILE** by Frederick Forsyth	$1.95
☐	11770	**ONCE IS NOT ENOUGH** by Jacqueline Susann	$2.25
☐	8500	**JAWS** by Peter Benchley	$1.95
☐	8844	**TINKER, TAILOR, SOLDIER, SPY** by John Le Carre	$1.95
☐	11929	**THE DOGS OF WAR** by Frederick Forsyth	$2.25
☐	10090	**THE R DOCUMENT** by Irving Wallace	$2.25
☐	10526	**INDIA ALLEN** by Elizabeth B. Coker	$1.95
☐	10357	**THE HARRAD EXPERIMENT** by Robert Rimmer	$1.95
☐	10422	**THE DEEP** by Peter Benchley	$2.25
☐	10500	**DOLORES** by Jacqueline Susann	$1.95
☐	11601	**THE LOVE MACHINE** by Jacqueline Susann	$2.25
☐	10600	**BURR** by Gore Vidal	$2.25
☐	10857	**THE DAY OF THE JACKAL** by Frederick Forsyth	$1.95
☐	11366	**DRAGONARD** by Rupert Gilchrist	$1.95
☐	11057	**PROVINCETOWN** by Burt Hirschfeld	$1.95
☐	11330	**THE BEGGARS ARE COMING** by Mary Loos	$1.95

Buy them at your local bookstore or use this handy coupon for ordering:

Bantam Books, Inc., Dept. FBB, 414 East Golf Road, Des Plaines, Ill. 60016

Please send me the books I have checked above. I am enclosing $_____
(please add 50¢ to cover postage and handling). Send check or money
order—no cash or C.O.D.'s please.

Mr/Mrs/Miss_____

Address_____

City_____ State/Zip_____

FBB—3/78

Please allow four weeks for delivery. This offer expires 9/78.

Bantam Book Catalog

Here's your up-to-the-minute listing of every book currently available from Bantam.

This easy-to-use catalog is divided into categories and contains over 1400 titles by your favorite authors.

So don't delay—take advantage of this special opportunity to increase your reading pleasure.

Just send us your name and address and 25¢ (to help defray postage and handling costs).